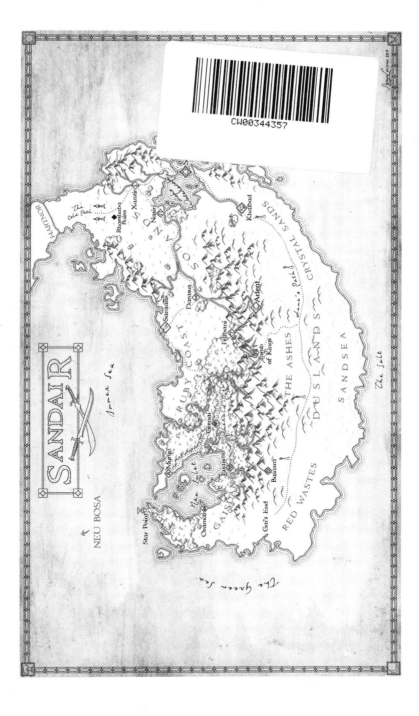

SANDAIR

NEU BOSA

HARNNOR

Amber Sea

The Green Sea

The Cold Reach

Rhaeshaba Ruins

Xanziri

Nourn

Kindbad

CRYSTAL SANDS

SOLANN

Sangathi

Darcius

Felbani

Ardent

Lenn's Reach

Tomb of Kings

THE ASHES

DUSLANDS

SANDSEA

The Salt

RUBY COAST

Gramat

Murut

Luin

Bakfont

Star Point

Oranmire

GAIS

Gai's End

RED WASTES

Explore more of the world of Sand Dancer

For short stories featuring characters from
this novel, appendices, pronunciation guides,
and other supplemental materials, visit:

TrudieSkies.com

SAND DANCER | BOOK TWO

Fire Walker

TRUDIE SKIES

Uproar Books

1419 PLYMOUTH DRIVE, NASHVILLE, TN 37027
UPROARBOOKS.COM

FIRE WALKER

Edited by Rick Lewis.

Cover illustration by Eduoard Noisette.

Map illustration by Soraya Corcoran.

Printed in the United States of America.

ISBN 978-1-949671-12-4

First paperback edition.

This book is dedicated to those who have sacrificed much during the 2020 coronavirus pandemic; to the lives lost, to the lives who have suffered, to the health care workers who have sacrificed their time and risked their lives, to the essential workers who have kept society together whilst our leaders could not, to the many who gave up their freedoms to help protect those dearest.

You've all walked through the fire.

Part One

Broken Oaths

1

BENEATH THE STONE

The High Priestess's rules for entering the Temple of Rahn were designed to punish and control. *No Fire Walker shall burn without permission, no clothing shall be worn to hide their marks, no weapons are to be brought inside the temple, no meat or fruit or wine shall be consumed, and no stone shall be disturbed upon penalty of death.*

Mina had broken each rule in her first week.

The tunnels underneath the temple were a maze. Mina had spent the past twelve weeks digging out blocked and collapsed passages and exploring where safe to do so. Many paths held signs of those who had last passed through: warnings etched into the stone walls, abandoned water canteens, bloody handprints, piles of ash. All were left by Fire Walkers who had attempted to escape imprisonment inside the temple. Some must have made it. Others weren't so lucky. It was those Mina sought.

The High Priestess of Rahn had forbidden Mina from digging up old bones—literal bones—and putting their spirits to rest. No amount of arguing had convinced her. Instead, Mina had gone over her head and petitioned the King of Sandair himself. Having saved his life and earned his reward this Rahn's Dawn, she'd expected King Khaled to be more forthcoming. But no. Their great king had waved his hand and declared the issue a matter for the temple to handle.

The High Priestess had made her stance perfectly clear.

The dead would remain buried. Their souls trapped in stone forever.

Such a declaration had only hardened Mina's resolve, and when the Priestess left the temple on a pilgrimage south, Mina knew this could be her only chance. The Priestess knew this, too, and left behind her two lackeys to keep guard. Today, Mina had managed to send one of them, Saeed, off on a wild chase into the city. But the other, a woman named Samira, wasn't so easily fooled. She was the reason Mina now ran in circles in the stifling dark.

Hunting Shadows was easier when the hunter wasn't also being hunted, but Mina's pursuer hadn't counted on her many years of experience running through Dusland alleyways.

Dust clouds rose from where Mina's hurried steps slapped the ground, disturbing layers of sand that had slumbered there for generations. She eased her breathing into a steady rhythm, tasting the salt and smoke that always lingered in the air. One hand carried a lit torch—its light necessary for navigation despite its oppressive heat—and the other gripped the hilt of her sword, Hawk. Only a year ago, she'd run through Khalbad's streets with a fishing rod tucked in her belt and dreamed of steel. Now she carried real steel strapped to her hip, but the scabbard slapped her thigh with each step. Swords weren't made for running. Neither was fire.

From behind her came the rasping breath of her pursuer. A woman clearly not meant to run, or hunt, or fight, but stubborn enough to try. That Samira hadn't given up or collapsed yet was impressive enough, and Mina hadn't made her path easy by leading her through twisting tunnels with uneven ground decorated in cobwebs. It would have been fun, if not for their priestess's parting threat: *"Touch those bones and you'll be committing treason, Mina Hawker, and your bones will join them."*

Mina had some experience committing treason, too.

She turned the corner to begin her loop again. A wall of fire burst from the ground, blocking the entire tunnel with blinding light. She dropped her torch and cursed, skidding to a halt.

"Enough!"

Samira staggered up from behind, her chest heaving. Her shiny bald head gleamed with sweat, and even in the flame-lit tunnel, her bronze Solander skin looked pale. "Stop," she wheezed.

Mina scooped her torch and re-lit it against Samira's flames. "Stop what? Running? Is exercise not allowed now?"

Samira sagged against the wall of the tunnel. "Don't—don't think I don't know what you're doing! I know your Rhaesbond is digging—"

"He has a name."

"—digging tunnels, that traitorous filth. You think you're so smart, tricking Saeed into running halfway across Solus, but you're not! He's fetching the guard."

"You summoned the *guard*? When did exercising become a criminal offense?"

"Don't play games with me. Do you realize how dangerous it is out there for our kind? Do you care at all? Fire Walkers are getting attacked in the streets, thanks to you and your worthless Rhaesbond. All it'll take is one spark and their hatred for our kind will ignite."

"You never leave the temple. How would you know what's going on outside?"

Samira and Saeed were fools who believed Fire Walkers belonged in stone cages. But the King had granted them freedom, and most Fire Walkers had returned to their families to resume the life they once had—or to begin a life they were denied. Only a small handful—including Saeed, Samira, and High Priestess Leila—had chosen to remain in the Temple of Rahn. The stubborn, scared, and pitiful, who'd spent their entire lives inside the temple and now refused to stand in Rahn's warmth.

At least the empty temple remained quiet. Peaceful. The perfect place for Mina to train in both sword and fire. Or it would have been, if Saeed and Samira weren't always stalking her.

Twelve gods-damn weeks had passed. Solus still stood. Sandair hadn't burned. Yes, there'd been rumors of Fire Walkers being harassed in the streets, and Mina planned to investigate those once done here. But the way Samira and Saeed spoke, it was as though they expected Rahn himself to crash down upon the city at any moment.

"You Housemen think you know everything. You have no rank in Rahn's domain." Samira snapped her fingers and a single flame danced in her palm. "I could burn you to ash."

Housemen?

It annoyed Mina whenever anyone named her a Houseman, but that's who she was now, no matter how deeply she'd feared and despised them as a child. Not that Samira understood the path Mina had taken from starving on a Dusland street to joining a House and gaining all the responsibilities that came with it. Mina let out an exasperated sigh. The heat of the wall of fire at her back burned too close, and Samira blocked the only other way out.

As was traditional for the temple's Fire Walkers, Samira wore no clothes, only a band across her chest and a loincloth. Red swirls resembling flame were inked across her chest, shoulders, and upper arms. She carried no weapon except for the power within her own blood—power that could be cut short with a quick slice of Mina's blade. A Fire Walker couldn't burn without their blood, but she'd rather not spill any. She removed her hand from Hawk's hilt.

"Burn me, then. But first, tell me why. Why can't the bones hidden in these tunnels receive a proper lurrite?"

Samira blinked. "They're traitors."

"Traitors for doing what? Trying to escape imprisonment?"

"Gods, nothing so simple. If they were fleeing, we'd merely cut them down and burn them."

"Then why?"

"For refusing to use their fire when called upon by the Bright Solara."

"What? The King locked people away for possessing fire. Are you saying he ordered those same people killed for refusing to use it? That's madness!"

Fresh sweat beads ran down Samira's forehead. Her wall of fire was taking its toll. "I was there in the last war. I saw how important blood fire was to the war effort—"

"You burned the enemy and killed your own people who wouldn't?"

"I didn't kill anyone! Fire Walkers tended to the camps and the wounded. And to the dead. We were the ones who burned the bodies. The battlefields needed to be purged, or they'd become stalking grounds for wraiths. The Shadows of our fallen men would have overrun both armies had we not cleared them."

"Then you understand what I'm trying to do."

"No. This isn't the same thing. Gods, do you listen? Rahn gave us a sacred duty. We must sever the bonds of the dead to the living world, especially in times of war, and it is not permitted to refuse."

Those were Lunei words. The tribe of her ancestors... and of High Priestess Leila. Perhaps she had passed on their tribe's teachings to her acolytes. "And what of the dead here? You don't fear they'll become wraiths?"

"The dead of this temple are aware of their sins. That is why they don't attack."

"You know that for a fact? Because I can see them. I hear what they're saying." Mina put a hand to her ear. "They don't sound too pleased."

A flicker of doubt danced across Samira's face, but then she hardened her eyes and her voice. "You don't scare me, girl. I've lived inside this temple since before you were born. And I tell you now, if you defy Leila's order, you'll be hanged for treason."

Mina snorted. "Treason? Do you really think the King cares enough about some old bones that he'd hang the champion of the Solaran Tournament? Or the daughter of his sorran? The King will have you hanged for wasting his time."

"The King doesn't care enough to grant you permission though, does he?" Samira tapped her nose. "Are you foolish enough to lie to your king?"

Mina rolled her eyes. She'd lied to the King plenty of times and kept her head intact. Her father Talin had done all the bowing and scraping necessary to win back royal favor, though she didn't want to push their luck further. Lune's protection only extended so far.

If Samira spoke true, guards could be marching toward the temple already. She didn't think they'd arrest her, least of all for treason, but they'd interfere with her plans. And time was running out. Her Aunt Iman had sent word that Prince Rais's entourage was seen approaching Solus, returning from their pilgrimage to the Duslands in celebration of his helbond. High Priestess Leila travelled with them; she could be back in the city as soon as tomorrow. This was Mina's best—perhaps only—chance to complete the one task she'd been forbidden from undertaking. She hadn't expected it to take this long, but the tunnels were vast and the Shadows haunting the temple had an annoying habit of passing in and out of the walls in a manner Mina couldn't follow.

Their bones needed to be burned. Their Shadows could not pass to the next world until they were. "I'm Lunei. You say Rahn gave us fire to use? Then Lune gave me her sight to see the dead. And if you don't let me pass, I'll order them to attack."

Samira blanched. "You can't do that. Leila said—"

"You want to test me?" She pointed her lit torch over Samira's shoulder. "There's a Shadow standing right... *there.*"

Dust crumbled from the wall, landing on Samira's shoulder. She shrieked and ran, and the wall of fire immediately snapped out.

Mina laughed and wafted the remaining smoke away. Shadows couldn't be controlled. Gods, she could barely commune with them, but Samira didn't need to know that.

A thick, dark column of smoke lingered, even when Mina's fingers passed through. It rippled, sending a cold shudder up her arm.

She'd been right after all. A Shadow *was* there.

She stepped back as the Shadow took the shape of a faceless man, though it floated unnaturally, its entire body made from midnight. She held up her torch, but the light made no effect. They were a void. A spirit lingering between death and the afterlife.

As a Lunei, her blood attracted the Shadows. Her silver eyes could see them when no one else could. And she'd learned from

Leila's own mouth that the duty of the Lunei, their shared tribe, was to help the Shadows find their way back to Rahn. Leila had let these souls down, but Mina wouldn't.

"Jonan's found you, hasn't he?"

The Shadow swept through the tunnel, its legs barely moving as it slid across the sand. Tendrils of black mist trailed behind it, leaving a cool, smoky residue that pricked her nerves. There was something familiar about this Shadow. The blood bond of her House stirred with Jonan's essence, with Rahnlight and heat.

Jahan.

This Shadow was Jonan's father, Jahan.

She followed him through the tunnels, and the *tock-tock* of a pickaxe rang louder and louder until she found Jonan at his work. He offered a grunt in welcome and nodded at a pile of yellow-white stones that glimmered in the torch light.

Not stones. Pale bones.

She crouched to get a better view. Bones of all types and sizes. She couldn't name them all. But she could name what this was.

"A mass grave."

"Yes." Jonan wiped sweat from his brow, smearing dirt and dust. His tunic was soaked through. Like her, he wore a purple sash across his shoulder, though that too was damp and marred with beige dust. He'd kept his hair at a stubble but allowed his beard to grow. It hadn't made much progress. Neither had her own hair since it had been completely shaved off by Samira all those weeks ago. "Are these all of them? Can you see?"

She set her torch down and ran her palm over the nearest bone. Another Shadow rippled into existence before her. She heard it then: whispers clinging to the wind, words no other mortal would ever hear.

Where is the light?

Those whispers had haunted her stay in the temple, but she'd caught only fragments, tales from another life. Many lives. Ten at least. Maybe more.

Jahan's Shadow watched his son, who leaned against the stone wall, unaware that his own father graced their presence. She opened her mouth to tell Jonan that his father's bones were among those he'd uncovered, but a sudden shiver raced up her spine. The Shadow didn't want to be revealed. For Jonan's sake, or its own?

Other Shadows rose from the bones in puffs of dark cloud. Watching. Waiting.

Jahan's Shadow approached her and reached out as if to touch her shoulder, though his hand passed through with only a chill. She shuddered as his soft words echoed in her mind: *Listen to their tale. No one has heard them speak.*

One of the Shadow's held out its hand. An invitation. She'd touched enough of the Shadows to know not all were friendly, and even those who wished her no harm might plague her with unpleasant thoughts, dreams, and memories. But Mina did not fear dark dreams and memories. She'd lived through her worst nightmares and survived to tell their tales.

Whatever this Shadow wished to throw at her, she was ready.

Mina grasped its cold hand.

Sky fire burned through her veins, and her legs buckled. Her eyelids fluttered into darkness.

2

CHILDREN OF SHADOW

I kneeled in black ash. I could still taste men floating in the smoke. My brothers and sisters kneeled beside me. One had tried to run, and his body left a smear of white and red upon the blackened ground.

Guards pointed their swords at us, but we weren't a threat. The leech at my neck made certain of that. I couldn't burn even if I wished to.

My thoughts turned to home.

I'd turned thirteen when Rahn blessed me. I'd burned in anger over something so inconsequential, I don't even remember it. I burned down our home. My da. My ma. Everything. When the men came for me, I was still alight. Half the townsfolk looked at me like the monster I'd become, but the guardsmen... they saw a weapon.

That's all they ever saw.

They should have cut me down there and then. I should have paid the price. But instead, they locked me inside Rahn's temple and taught me to use his gift on command. I did so. I obeyed. We all did. The strongest among us were rewarded in lamb or silks. Nothing extravagant, small gifts that we could keep inside the temple. I took no reward. I served Rahn as penance.

I watched my brothers and sisters toe the line between monster and weapon.

They died in battle. By sword, by arrow, or by their own fire bleeding them dry.

I pointed my fire where they told me.

Until I couldn't anymore. Rahn forgive me, I couldn't.

My flame had burned flesh from bone and bone to ash.
I closed my eyes as the sword made its way down the line. No one ran. They didn't whimper. They didn't cry. My brothers. My sisters.
Cool steel rested atop my bare shoulder, an inch from the leech. "Why won't you obey?" the guard asked. "Rahn has given you this gift."
I kept my eyes shut tight. "Rahn can take it back."
A sharp sting cut into my neck. It threatened to topple me, but I remained kneeling, fists clasped in my lap. Farther it pushed, strong enough to feel its bite, but not fast enough to remove my head.
Warmth ran down my neck—my life's blood and the gift contained within.
Emptiness replaced the fire inside. Why did it feel so cold? So dark? Where was the light?
Where was the fire that was promised?
Where was the light?

Mina found herself curled on the ground. Her nails dug into the sand and scraped across the stone beneath, grabbing hold of reality. The emptiness of the memory sapped the warmth from her blood, as though it stripped her naked and left her squirming in the dust. She brought her knees into her chest and hugged them tight with shaking arms.

Jonan crouched beside her and grabbed her shoulders. "What happened? A memory?"

More Shadows filled the cramped tunnel with their unnatural darkness. All held their hands open, waiting to be touched. Wanting their tales to be heard.

She shuffled back until her head bumped the wall. "Don't let them touch me!"

That wasn't any of her memories, but... the Shadow's? Gods, she'd felt the leech suck at her skin, felt the sword slice through her neck, felt her life's blood spill. It had felt real, all of it, and she'd experienced every moment.

Jonan squeezed her knee. "Are you still with me?"

Footsteps and shouts echoed in the tunnels above. They were

running out of time, and the Shadows still lingered. Ten of them. She couldn't touch them all and relive ten deaths in a row. "I can't do this."

"Do you want me to burn them?" His words were gentle.

"No, I… They want me to touch them. I—I don't know why. I don't know what they want. A lurrite?"

"We don't have time."

Weeks of planning, searching, and digging… and now, time was up. A flicker of light drew her gaze to a torch beside the bones. A face smiled within the flames. Tira, Mina's mother. Long dead, but somehow still able to watch from the world beyond. No one else could see her. Mina assumed this to be another gift from Lune, but the only other Lunei she knew to ask was Leila.

"My mother helped the Shadows. I've seen her in my dreams. What did she do?"

Jonan sat back on his heels. "She calmed them. I watched her, once. She soothed their spirits. Absolved them of whatever guilt plagued them." He gave her an odd look. "Is this who you want to be?"

Mina stood on shaking legs. "It's what Lune wants, isn't it? You fought in the last war. Were Fire Walkers forced to fight? What happened to those who refused?"

Jonan took her arm and steadied her balance. "What do you want me to say?"

"The truth."

The shouting grew louder. Jonan released her and grabbed his scimitar. "Discuss it later. Are you sure you can burn them?"

From the torchlight, Tira nodded.

"I'll be fine. Samira said Saeed was fetching guards."

Jonan hissed a curse. "Then be quick. I'll hold them off. Breathe, Master Malik. Remember, when you feel your limit—"

"Pull back, I know." She rolled up her sleeves, exposing the silver tattoos that swirled around her bare arms. The hairs stood on end, though not from the air. Jonan ran through the tunnel, passing right through Jahan's Shadow that he couldn't see.

She approached the group of Shadows and held up her palms. "We don't have time for a lurrite. I'm not a priestess. I don't even know the words." She sucked in a breath. "You didn't deserve this fate, and I swear it will never happen again. I'll send you back to Rahn. All of you. I'll send you back to the light." It was the least she could do.

Jahan's Shadow brushed her arm. *They'll follow your lead*, his voice echoed in her mind. A smile bloomed through their shared connection. *I wish I could have named him mine. Tell him.*

She stared into his faceless darkness. "I'll tell him, I swear."

The Shadows moved back, giving her space. She rolled her shoulders to regain her composure. Finding them had been a test of her Lunei abilities. This would test her control. Weeks of training had led to this moment.

Every Fire Walker had a trick to summoning their flame, so Jonan had taught her. Some could summon it with a single thought. Others needed a physical action, such as a snap of their fingers. She'd discovered early on that emotion manipulated her blood's magic.

She thought of her father. Talin.

He was travelling now with Prince Rais—and with High Priestess Leila. He'd be back with her as soon as tomorrow. Her inner embers warmed at the thought.

In the few short weeks before he'd left with the Prince's caravan, Talin had joined Mina inside the temple every morning, and they'd kicked off their boots and danced within the main sanctum. Sometimes to an audience—Fire Walkers eager to see the legendary *Sand Dancer* who'd won the tournament. She could still feel the swish of air against her knuckles, the sand between her toes, the gritty salt on her tongue, and her father's dark eyes upon her, proud and intense, as their swords curved side by side.

Her father. She woke each dawn and still didn't believe it. All those years spent idolizing the Protector of the Path, and he'd been her father all along. She'd wanted to travel back to the Duslands with him—to not let him out of her sight in case it had all been a mirage, some trick of the gods. But some duties were more urgent than blood and bonds.

The tingling under her skin turned to prickling heat as her own blood began to boil—the oil to ignite her fire. A red flicker of flame sparked in the palm of her hand.

It didn't hurt. Even pressing the flame against her cheek didn't burn, but tickle. Of course, just because it didn't hurt her, didn't mean it couldn't hurt others. This power had been cursed and feared for hundreds of years for a reason.

Flames spread around her entire fist. She hadn't wanted this gift. No one did. Being born with blood fire was both a sin and a crime—or it had been until twelve weeks ago. The law was different now, and the hearts and minds of the people would follow in time. Mina and her House would make sure of that. Yes, High Priestess Leila and her foolish acolytes would oppose her every step of the way, but so long as Mina drew breath, Fire Walkers would never be imprisoned again.

Never again.

"Rahn, guide these lost souls home."

Heat poured from her hand and engulfed the bones in a blazing bonfire. She squinted against the light and gripped her shaking arm with her other hand, holding the flames steady. The fire pulsed with her heartbeat, and an ache soon throbbed in her forehead. It wasn't just fire leaving her body, but her own blood. The cost of Rahn's gift. It was almost poetic that only blood fire could burn *all* traces of bone. Life's blood in exchange for death's passing. But with so many bones... the cost would be high.

Tira frowned in the flames. She mouthed one word: *Stop.*

Mina kept her trembling arm up. "Not yet."

Again, the command: *Stop.*

Mina looked inside herself at the bright glow of her inner embers and tried to calm them. The bones called to her, latched onto her, and pulled at her blood like a thread. They were stronger than she, and the fire responded to their will, not hers.

Jahan's urgent voice whispered into her mind: *Trouble is coming.*

"I know! I'm trying to control it—"

Footsteps echoed in the tunnel.

Trouble is coming, the whisper repeated.

Mina glanced over her shoulder as Samira came running.

"Stop!" Samira yelled, and flame burst from her outstretched hand. The force almost knocked Mina off her feet.

But Samira's flames weren't aimed at Mina's body. Instead, they formed a shield around the bones, blocking her fire from reaching them.

Mina chewed her lip and pushed against it.

Samira stood calm as her flames poured in a steady, controlled stream. "Stop, or you'll bleed yourself dry."

"You first."

"Don't be so stubborn!"

In a contest of blood fire, Mina stood no chance against a trained acolyte, but she couldn't stop now. She stoked her inner embers and a torrent of blood fire poured upon the shield. It did nothing but send spasms of pain shooting up her arm. The throb in Mina's forehead rose from an ache to a hammer's blow; she was pushing far beyond her limit.

By the smirk creeping across Samira's face, she knew it.

Then Jahan's Shadow fell upon Samira, swallowing her in darkness. Samira couldn't see the Shadow and barely flinched at the touch, but her flame flickered, giving Mina her only opening.

Heat surged through Mina's veins and she squeezed every drop of blood into one final push. Blinding light tore through the shield and absorbed the bones. Samira stumbled back.

It is done, Jahan's voice whispered.

Mina's flames sputtered out and she collapsed into the dust. She tried to sit up, but the tunnel spun and her limbs were heavy as stone.

"You fool, you've burned through all your blood, haven't you?" Samira said, brushing dust from her arms. "Well? Was it worth it?"

The smoldering bones turned to glowing red ash. One by one, the Shadows faded and disappeared from sight.

"Yes."

"That kind of blood loss is impossible to recover from. Didn't your Rhaesbond teach you that?"

Mina shuffled back and leaned her head against the wall. Her heartbeat fluttered, fast and shallow. Samira was right—she'd given too much. "Duty—"

"Duty? What do you know of duty? You think you're so smart, coming into our temple and telling us how to live. You want to help us, but what have you ever done for us?"

"The Prince—"

"We don't need you to win some foolish tournament to protect us from the Bright Solara or his scheming whelp. You House-men understand nothing of our people, or our duties, or what it takes to keep us safe! Why else would you care more for the dead than what's going on in the real world? You think Leila cares for some old bones? She protects the living! Everything she does is for the good of our people." Samira sauntered forward. "You thought you were tricking Saeed and me, distracting us. But whilst you and your Rhaesbond were digging tunnels, Saeed took Leila's place on the Council. You have no idea what's coming, do you?"

"What?"

"You're dying, Mina Hawker, and it's your own fault. I didn't force you to burn through your blood. It was the hubris of youth. And you're so far down in these tunnels, no one will find you in time. Your Rhaesbond's too busy trying to keep Saeed *out*." She chuckled. "You're not so smart now."

Mina lifted her heavy arm and twisted it to show her silver tattoos. "You marked me." Her arm fell into her lap. "You know what I am."

A Lunei.

It was why Samira chose to paint her silver, and not the traditional red of other Fire Walkers.

Samira crouched and ran a soothing hand across Mina's scalp. "I'm no monster. I'll burn your body. Don't fear Rahn's light when he calls for you. And don't fear for the Fire Walkers. They'll be safe in Rahn's temple, where they belong."

Gods. What a fool she'd been. Did Samira and Saeed truly hate her that much? For freeing the Fire Walkers? No, they were acting on Leila's orders. Mina tried to shove Samira away, but her blood, her life, drained from her. She'd given everything so the dead could find peace. Was that all Lune wanted her for?

"Unhand my niece!" a woman bellowed.

Samira leaped up. A large figure took up the entire width of the tunnel, a hand on her sword hilt. Mina's heart soared. Her Aunt Iman.

"Stand aside, or by Rahn, I'll cut you in half!"

Samira summoned a small ball of flame. "I am an acolyte of Rahn. How dare you threaten me!"

Iman drew her sword an inch—there wasn't enough space to unleash it fully, but the effect made Samira shrink. "And I am the stewardess of House Arlbond." The dim light made Iman look even larger and more intimidating. "What are you doing to my niece?"

"She used too much blood fire, you fool. I was help—"

"Touch her and I'll drag your sorry carcass to the sandsea for the goats!"

Samira shook her flame out. "Fine," she snarled. "There's nothing to be done for her anyway. I'll leave you to perform her lurrite." With that, she turned and marched away into the far tunnel.

Mina toppled over and would have hit the ground if Iman hadn't caught her. "Easy, girl. Easy. Did that wretch—"

"How did you find me?" Mina gasped.

"I felt you through the bond. It's useful for something."

Iman lifted her up. Mina leaned into her aunt's warm, soft curves and breathed in her familiar essence of spice and wine. She had no strength to walk as Iman half-carried her to the main temple sanctum and lay Mina on the stone steps that encircled the deeps sands covering the sanctum floor.

Mina closed her eyes. Use too much blood fire too quickly, and it *hurt*. Headaches were the first sign, followed by dizziness and nausea. It reminded her of Lune's bloody visits. But the pain now was different than anything before—smothering and yet also distant, as if her mind had somehow separated itself from her spent and useless body.

"I'm not impressed with either of you," Iman snapped. "You were supposed to watch her! Look at her, she's barely got enough blood to stand."

Mina forced open one eye. Iman's anger wasn't directed at her, but Jonan. When had he returned? A soft cooing rumbled against her thigh and she glanced down. A blanket had been wrapped around her shoulders and Fez curled in her lap. The little fennec fox often slept by the braziers in the sanctum. The Solus temple was as far from the Duslands as she could get, yet it reminded her of home, a miniature desert in the heart of the city. It was one reason why Mina chose to remain here instead of the Keep.

And she didn't need to fear running into a certain pompous prince who remained locked inside his palace.

Jonan gently roused Mina and shoved a canteen under her nose. "Drink. Don't sleep. If you sleep, you may not wake up."

She complied. The water tasted crisp and refreshing with a hint of cooling mint.

"That kind of blood loss will take a season to recover from," Iman said.

"I'll deal with it. Go," Jonan answered.

"Where's Talin?" Mina mumbled.

Iman leaned over and planted a wet kiss on her forehead. "Drink as much water as you can, and try not to move." She used her thumb to gently dry Mina's forehead from her kiss. "I'll be back soon." She stomped away from the sanctum.

Jonan sighed and shuffled into position beside Mina. "You used too much blood."

"Didn't."

"We discussed this." Jonan poked her bicep and she keeled

over. He grabbed the shawl around her shoulders and pulled her upright. "I should have burned them."

"If I can't master my fire, what use am I?"

"If you burn through your blood, what use will your corpse be? We trained for this, Master Malik. What went wrong?"

She took another gulp of water and stroked Fez's soft nape to steady the nausea now rising in her stomach. "Samira, she... She tried to stop me."

His anger snapped taut through their shared House bond. "Samira did this?"

"She said something about the Council. I—what are you doing?"

Jonan pulled a knife from his sahn and took her hand. "Stay calm. This will last but a moment." He nicked her palm with a sharp sting, and then his own. He pressed the two wounds together.

Sky fire burned through her arm as it travelled up into her chest. She yelped and tried to pull free, sending Fez screeching from her lap. "What are you doing to me?"

Jonan's grip tightened around her hand and his eyes burned bright red. "Giving you my blood."

Just as he'd saved King Khaled's life. The King would have bled to death if Jonan hadn't been there.

Jonan's life essence pulsed in her veins. Like Rahn Himself—pure heat and light and righteous anger. But her nerves were frayed. Sheer panic gripped her heart, followed by guilt and shame.

Guilt? Why? What did she—

No, these were Jonan's emotions.

He thinks he failed me.

With each heartbeat, she felt his strength bolster her own. "How are you doing this? How is this possible?"

His expression turned somber. "This is forbidden blood magic. You and I will not speak of it again."

"How can it be forbidden if you know about it? You saved the King—"

"Fire Walker priests know it. They keep this knowledge from the rest of Sandair."

"Why hide it? This can save lives!"

"Blood bonds are not to be played with. Only experienced priests can administer blood. Anyone else could risk forming a marriage bond, or draining a body of its blood, or worse."

"What's worse than marriage or death?"

His eyes narrowed. "There are worse things than death." His grip tightened around her arm. "Swear to me you will never attempt this."

"If it can help people, I want to learn—"

"*No.* This is dangerous beyond your understanding. I trained in the temple under the old High Priestess for years before I fled, remember?"

"What if I become a priestess?"

"You're no priestess, and this is no laughing matter. Swear to me you will *never* give your blood. Even if the King is dying. Even if it's one of us. Swear to me you will never do this."

"I won't—"

His grip crushed her bones. "Swear it on Talin's life."

She swallowed dry air. "I swear it."

He released her arm, apparently satisfied with her answer. She examined the damage to her palm. The cut had cauterized into a single scar, another for her collection, but her veins still tingled.

The sanctum doors swung open. Iman came bounding back inside, her face flushed with sweat and her anxiety ringing through the bond.

"What's happening?" Jonan climbed to his feet and tucked his hands into his pockets, though not quickly enough to hide their tremble. He'd given too much of his blood.

"Talin's back—" Iman began, but seeing Mina's face light up, she raised her hand to keep from being interrupted. "But he's been called to the Keep. Leila too. They all have."

"What's going on?" Mina asked.

"Ships," Iman gasped. "Hartnord ships approaching the harbor."

3

THE GRAY OF DAWN

Crowds of city folk flooded the streets of Solus. All ran in different directions—some for the docks to see what the commotion was about, though others ran the opposite way, fleeing for the safety of their stone townhouses. Mina found herself awash in a sea of panicked voices as she, Iman, and Jonan elbowed their way through the market quarter. Stall owners hurriedly packed away their wares and fought off opportunistic thieves. The city guard barked for order but went unheard.

Iman grabbed Mina's sahn and pulled her into one of the side alleys leading to the Neu Bosan quarter. She was glad she'd left Fez behind in the temple. With so many feet trampling the streets, Fez could have gotten lost or hurt.

"Gods-damn fools are going to start a riot," Iman muttered.

Jonan lingered behind with a hand to his sword hilt. "Can't blame them. Most still remember the last time Hartnord ships graced our shores. You should both return to the temple."

"If we're being invaded, there'll be plenty of guards at the docks. And someone there will know what's going on."

"What have you heard at the Council meetings? Anything that could explain this?"

"I've been busy distracting those two fools whilst the two of you

were running around underground. I can't be in two places at once."

"You didn't attend the meetings?" Jonan sighed. "You've heard nothing in the Keep? No whispers of Hartnords?"

Iman shook her head. Unlike Mina and Jonan, Iman had elected to remain in the Keep. She was supposed to take Talin's place on the King's Council whilst he was away, but they'd needed help distracting Samira and Saeed—or so Mina thought.

"Saeed and Samira know what's going on," Mina said. "Saeed took Leila's place on the Council. Samira told me as much."

Jonan glared at Iman. "If you'd attended those meetings *as discussed*—"

"So I could listen to Salasar and Farzad Fellbond argue who has the biggest sword? I get enough of that nonsense in my own House. And don't you lecture me about responsibilities!"

Mina pushed between them. "Can we argue later?"

Both her elders muttered a curse but otherwise held their tongues. The pair of them were stubborn as goats. Mina had learned to follow Talin's lead when they bickered—he stood by and let them sort themselves out, knowing the shouting would end in agreement eventually. Jonan was a grumpy cub at heart, and Iman could be placated with a little wine.

They continued through the back alleys of the Neu Bosan quarter. Mina knew these alleys. They led to a tavern she'd frequented often with her Academy friends Alistar and Raj. Both had left for their homes in Gaisland after Mina's victory in the tournament but promised to return for Prince Rais's helbond ceremony. She passed a little teahouse that Raj had managed to drag them into once, and which had become a favorite place for Mina to spend afternoons with Iman.

Over mint and honeyed teas, she'd been able to ask Iman questions about her mother that would have been too awkward for Talin to answer. And now that Talin had returned and they'd finally have time to spend together as father and daughter, gods-damn northerners were invading.

Mina jogged ahead with a spring in her step. After receiving

Jonan's blood, she'd never felt more alive, though she noticed Jonan lagged. His fatigue ached through the bond.

Iman bounded up beside her. "Are you going to tell me what happened? I'll need to know if Talin's likely to burn the temple down along with its wretched acolytes."

Mina rolled her eyes.

"Don't give me that look, girl." Iman's breath rasped. "If anyone hurt you, he'd cut them down before you or I could blink."

"They tricked us. I don't know why, but… it's something to do with the Council. They might know about the Hartnords. How is this going to affect the Fire Walkers?"

"If this is the start of another war, the King will likely demand the temple send Fire Walkers to support his army. That's how it has always been."

"The law changed. They're free now."

"If it's war, all men are called."

All men? That would mean Talin, Jonan, Alistar, and Raj… But Samira had looked so gleeful. She couldn't want Fire Walkers drawn into another war?

The alleyways opened to the canal, which they followed down to the docks. Here, the streets were eerily quiet. The Neu Bosan who wanted to lock themselves in their homes had done so by now, and the rest were already at the docks, which came into view. The loud seagulls and stench of fish reminded her of the little wooden shack of Khalbad.

A whole lifetime ago.

Hundreds of boats remained tucked into the docks, both the larger Neu Bosan trade ships and the smaller Sandarian fishing boats. No doubt they'd headed straight back to shore at the first sign of a Hartnord fleet. Sailors stood by their vessels, waving their arms angrily, but the city guards in their royal crimson tunics and bronze chest plates handled the crowds efficiently. A flash of turquoise among them seemed the reason why. The Sword of Solus was in charge.

The crowds yelled and pointed out to sea. Two tall ships rolled toward the city. Wooden, like Sandarian ships, but twice the size. Gray sails were held taut by the wind and their masts disappeared into the clouds.

"Those aren't war ships," Jonan said, coming up behind her.

Mina whirled round. "You've seen Hartnord war ships?"

"In the last war. I watched them burn."

A loud clanking sound rang in Mina's ears. The harbor chain was being lowered. Not to allow the Solus ships out, but... to allow the Hartnord ships in.

The ships lowered their sails as they entered the harbor. Space had been cordoned off at the far end of the docks, and the city guards threatened any who came near. As the two ships began the slow process of docking, a group of Neu Bosan in lime green robes marched through the crowds and met with Salasar and his small contingent of royal guards.

None of the Neu Bosan carried a sword, except for a younger man skulking at the back—Alistar.

"I'll catch up later." Mina raced down the stone steps leading to the docks before Iman or Jonan could stop her.

The guards must either have recognized her face as the tournament champion or her purple sahn marking her as a member of House Arlbond, because they let her pass straight through their ranks and catch up with the Neu Bosan delegation. She slipped in behind Alistar and gave him a gentle push.

Alistar spun around. His emerald eyes opened wide. "Malik!" He cringed. "Mina. I forget." A sly smile spread across his lips, and he pulled her away from the crowd. "Thank the stars! You're here to save me."

Despite being born Neu Bosan, he and his family were Sandarian citizens—Housemen, no less—and he wore his House's lime green sahn. But there was something different about him. His hair had been cut short, other than his single braid, and a thin layer of fuzz coated his chin. The overall effect made him look... mature.

She leaned into his side. "What's going on?"

"Your House didn't tell you? Don't they sit on the Council?"

"Ali!" a Neu Bosan man shouted. "Where are you going?"

Alistar held up Mina's arm. "Sorran business."

"You're not my sorran," she said.

Alistar prodded her side and grinned through clenched teeth. "They don't know that. Stars above, you can't condemn me to this."

"To *what*? I don't even—"

"To all this posturing! It's all they've talked about for weeks and I'm sick of hearing it. How haven't you heard?"

"I've been busy."

"Doing what? Hiding underground?"

She pursed her lips. *In a manner of speaking.* Outside her House, she hadn't explained the Shadows to anyone, or how her Lunei blood attracted them. Her friends wouldn't understand. To them, Shadows and wraiths were tales, though they'd witnessed the destructive force of sand wraiths during the Solend. They already thought her odd for pretending to be a man while they attended the Academy. What would they think if they knew she could see and speak to the dead?

Alistar nudged her and pointed. "Look."

The first of the Hartnord ships finished docking and lowered its boarding ramp. Statues of silver began descending upon the dock— no, these were men! Giant men with golden hair and pale faces and steel armor covering every other inch of them. Each carried a large triangular shield, the design of which she'd never seen before.

How could they move?

But move they did, and their limbs clinked as they walked.

If Solus were being invaded, this was a strange way to go about it.

Salasar and his guard welcomed the foreigners and formed a protective circle around them, not that the metal giants needed their protection—they towered over Salasar.

The circle of guards and the men in steel marched together toward Bloodstone Keep, with the Neu Bosan delegation trailing behind.

Mina waved at Iman and Jonan to let them know she was safe

but kept her position by Alistar's side among the Neu Bosan procession. The crowds parted for the royal guards, some more willingly than others, but eventually they made it to the Keep's gates. Housemen and servants stared as Salasar led the Hartnords inside.

"Where are we taking them?" Mina whispered to Alistar, though her question was soon answered. Their march led straight to the throne room. Guards at every corner turned back oglers, but none hindered Mina until she reached the throne room door.

Alistar flashed his lime sahn. "We're with the delegation. Houses Myrbond and Arlbond."

The guards allowed them inside.

The throne room was full of Housemen in their rainbow of sahns, just as it had been the first time she'd stepped foot here after winning the tournament. But this time, Neu Bosan also filled the room. "We're here to make sure no one starts another war," Alistar whispered.

"They're not invading?"

Alistar raised his eyebrow and the three silver stars inked above. "You really don't know? Look—" He pointed to an older Neu Bosan man dressed in a long, flowing shalwar kameez and bearing the lime green sahn of Alistar's House. His hair was still dark black, despite his age, and his beard curled into a thin wisp, a style common among men of the Neu Bosan quarter. "That's the ambassador to Neu Bosa. And he's, uh, my father."

"Your father's the ambassador? You never told me this."

"It's a new thing. Times change fast in Neu Bosa. You know, politics." He shrugged as the room fell silent.

King Khaled rose from his hulking stone lump of a throne, *Rahn's Cradle*. As he stepped from it, a faint red glow inside the rock faded. Then, the blood bond warmed in Mina's chest and her heart skipped a beat. On the King's right stood her father, Talin. The King's Right Arm. He was still dressed for travel, his purple sahn coated in the beige sand of her homeland. His eyes found hers across the crowd of Housemen and he smiled. His calming presence soothed through the bond. Whatever this meeting was, he wasn't concerned.

Good. They'd suffered enough foolishness chasing Shadows. The gods owed them a reprieve.

All of the Hartnords save one bowed deeply before King Khaled. Salasar said something she didn't hear over the murmurs spreading throughout the throne room. A hush descended as the King raised his hand to beckon the one standing Hartnord to step up onto the dais and join him.

"You honor us with your visit, King Reinhart. I, and the people of Sandair, welcome you to our great city."

Muffled whispers ignited once again in the crowd. The King of Sandair looked resplendent in his three-gemmed crown, ruby sword, and crimson sahn. He bowed and spoke words in a language she didn't understand.

"What is he—"

"The King's speaking Hartnord," Alistar whispered.

A glint of silver shone in the Rahnlight as the giant steel Hartnords parted for their king to pass. He stood as large as his guards, and he too wore steel wrapped around his body. A blue cloak dangled over his shoulder like a sahn, and a sword hung by his hip. An odd weapon. The blade looked straight, not at all curved like Sandarian swords. Like King Khaled, he was an older man with that strong sense of authority that could command a whole kingdom and bright eyes that spoke of a lifetime of tales. Golden hair curled about his cheeks, streaked with silver like his beard. Odder still, his pale skin looked as bright as Lunelight.

The Hartnord King bowed and said strange words in return. His voice snapped short and sharp, like the thrust of a dagger. Not at all like the smooth melody of the Sandarian tongue.

Alistar bent his head close. "That's King Reinhart, ruler of Hartnor. He's saying he's honored to be here—"

"You understand them?"

"My Hartnord is a little rusty, but I get the gist."

King Khaled spoke in Sandarian: "We celebrate a renewed

peace between the lands of Hartnor and Sandair. King Reinhart has travelled far to sign a treaty between our people and usher in the dawn of a relationship to benefit us both."

A repressed cheer sounded in the crowd. More Hartnord words were exchanged. It was so strange to see two kings in one room. Beside them, King Khaled's Hartnord sorran Gareth—the King's Left Arm—shifted uncomfortably. His face twisted, as though trying to force a smile and losing the battle.

"What are they saying?" she asked Alistar, but he didn't get a chance to answer.

With a loud *thud* the throne room doors opened, silencing the two kings' pleasantries in that strange, harsh tongue. All eyes turned to the late arrival. The crowd parted, and a familiar taunting stride approached.

Prince Ravel, the former heir to Sandair's throne.

The King did not acknowledge his son, but immediately returned to his conversation in Hartnord. If the foreigners noticed the slight, they had the grace not to show it. The crowd muttered and turned their attention away from the Prince and back to his father.

The Prince of Poison didn't look any worse for wear for being imprisoned in the palace these past twelve weeks. He wore the same lavish red tunic embroidered in golden flames, and his beard had grown a couple of inches, long enough to support a single ruby bead. No sword hung at his hip, she noted with satisfaction. And a crescent scar branded his left cheek—a scar she'd caused with her own flame. A mirror to the scar he'd sliced into her the day he'd murdered her uncle—the man she'd called her father for seventeen years.

"They're saying they look forward to negotiating trade agreements, Lady Arlbond."

Alistar bowed to the Prince.

She did not. "They let you out?"

A shadow of a smile graced the Prince's lips. "My father occasionally allows me out of my cage."

His golden palace hardly served as a cage, not like the dusty temple the Fire Walkers were forced to endure. "Without your sword."

"An astute observation. And yet you carry yours, Lady Arlbond, and, ah, whatever that is you're wearing. Are you still pretending to be a man? You'll confuse our Hartnord guests into believing such customs are normal. But I don't recall seeing your name on the list of dignitaries."

She rubbed Hawk's hilt. "I attend as winner of the tournament. Why are you here?"

"Visiting dignitaries are a grand occasion, and it would be odd for the heir to be seen hiding."

"Yes, where is Prince Rais?"

"My dear brother doesn't appear to appreciate the importance of our esteemed guests. This visit could shape the course of our history. Though if you'll excuse me, I have Council meetings to attend. Meetings neither your House nor my brother consider important, Lady Arlbond. A pity."

No one paid attention to Prince Ravel as he strode among the Housemen. Surely they wouldn't have forgotten the Prince's crimes so soon? Locking him in the palace and taking away his sword wasn't much of a punishment for the lives he'd taken and the people he'd hurt, especially not if he could come and go as he pleased *and* attend the Council.

Seeing his smug face made her ill at ease. She knew she wouldn't be able to avoid him forever. What interest did he have in these Hartnords?

It had something to do with the Fire Walkers. Mina just didn't know what.

4

A PROPOSAL

Days passed in a bustle of multi-colored faces. Housemen swarmed Bloodstone Keep, and not just for Prince Rais's impending helbond ceremony. From the whispers Mina could glean, the foreigners were locked in meetings for most of their visit. As the King's sorran, Talin could only spare brief moments to confirm there was nothing to fear, but a nervous energy filled the Keep like sky fire ready to crack.

Mina lingered in the palace gardens. With High Priestess Leila back in Solus, Jonan decided it would be safer to leave the temple and rejoin life in the Keep. All of the spare palace rooms were occupied by Hartnords and Neu Bosan dignitaries, forcing Mina to share a room with her aunt in the Keep's apartments again, while Jonan roomed with Talin in his quarters in the palace.

House nobles sat on the marble benches beside the water fountains, gossiping. Mina wandered the path between the fountains and rose bushes with an eye to the palace as Fez explored the gardens, diving in and out of bushes. The little fox hadn't been pleased to be plucked out of the warm temple sands and brought back to the gardens, nipping her hand to say so, but he soon kept himself busy hunting birds and bugs. Samira never liked him anyway.

Mina hoped to catch either Talin or Alistar on a break from their meetings, but no one emerged. As the midday heat settled in, she gave up. Even Alistar had been snapped up by his House to perform duties, despite pretending to be her sorran. It grated her nerves that Prince Ravel and Samira knew why the Hartnords were here. And they seemed *happy* about it—which couldn't be good. How could Mina prepare for a threat when she didn't know what it was?

There was only one way she *could* prepare.

She left the garden path and found the clearing where Prince Ravel had cultivated Rahn's Breath. The charred grass had grown over since then, and the hidden space gave her some peace. She drew Hawk and loosed her limbs in a series of controlled spins.

To dance was to become her sword, body and blade as one. Each movement served a purpose as though guided by Lune herself. Working through the motions relaxed her muscles and uncoiled the tension in her gut, easing whatever fears festered in her spirit. When she danced, she felt Lune's hand—and the goddess's permission to breathe and let go.

Mina became the master of her own self.

The blood bond warmed before she heard the rustle of leaves. She lowered Hawk as her father ducked under palm fronds.

"We do have training rooms you can use."

"The palace is overrun. Shouldn't you be guarding the King from our enemies?"

Talin's lip quirked. "The King's enemies are taking a break for prayer. Khaled suggested I rest whilst it's quiet. It's going to be a long night."

She sheathed her sword. "Who do they pray to?"

Talin led her to an empty marble bench and sat, stretching his legs. A fountain splashed farther down the path. This part of the palace garden seemed quiet enough as Housemen retreated indoors to rest through the midday heat, not that Solanders knew anything about heat.

"They have only the one god. That's convenient, I suppose, except Gareth tells me they're required to pray twice a day, at dawn and dusk, and whenever they seek counsel. Gareth was saying—"

"Why are they here?"

"They're not here to start a war."

"Seems a long journey for a Hartnord king to come and talk about trade."

"It's not just about trade. For hundreds of years, our countries have been at odds. Establishing a foundation of friendship is the first step toward lasting peace."

"Why now? What do they want?"

"It's… complex. Gareth is helping me make sense of it." He glanced over his shoulder, but no eavesdroppers lingered. "You cannot repeat what I am about to tell you. The Hartnords are afraid of us. Of our blood fire."

A cold sense of dread weighed in her stomach. "I knew this had something to do with the Fire Walkers."

"According to King Reinhart, there are Fire Walkers crossing his border and they've caused some disturbance. He wants a stop to it. He's also concerned with Khaled's recent concessions regarding them. The Hartnords weren't so bothered when we were locking them away. Now that they're free to live as they please, the Hartnords see it as an affront to their god, so Gareth tells me. They want the law changed back, or at least some restrictions placed on those with blood fire."

There it was—the reason Samira danced with such glee. "Who are they to demand that of us?"

"Naturally, Khaled does not wish to bow to outsiders. But they're offering unrestricted trade as compensation—a gesture of good faith, so they call it. Most of the Council are pushing for this, and it's not just about gold—nations that trade openly rarely go to war. You know how tense things have been." Talin rubbed the creases on his forehead. "Most Houses aren't happy with Khaled's reforms, and public safety is only one of those reasons. Gold is another. They used to have a temple full of Fire Walkers who had no choice but to perform certain duties, but now they're required to hire additional hands. There are many Housemen who want things to return to what they were before, and they've latched onto the Hartnords' proposals. It's a divisive issue."

The subject of the Fire Walkers' freedom shouldn't have been divisive at all. "Don't they remember the King is a Fire Walker, too? They're his Council, can't he control them?"

"Khaled is putting his foot down and trying to convince the Hartnords that Fire Walkers are no threat. It's a hard sell, as they'll be attending Prince Rais's helbond ceremony tonight and he has the scars to prove their danger. That's why Rais has been absent from these initial meetings for now. Fire Walkers will be performing at the ceremony, at the King's suggestion, to show they can be trusted to control their power. We'll all need to be on our best behavior."

"You can't let Leila or her acolytes near the ceremony—"

"Leila is High Priestess. The ceremony is hers."

"One of her acolytes left me to die. You can't trust them."

"We'll take every precaution, don't fear. I've asked Jonan to watch them, in any case. Once this is over, I'll be bringing my own concerns to the King regarding Leila and her acolytes. Don't think I'm going to let them get away with mistreating you."

She'd keep an eye on them, too, but it didn't feel like enough. Stopping Prince Ravel from winning the tournament had been straight forward, but how could she convince an entire foreign kingdom to leave the Fire Walkers alone?

"There is another matter I must discuss with you," Talin said. "The Council has made its own proposal to placate the Hartnords. Their crown prince needs a wife. Princess Aniya is at an eligible age for marriage. An alliance would strengthen ties between the nations."

A marriage between Sandair and Hartnor? Mina knew little enough about politics, but this marriage didn't sound like something any woman would desire. "Does Aniya want to marry a Hartnord?"

"She knows what's expected of her."

"That's not an answer. Doesn't she get a say?"

Talin tugged at his braided beard. "Khaled is... uncomfortable with the prospect of his daughter marrying a Hartnord. Not after he lost his dear sister on Hartnord land seventeen years ago. But he needs a strong reason to reject the Council's proposal. He has another marriage candidate in mind for Aniya, and she has agreed."

"That's good, isn't it? If she's happy with the choice—"

"It's your sorran. The Neu Bosan boy. I'm afraid you'll need to release him."

Alistar? *He* was a marriage candidate for the Princess? Since when? He'd barely left the Academy, hadn't even won the tournament, and yet he was being stolen for marriage? Mina squeezed her hands together. "Does he know?"

"Not yet. The King has been in talks with his father. All parties have agreed to the match."

"But Ali—my sorran doesn't even know? They've not asked him? What happened to building alliances between Sandair and Hartnor?"

"A marriage between Sandair and Neu Bosa would be equally favorable. Neu Bosa don't have royalty to speak of, but House Myrbond has recently gained enough political power in Neu Bosa to raise them to that level. As the ambassador's son—"

"We're already allies with Neu Bosa!"

"This would strengthen that alliance. And Khaled would feel happier if Aniya was tied to a Sandarian House rather than a foreign power."

This was why Alistar was too busy to see her. He was being groomed for life as a pampered prince. He, Princess Aniya, and the Fire Walkers were being offered up as sacrificial lambs on a political platter just to make some Housemen happy. Did Alistar get any say in how to live his life? Did the Princess? None of it seemed fair.

"When?" was all Mina managed to say.

"The proposal will be drafted shortly, whilst our Hartnord guests are with us. The actual marriage will likely take place in the coming Gai's Seed."

Gai's Seed, the season of renewal and growth. They still had the rest of Rahn's Dawn and then Lune's Shadow to get through.

That meant Alistar would be married off in less than half a year. Gods, he'd become a prince. Would Alistar accept or flee? She'd always thought Alistar valued training as a warrior more than marriage. He spoke often of the isles of Neu Bosa and the adventures they could have at sea together—him, her, and Raj.

Talin patted her shoulder. "I know you two are close—"

"We're not close."

"He's your sorran. That kind of bond is always close."

Except the sorran bond had never worked for them, though they'd kept it hidden. Only Raj knew the truth.

"Once the proposal has been made, he cannot remain as your sorran," Talin said.

"Why not? If the marriage isn't until Gai's Seed—"

"It wouldn't be proper, Mina."

"What, because I'm a girl?"

"Essentially." The word was laced with sympathy.

Her gut warmed at the implication that she would be anything but *proper* with her sorran. *No one cared before,* she wanted to argue, but she bit her tongue. She wasn't a girl before, and it wasn't Talin's fault this foolishness was being thrust upon her.

"If you're interested, Prince Rais was asking after you." Talin nudged her.

"Me?"

"He wants you to serve as his sorran. It's all he spoke about on the journey south. He mentioned something about a pact the two of you made."

Heat flushed her cheeks. She *had* offered to serve as his sorran Vif he agreed to help keep Prince Ravel from the throne, but that was before the Prince of Poison had been placed under house arrest for his deeds—and before she'd revealed her true sex and blood fire to an arena full of people. She hadn't expected Prince Rais to remain committed to their bargain.

"Wouldn't that be improper?"

Talin chuckled. "I don't think Rais cares. I'm warning you now, he'll try and corner you after his ceremony. It's your choice, but

Rais would appreciate having a tournament champion for a sorran. And, I think these next few days are the beginning of a new dawn. Times are changing fast and you'll need to decide who you wish to be."

She stared into his dark eyes. "What do you mean?"

"Once things have settled, Iman will need to return to Arlent. No doubt she'd welcome your company, and as my daughter and heir, I'd like for you to take a more active interest in our House and its future. But…"

Her stomach fluttered whenever he spoke of her as his daughter. "But?"

"You're young, and there's plenty of time for that. The King needs me to remain as his sorran whilst this transition with the Hartnords takes place. I would appreciate your company, as well. I don't want you to be bored. We'll need to find you something to do."

She shuffled into his side and leaned her head against his shoulder. "If you want me to stay, just say so."

He wrapped his arm around her and squeezed. "Is it selfish that I want my daughter close?"

She strained a look up and grinned. "Not at all."

"Times like these may be rare."

"Then we'll treasure them."

Talin's essence bloomed through the bond like the first rays of dawn. "Do you want to dance? I can spare a little time before the ceremony."

Mina slid off the bench and gripped Hawk's hilt. "I'm already warmed up."

Talin stepped beside her, his height dwarfing her own. He put his left hand on his own sword and drew it in a single flourish. The action was smooth, powerful. Of a warrior. The greatest warrior in all Sandair, and he was her father. It sent a thrill through her spine.

If the Fire Walkers were facing another battle, then Mina would be ready.

5

THE HELBOND CEREMONY

The afternoon sky burned a deeper shade of red. Mina returned to her shared room sweaty but satisfied. Iman sat at the dresser wearing a silver dress and her purple sahn tied around her waist. She forwent her usual turban and let her shoulder-length hair rest naturally, with two silver hoops dangling from her ears. The effect looked feminine, but Iman still cut a formidable figure. Her attention was fixed on a scroll in one hand—a glass of wine held in the other.

Iman glanced up. "Did you almost forget about the ceremony?" She nodded toward their shared cistern. "Go wash but be quick about it. You stink like a camel."

Mina pulled a face and skipped into the cistern. Iman had already lit a few lamps, enough to light their tiny room. It was just as cramped as their shared lodgings during the tournament— barely big enough for Iman's bed and Mina's lounger—but at least the furniture didn't look like it was about to fall apart. Mina unbuckled her scabbard and sword, carefully placing them on a stool beside the bath, and shrugged off the rest of her clothes into a heap. She slipped into the water. It wasn't cool like she expected, but warm. "Did you heat this?"

"I heat all my baths," Iman called back.

Iman had the gall to complain about Mina using her fire frivolously when she wasted her own blood on petty comfort? She tutted and sank until the waters lapped her chin. Its warmth soothed and eased the tension in her muscles. Perhaps she'd try heating her own baths. She grabbed the lavender-scented soap and scrubbed her underarms.

Did Prince Rais truly plan to ask her to serve as sorran knowing who she was?

It meant making a bond and serving a master—neither of which appealed to her. Prince Rais would be able to order her to do whatever he wished. How was that any different from a forced marriage? From being forced to use blood fire as a Fire Walker? She wouldn't be her own man—*woman*. She wouldn't be able to make her own choices.

And would it be *proper*? For a woman to serve a man? She sat up, splashing water. Life had been less complex when she'd been hiding behind Malik. Now she had to worry about being proper, for Lune's sake.

Could she refuse a Prince she'd sworn promises to?

Would Talin be disappointed if she did?

Iman opened the cistern door and leaned against the archway. "Taking your time, girl. Have you thought about what you're wearing tonight?"

"I have those black robes from my bondrite."

Iman offered her a towel. "I've got something else in mind."

Mina climbed out of the bath, wrapped the towel around her waist, and followed Iman back into the room. A purple silk dress hung from the dresser's edge. Its color matched House Arlbond, and the silks flowed in layers, thin at the top and then spilling into ruffles at the bottom. Tiny silver crescents stitched into the fabric glittered like stars.

It was beautiful.

Mina ran her finger down the soft silk. "You made this?"

Iman poured herself another glass of wine and sat on the edge of her bed. "Not me, girl. Your mother. She had a skill for sewing, did Tira. It was the agreement we had between us: I'd do all the cooking and baking, and she'd do all the sewing and embroidery.

She spent many nights on this design but didn't get a chance to wear it. It's yours."

A lump caught in Mina's throat. She hadn't returned to Arlent since learning the truth of her mother and owned nothing from her mother's life, save the dagger gifted by Talin.

"I've adjusted the sizing," Iman said. "You're a little taller than Tira."

"*I'm* taller than my mother? How could I possibly be taller than anyone?"

"You're Talin's daughter, girl."

"I don't look anything like him."

Iman chuckled. "Hawker blood is strong, but you're his daughter through and though." She raised her glass to the dress. "Try it on."

"It's... it's beautiful, truly, but I can't wear this. Not tonight."

Iman raised a thick eyebrow. "And why not?"

"Because I'm the winner of the tournament." *And Prince Rais will be there.* "Warriors don't wear dresses."

Iman sighed. She placed her wine glass down and patted the bed beside her. "Sit, girl."

Mina sat on the bed, tugging the towel tight.

"Being a woman doesn't make you any less of a warrior, nor does being a warrior make you less of a woman. You won the tournament. You. A girl and a Fire Walker. What message do you think that sends?"

"That the King is easily fooled?"

Iman snorted. "No woman has fought in the tournament in hundreds of years, and you won. No Fire Walker has received the King's blessing, and you did. Other girls, other Fire Walkers, they'll look upon you and see what they could obtain for themselves. Be proud of what you've achieved. Be proud of who you are. By hiding those aspects, you dishonor yourself."

"The Housemen will look at me and see a girl in a dress. Not a warrior."

"Pah. Housemen find any reason to belittle women. Why do

their job for them? Tonight isn't about them. Those Hartnords will look upon you and see a brave woman—and a Fire Walker who has achieved great things. We need to show them who Fire Walkers really are."

In truth, Mina had never worn a real dress before. The rags and castoffs she'd taken from the Temple of Gai in Khalbad were patched together, and after a while she'd chosen boys' clothes because they were easier to run in and fight. Boys' clothes were comfortable, but girls'... their designs could be completely impractical.

Prince Rais wanted her for a sorran knowing she was a girl and a Fire Walker, and Alistar was still hers, despite it being improper. She'd show them *improper*. "What about my sahn?"

"Noblewomen don't need to wear one. But you can wrap it around your waist if need be."

"I need my waist free for my belt."

"Your belt?"

"For my sword."

"For your..." Iman rubbed her forehead. "Can't you leave it behind for one night?"

"No warrior leaves home without their sword."

"Who do you expect to fight, girl?"

"There'll be Hartnords at the ceremony."

"Who'll be under watch by guards—"

"And is Prince Ravel going to be at the ceremony?"

"Yes, I'd imagine—"

"Then I'm taking my sword."

"You'll scare off the boys." Iman's raised brow implied a certain younger prince, but Prince Rais's interest was in her sword, nothing else.

"If I wanted to attract a boy, I'd attend the ceremony naked."

"Fine, fine. Get dry so we can begin this farce."

Mina kissed her aunt on the cheek and twirled the silk dress in the light, getting a better look at the twilight of colors and sparkling silver. Tonight, she'd keep her promises to the Fire Walkers and make her mother proud.

In the lamplight, Mina caught a glimpse of her mother, always watching through the fire. Tira smiled and nodded her blessing.

Mina followed Fez along the marble path into the palace gardens, breathing in the scents of rose and jasmine. The royal gardens were a hidden paradise within the Keep, but tonight they buzzed with activity. Housemen sat on the benches or stood beside the fountains, chatting and enjoying the early evening Rahnlight. They were all dressed in their finest silks and colorful gemstones. Iman had once offered to pierce Mina's ears, but jewelry could be grabbed in a fight and turned against her.

The dress covered her chest well enough, but ended shorter than she would have liked, exposing her legs below the knee and the silver tattoos on her arms. Its length offered one key advantage—she'd be able to draw her sword, bend her knees, and move in a fight. Not that she expected trouble, but as Iman said, her choice of clothes sent a message, and she wanted that message to be that she'd be ready for battle no matter the occasion.

Fez screeched and ran from underneath a bush. The fronds parted and a tall Gaislander boy waddled out. Leaves clung to his fine green silk robes and the lilac sahn wrapped tightly across his shoulder. He ran a hand through an unruly bunch of curls on his head.

"Mina? Is that you?" Raj's eyes opened wide and he grinned. "It is you! I knew Fez wouldn't lead me astray." Raj bounded to Mina and grabbed her hands, squeezing them. "You look healthy! How have you been—no, tell me later. Ali is around here somewhere."

She plucked leaves from Raj's sahn. His chin also bore a patch of hair, like Alistar's. Both of her friends were growing into men. "It's good to see you too. Have you been crawling in bushes?"

He gave a bashful smile. "I, um, I was admiring the flowers."

She looped her arm around his. "Course you were."

Raj beamed and allowed her to guide them back to the path.

They joined the main crowd of Housemen headed to the throne room where Prince Rais's helbond ceremony would take place. Jovial chatter and laughter lightened the air, much different from when the Hartnords first arrived, though this number of people hadn't visited the Keep for Prince Rais alone.

Through the bond, she could tell Iman and Jonan were close by, and Talin waited farther on ahead, no doubt by the King's side. The Housemen gave her and Raj odd looks. She supposed the two of them made a strange pair. Raj stood at least two heads taller than she, and he carried no sword. He'd never been one for the fighting arts like Alistar and her, but his skills as a Green Hand won different types of battles. He pointed out flowers in the garden as they walked, explaining which were native and which had been imported from Gaisland. She wasn't following his words—her attention remained fixed on Fez running in and out of the bushes—but she chimed in where necessary if only to elicit a smile.

The crowd poured into the throne room. Saeed and Samira stood guard by the main archway, scanning people as they entered. Both glared as Mina approached. The pair of them looked almost like twins with their bald heads and identical red flame tattoos and matching scowls, only Samira stood a few inches taller. Samira whispered something in Saeed's ear and shot her a scathing look.

Saeed stepped before her and held up his hands, blocking her entry. "You recover from blood loss remarkably quickly. Is your Rhaesbond aware that it is a perversion to partake in rites protected by priests?"

She ignored Raj's confused stare and offered her sweetest smile. "I trust a Rhaesbond to do the right thing more than your priests."

A couple of Housemen muttered as they walked past. Mina moved to join them.

Saeed grabbed her arm. "What do you hope to achieve here?" he whispered.

"To support the Fire Walkers, same as you." She yanked her arm free.

"Then you've heard the rumors of Fire Walkers attacking

Hartnords by the border? Or Fire Walkers burning trees in Gaisland? Or Fire Walkers threatening families in the lower city?"

Mina swallowed. She hadn't heard all of those rumors. "Fire Walkers aren't monsters."

"No, but they're angry. And angry men with fire in their blood make a dangerous combination. It will take one spark for our entire kingdom to burn itself to the ground."

"You're being dramatic."

"Am I? You've not spent your entire life in the temple. You're nothing but a pampered noble sticking your nose into matters you can't understand." He fixed a smile as more Housemen walked by.

"You don't know my life. My uncle was murdered for being a Fire Walker, so don't you dare—"

"It always has to be someone's uncle or parent or child before people care enough to take action. Your heart may be in the right place, but that's no excuse for ignorance—"

"*I'm* ignorant? You're the one who believes Fire Walkers deserve no freedom!"

"Our people are safer in the temple. They have no one to protect them from hatred—"

"They have me."

"Do they?" Saeed crossed his arms. "And what will you give up to protect them?"

She wanted to laugh. She'd almost sacrificed her House, her family, her own life to keep Prince Ravel off the throne and save the Fire Walkers from genocide. "Haven't I done enough?"

"An answer I'd expect from a Houseman. You can't just change a law spanning hundreds of years without transition and care."

Raj gently nudged her. Some Housemen were staring at them. Mina matched Saeed's disdain with her own. "Are we done?"

Saeed stepped to one side and swung into a mocking bow. "I hope you'll be there for them, Mina Hawker, when the kingdom burns."

She brushed past him and scowled over her shoulder.

Raj hurried to her side. "What was all that about?"

"Just another fool."

They followed Housemen inside. Space had been cordoned off in the middle, presumably for Prince Rais. From what Iman had explained, the point of the ceremony was to recreate his bondrite for the benefit of the Houses. Then a night of feasting and celebration would await. It promised to be as eventful as the Solend, more so since they'd be entertaining foreign guests.

A troupe of Neu Bosan musicians played a soft melody on their flutes in the corner. Raj tugged her arm and pulled her toward a Neu Bosan standing close by, listening to the music.

"Ali, look who I've found!" Raj said, tugging her along.

Alistar spun round. "Who's your frien—" His mouth opened wide. "Malik?"

Raj giggled. "It's Mina, remember? Doesn't she look—"

"Why are you wearing that?" Alistar blurted out.

Heat filled her cheeks. "Warriors don't leave their sword behind."

Alistar's emerald eyes traced down to her hip. "You brought your sword?"

She crossed her arms over her chest. "You're wearing yours."

Alistar wore a black silk shalwar kameez in the Sandarian style with a green trim embroidered into the edges, matching his lime sahn. They were richer clothes than he'd normally wear, and his hair looked different too. Slick and brushed back. The green beads that usually dangled on a braid beside his neck were missing, and his chin had been clean shaven. He looked like a prince.

Did he know of his fate?

Raj pointed to the dais. "The Hartnords are here."

The silver giants with their pale faces strolled into the room. Only their King had forsaken his armor, graced instead in cobalt blue, the Water Bearers color—the color of death and mourning. Inappropriate for Prince Rais's helbond. Didn't these Hartnords know anything about Sandarian culture? Seats had been placed on the dais beside the royal throne, and the Hartnords moved for the ones at the far side.

The Queen of Sandair stepped onto the dais next, earning a cheer from the Housemen. Her round belly looked ready to burst with child any day. As the young Princess Aniya helped the Queen to her seat, Mina spared a glance to Alistar. He stared into the distance, frowning. She wanted to say something, but what? He wasn't technically her sorran; there was no bond between them that she could pull, but she didn't need a blood bond to understand his mood, nor did she blame him. His life was being dictated, and who'd want Prince Ravel for a brother-in-law?

A loud cheer filled the room next as Prince Rais walked onto the dais and waved to the Housemen with a broad smile. He wore his hair tied back, revealing his scarred face to the world, and his hand gripped the sword strapped to his hip—the sword that now named him a man. He looked so different from the skulking boy who had once hidden in his brother's shadow.

That shadow stepped into the hall next. The disgraced Prince himself.

Losing the Solaran tournament hadn't dulled Prince Ravel's polished charisma. He paraded his fake smiles with all the enthusiasm of a snake charmer. The crowd welcomed him with a cheer as well, and not even a subdued one. Mina felt the embers in her gut surge and heat flooded through her arms, making her fingers tingle. She flexed them and took a steadying breath. This night wasn't about him.

The loudest cheers welcomed King Khaled, who was followed by his two sorrans—Gareth and her father. The Bright Solara sat. Each wore varying shades of reds and gold to match the banners and braziers above. Both the King and his sons dominated the space with their presence, as though in competition with each other.

Housemen continued to fill the throne room. The Sword of Solus and Guardian of Gai guarded the bottom of the dais, both dressed in their finest scale armor as guests and warriors of the King. Salasar eyed the crowds with a wary expression. No doubt he remembered the disaster of Prince Ravel's helbond ceremony a year prior.

A Houseman bumped into her and cursed. Some commotion was going on behind her. A noblewoman yelled something about a rat. Mina grabbed the hilt of her sword and waded through the crowd.

An orange furball had grabbed hold of the woman's scarf and was tugging it with his teeth. A few of the Houseman pointed and laughed as the woman struggled. Another girl pulled at the scarf and tried to shoo the fox away. Gods damn it, he must have followed her inside.

Mina leaped into the fray. "Fez, stop it!"

The fox refused to drop his prey. Raj fished out seeds from his pocket. "Here."

Fez's ears sprang up at the sight of food. He abandoned the poor woman's scarf and attacked the seeds instead. Mina mumbled an apology and scooped the fox. Her dress did nothing to protect against his sharp claws. "You're not on the guest list, you little bug-biter. Stop ruining my dress."

Fez screeched in protest as she carried him away from the crowd.

A girl followed her—the same Solander girl who'd tried to help. "He's a feisty one. And you're the Sand Dancer, aren't you? Tamina Arlbond? I watched you win the tournament dressed as a boy."

Mina's heart skipped a beat. Iman had said winning the tournament would send a message. "That's right."

This girl stood taller than Mina and wore a flowing turquoise dress and matching ribbons braided into her long black hair. Two silver doves dangled from her ears, but compared to the other noble girls, she didn't flaunt her wealth. "And you studied in the Academy. As a boy."

Where was she going with this? "They don't let girls into the Academy. I did what was necessary to get inside."

"But that's not right. Girls are capable of learning academics and swordplay. Why shouldn't they be allowed in the Academy? You're proof we have a place there."

"Tell that to the King."

The girl's cheeks flushed pink. "Yes, exactly! I—forgive my manners. I'm Kasara." She dipped into a quick curtsey. "I was hoping you'd be here tonight. Would you be willing to lend your voice and help me convince the King to admit girls?"

"I've already asked. The King refused to—"

A flickering brazier caught Mina's eye. Tira waved at her from the flames and pointed to the throne room entrance. A pale-skinned man dressed in blue silks slid past the doors to the gardens outside.

A Hartnord.

Alone, without a guard or chaperone.

She'd not been able to approach a Hartnord yet. Everywhere they walked, they were accompanied by the palace guards, and they didn't eat in the dining hall.

But this could be her chance to speak to one.

She juggled Fez in her arms. "If you'll excuse me, I should take him outside."

Kasara blocked her path. "Perhaps if we drew up a petition and approached the King together—"

"Another time." Mina brushed past her and carried Fez outside into the gardens.

She shuffled between late-arriving Housemen, but the Hartnord had vanished. Fez wiggled free and she let him down between the bushes. A passing firefly caught his attention and he crouched into a hunt. She brushed stray strands of fur from her dress and straightened its ruffles as best she could. He'd left a few superficial scratches on her bare arms, but no one would notice those among her silver swirls.

It had been a foolish plan anyway. How could she even speak to a Hartnord? She knew nothing about them or their language, only that their land was supposedly hard as stone and devoid of warmth.

The bushes rustled behind her. Alistar and Raj must have followed. "We best return now before Fez notices—"

Mina jumped. The Hartnord stood before her.

6

THE SILVER PRINCE

"You have the Hartsire gaze," the Hartnord said with a lilting accent like the pitter-patter of rain. He stood tall in a blue silk tunic edged with silver embroidery that matched the shimmering stars of Mina's dress. It hugged his slim body and the top collar flopped open, exposing a tuft of light hair. His pale face was clean shaven and smooth, making him look young—certainly no older than Prince Ravel—and his short-combed hair glowed white in the early evening light.

His bright silver eyes mirrored her own, cut from starlight.

He was Lune in male form.

Mina stared at him. "You speak Sandarian?"

He smiled with perfect teeth. "I am ill-practiced in your speech, but learning."

There was something unnerving about him and his silver eyes. "Are—are you lost? The other Hartnords—uh, your people, they're waiting in the throne room."

"Your palace is hot, even at night. I was in need of air. Are you one of them?"

"One of who?"

He pointed to her arm. "They all have markings, yes?"

"I'm a Fire Walker, if that's what you mean."

"They've been hiding you. Your kin. They wouldn't let us meet you, but your King says you are safe and can be trusted."

"My King speaks the truth."

"Then why hide you? It's why I came. To see you for myself and know if the stories are true."

This was it. Her one chance to convince these foreigners that Fire Walkers were no threat. "The tales are... exaggerated. Fire Walkers are normal men and women who wish to live their lives in peace. None of them asked for blood fire. They'd give it back if they could."

"Then where did it come from? How does it work?"

"It's in our blood as a gift from Rahn—our god."

"The stories say you stole it from god."

Even Hartnords told the same children's tales of the Fire Walkers? She tried to imitate Talin's reassuring smile. "I'm no thief. I wouldn't know how to steal from a man, let alone a god. He'd surely notice if we all stole his fire, wouldn't he?"

The Hartnord didn't return the smile. "When one of your people cast your magic, it takes from the sun. And so its light diminishes, and the days get shorter, and the nights longer, until at last there will be no light at all. Only darkness. So our prophet speaks."

"Forgive me, what do you mean by the sun?"

"The light in the daytime sky. Rahn, I believe you called it?"

When her childhood tales spoke of Fire Walkers stealing their power, she'd never considered what it meant—that they were literally stealing Rahn's warmth and light. If that were true, then Rahn would have shrunk over hundreds of years, wouldn't he? "But the days and nights are the same. They don't change."

"They do in Hartnor. Our days shorten and our fields turn brown. Come winter, the darkness presses heavy and our lands freeze. Only by prayer, and by committing to the laws of our god, do the light and warmth return."

What was he saying? That Sandarian blood fire was responsible for their seasons? Surely Hartnords weren't foolish enough to believe that. "We don't steal Rahnlight from your lands. How could we? Our fire is something else. It's part of us, it's part of our blood."

"May I see it?" The way he looked at her wasn't with apprehension, but eager curiosity. He wasn't scared of her. Perhaps she'd misread him and he was as skeptical of childhood tales as she was.

She held up her palm and summoned a single dancing flame. It lit up his face, and he stared at it with wide eyes. "How is that possible? Does it not hurt you?" He reached out to touch it.

She snatched her hand back before she could accidentally burn him. "It—it doesn't hurt me, but I wouldn't want to hurt you." She cringed at her own words—she hadn't meant it to sound like a threat.

He cocked his head. "Wouldn't you? Your people march on our land and burn our homes."

"Fire Walker aren't monsters. We use our fire to cook or light lanterns, not to hurt others."

"But your people *do* hurt others."

"There may be the odd criminal who does, but they don't represent the rest of us. They're no different from a man who chooses to turn his sword against an innocent. Are there no criminals in Hartnor?"

That drew a smile.

The bushes parted. She shook out her flame but swallowed her relief—another Hartnord. No, Gareth, the King's sorran. "You shouldn't be out here."

The young Hartnord placed a hand on his chest and inclined his head. "Your friends are stifling. I needed air."

"The ceremony is beginning shortly. You don't want to miss it." Then Gareth spoke sharp Hartnord words, the first time she'd ever heard him speak that way, and their Hartnord guest responded in kind.

The young Hartnord buckled his collar. "But of course, I am a guest at your mercy." He held out his hand to her. "Will you join me? I am still new to your kingdom. It appears there is much we could learn from one another."

She stared at his hand. Did he mean for her to kiss it? She

didn't even know who he was! But he belonged to the delegation, and if she could convince him that Fire Walkers truly meant them no harm, perhaps the Hartnords would return to their home in the north and drop all notions of pressuring the King and his Council.

She took his hand. "I'm Mina of House Arlbond."

"A noble lady? Ah, I did not realize. Forgive my lack of courtesy." He bowed and brushed soft lips against the back of her hand before she could react. Her heart fluttered. "Call me Wulf. Shall we?"

Wulf? An odd name. He looped his arm around hers and guided her back to the path. Her heart thumped with each step. It wasn't like walking with Raj. He was her friend, the boy she'd trusted with her biggest secrets, and this was a stranger, a foreigner, a man whose body heat burned uncomfortably close despite the tales claiming Hartnords were cold and hard. Gareth trailed them, though he was out of earshot.

She glanced over her shoulder to make sure before whispering, "Do you know him? Gareth?" Something in the way they'd exchanged words in the Hartnord tongue suggested familiarity.

"He once served my father."

"Your father? In Hartnor?"

"Yes, many moons ago."

Talin had told her that Gareth had come into King Khaled's service during the last Hartnord war seventeen years ago, but he'd never revealed the details of Gareth's defection. Did his own people consider him a traitor? It was a question she'd ask Talin later. "What are moons?"

"I forget what you call it." He pointed to the silver crescents tattooed on her arm. "Moon."

"Lune?" She stifled a giggle.

He smiled. "Lune."

The two of them walked arm-in-arm into the throne room. She feared the stares and whispers as they entered, but none of the Housemen were looking in her direction. Their attention remained

SAND DANCER | 51

fixed on the center of the room.

"We're arrived in time." Wulf released her arm.

Six Hartnord men stood in the cordoned-off section of the throne room, wearing nothing but leather pants, their pale chests bare and oiled.

"What are they, Hartnord Fire Walkers?" someone beside her said, and laughed.

The Hartnord men paired off. Whispers and giggles rippled through the crowd as the Hartnords raised their fists into a fighting stance.

They leaped at each other. She stared open-mouthed as the Hartnord men fought with a flurry of fists and feet instead of steel. They grappled, flesh connecting with flesh. It looked less of a battle and more of a dance.

"Incredible," she whispered. "Do all Hartnords fight this way?"

A shadow stepped beside her. She hadn't noticed Prince Ravel leave the King's side. "They fight with steel, Lady Arlbond, and they know how to use it. Isn't that so, Prince Wulfhart?"

She bit her lip to hide her shock. Gods, she'd been talking—and walking arm-in-arm—with a prince of Hartnor? She silently ran through their conversation in the garden, trying to remember if she'd said anything grossly inappropriate.

He greeted Prince Ravel with a brief tilt of his head. "Indeed. It's a shame we missed your tournament. We would have liked to have tested our steel against yours. Your warriors move fast, so everyone says, but they cannot match Hartnord metal. Our weapons are designed for strength, and our armor can deflect any blade."

Prince Ravel returned the modest bow. "We move faster because we don't hide behind thick armor. It's a burden that holds you back. Whilst you're still lifting your blade, ours will be at your throat."

"The Sandarian need to spill blood is barbaric to us."

Prince Ravel smiled as pleasantly as always, but his charm hid a viper's fangs. "Such is the way of the warrior. What man can name himself a man without spilling blood?"

"Nothing bleeds faster than a Sandarian. Isn't that what they say?"

"No corpse is colder than a Hartnord's."

Prince Wulfhart's cool silver eyes met Prince Ravel's fiery amber. "We find it interesting that a woman won your tournament. Are there so few men who pose a challenge?"

She clasped hands behind her back and itched to leave. Dealing with one pompous prince was bad enough.

Prince Ravel regarded her then, as though remembering she stood among them. "Lady Arlbond is a rather unique woman, wouldn't you say? Less of a woman and more of the man she masqueraded as. As you can see—" he waved a hand at her dress. "It's rather hard to tell."

She scowled and her hand twitched for Hawk's hilt. The crowd erupted with cheers. The Hartnord dancers finished their routine with a series of flips and jumps and rolled into a bow.

Prince Ravel clapped once. "If you'll excuse me, Prince Wulfhart, Lady Arlbond. Our entertainment is about to begin. It promises to be... fiery." The Prince winked at her as he strode back to the dais. She pulled a face.

"*You* won your tournament?" Wulf gave her an assessing stare.

A flicker of warmth stirred in her gut. What could he see with those eyes, so alike her own and Gareth's? Did he have the Hartnord Sight, too? The ability to see more than most men, as Iman once put it. "It's why I carry a sword, my Prince."

"Please, just Wulf. I did wonder if it was Sandarian fashion. It seems most of your people carry weapons."

"They don't in Hartnor?"

"No, only knights and guardsmen."

"Then how do you duel?"

"With sharp tongues, not sharp blades." He pointed to the center of the room. "Is that one of your kin?"

Saeed entered the space and stood alone. Surely, he wasn't the King's suggested entertainment? She scanned the room. High Priestess Leila stood at the back with Samira. Jonan lingered close by, watching them as promised. She caught a flicker of Alistar's lime green sahn and Raj's lilac in the crowd. Prince Ravel had returned to his seat on the dais beside the King and Prince Rais. On the other side sat King Reinhart. His silver giants towered behind him. Talin, Gareth, and Salasar were all lined up at the front—no trouble would get past them.

"Shouldn't you be with your king?" she asked.

Wulf half-shrugged. "I learn more with my ear on the ground. Is that how you say it?"

"Close enough." For a prince, he didn't seem so pompous. Perhaps he and Prince Rais would get on and forge a true alliance between their nations. Free trade and no more wars. So long as Prince Ravel kept his slimy face out of it.

Saeed raised his fists and they both flickered into flame. The crowd muttered, speculating what the Fire Walker would do next.

"For too long, my kind has been forced to hide the gifts that Rahn bestowed upon us," he proclaimed. "For too long, we buried our Rahnlight underground and allowed Rahn's gift to die. We are grateful for our King's mercy, and his wisdom that allows Rahn's light to flourish once more. We are honored to serve you, my King."

Mina's eyes narrowed. Those words might have come from her own mouth.

He bowed to King Khaled with an exaggerated flourish. His flame swished through the air as he did so, earning polite clapping and whoops from the crowd.

Next, Saeed approached the Hartnord king and repeated the same bow, to more cheers. "And we are honored to have such guests in our company, but also confused. You come here with unfounded prejudices against my kind. You come here and make demands of us which aren't wanted or warranted."

The cheers fizzled out into nervous murmurs. What was that fool doing? Insulting them wasn't going to win their favor.

"Is this part of your entertainment?" Wulf whispered.

"I—I don't know."

She tried to catch Talin's eye and his unease rumbled through the bond, echoed by Jonan, who slowly edged through the crowd. This wasn't part of the entertainment. Not at all.

"Blood fire has existed since the dawn of time," Saeed continued. "So long as Rahn burns, so will every Sandarian child born. His fire is in our blood. It cannot be suppressed. It cannot be denied. Only one great House in history has acknowledged this, and it is they I honor this night. It is they I burn for."

The silver giants stepped from behind their king, subtly removing their triangular shields from their backs, though not subtly enough. Whatever jest Saeed planned, the Hartnords weren't impressed.

Saeed dared a step toward King Reinhart and the silver giants slammed their shields onto the dais with a deafening clang.

Flame swirled around Saeed's fists. He lifted them as though examining the wondrous power bestowed to him. "May you burn bright, my King. For House Rhaesbond!"

Fire burst from Saeed's fists at King Reinhart.

7

THE CURSE OF HOUSE RHAESBOND

Screams erupted in the throne room. Mina grabbed her sword hilt and pushed passed the Housemen, fighting her way through the panicked mob to the center.

Saeed summoned a blazing wall of fire, blocking Talin and Salasar from getting through. Another burst of flame attacked it; Jonan came running, his own power colliding with Saeed's. The wall split for a heartbeat and allowed Talin to leap inside.

"Father!" She ran after him.

The wall of flame vanished.

Talin's blade had cut clean through Saeed's neck. He sank to his knees, blood already pouring down his bare back onto the pristine tiles. His fire had left its mark—a black line scorched its way up the dais steps to its intended target.

She covered her mouth and gagged.

Two of the Hartnord giants sagged to the ground, their metal armor blackened and twisted; Saeed's flames had melted through them, boiling the men inside their shells. Their triangular shields were molten, crumpled lumps. Hunched between them lay the Hartnord king, or what remained of him. He hadn't worn armor, not that it would have helped. His pale skin had been reduced to a pulpy red and black mess. Her hand dropped from Hawk's hilt.

Gods. Saeed had killed the Hartnord king.

A woman screamed behind her. Mina turned to find Samira

had collapsed to her knees, her body rocking back and forth, her wide, tearful eyes pinned on Saeed's twitching form. Housemen fled past her, knocking her over, not caring for her plight, or that the threat had now been put down. Leila came to Samira's side, but her eyes lacked warmth or sympathy.

Salasar waved his sword in the air. "Calm yourselves!" he yelled, his voice ringing around the room. "Rahn's blood, you're Housemen, not startled geldings! Get a hold of yourselves!" He barked orders at the guards.

They obeyed, rounding up Housemen like cattle. Alistar, Raj, and Iman were swept along with them. Some hurried and tripped over their own feet in their rush to leave, whilst others lingered, their jaws slack as they stared, their lips muttering silent prayers.

On the dais, Gareth tried to move the Bright Solara to safety. Guards escorted the Queen and Princess Aniya through the rear door to the royal offices, but the King and Prince Ravel remained locked in a heated argument Mina couldn't hear over the stomping Housemen and fearful murmurs.

The remaining Hartnords surrounded their dead king with their swords drawn, their pale faces a mixture of anguish and rage. What in Lune's name had possessed Saeed to do this? He was supposed to protect the Fire Walkers! He was their ally! This wouldn't just give the Council a justified reason to agree to the Hartnords' demands—it gave them cause to lock the Fire Walkers away forever, if not *worse*.

How could he have done this?

How could he?

A whoosh of fire made everyone jump. Leila stood over Saeed's body, burning it with her own hands.

Mina ran to the High Priestess and grabbed her arm, yanking her back. "Stop! What are you doing?"

Leila's fire snapped out and her silver eyes glared. "I'm burning a traitor's body—"

"If you burn him, we can't question his Shadow!"

"And if we don't burn him, his Shadow will form a wraith and attack. I can't risk that."

"I need to know *why*! Why did he do this? I need to ask—"

But it was too late. Saeed's body had crumpled into ash and no Shadow rose. The irony of it made her sick. Oh, it was acceptable to burn *his* body? Now she'd never know why he did it. Why he'd condemn his own people with a single burst of flame.

It was the curse of House Rhaesbond all over again.

Salasar stomped past her and reeled to a halt. The filthy curse he muttered wasn't aimed at Leila or Saeed's smoldering body, but the Hartnords by the dais.

Wulf had Prince Rais in his grip—a knife at his throat. "Stay still," the prince warned in rough Sandarian.

Salasar brandished his sword. "You spill a drop of his blood and none of you will leave this room alive."

The remaining silver giants guarded their prince, swords and shields raised, but no one dared move. Prince Rais's eye met hers. He bit his lip, and his chest rose in shallow breaths. His scabbard was empty, his sword discarded somewhere out of reach. At least he had the sense to remain still.

King Khaled came to Salasar's side, but no farther. His sorrans and Prince Ravel followed. The King held up his hand, halting them. "Stand down, Salasar."

"My King—"

"That is my command."

Salasar bowed and moved behind the King, though his sword remained drawn.

"My father is dead!" Wulf yelled, his voice breaking. "Your fire kin killed him! Cooked him like a pig!"

"You have my deepest condolences, Prince Wulfhart. I and my people never imagined this could happ—"

"Liar! You invite us to your home, you offer your wine, and you burn us with your blood! I see it within you, King Sandarian."

"Then look at my words and see their truth. No one is more saddened by this tragedy than I."

"Words will not bring my father back. Sandarian law is clear,

is it not? An eye for an eye? Blood for blood?" His hand flinched.
Prince Rais gasped. A single line of blood ran down his neck.

"Enough, Wulf," Gareth said. "Your father wouldn't want—"

"Don't speak of my father," Wulf spat. "Was this your plan?
Play the long game? Trap us here to enact the revenge you wanted
all along?"

Revenge?

Her eyes darted between them. In the light, they had more than
a passing resemblance. The same bright hair, silver eyes, and strong
jawline. She'd assumed all Hartnords looked like that, the way all
Sandarians had the same dark hair and hooked nose...

"Rush them, my King," Gareth murmured. "They won't back
down."

"And risk war?" Talin whispered.

"It's too late for that."

"Let them go, my King," Talin urged. "Forgive this matter, or
more blood will spill."

The King held up his hand and his sorrans fell into line. "The
man responsible lies dead. Release my son. Take your father's
body and return to your home. My men will escort you to your
ships unharmed, I give you my word."

"Your words belie the true cause. Your fire kin cannot be
trusted. Our prophet warned death would follow should we pursue
our treaty with you. My father ignored his warnings. He thought
enough years had passed between us. He thought our priests to be
fearful old men." He laughed joylessly. "He thought wrong."

Prince Ravel cleared his throat. "There are those in Sandair
who share your concerns, Prince Wulfhart."

What was that fool doing?

The King glared at his son. "Stand down," he said through
clenched teeth.

"I will not."

Prince Ravel stepped away from his father and approached the
Hartnords with his hands open, palms up, seemingly unbothered
by his brother's position as hostage. The silver giants shifted their

swords into a thrusting stance.

Wulf barked a few words in Hartnord. His guards lowered their swords. "A Sandarian with a spine."

Prince Ravel bowed low, the most respect she'd ever seen him grant anyone. "I regret your suffering, Prince Wulfhart, and I am deeply ashamed. You are not the first to suffer at the hands of a Fire Walker, and you won't be the last. You've seen my brother's scars. I, too, have been scarred by a Fire Walker." He lifted his chin, twisting his cheek to show the burned crescent she'd inflicted. "The Fire Walker responsible stands in this very room."

Wulf's eyes snapped to hers, as though he'd heard the beat of her heart and read the truth on her face.

Prince Ravel would twist this tragedy to suit his needs, but not whilst she still stood here. She released her sword hilt and took a step forward.

"Get back, you fool," Salasar hissed.

She stepped in line with Prince Ravel, and not another inch. "Saeed was a monster. But he didn't speak for me, or any of the Fire Walkers—"

"You warned me your fire could harm," Wulf said.

"So could my sword."

The Prince's guard once again thrust their blades forward. She didn't need Hartnord Sight to know they were a heartbeat from ending her life.

"I mean you no harm. Not by sword or flame. But Saeed did. Does it matter that he used fire rather than steel for murder? The method doesn't change the intent of a criminal—"

"Such a constructive point to make at this serious time, Lady Arlbond," Prince Ravel said with a sneer. "Perhaps some Fire Walkers mean no ill intent, but as we have seen today, some mean to murder. Such power is deadly and impossible to defend against."

Her eyes flickered to the melted metal shields. Their silver armor had done nothing to save them.

Behind her, Samira sobbed. She'd been left abandoned on the floor. Forgotten. Mina couldn't let the actions of one lone man cost more lives. "Fire Walkers spent hundreds of years locked away because of the actions of one House—"

"And yet, peace reigned in those hundreds of years. There were no wars of a Fire Walker's making, no cities burned, no kings murdered. My apologies, Prince Wulfhart. This is no time for political debate, and it is despicable for Lady Arlbond to be pushing her agenda onto a grieving man. You deserve justice."

She wanted to laugh at the Prince's blatant hypocrisy. Surely the Hartnords would see through it?

"What justice would you offer me?" Wulf said. "What justice would be worth the life of my father, of my people's king? You wield your Fire Walkers as weapons against my people."

"Release my son," the King said, his voice carrying across the hall. "And we will discuss what we can do to put this right."

The King's words squirmed in her stomach. What did he mean by putting it right? Imprisoning the Fire Walkers again? Killing them?

By the slight smile on Prince Ravel's face, that's what he had in mind.

Wulf lowered his knife. The room breathed with a collective sigh as Prince Rais staggered down the dais steps and into his father's arms. Salasar kept his sword drawn, but his face sagged in relief. Only Gareth and Talin remained tense, ready for anything.

"We will return home and bury my father," Wulf said. "Then we shall discuss your Fire Walkers. You will listen to us, fire king, or we shall consider this attack a declaration of war."

"We will listen, Prince Wulfhart. You have my word," the King said.

Both sides lowered their swords. Mina joined Talin and they watched as Salasar personally escorted the Hartnords out of the throne room. The silver giants carried their dead, and as they left, a smoky mist trailed behind their bodies—their Shadows. Why hadn't they communed with her, or turned into wraiths to gain their revenge? Was it because they were Hartnord Shadows?

Jonan came to her side and wiped sweat from his brow. "That

could have gone worse."

Talin forced a weak smile. "It could have gone better."

Prince Ravel approached them with a trail of guards. He pointed at Jonan. "Arrest him."

She stepped in front of him. "What? Why?"

"The Fire Walker who murdered King Reinhart claimed allegiance to the great old House Rhaesbond. I don't believe in coincidence."

"Are you a fool? Saeed wasn't a Rhaesbond—"

"And yet he burned in their name. He made it quite clear. Stand aside, Lady Arlbond, and allow me to prevent our kingdom from falling into war."

She grabbed her hilt and drew Hawk an inch. "You're not touching him."

The guards responded in kind. The action caught the King's attention. "What's going on here? On who's command do you act?"

Prince Ravel didn't flinch. "On mine. A great injustice has taken place here this night, and I intend to set it right in the name of peace. That Fire Walker claimed to speak in House Rhaesbond's name—"

"To pin the blame on them!" she yelled.

"I mean Lord Jonan no harm. I merely wish to question him. Are you so frightened of mere words, or is your House hiding more secrets from their king?"

Jonan put a hand on her shoulder. "It's fine. I have nothing to hide."

"No, this is foolish—"

"There are no secrets of House Rhaesbond that you yourself don't already know, my Prince," Jonan said. "But if my testimony will prevent war, I will assist."

Jonan patted her shoulder and approached the guard. They gestured for his sword, and he unbuckled it with a casual smile. It was all a show to put her at ease, but his anxiety, and Talin's, rang through the bond.

Prince Ravel didn't even carry a sword and yet he commanded

this crisis as though the crown sat on his head.

"What about her?" Mina pointed to Samira still slumped on the tiled floor. "She was in league with Saeed all this time. If anyone can explain Saeed's attack, it's *her*."

Samira scrambled to her feet. "My Prince, my King, I know nothing, I—I swear it! Saeed would never—"

"Yet he did!" Mina roared. "You and Saeed planned this. All of this."

Leila sprawled into her usual, pointless bow. "My Prince, this will not be necessary. As you can see, my acolyte is distraught—"

"This ceremony was your responsibility!" Mina shoved a finger into the High Priestess's face. "*You* let this happen. Perhaps you should be questioned, too?"

Leila spluttered.

Prince Ravel gave Mina an odd look. It was almost a look of admiration. "Take the Fire Walker acolyte. She'll be questioned. I'll require your assistance on this matter, High Priestess. I plan for my investigation to be thorough."

Samira pleaded as the guards grabbed her arms and dragged her from the throne room. Mina's gaze was drawn to the pile of ash that had once been Saeed. A Fire Walker who believed protecting his people meant locking them up for their own good.

Now their continued freedom might mean war between the two kingdoms. That couldn't have been his plan all along?

"I hope you'll be there for them, Mina Hawker, when the kingdom burns."

8

THE BAKER'S BOY

The evening streets of Solus were quiet. The drunks kept to their taverns, the families to their homes. Mina heard whispers as she passed—city guards at their posts. They fell silent when she turned to face them. As though it was all her fault, somehow.

It felt it.

Alistar and Raj followed her wordlessly into the back alleys that led to the Neu Bosan quarter. It remained just as quiet here. Alistar chewed on a nail, lost in thought. Raj kept opening his mouth to say something, but stayed silent. None of them had the strength for idle talk.

She turned the corner away from Alistar's favorite tavern and toward the lower city.

"I thought we were getting a drink?" Alistar said.

"I never said that."

"You haven't said anything."

She came to a halt and rounded on them. "I'm getting some air. If you want to drink, go ahead. I'm not stopping you." She turned heel and strode down the alleyway.

The alleys here were cramped; Sandarian braziers stuck out from sandstone walls on one side and Neu Bosan glass lanterns hung from brass posts on wooden walls on the other. A mismatch of cultures.

"It's dangerous to be wandering the streets at night," Alistar said, with Raj trailing behind him.

"I have my sword," Mina snapped. "You're more likely to be attacked than I."

Alistar pulled a face. "What's that supposed to mean?"

"You look like a Houseman, that's all."

"And you look like a girl."

"Do I?"

Alistar frowned but didn't answer. Dressed in her male clothes—a black shalwar kameez, boots, headscarf, sword—she looked no different than Malik. She still bound her chest, for comfort more than anything, and being revealed as a woman hadn't suddenly changed who she was, the way she spoke, or the way she walked. Wearing a dress and pretending to be a girl had been the disguise. Perhaps Mina had been Malik all along.

Neither Alistar nor Raj had bothered to change out of their fancy noble clothes, but they had the good sense to tuck away their sahns. Wearing a sahn signaled status, but also painted a target. There were men desperate enough for gold to risk threatening a Houseman. She'd chosen her clothes carefully to avoid such attention, but Alistar and Raj... they stuck out like shiny gemstones in a clay pot.

She wove in and out of the alleyways, pausing at each corner to spy who else sneaked amid the shadows. No one lingered. And no light followed. Night swallowed Solus whole and not even Lune saw fit to grace them with her presence. As Mina moved away from the Neu Bosan homes and their canals, the scent of brine and fish and salt were replaced with more repugnant smells. Ale, sweat, piss, rot. Dirt and grime coated the walls of the lower city and the darkness here felt thicker. Not all of the braziers were lit, and guardsmen were few and far between.

It was her first time venturing into the lower city. She'd heard tales of its crime-infested streets, of pickpockets and beggars latching onto any Housemen who'd lost their way, and of guardsmen making hurried patrols either to win some bet or as punishment.

When she first came to Solus, she'd never expected a city as great and rich as the jewel of Sandair would be home to street rats. Surely the crown owned enough gold to pass on their riches? But no. Besides Arlent, it seemed every city was host to its own nest of rats. And, as Mina knew from personal experience, any city that tried to flush out their rats only sent them down the gutter. To the docks and waterways. Solus's street rats hid within the underground cisterns and aqueducts of the island.

Alistar grabbed her arm and pulled her into the alcove of a boarded-up townhouse. "What are you doing?"

"I told you, I'm getting some air."

"Air? In the lower city? What's this about?"

Raj ducked into the doorway beside them, forcing them to shuffle aside. "Um, we shouldn't be here."

"Mina?" Alistar prompted.

"Saeed said Fire Walkers were threatening families in the lower city. He said they were burning trees in Gaisland, too, but I can't very well get to Gaisland in one night. Would either of you know anything about that?"

"Stars," Alistar hissed. He ran a hand through his hair, messing up their sleek threads. "Why would I know anything about Fire Walkers?"

"Because your father is apparently the ambassador now. Surely you'd hear news if Gaisland was on fire?"

"I hear reports about trade, mostly—"

"Raj?"

"Um… I don't really listen to news."

Mina threw up her hands. "Well, you're both helpful." She shoved between them and continued her walk.

Alistar strode beside her. "You're looking for trouble? Is that it? You think finding some Fire Walkers in the lower city is going to fix what's happened? Because it won't."

"I don't expect you to understand."

"Then enlighten me."

She stomped around a corner. Nothing. No one. She'd found no signs of trouble, not even a street rat or a pick pocket. No Fire

Walkers. No proof behind Saeed's accusations. She sat on a crumbling stone wall and cradled her head in her hands.

Raj sat beside her. "Talk to us."

The words churned in her gut. Twelve weeks of freedom... Is that all she'd earned for her people? Saeed had destroyed it all. He'd reignited those old prejudices. He'd practically signed the laws that would imprison the Fire Walkers, or see them executed. He'd condemned Jonan to arrest *again* because he shared blood with a traitorous House long dead. Saeed had looked her in the eye and blamed everything on her, on the freedom she'd earned for them.

Had any of it mattered? Her tournament win? Keeping Prince Ravel off the throne? The King embracing his blood and denouncing an ancient law?

"*I hope you'll be there for them, Mina Hawker, when the kingdom burns.*"

"Do I really need to explain? It's going to happen again. They'll be locked away, and what then? Prince Ravel wanted to kill everyone with blood fire. Isn't that the next step?"

Alistar leaned on the wall. "You don't know that. The Hartnords want sanctions, not genocide—"

"You weren't there. You didn't see. That Hartnord Prince latched onto Prince Ravel like a leech." She shuddered at the thought of the two princes' embracing their mutual hate for Fire Walkers. "Sanctions first, imprisonment next, then genocide. That's what Jonan told me—that oppression of the Fire Walkers took time. Saeed... he just sped it up."

"The King won't let that happen."

"The King's a Fire Walker. He'll be the first to go." She looked Alistar in the eye. "And I'll follow."

"Don't say that."

"It's true, isn't it?"

"The other Houses—"

"Support the Prince. They don't care."

"Um, my House doesn't," Raj said. "We support the King. We

support the Fire Walkers."

"What does your support mean, Raj? Didn't your House lock up Fire Walkers and persecute them like the rest?"

Raj shifted on the wall. "Well, um, we followed the King's law. We all did. But my House never hurt them. We let them serve as gardeners—"

"You let them serve. How nice of you."

"That isn't fair," Alistar said. "We all followed the King's law because it was the law. Of course we locked Fire Walkers away. We live in Gaisland! Can you imagine a Fire Walker on the loose in our forests? Can you imagine the destruction they'd cause if they lost control?"

"Weren't you paying attention over the Solend? Fire Walkers don't lose control for no good reason, Ali. They were poisoned."

"Saeed wasn't."

She scowled at him.

"Look, all I'm saying is that people are frightened." Alistar reached to tug a braid that wasn't there and his hand dropped uselessly. "Some people think Fire Walkers want revenge for their imprisonment and that's why they've started burning people. That's why Saeed did what he did."

"No Fire Walker wants that! What Saeed did was unforgivable, but he doesn't speak for the Fire Walkers. They just want to be left alone."

"Do you know that for sure?"

She leaped off the wall and stomped away.

"You think you're the only one to be hated for who you are?" Alistar called.

She whirled around. "Oh, so you're a Fire Walker now?"

Alistar strode an inch from her nose and his emerald eyes sparkled in the dark. "There are plenty on the King's Council who would see my House burned and my people run from Solus. We're Sandarian, too—no matter where our ancestors came from."

"That's not the same!"

"How isn't it? Because we don't have power, like you?"

"Power? What kind of power do we have when we're imprisoned for it, *killed* for it?"

"My people have been imprisoned, too. Killed in the streets—"

"I've not heard of any Neu Bosan being murdered—"

"Why would you? You don't hear about it because who cares about us? The King likes to pretend we're close allies, but he turns a blind eye when we need his support. How is that any different from Fire Walkers?"

Raj pushed between them. "Stop fighting, stop it!" He held them apart with his long arms. "Why are you fighting about this? Just stop!"

She took a deep breath. "Look, I—"

Shouting echoed down one of the alleys.

"We *really* shouldn't be here," Raj said.

"It could be a Fire Walker."

Alistar made a face. "It could be a Bosan."

They both ran into the alley. Raj moaned and ran after them.

A woman screamed as Mina turned the corner and skidded to a halt. A small group of men surrounded a young Solander boy. His flaming fists lit up the alley. A Fire Walker.

The mob brandished knives and sticks and thrust them at the boy. He spun his fire in a circle to keep them back.

"I beg you!" a woman cried. "Leave him alone!"

Mina recognized her—and her son. The baker's boy. The one Salasar had arrested on the day Mina first arrived in Solus. He wasn't a threat to anyone, certainly not to these men.

Mina drew her sword. "Stop in the name of the King!"

The men whirled their weapons at her. They were older men, but Solander street rats nonetheless, clothed in patchwork rags. None carried a sword at his hip. Green Hands like Raj might walk around without a proper weapon, but other than priests and healers, no respectable man would be caught dead in public without a sword at his belt—which could only mean these were criminals, forbidden by law from carrying a blade. Pickpockets, thieves, or worse.

A skinny rake of a man sneered with missing teeth. "It's a little

far out for you, isn't it, Houseman?" He brandished a sharp shiv.
Alistar and Raj flanked her. Even if they weren't wearing silks
worth a season of food in the lower city, the way they walked and
held themselves spoke of wealth and confidence—the swagger of a
Houseman.

One of the men pointed a sharpened staff at Alistar. "His face
isn't welcome here."

Alistar drew his sword in response.

The mob began to spread out, each dark eye assessing Mina,
Alistar, and their swords. There were seven of them in all, not
counting the baker's boy or his mother cowering by the wall.

She raised Hawk into the Solaran stance: hilt above her head,
blade tilted down across her chest. "Return to your homes and
leave these people be."

"What homes?" The street rat pointed his shiv at the baker's
boy. "That there fire-breather burned down my shack."

"It was an accident!" the boy yelled.

"If you've come 'ere waving your swords, you best be waving
them at *him*. There's been fires all over, not that you Housemen
care, so long as it's not your homes burning."

"He's just a boy," said Mina. "Let him go, and I'll escort him
away from here. No one need be harmed."

The street rat spat. "Not good enough. Damn Fire Walkers
'ave been burning *people*, not just homes! They burned a little girl
until she was nothing but soot. Her da tried to find the burner who
did it and they melted his eyeballs right out his sockets."

Raj gasped. Alistar tried to disguise his gagging with a cough.

A tale spun to sow fear, no doubt, and it was working. "Saw this
yourself, did you? Or are you parroting any old tale you hear?"

"It's the truth!" He waved a man over. "Show 'em your scar."

One of the men raised his hand. In the light of the boy's flames,
the skin looked wrinkled, and some of the fingers curled in unnatural
ways.

"See? A Fire Walker did that," the street rat said triumphantly.
"You let 'em out. You let 'em infest our streets. And we can't tell

who's cursed with that gods-damn fire blood when they hide their
damn marks. Could be anyone. How'd we know?

Her heart thumped. Not all Fire Walkers were good men—
Saeed wasn't—but none of the Fire Walkers she'd ever met went
around deliberately burning people. If a Fire Walker had done that,
then it was in self-defense.

Alistar nudged her side. "There's too many," he whispered.
"We need to get out of here and let the guards handle this—"

"I'm not letting them hurt that boy."

Raj cleared his throat. "Um, if you go to the Temple of Gai,
they'll bandage your hand."

The street rats exchanged a glance. "Green Hands don't help
us. They don't even give us water—"

"I'm a Green Hand. Tell them I sent you—Rajesh of House
Enaibond. We'll give you food, water, and salves if you leave this
boy alone."

Both she and Alistar stared at Raj. When had he grown into a
man?

"And why should we trust you, Houseman?"

Mina sheathed her sword. "I swear to you. Release the boy and
his mother to us, and we'll go quietly. Don't, and the full force of
the King's guards will march on these streets."

The men muttered among themselves, considering her and
Raj's words. A hundred heartbeats thudded in her chest before
they stepped aside and let the boy and his mother go.

The baker's boy dulled his flames and ran to Mina. "Sand
Dancer!" he exclaimed, and then clamped a hand over his mouth.

Too late.

The street rat cursed. "It's that woman who won the tournament and freed them! This is all her gods-damn fault!"

The mob raised their weapons and stalked forward.

Mina grabbed the baker's boy's wrist and yanked him behind
her. "Run!"

9

RIOT

Angry voices chased Mina through the alleyways.

Alistar took point, with Mina guarding the rear. The boy's mother hoisted her skirts and ran faster than Mina anticipated, but the winding alleyways of the lower city impeded their pace. Mina could almost feel the hot breath of their pursuers.

"This way!" Alistar yelled, and they tumbled out into an open courtyard.

Wrong way.

Street rats blocked every exit, brandishing knives or wooden batons.

Raj nearly slammed into Alistar. "Oh Gai, what do we do?"

Mina and Alistar drew their swords and stepped in front of the baker's boy and his mother, forming a human shield around them and Raj. The street rats edged closer. More had joined them—ten at least.

They were woefully outnumbered.

The street rats' weapons were crude, but their eyes shone with rage and desperation. She knew well enough from her childhood on Khalbad's streets what desperation could do to a man. Mina and Alistar couldn't take them all on, nor was she keen on spilling blood. These were ignorant fools who'd yet to commit a deed worth blood as payment. She hoped it wouldn't come to that.

"Get back in your temple, fire-breather!" One of the men threw a rock.

She side-stepped it with a quick hop. More rocks flew, forcing her group to shuffle closer to the wall. They were being penned in, and then she'd have little room to dance.

The boy's mother shrieked as a rock pelted her shoulder.

Gods, Mina needed to get them out of here. "Ali," she whispered. "I'll cause a distraction. Get them to the Keep."

Alistar jumped out of the way of another rock. "Stars above, I'm not leaving you to fend off ten men—"

"We don't have time to argue. Trust me."

"What are you going to do?"

"Give them what they want."

Mina stepped into the center of the courtyard. She lifted Hawk into the Solaran stance. "You want fire? I'll show you fire."

She held up her left hand and bright orange flames burst from her flesh, filling the courtyard with Rahn's fury. Her fire had never been this bright or easy to summon before, and she blinked at its raw intensity. Jonan's blood still lingered in her veins, and it was his essence she'd summoned. The power of House Rhaesbond.

The men staggered back and cursed, as she'd expected. She didn't give them chance to recover their senses. She spun her sword in a miniature whirlwind, allowing her flaming hand to trail Hawk's silver with a tail of fire. The effect held their attention.

One man swung his wooden baton. She deflected the strike with ease, hacking the wood in half with her blade. Another baton came down next, and she set it alight with a single touch.

Some of the men scattered in fear. Others, the ones with real steel, remained. But enough of their number had run to give her friends a chance to flee.

The glint of a knife thrust toward her.

Mina evaded the blade and danced around its deadly jabs. Fighting off a knife was different than a curved blade, its movement more erratic. She knocked the man's wrist aside with the flat of her sword and shoved her flaming palm against his chest.

His rags caught alight, and he fell back screaming.

A shadow came up behind her and she whirled around. The street rat with the shiv. He stabbed it at her chest. She raised Hawk, but not quickly enough. His knife sliced across her forearm, drawing blood. The embers in her gut pulsed, and her flames puffed out.

The man sneered. "Burners can't burn without their blood, can they?" He thrust his shiv again.

She ducked under his arm. Another man grabbed her shirt and yanked her back. She tripped over her feet with a curse.

The street rat shoved her against a wall. The second thug grabbed her sword arm and bashed her wrist against the stone, attempting to pry away her blade. Dull pain throbbed through her hand, but her grip around Hawk tightened. A third man grabbed her other arm.

The street rat's body heat pressed close. Hot, sour breath blew across her cheek and his filthy nails dug into her wrist. "You hiding marks under here, burner?" He leered and tugged up her tunic.

She stomped down on his sandaled foot. He howled and fell back, giving Mina room to drive her knee into the second thug's groin. He released her wrist with a high-pitched whine, and she slammed Hawk's pommel into his nose with a sickening crunch.

The third street rat skittered back, terror flashing in his eyes. She didn't hesitate and ran for the nearest alley. Her heart pounded along with her feet as she raced down alley after alley. That was too close—she didn't even want to think about what could have happened. Nothing as quick as death.

She spun out of another alley and leaned against a doorway to catch her breath. The lower city streets all looked the same and it was too dark to tell which direction she originally came from. She was running in gods-damn circles! Lune wasn't out to guide her path; neither was Rahn. If she weren't careful, she'd run straight back into her assailants. She tried to summon a flicker of flame, if only to guide her way, but the cut on her arm and her frantically beating heart made it impossible.

I am the master of my own self. Calm.

The blood bond tugged in her chest. Talin. His concern nudged her, even from this far away. None of her family were nearby, but she could sense roughly which direction they—and the Keep—were.

She followed the thread through dirty, cramped backstreets until they opened out into the colorful bunting of the Neu Bosan quarter. Shouts and noise came from ahead, but not the usual cheer of a living city at night. She jogged alongside the canal, heading north, and came out into the market quarter.

Her heart leaped to her throat.

A mob of city folk stomped through the streets, brandishing lit torches, swords, brooms, cleavers, anything that could be turned into a weapon. Hundreds of them. They marched north to the Keep, and their chants left her blood cold.

Bleed the burners. Bleed the Fire Walkers.

A group of them were dragging a dirty sack though the streets. No, not a sack—a man. His shirt had been ripped to shreds, exposing the red flaming tattoos of a Fire Walker, but the smeared dirt and dried blood made them difficult to see. The mob dragged his lifeless body by a rope around his neck, hauling it awkwardly over bumps in the road, and his dull eyes stared at nothing.

Gods no.

"Here!" a voice hissed. Alistar leaned his head out from the safety of an alleyway.

She rocked on her heels. Someone needed to go after them, stop them, burn the body—

Alistar grabbed her wrist. "It's not safe out here." He pulled her into cover before she could protest. "They're after Fire Walkers."

"How—how did this happen?"

"One of the street rats came running out of an alley with his clothes on fire, screaming about… well, you. That set the mob off. They…" Alistar ran a hand through his hair. "Stars above, I saw them lynch a man."

This couldn't be happening. "Did he attack them? The Fire Walker? Did he start this?"

"He didn't burn, but he had tattoos, and that was good enough for them."

"The city's scared," Raj whispered. "They heard about the Hartnords. They're blaming the curse of House Rhaesbond—"

"Their foolishness is going to cost lives!" Mina leaned her head against the wall with a *thunk*. "We need to get back to the Keep and stop this."

Alistar jerked his thumb over his shoulder to where the baker's boy and his mother huddled beside a doorway. "We need to get them to safety first."

The woman trembled, anxiety plain across her face, though the boy looked more annoyed than afraid. Mina couldn't blame him there.

Raj took her arm and examined it. "You're hurt."

"It's just a scratch. Where can we go from here? What about the tavern?"

Alistar shook his head. "I tried. They won't take us. They're scared, too—they don't want a mob of angry Sandarians breaking down their doors."

"What about the Temple of Gai?"

"Um, that's not a good idea," Raj said. "They're not fighters. Someone could get hurt."

"Temple of Lune?" Alistar offered.

"They wouldn't take you," the woman said behind them. "They won't shelter men."

"Then we have only one choice," Mina said. "The only place Fire Walkers will be safe, and the one place not even that mob will dare enter."

The Temple of Rahn.

The mother wrapped her arms around her boy's waist. "You can't mean to lock him back in there?"

"We're seeking shelter, that's all—"

"You took my boy away! You can't take him again!"

The baker's boy shrugged from her grip. "It's fine, Ma. It's not so bad inside."

"It's the safest place right now," Mina said. "What's your name?"

The baker's boy rubbed his nose. "I'm Kamran."

Mina forced a smile. "Well, Kamran, you stay close behind. I'm Mina, and these are my friends—Ali and Raj. They'll keep you safe."

Kamran nodded and dragged his ma along. With the mob in full force tramping through the market, they kept to the back alleys and shadows of townhouses. The sheer number and noise of the enraged crowds made it easy to steer out of their way.

Outside the Temple of Rahn, a handful of angry men threw rocks at the pyramid walls but they didn't dare enter. She needed to sneak Kamran and his mother inside, somehow. Perhaps with another distraction.

"That's the baker!" someone yelled. "He's one of them!"

So much for a distraction. The mob turned on them. The bravest among them hurled a rock at Kamran's head, missing by inches.

Mina cursed and drew her sword.

These men were no mere street rats. She recognized some of their faces. One was a merchant with a fruit stall in the market. Two were gardeners in the Keep. Another was a guardsman with a post in the Neu Bosan quarter. Their friendly faces and smiles were gone, replaced by a flame-lit mask of hate.

"In the name of the King, stop!" She tried to imitate Salasar's commanding voice. "Look at yourselves!"

Their dark eyes didn't see her. They didn't see Tamina Arlbond, daughter of Lord Talin, sorran to the King. They didn't see the *Sand Dancer*, winner of the Solaran Tournament. They didn't see a person at all.

They saw a Fire Walker.

A monster.

Alistar drew his sword and stepped to her side. "I'm not leaving you this time."

"Are you sure you want to get cut down protecting a Fire Walker?"

"Who said anything about protecting Fire Walkers? I just want to fight some Solanders." His lower lip trembled, betraying his bravado.

The mob struck first, hurling stones and shards of broken pottery. A rock caught Mina on her sword arm, sending a spasm of pain. She yelped and dropped her sword.

Kamran ran to her side and picked up the rock. "Leave her alone!" He hurled it back at the crowd.

Another stone whooshed past and smacked into Kamran's forehead. He crumpled to the ground. She grabbed him before his head hit the dust. Blood ran down his face, over his eye.

Gods, don't let him have lost an eye.

"Bleed the burners!" a man yelled.

"Bleed their fire dry!" screamed another.

The mob marched right at them with relentless fury.

"Stop!" Mina called, but it was futile. They weren't listening.

Alistar raised his sword into a block and stepped before Mina, planting himself between her and the mob, but there were too many of them. Raj pounded on the temple doors, yelling at them to open, as the mob inched closer.

What would these madmen do? Beat them. Lynch them. Hunt down every Fire Walker in the city. Prince Ravel didn't need to enact laws when the people of Solus were ready to kill strangers in the streets for him.

A wall of fire erupted around them, forcing the mob back. Mina squinted as a flaming figure stepped through the wall, its body cloaked in red and orange.

"Jonan?"

The flames parted, revealing the woman underneath. Leila. "Get inside. Now."

Mina didn't need to be told twice. She grabbed her sword and awkwardly lifted Kamran to his feet. He roused, and she guided him to the temple doors as Alistar protected their rear. Leila wove her wall of fire, holding the shrieking mob at bay.

Men and women were gathered inside the main sanctum. Some were Fire Walkers who'd chosen to remain in the temple, but others wore clothes—Fire Walkers who'd left but had also been forced to seek shelter.

She helped Kamran to the stone steps and gently lay him down. His mother held his hand tightly as Raj examined the bloodied gash above his left eye.

Leila entered the sanctum, followed by a flurry of guards and a familiar brute wearing a turquoise sahn—the Sword of Solus.

The guards were dragging men inside. Not the mob, but people she recognized as Fire Walkers. Clothes hid their tattoos, but their short hair and terrified faces were plain enough.

Leila engaged Salasar in some heated conversation as more and more Fire Walkers were marched inside.

Mina jogged over to them. "What's going on?"

"There you are," Salasar said. "Talin's looking for you. Wait until I'm done here, and my men will escort you to the Keep."

"Done doing what?"

A woman yelped as a guard shoved her roughly. Mina turned to shout, but Salasar grabbed her arm. "This isn't your jurisdiction, Arlbond."

"And this isn't your temple. There's a mob out there! Shouldn't you be waving your sword and breaking them up?"

"The mob isn't my concern. I'm here under orders from the King."

Dread washed over her like the cooling rains of Lune's Shadow. "What orders?"

"All Fire Walkers are to return to the temple immediately. Those who resist will face the King's justice."

10

THE KING'S JUSTICE

The city guards dragged more men, women, and children into the temple. Fire Walkers. None refused—they remembered the old law and what would happen to them or their kin if they didn't comply. None were angry, but they looked confused. Afraid. Sad. These were Mina's people and she couldn't bear it.

Salasar marched back and forth, barking orders at Leila and his men. He ignored Mina, likely out of guilt, until she forced her way into his path. He came to a halt and cursed.

"For how long?" she demanded. "You can't tell me the King has overturned the law over one incident?"

"One incident? That's what you call the assassination of a king? It was the attempted assassination of a king by House Rhaesbond that led to Fire Walkers being banished to the temples in the first place. You think it's so farfetched that another madman acting in their name wouldn't have the same effect?"

"Saeed wasn't a Rhaesbond—"

"No, but he's put the fear of them in every Houseman in the Keep and every father in this city. You faced the mob. I'll wager my firstborn that's only the start."

Salasar turned to walk away. Mina grabbed his sahn, holding him back. "How long will this last?"

Salasar looked down at her hand gripping his sahn. "Indefinitely."

She released his sahn, hands dropping uselessly by her side. "Then why am I allowed to leave the temple?"

He straightened his sahn. "Housemen and their families are exempt."

"Exempt!" She wanted to laugh. "How is that fair?"

"The King wants control of this situation, you hear? Housemen aren't a threat. But these are." He waved a hand at the men and women cowering on the stone steps.

"You're a gods-damn fool. Look at them. They're no threat. The real threat is out there, running through the streets with torches! Or sitting in Council meetings, drinking wine and stealing the freedoms of innocent people!"

"Rant all you want, child, but that doesn't change what's happening here. Go back to the Keep and tell the King yourself just how gods-damn foolish he is. Wait until I get there so I can see which of your House gets executed for treason first. My bet's on you."

"You're a Fire Walker, same as I. If the King ordered you to give up your sword, your family, and your House to join the temple, would you?"

"Willingly. I'm a Houseman, I obey my King." He returned to his men.

Leila flitted between groups of Fire Walkers and sent them down to the dormitories below. The night grew late, and with this many returning to the temple, Leila would need to find clothing and food. She no longer had her lackeys to help. Saeed was dead, and Samira remained locked away.

Alistar caught her eye from across the room, his face a picture of concern. She swallowed the flaming bile in her throat. It was men like him, fools scared of fire, who demanded Fire Walkers be kept out of sight. And it was Housemen like him and Raj who turned a blind eye to their abuse. There were plenty of Housemen with fire in their blood and enough gold to keep their dirty secrets hidden. Especially when they themselves were exempt from the law.

They hadn't learned a gods-damn thing. Fear and hatred had driven a pompous Prince to poison his own people in order to root out the Fire Walkers hidden in plain sight, and now it was happening again—not with poison this time, but with an angry mob.

But she was a Houseman now. She had a voice, where those locked inside the temple did not. And by Rahn, she'd shout it to the skies.

No one stopped her as she left the temple. Leila gave her a look of disgust, as though this was Mina's fault, but didn't say a word. Alistar and Raj jogged after her and kept pace with her furious march back to Bloodstone Keep.

"Listen, Mina, I heard what's happening," Alistar said. "I'll speak to my House. I'll ask my father to put pressure on the King."

"Will he listen to you?"

"Yes, if he wants our House to be the bond tying Sandair and Neu Bosa together," he said with a trace of bitterness.

Alistar knew about his family's bargain with the King, then. Would marriage between the two nations be more vital now that the peace talks with Hartnor had failed?

"I'll speak to my mother, too," Raj added. "I'm, um, I'm her only heir. Sitting on the Council is something I'll have to do, someday. She'll listen to me. I know it."

She wanted to thank them, but the words caught in her throat. Even with their Houses supporting the Fire Walkers, that was only three seats on the Council. It wasn't enough to convince them, or the King.

Inside the Keep's gate, Raj and Alistar turned left to find their families and begin their pleading. Mina marched straight for the palace.

Burning braziers lined the halls. Each flame she passed increased the warmth in her gut until her embers threatened to burst and create a few flames of their own. How could the King turn his back on them, on his own word, when he possessed blood fire?

How could everything have fallen apart this easily? The mob was out there attacking people—*murdering* them—because of one crazed man, and she felt powerless to stop it. She rubbed her burning eyes and swallowed the urge to scream.

The blood bond warmed and Talin stepped out into the corridor, blocking her path. "If you're looking for an audience, it's rather late."

"That didn't stop the King from condemning the Fire Walkers."

"Come. We'll talk."

She swallowed her burning rage and followed Talin into the royal gardens, which were quiet except for the chitter of insects.

"Are you hurt?" Talin said, eyeing the cut on her wrist.

"It's nothing."

"I sent Iman to look for you once I heard about the mob. I would have come myself, but the King forced me to stay close. I see Salasar found you first."

"How do you know Salasar found me?"

"Because your anger burned through the bond with such strength, I had to sit down and pour myself wine."

She bristled at his tone. "I don't see what's amusing about it."

"No. It's not good. But charging into the Keep and demanding an audience with the King in your state would lead to the sacking of our House a lot quicker. Let us calm down and discuss it."

"What's there to discuss?"

"Our plan of action, for one." They neared the east entrance of the palace, where Talin's apartment lay. "So calm yourself. I'm not letting you inside until I hear you say it."

She scowled but obeyed. She took a deep breath and allow the night's cool air to soothe her inner embers. "I am the master of my own self."

"Good. Now come."

The palace corridors were also quiet this night, and the eerie silence chilled her bones. Everything had been so hectic and bustling while the Hartnords were here. The entire world had changed in a single cursed evening.

She'd been so concerned with the Fire Walkers' fate, she'd paid little heed to the Hartnord prince or the father he'd so brutally lost.

She knew what it was like to lose a father—or at least the man she knew as her father for so many years. Watching him cut down without mercy had fueled her anger and given her purpose. It forged the reason she stood here in this golden palace, the reason she had a family and people to protect. She understood that drive for revenge—and its cost. What would be the cost of Prince Wulfhart's revenge?

Talin beckoned her into his room decorated in shades of Arlent's purple, and he lit lamps to ward off the dark. She sat on his lounger and examined the tear in her sleeve as Talin busied himself pouring wine. The cut stung, but only the shirt would need stitching.

"Iman warned me young girls burn through their clothes, but I thought she was being facetious." Talin sighed as he placed two full cups on the table and sat beside her.

Mina couldn't bring herself to meet his eyes. "They were trying to kill Fire Walkers. They—they were so full of hate. How can we go back to that again? How can anyone live like that?" Horror and panic shook through her in equal measure and she struggled to contain the anxiety bubbling in her blood.

Talin thrust a cup in her hands. "Drink. It'll help."

She took a sip and gasped at the burning alcohol. It was stronger wine than she was used to. Her father's calm demeanor settled over her like a cloak. How could he remain calm in a time like this? It was a warrior's calm. A calm vital to surviving even the direst battle.

And that's what this was. A battle.

"Why is the King doing this?"

"Khaled has to be seen doing something. At least this will buy us some time. I know it's not fair, but the temple is the safest place for them until the King can decide what to do."

"Decide on what? He gave Fire Walkers their freedom—"

"Do you remember what he said during his speech at the Solend? He said we needed to work together to find a balance. He's not reneging on his promises, but there is pressure from the Council, from the Hartnords, to find that balance quickly."

"You mean sanctions. Prod Fire Walkers with tests to prove who is safe and who should be locked up?"

"Yes, to a degree. But the King listens. Our House will guide him to the correct balance. Iman and I have offered to pass on our methods for keeping the Fire Walkers safe and free within Arlent. None of that involves testing them or locking them up, but training them to correctly channel their power in safe ways. In time, the people will come to understand that our gifts are far less dangerous when embraced rather than suppressed. It's safer, and healthier, both to ourselves and the people around us. Do you understand? We can work toward restoring Fire Walkers to their rightful place. We can make them respected once more."

Arlent as a model for the rest of the kingdom? It sounded too good to be true. "The Council will never allow it."

"The Council is split. There are some who believe in the good of Fire Walkers and others who take Prince Ravel's side. He has the Hartnords' ear, it seems. Prince Wulfhart demands action. He mourns his father, and rightly so. We will find a balance. But for now, the Fire Walkers must remain where there are, as a precaution. Time will heal this wound."

Of course Prince Ravel was using this tragedy to further his own agenda. He didn't care for Prince Wulfhart—he'd insulted the Hartnord to his face. "What if the Council takes Prince Ravel's side?"

"Khaled is still king. If the Council had its way, even Housemen with blood fire would be locked away—Salasar and myself included. But Khaled put his foot down. He said if Housemen were to be locked away, then he'd personally oversee the testing of all members of Houses to ensure all were treated equally. That shut them up."

She stared into her cup at the bloodied color. "So, what do we do? Just sit and wait until Prince Wulfhart forgets we murdered his father?"

"Jonan has volunteered to help investigate those responsible for King Reinhart's death."

The wine churned in her stomach. "What do you mean? It was just Saeed."

"We've had reports for weeks now that a group of rogue Fire Walkers claiming to be House Rhaesbond have been causing fires. The reports stretch as far as Gaisland and even across the border into Hartnor. Saeed may or may not have been in league with them. We'll never know."

She took another sip of wine to calm her nerves. "House Rhaesbond are long gone."

"So Jonan believes. Someone is using their name to stir hatred. If we deal with them, I think the Hartnords and the Council will be appeased."

"What about Samira? Does she know anything?"

"She's been questioned. Neither she nor Leila are culpable."

Mina leaned back against the lounger and cradled her cup. She didn't believe Leila was completely innocent; her acolytes were too devoted to her, too loyal. "What can I do to help?"

"If I told you to keep out of trouble and let me handle this, would you?"

She scowled and he laughed.

"No, I thought not. The Fire Walkers will need you. These next few weeks will be crucial in winning hearts and minds. Many saw you during the tournament—Housemen and city folk alike—they saw you win, and they saw you burn to protect the Prince."

"They also saw me naked."

"And they witnessed you receive the King's blessing. It's not a burden you asked for, but when the city folk speak of Fire Walkers, they speak of you. I'd like you to keep on showing them what good Fire Walkers can do, and that means keeping out of mobs and not storming the Keep with your temper ready to burst."

"You want me to represent the Fire Walkers?"

"Yes. And... I want you to consider what I'm about to propose next. For our House. And for the Fire Walkers." Talin's anxiety rang through the bond.

"Why do I suddenly want to thump you?"

He wore an uneasy smile. "It's Khaled's idea. He still wishes to marry Aniya to your sorran, to build those bridges between our nations. But he's suggested that marrying Rais to a Fire Walker would also build bridges. It would show the faith he has in Fire Walkers, and that Rais has overcome his own grievances with them."

She gawked at him. "You're not serious?"

"Marrying into the House of the Bright Solara would protect us, elevate us, and give us a stronger voice on the Council. I, ah, spoke briefly with Rais. He approves of the match."

"Prince Rais wants to *marry* me?"

Talin took his cup and swirled it. "You asked how you could help."

11

THE GRAY OF DAWN

Marriage.

Mina stared at the slither of Rahnlight creeping across the ceiling. *Marriage.* Gods. She'd been outraged the first time Talin had suggested it during the tournament, but that was different—an attempt to keep her safe from Prince Ravel and out of the tournament. This time, it was to protect their House and Arlent from inevitable backlash, and to send a message that the Bright Solara wasn't afraid of Fire Walkers.

But her? And Prince Rais? She barely knew him! He seemed an honorable man, willing to stand up to his brother. And he'd trained with Salasar so he wasn't completely helpless with a sword. He'd even helped protect his father during the Solend.

He wasn't unattractive, despite his scars—she had plenty of her own.

But those amber eyes still haunted her dreams.

Now she understood how Alistar must feel. The hopes of his entire family—and an entire country—were pinned on his marriage into the Bright Solara. At least Princess Aniya and Prince Rais were noble in their hearts as well as in their blood. Gods help the woman who'd be forced into marrying Prince Ravel. At least he wouldn't become king with Prince Rais to deny him...

She sat up on the lounger. Prince Rais could one day become king.

Which meant she could one day become his queen.

"I don't want to be queen!"

Marriage was one beast, but to become queen? Of all Sandair? Impossible! Surely Talin must realize what marrying a crown prince entailed... but of course he did. If she were queen, she'd have the power to protect the Fire Walkers better than anyone, and no one would question her House's legitimacy.

All it would cost is her freedom.

They'd expect her to give up her sword. They certainly wouldn't approve of her masculine clothes. She'd never hold Hawk. Never ride Luna. Never dance. And they'd expect her to live in Solus. She'd never see the Duslands again.

She hugged her chest. This brought back her fear of entering the Temple of Rahn for the first time, only the prison was now made of gold instead of stone.

"Most girls would give their right arm to be in your position." Iman sat at the dresser with another stack of scrolls—reports from Arlent—and a half-empty wine glass.

"Why, so they can let foolish men dictate their entire lives?"

"Being queen is a position of power and responsibility. You think it's about lying on your back and pushing out heirs?"

Mina's cheeks warmed. Gods, if she married a man, she'd be expected to birth children, too. "That's all the queen's good for, isn't it?"

Iman put her scroll down and turned to Mina with a raised eyebrow. "Queen Vida sits on the Council and helps run the common court. Certainly, she's taken some time away whilst carrying a child, but that was conceived out of love, not duty. She takes her role seriously to carry on the work started by the late Princess Aniya."

"Who?"

"The King's twin sister. It was her death that caused the last war seventeen years ago. And she wouldn't abide you talking such nonsense. Solaran princesses and queens have more power than you realize. More power than Housemen care for. Aniya, now she was a woman."

"You knew her?"

Iman swirled her wine glass. "Ah, Aniya was the most beautiful woman in all Sandair. A real princess. All women wanted to be her, and all men wanted to bed her. But she never married, much to her brother's annoyance—she had enough suitors to fill the Keep. She introduced me to Solus's famous wines. And she petitioned Khaled for my entry into the Academy, too, and probably would have convinced him in time, had she not passed. It's thanks to her that the Temple of Lune can support so many women. And it's thanks to her that each high priestess owns a chair on the Council. You would have liked her. She would have been the first to stand up for the Fire Walkers." Iman took a gulp from her glass. "Shame she's gone. She was the only one who could talk sense into the King. She'd be yelling at him now."

A flicker of flame caught Mina's eye. She turned to the lantern on her bedside table. Tira was listening to Iman's conversation. "How did she die?"

"She travelled to Hartnor as our ambassador with a peace treaty in hand. She never returned, and her body was never recovered. King Reinhart denied all involvement, but Khaled saw blood and declared war."

"She was murdered?"

"It's one of those mysteries we'll never discover the truth of, girl. No point speculating it."

Now Mina understood why the King was so uncomfortable with his daughter marrying a Hartnord. "Do you think I should marry Prince Rais?"

Tira shook her head in the flames.

"Talin won't force you, girl. He'd have to go through me first."

"That's not what I asked."

Iman emptied her glass and busied herself pouring another. "You're the daughter of a Houseman, but also a tribe rat that spent too long scrimping in the dirt and swaggering around like a boy. You're too sharp."

"What's that supposed to mean?"

"You'll offend half the Council before you reach your wedding night. Talin's an optimist. He thinks you'll adapt, but you can't be dulled, girl. You'll cut the first man who crosses you, and bleeding nobles aren't a good look. Boys like Prince Rais—royal boys—they expect women to behave and act a certain way, and then get upset when their wives disobey. Talin believes Prince Rais has the fortitude to put up with you, but Talin has a task on his hands."

"Talin seems awfully keen on the idea."

"What father wouldn't give their daughter the world? You can't blame him for trying. But you need to put your foot down, girl, and make it clear what the world means to you."

Tira nodded.

Mina held her mother's stare. "What do you think my mother would say, if she were here?"

Iman rubbed her chin. "To take your own path. It's what she wanted for you. She wouldn't care if you chose to find a suitable husband, so long as that husband was worthy of you. Nor would she be disappointed if you didn't follow in her footsteps. There are expectations of noble girls, but she always wanted you to choose your own path, whatever that may be."

Tira smiled and nodded.

"Though," Iman continued, "I doubt she'd find a Solaran prince to her tastes."

At that, Tira grinned.

"I could help the Fire Walkers," Mina said.

"We'll find ways to help them. If you want to marry a man, find one who is worthy of you."

"A prince isn't worthy enough?"

"Only you can answer that."

"And what about you? Are there no men worthy of you?"

Iman took a sip from her cup. "There's no man in the whole of Sandair worthy of me, girl."

"Isn't that convenient."

Iman barked a laugh and returned to her scroll.

Mina hated the implication that marriage was the only way she could be useful. Malik certainly wouldn't be forced into marriage just to gain power. She rested her head against a cushion and stared at her mother, always present in the flames. Watching the lantern oil fade to darkness had become her bedtime routine, both here and inside the Temple of Rahn. If Iman found her habit odd or childish, she hadn't mentioned it. It comforted her to know her mother watched over her, that she was close by and willing to listen to whatever fears Mina whispered.

Tira pulled a silly face. Mina stuck out her tongue, and Tira laughed in soundless joy.

The next few days passed quietly. Talin remained by the King's side and locked in Council meetings. The Fire Walkers remained locked inside their temple as Salasar rampaged across Solus and rounded up the stragglers. The declaration rang loud—any who refused to return to the temple would be in defiance of the King's law. Most willingly entered, though some were ousted by family members or neighbors. Some put up a fight, but none were killed. All submitted once the Sword of Solus turned up and flashed his sword. Mina had accompanied him on a few of these excursions to ensure no blood would be spilled. Salasar could bark loud, but she knew he didn't truly mean harm to the Fire Walkers.

The Fire Walkers weren't happy, and each one forced to pass the temple threshold weighed on her heart.

She didn't want to marry Prince Rais.

Gods, she couldn't stomach the thought of being his sorran, let alone his wife and queen.

But if marrying him gave her a seat on the Council and the power to influence the law and create a future where Fire Walkers weren't blamed for every injustice, wasn't it worth the sacrifice? Wasn't this what it meant to be a Houseman? She'd willingly risked everything to stop Prince Ravel gaining the throne, and that was arguably more personal than *marriage*.

But if she'd lost her House, been stripped of her sword, and been condemned to the Temple of Rahn for the rest of her days, she'd still be Mina.

Who would she be as queen? As someone's wife?

She distracted herself from such thoughts the only way she knew how—sword training. Raj had returned to the Temple of Gai to help with the influx of wounded from the riots, leaving Alistar. He often managed to slip away from his House and was in need of distraction as much as she was. It felt wrong—improper, even— that the two of them were forced to sneak into the Keep's gardens and find a quiet clearing just to train together. Neither of them mentioned Princess Aniya or Prince Rais.

Hiding in the gardens served another purpose. She had no intention of speaking with Prince Rais yet, though she knew he stalked the Keep, perhaps in search of her. He'd come awfully close to finding her training spot once. Alistar had said nothing when she'd shushed him into silence, like a master ordering her sorran. If he knew what she was doing, then he played along for similar reasons. Though she wondered if he felt as awkward as she did— sneaking around like young lovers cheating on their betrothed.

She couldn't avoid Prince Rais forever.

The Keep carried on as normal, as though the riots, the dead Hartnord king, and the Fire Walkers were passing gossip. More Housemen filled the dining hall than normal, however, as their lords remained in the Keep for the Council meetings. Most nights, it made it easier for her to sneak in and out of the hall without the notice of the crown prince or his family. But on this night, the only spare seats were near the front, close to the dais where the Bright Solara sat.

Raj had saved seats for her and Alistar, and waved them over with an apologetic shrug. "It was the only table left," he said, as she sat awkwardly.

She was readying an excuse to leave when an amber eye caught her gaze. Prince Rais was staring right at her, chewing his lower lip. To his left, Prince Ravel leaned in close, whispering dark portents into his younger brother's ear. He too stared at her, a sardonic smile stretching across his face. They were talking about her.

She stood. "I have to find my aunt. She needed my help with something."

Alistar said nothing and returned to his wine. Both her friends looked glum, for their own reasons, no doubt—the stress of the riots likely played on Raj's mind, whereas Alistar had the same marital woes as she.

Mina made her way to the edge of the dining hall. She'd almost reached the exit when a voice called after.

"Lady Arlbond, a moment."

She considered running ahead, but that would only offend Prince Rais further, and then she'd have to admit she *was* avoiding him. She turned around into a bow. "My Prince."

Prince Rais seemed to have grown a few inches since she last saw him up close. His long hair was tied back, the same fashion as Prince Ravel, and his facial hair had developed into a small, cropped beard, though not long enough to braid or adorn. He wore fine red silks with silver embroidery in the shapes of Lune and her stars—a subtle nod to her. The silks hugged the muscles across his chest and upper arms, and the crimson sahn across his shoulder was pulled taut. A sword hung at his hip and his hand displayed the bloodstone ring of his bloodline.

Her stomach fluttered at his smile. *Gods.* Solaran boys grew into men quick.

"I was hoping to catch you after my helbond ceremony. It's unfortunate that events transpired as they did."

She linked her hands behind her back. "Most unfortunate, my Prince. You look well."

"Will you walk with me a moment?" He held out his hand.

She hesitated but took it. It was warm and soft. Only Prince Wulfhart had dared act so forward with her, and she didn't know what to do with her other hand.

Prince Rais guided her to a private alcove overlooking the gardens. Thick red curtains hid them from most of the dining hall, though she could still see the royals. Prince Ravel leaned on a fist, his amber eyes watching her.

She turned her back and admired the garden in the golden Rahnlight.

"You haven't returned to the palace," Prince Rais said, his hand still clasped around hers. "There are rooms available."

"My aunt needs my company. It wouldn't be fair to leave her alone, my Prince."

"She could join you. I'm sure we can find her a room."

"That—that would be most generous, my Prince." Something tugged through the blood bond and she spared a glance to the dais. Talin sat speaking with the King and Queen, and Prince Ravel was fingering his bloodstone ring, lost in thought. An oddly human gesture coming from him, but nothing concerning. What was her blood reacting to?

Prince Rais squeezed her hand. "Your dress was beautiful."

"My dress?"

"At my ceremony. Why don't you wear it again? My sister says girls can't be seen wearing the same thing twice, which is nonsense. Men always wear the same old leather." His Solander cheeks reddened and he bloomed with a shy smile reminiscent of Raj. "But my sister knows more about these things than I do. I could introduce you, if you'd like."

"I'd like that, my Prince." A subtle lie—she had no intention of cozying up and playing princess. Prince Rais was making his move, so she needed to make her own. "Dresses don't always match with swords."

"Well, you don't need your sword. The palace is safe."

"I need it to train."

"What are you training for?"

"It's good exercise, my Prince."

"There are safer ways to exercise. The gardens are ample for walks, and the palace has a cistern large enough to swim. I could take you."

"I prefer my sword."

"Do you train with your sorran?"

His single amber eye turned hard. She couldn't lie—she'd lied enough and he'd catch it. "He's my sorran, my Prince. We train together."

His grip tightened around her hand. "Privately?"

"Yes, my—"

"What does your training entail?"

"The same as when we were back in the Academy, my Prince."

"You're no longer in the Academy. The Code of Honor doesn't allow women to have sorrans."

She'd read the Code of Honor, all one thousand and one pages of it. It said nothing about women's rights where sorrans were concerned. Well, it didn't mention women at all, which she understood to mean there were no rules. "That's not true, my Prince—"

"Are you close to your sorran? You must be. That's how the bond works. Even grown men have been known to bed their sorran. Your father beds his."

She yanked her hand from his grip. "Who told you that? Your brother? Ali is my *friend*."

"Why are your friends men? The Neu Bosan and the Gaislander."

She sucked in a breath. How had this conversation burned to nothing so quickly? "You're welcome to train and eat with us if you can climb down from your throne, my Prince."

Prince Rais gawked. Now she'd gone and offended another potential king, but she couldn't let that insult to her character or her father stand. Who was he to control her life when she hadn't even agreed to become his wife?

He paced to the window, drawing a deep breath of air. He glanced over his shoulder; his sullen expression sagged into embarrassment. "Forgive me. You wound my feelings, Lady Arlbond, when you hide from me. Is it my face? Are you afraid of a man that looks like... like this?" He stroked a trembling hand under his scarred cheek.

Oh gods. Prince Rais thought she'd been avoiding him because of his scars? She took his hand and placed her own over his cheek. "No, my Prince, I'd never think that."

"Then why? I thought, perhaps, you preferred your sorran, given the bond—"

"The bond doesn't work, my Prince."

"Doesn't work?"

"For a Neu Bosan."

He took her hand and lowered it. "You lied?"

Her cheeks flushed. She didn't want to admit the lie laid with Alistar. "To protect myself from your brother, my Prince."

"You don't have to lie anymore, Tamina." He pulled an item from his sahn. His fist uncurled to reveal a large unblemished ruby the size of his palm and attached to a golden chain. Its shimmering surface reflected his amber eye. "I want you to have this."

Was this... a proposal? "My Prince, it's beautiful, but I couldn't—"

"It will show the people you have my support."

She forced a smile as he placed the ruby around her neck, but words wouldn't come. She kept her tongue leashed, lest she say, *I don't want to marry you. I don't want to be your queen. I'd sooner set myself on fire.*

Since when did wearing dresses allow delicate princes to be so forward with her? She was a warrior, not someone's wife. Gods forbid. She'd find a way to help the Fire Walkers without throwing away anyone's freedom, hers or theirs. But first, she needed to find the right words to escape Prince Rais without insulting his honor or wounding his ego.

Delicate princes indeed. Let some other fool marry into the Bright Solara.

Concern nudged through the House bond, but it wasn't about her—Talin was worried about something, and his anxiety rippled through her gut.

Prince Rais rubbed his stomach and grimaced. "Mother?"

Mina shoved the ruby necklace down her shirt and pushed past the Prince into the main dining hall. Mutters and stares were all aimed at the front. The Queen squirmed in her seat, her trembling hand clutched tightly around the King's arm as sweat ran down her brow. Talin kneeled beside them, his expression neutral, as though engaging in some pleasant conversation. But the whining screech through the bond said otherwise.

"Could it be her baby?" Prince Rais said with awe. "I felt something stir in the bond. Father warned I might experience her labor."

No. Something was wrong.

Gareth snatched the Queen's discarded wine glass. He sniffed its contents and his eyes snapped to the Queen.

A cry escaped her lips. She rocked back and forth, clutching her stomach.

"Send for a Green Hand, now!" Talin yelled.

The dining hall erupted into a flurry of activity. Housemen and their families stood as guards shuffled between them, pushing them away from the Bright Solara. Raj fought through them as the nearest Green Hand in the hall. Mina ran after him, accompanied by Prince Rais. Salasar was there, barking orders and clearing space for the Green Hands. Thank the gods for the brute—he had the dining hall emptied in a heartbeat.

The Queen shrieked.

Green Hands surrounded the Queen and attempted to carry her from the hall. Darkness seeped through her dress and ran down her legs, staining the floor red. She sagged in their arms, her skin as pale as the Hartnord who stood beside her. The Queen's goblet shook in Gareth's grip.

Prince Ravel sniffed his own cup and tossed it. Alistar took the Princess's arm and led her away from the commotion.

The King shoved Raj aside. "She's bleeding too much. She's losing blood."

Talin wrestled the King back. "Let them work, my King—"

"She needs blood, Rahn curse you!"

The Queen didn't stir. Her limbs slackened.

Prince Rais leaned into Mina's side and whimpered. "Mama?

She's... Gods, it's gone. I can't feel her essence. I can't feel it! It's gone!"

The lit braziers of the hall flickered out, as though the heat and light of Bloodstone Keep had been stolen.

Fire erupted from the King's chest, knocking back Talin.

The roar of the King's flames was not enough to silence his howl of grief. A sharp pain seared behind Mina's left breast. The King's flames suddenly disappeared in a *whoof* of hot air, and his body fell limp to the ground.

12

POISON

Mina ran for her father. Talin kneeled on the ground, hand clutching his chest. He still lived, thank the gods.

"The King—he needs a Green Hand," Talin croaked. Whatever pain the King felt, his sorrans suffered in equal measure. And if a sorran's master died...

Salasar shouted for the Green Hands, who quickly but gently lowered the Queen to the ground—there was nothing they could do for her now—and ran to their king.

"I warned you!" Prince Ravel yelled. "I warned you this would happen!"

Salasar stomped to Talin's side. "Gods, is he—"

"Still breathing," Talin gasped. His face had turned ashen, and pain still burned in Mina's chest—an echo from what Talin felt as the King's sorran.

Iman grabbed her shoulder and pulled her away. "Come, girl, there's nothing we can do—"

"No! Talin!" Mina reached out for her father.

He shook his head and a little color returned to his cheeks. "Go."

"I'll watch over him," said a gruff voice. The King's other sorran, Gareth. His face showed no pain, and no fear either—only the same calm, cold expression as always. She'd often wondered if the King's attempt to make a sorran out of a Hartnord had been as ineffective as her own attempt with a Neu Bosan, but she'd never dared ask. Watching him now, it was clear Gareth didn't feel the same ripples of pain, the tightening in his chest, and the breathlessness that Talin did.

And he wouldn't die if the King didn't recover.

Iman dragged Mina away from the dining hall, through the Keep, and back to their shared room. Mina sank onto the lounger as Iman poured wine. She sniffed the cup and sighed, placing it back on the dresser.

Mina wiped tears from her eyes. She could lose Talin. She could lose another father, and she'd had barely any chance to spend time with him. "Iman?"

Iman sat and put her arm around Mina, pulling her tight. "I've got you, girl. I've got you."

"What do we do?"

"We wait. It's all we can do."

The Queen had been poisoned, but why? Revenge? And by whom? By the Fire Walkers for their return to imprisonment or by the Hartnords for the assassination of their own king? Whatever peace they'd tried to build was gone now, burned to ash. They'd march to war—there was no stopping it now. But against whom? Their pale-skinned neighbors to the far-off north or their own brethren right here in Solus?

And who would lead the march?

If the King didn't recover, neither Prince Ravel nor Prince Rais were ready to take his place. Prince Rais was too green—untested and unknown. Prince Ravel had allies in the Council, but the people of Sandair hated him for his crimes.

Or they had. Before the riots.

Did they still?

No Fire Walker would have poisoned the King—they weren't a threat to their own people, whatever the angry city folk thought. Which meant it could only be the Hartnords.

But there were no Hartnords left in Solus. They'd fled back to the north.

There was only Gareth.

Mina leaped up. "It's him. He did it. He poisoned the Queen. Gareth!"

"What are you talking about, girl?"

"Gareth poisoned the Queen! He's a Hartnord—"

"Have you lost your senses? He's the King's Left Arm—"

"Which means no one would suspect him! Prince Wulfhart knew him, said he served King Reinhart. Who's to say he's not serving them still? Spying on us? He could have sought revenge—"

"Sit down and cease your nonsense!" Iman bellowed. "You know nothing of his past, and if you did, you'd not make such foolish accusations."

Mina crossed her arms and leaned on the dresser. "Then tell me. Why does a Hartnord serve the King? What's in it for him?"

"Gareth may be a Hartnord, but that doesn't make him the enemy. Don't give me that look, girl. Talin knows him, and his loss. They fought side by side during the last war. Gareth was Princess Aniya's lover."

"The King's sister? Who died on Hartnord land?" As she said it, the lantern's flame flickered and Tira appeared. She nodded confirmation.

"Yes. Gareth served King Reinhart as his ambassador back then. He was a charming sort, and Princess Aniya took a shine to him. They kept their entanglement quiet, or Khaled tried to—he wasn't keen on his sister bedding a Hartnord. But there was no stopping Aniya from getting what she wanted.

"It was Gareth who suggested Aniya act as envoy for Sandair, and they travelled to Hartnor together. As soon as they crossed the border, they were attacked and separated. Gareth blamed Reinhart, but he also blamed himself. When they couldn't find her, he threw himself at the King's feet and begged for death."

"Did Gareth kill the Princess?" Mina asked to her mother more than Iman. Tira shook her head.

"Was he responsible?"

Again, another shake.

"The King didn't believe so," said Iman. "He told Gareth he'd be more useful gaining vengeance than throwing his life away, so Gareth fought by our side in the war. He turned his back on his own people and gave us every advantage." Iman took a deep sip of her wine before she continued. "We decimated the Hartnords. In battle after battle, city after city. It was King Khaled himself who ended the slaughter. Who tired of it. Killing Hartnords was never going to bring his sister back. Gareth has remained by the King's side ever since."

Mina stared into the lantern's flames. Her mother gave a solemn nod, confirming Iman's tale.

How did she know so much about Princess Aniya's death? Were they together in the afterlife? Not for the first time did Mina wish she could hold a proper conversation through the fire.

Hours passed in silent agony with only a faint fluttering of anxiety detectable through the bond. Still, Mina jumped at every noise. Neither she nor Iman managed to sleep.

Dawn rose before a knock rattled the door. Mina leaped up as Talin pushed through. She wrapped arms around him, and Talin squeezed her tight. "I can't stay. You must both pack and leave for Arlent immediately."

She let go and stared into his dark eyes. "What? Why?"

Iman stood. "The King?"

"Sleeping, for now. He's... it's his heart. A soul wound from Vida's..." His voice hitched. "He's alive, but at his age—he's taken ill and may not recover."

"The Queen's really gone? And the babe?"

"The Green Hands couldn't save either of them."

Iman rubbed a hand down the full length of her face and hissed a soft curse. "Vida didn't deserve this. What caused it?"

"The Green Hands are still examining her, but they believe she ingested something which triggered a false labor. I'm not sure if the intent was to target her or her child, but she lost too much blood. I... felt it. Through Khaled's bond to her, I felt her life leaving her. And Khaled... gods."

A gut-wrenching cry whined through the blood bond. Talin alone would understand what it meant to lose a wife and child.

"Does Gareth believe the Hartnords did this?" Iman asked.

"Yes."

Another curse. Iman sank onto the lounger. "How?"

"There's a drug the Hartnord royal family uses to end unwanted pregnancies and keep their bloodline pure, so Gareth says."

"Why would Hartnords have such a thing?" Mina said, aghast.

Iman gave a bitter laugh. "Seriously, girl? Young women do sometimes get pregnant when they don't intend to, even in royal families."

"Then Prince Wulfhart did this," Mina declared.

"Perhaps," Talin said. "Gareth thinks so, although he doesn't believe Wulfhart intended to kill the Queen."

Blood for blood. But an innocent unborn child? She'd thought Prince Wulfhart odd, but not a murderer. An assassin. A child killer.

"As the King's Right Arm, I've assumed command. We're holding a Council meeting shortly. The King is in and out of consciousness but had the clarity to give one command."

"Which is?"

Talin's eyes burned with a dark intensity. "War. We must prepare for war."

The blood bond went cool as though steel had sliced through it. War.

They'd be marc hing north to once again face Hartnords on the battlefield—an enemy she knew little about. It wouldn't be the same as fighting a duel or winning the tournament. No, this would be real fire and blood and death. Her hands shook by her sides.

Talin squeezed her shoulder. "Return to Arlent now. Don't wait for me. Lune guide you and keep you both safe." He released her and strode from the room before she could object.

Iman stomped to the dresser and pulled out clothes. "You heard the man."

"We can't just *leave!*"

"Talin knows what he's doing." Iman shoved clothes into a sack. "Hurry it up, girl."

"What about the Fire Walkers? What about the King? What if he—he..." She couldn't say the words. "What we are doing? Running back to Arlent and letting Talin fight a war on his own? He'll need us."

"He'll have Jonan. Arlent will need us. War won't reach the Duslands, but raiders always take advantage. Someone will need to protect Arlent. You'll get your glory then."

"This isn't about glory!" She flapped her arms. "He's my *father*! I'm not running to the desert when my family and friends are marching to war!" Iman had said all men would be called to war; that meant Alistar and Raj, too.

Iman grabbed a spare boot and brandished it like a weapon. "Does it not occur to you that if you stay, you'll worry him? Distract him? He's the King's Right Arm. This war will be on his head—"

"He doesn't have to worry about me. I can take care of myself."

"And Rahn doesn't have to rise and set each day. But he'll do it anyway."

A knock sounded at the door. Mina took a deep breath and strode to it, throwing an angry glare over her shoulder. She jumped back at the face waiting there.

Zavar Xanbond twitched as he eyed Iman behind her. Prince Ravel's sorran still bore a scar across the bridge of his nose from where Iman had smashed it during the tournament. Mina held no sympathy for him; he'd poisoned her in their match and earned his own disqualification. Her shoulder bore the scar from his blade.

He straightened his silver sahn, regaining his composure. "Prince Ravel requests your presence at the Council meeting, Lady Arlbond."

Iman threw the boot across the room and it smacked the wall with a thud. Her scowl twisted into something sour.

Zavar's face puffed into that of a smug fig merchant. "Now, if you would, Lady Arlbond. The Council can't wait." His grin grew positively wolflike. "Or shall I pass on your refusal to our new king?"

13

THE COUNCIL

"*Our new king.*"

Those words stole Mina's breath. She hadn't fought through the tournament, risked her honor, her House, and the lives of hundreds of Fire Walkers to throw that all away. "King Khaled is still alive," she spluttered.

Zavar strode down the hall and she jogged after him. "For how long? The King is rather unwell. He's not fit to rule—"

"And you think your master is?"

"My Prince has trained his entire life for this role. He understands the concerns of modern Sandair, whereas his father, Rahn guide him, refuses to see the danger." Zavar stopped and rounded on her. "We live in dark times, Lady Arlbond. The Hartnords have killed my aunt. She was—" His voice cracked and he cleared his throat. "She was kind to me." Zavar closed his eyes for a moment, and when they opened again, hatred burned bright in them. "I grew up beside the border. I saw Hartnord savagery with my own eyes. No one understands the threat of a Hartnord better than my House and I. We need a man of strength to lead us."

Prince Ravel was not that man. She clenched her teeth and followed him through the Keep's many corridors. A dead Hartnord king and now a dead Sandarian queen. Everyone was out for blood.

She understood that need for revenge, but this was going to tear their kingdoms apart.

As they strode through the gardens, they bumped into Alistar. He slid to her side and kept pace with their march. "What's going on?" he whispered.

"War."

He hissed a curse.

They entered the military court. This part of the Keep was occupied by the King's personal guards, the soldiers, and the city guards. She'd wandered here once looking for training space before the tournament, but they had no patience for former Academy students. This was where the King and his three wardens spent most of their time, so Talin had informed her. And where the Council of Housemen convened.

The courtyards here were not filled with flowers, trees, and water fountains, but with racks of silver swords. Even at this early hour, men in bronze scale armor worked through drills. Their war cries and the stench of sweat sent a shiver down her spine. How many of these men would bleed in the coming weeks? How many would die? Each yard they passed held a different group of men, and the quality of their blades and armor increased until they reached men in golden armor and red leather. The King's own royal guards.

Zavar stopped before a marble double door, reminiscent of the wooden entrance to the Academy with its carved symbols. Fourteen sigils had been etched into the marble, some more worn than others. The newest was Lune's crescent—the symbol of House Arlbond. And one had been scratched out, erased, though its outline remained—a three-forked flame. In the middle, split between the two doors, was the large round symbol of Rahn. The Bright Solara. Two royal guards stood on either side and parted the doors, allowing Zavar to pass.

Mina followed him into a cavernous room, its glittering marble walls Lune-white with tall windows. Housemen were gathered around a large triangular table with points colored in faded red, orange, and green representing the regions of the Solands, the

Duslands, and Gaisland. Scrolls, maps, and wine cups covered the table's surface.

Behind them stood their sorrans, and, to Mina's surprise, chairs for each of the three high priestesses of Sandair. Leila sat in the middle in her flowing red robe, her face already hardened into an unwelcoming glare. On her right was an old Gaislander woman in a green robe with a sash covered in knots to indicate her status as a trained Green Hand. And to her left sat a heavily pregnant Solander woman in a blue hooded robe. The High Priestess of Lune.

The blood bond pulled her attention to Talin, who sat near the red point of the table, which was marked with the symbol of Rahn. His own chair, beside Lune's crescent, was empty. He didn't look surprised to see her; no doubt he'd felt her approach through the bond, though his expression looked weary. Defeated. Beside him, Prince Ravel rose to his feet.

"My lords and ladies. I saw fit to invite our tournament champion. Before we begin what is destined to be a profoundly difficult meeting, I wish to put forth an addition to our agenda—a vote of no confidence in my father's ability to rule as king."

Mutters rippled through the room. Alistar stiffened beside her, and she followed his gaze to his father by the Gaisland point of the table. This close, the resemblance between Alistar and his father was uncanny.

A chair scraped across the tiled floor. Salasar stood. "My Prince, your father fell ill only a short time ago. Give him time to heal and grieve. His Right Arm can handle his affairs until—"

"The Green Hands say my father's heart is weak and beyond repair. He may never wield a sword again, Lord Sarabond, and what use is a king who cannot raise a blade and ride into a war that he has declared?"

A short Gaislander in a green sahn and matching turban stood. The Guardian of Gai. "Now is not the time for rash action, my Prince. Our Queen was taken from us—"

"My mother was murdered before my own eyes, Lord Nazim.

I felt her dying gasps through my own blood. There will be time to mourn. Now is the time to act." The Prince's amber eyes flared. "I will honor my father's dying wish. Blood for blood. But my father cannot lead the charge. As much as I respect the great Lord Talin, it is the blood of the Bright Solara who should lead our kingdom. *I* can lead us. Let me avenge my mother."

His speech sent a shiver down her spine. Prince Ravel wielded his anger as a weapon, and the Housemen fed off his emotions. She could see it reflected in their tired faces.

Their mutterings renewed. Some Housemen nodded; others looked less convinced, their faces pulled taut into uneasy grimaces. How could anyone have forgotten the Prince's crimes so soon? Talin sat expressionless, considering the Prince's words, but she felt his anxiety. Who would dare stand against the Prince? This was the Solaran Tournament all over again, with no combatant willing to face him.

Criticizing a grieving son would make her a monster. But if she needed to become a monster, then so be it. She stepped up to the table. Alistar grabbed her arm and pinched sharp. She bit back a yelp and glared at him. He mouthed one word: *Don't.*

The pinch pulled Talin from his stupor. He rose to his feet with slow, considered movements, and the murmurs died out. "We are all shocked by Queen Vida's death, none more than I. She was a dear friend who supported me through the loss of my own wife. I, too, wish to see justice. I stand here today as the King's sorran, as his Right Arm, to fulfill his commands. I do so in line with our Code of Honor, and with rules abided by for generations and generations of my King's bloodline. It is that same Code of Honor which states a prince must win the Solaran Tournament before he can hold the crown."

She swallowed a sigh of relief.

Talin smiled. "The tournament my daughter won."

The Housemen leaned over the table to get a better look at her. Blood rose to her cheeks, but she held her chin high.

The Prince's lips churned with a repressed sneer. "Lady Arlbond should never have been allowed to compete in the tournament, my lords. Her victory should not be recognized."

Heat flared in her gut. "The King recognized my victory, Prince."

"Yet the Code of Honor does not. Women have no place in the tournament."

"A woman still won fairly, my Prince," said one of the priestesses—the pregnant High Priestess of Lune. "She won to your rules."

Prince Ravel turned to the priestess and inclined his head a fraction. "With respect, Lady Sarabond, this is not a matter for the temple."

Lady Sarabond? Mina flicked her gaze to Salasar, who'd returned to his seat and was now grinding his teeth. Salasar's wife was the High Priestess of Lune?

The priestess—Lady Sarabond—didn't look impressed, nor cowed by the Prince's dismissal. "The Temple of Lune represents all of Lune's daughters, my Prince. That includes her."

"Yes, yes, we're not here to discuss the validity of some woman's accomplishments," drawled a familiar voice. Lord Farzad Fellbond. A hefty man Mina had defeated in the tournament. He dismissed her, and Lady Sarabond, with a flick of his wrist. "It's irrelevant if this girl cheated her way through the tournament—"

"I didn't cheat!"

"—to make some sort of tale for the crowd to eat up. We all know Prince Ravel would have won, *should* have won, and that the King named him his heir."

"Are you forgetting the crimes he committed?" Heat tingled her fingers and she flexed them into fists by her side. "He poisoned people. His own father!"

"An unfortunate accident, yes, but he has been punished enough."

"What, by being locked inside his golden palace and pampered like a child?"

Some of the Housemen muttered and shot glares her way. A

warning burned through the blood bond, and Talin shook his head subtly, enough for her to catch it.

"My mother has been murdered, Lady Arlbond," Prince Ravel snarled. He let his eyes drift from Houseman to Houseman. "I have spent these past weeks making amends to prove to you all how deeply I regret my actions. Know they came from a place of fear. Not fear for myself, but for my kingdom. You all witnessed my helbond ceremony a year ago, when my dear brother was so terribly injured. I could not abide the threat posed to the people of Sandair by Fire Walkers hiding among us. And look where we are now. A Fire Walker set in motion this chain of events that killed my mother and brought us to the brink of war." The Prince closed his eyes, took a deep breath, and opened them again. "But the Fire Walkers are not the point of this meeting. We must move forward. I ask you to place your faith in me."

The Housemen murmured their agreement. How had he won back their hearts and minds so quickly? The city folk in the taverns still cursed his name.

But it was Housemen who decided the fate of their people, who voted at Council meetings and forced laws on the rest of Sandair. By dropping bribes in a few choice pockets, he could have bought his support back. Whilst she was avoiding the palace, sure he was locked safely away in his room, he could have been using that time to his advantage. Gods, how could she have been so foolish?

"No one doubts your courage, my Prince," Salasar said. "But you lack the experience needed to lead men into battle—"

"I graduated from the Academy with your blessing, Lord Salasar. You trained me yourself and named me your most promising student. Did you lie?"

"No, my Prince, but you are young—"

"My father was eighteen when he assumed the throne."

"Your father had fought in real battles and killed men by the time he took the crown. I speak as a commander, as Sword of Solus, when I say you're too green, my Prince. Boys who rush into war rarely become men."

Shocked whispers whipped around the room. The Prince's face contorted with anger for a heartbeat before returning to its mask of perfection. The Sword of Solus had said the words no one else dared. By the grimace pulling on Salasar's face, he knew he'd overstepped.

"Forgive me, my Prince," Talin said. "The Code of Honor still stands."

Farzad Fellbond slammed his fist on the table, making everyone jump. "Gai's teat, if you're going to blather on about the Code of Honor, then don't pick and choose. If the King isn't fit enough to chair this meeting, then he's not fit enough to rule. How can he organize a war from his sick bed? Our Prince may be young, but he's shown more courage than the lot of you."

Murmurs of agreement lit a fire in her stomach.

"Khaled is still king," the Guardian of Gai said, his voice as sharp as a bird's cry. "I have every faith Lord Talin can manage his affairs—"

"And what if the King passes on?" said a man in a silver sahn. House Xanbond. Zavar's father? "Talin would die with him. We'd lose our commander in the middle of a war! If the King's life is in danger—and we all know that it is—we can't march into Hartnord land with his sorran in command of our army. We need the King's heir to lead us. And Prince Ravel is his chosen heir."

"But he lost the tournament!" Mina said.

"That only matters when the King surrenders the throne to his heir while he's still alive. The Code of Honor says nothing about the tournament when a king dies."

"For shame! The King isn't dead yet," tutted a small Gaislander woman in a lilac dress. House Enaibond. Raj's mother.

If the tournament didn't matter, then another prince could challenge the throne. "What of Prince Rais?" Mina called out.

"He's passed his helbond—"

"My brother has taken the death of our mother to heart," Prince Ravel said. "I'm afraid he has no capacity to lead. Nor, as you are aware, my lords, has he ever taken an interest in this Council."

She chewed her tongue. Prince Rais *should* be here. She couldn't win this battle for him—no one could. Who could take him seriously as a challenger for the throne when he didn't even show up to argue for himself?

"Then we hold a vote of confidence as the Prince suggests," the Xanbond Houseman said.

"A vote is unnecessary. Of course we have confidence in the King," the Guardian of Gai countered.

"Must be comfortable in Gaisland, Nazim," Farzad Fellbond drawled. "Battle never reaches your forest. It's Fellbani land that the Hartnords will raid. It's our towns they'll plunder, and our people they'll slaughter. Same as it was seventeen years ago." Lord Farzad's voice dropped to a low growl. "I lost my brother on some foolhardy mission to protect the King's Hartnord sorran. Is that the same leadership we can expect from you this time, Lord Talin?" His face turned a blotchy red. "You led that mission yourself. I'd sooner place my faith in fresh blood than some withered old man—"

Chairs crashed backwards—Salasar was on his feet, shouting, hand on his sword hilt. So was the Lord of House Xanbond. And the Guardian of Gai. And two other Housemen who seemed to be taking House Fellbond's side, in sahn's of deep blue and bright yellow, though it was hard to make out who was shouting what. Prince Ravel watched, absorbing the chaos with a subtle smirk. He was enjoying this.

Talin raised his hand. "Enough!"

The men fell silent, like Academy children scolded by their teacher. Even Salasar.

"We'll hold a vote," Talin declared. "All those in favor of the Prince's proposal and his claim to the throne, sit. Those who support the King and agree to follow my command as his Right Arm, stand. Are we clear?"

Prince Ravel inclined his head. "As my father's Right Arm, it is only fair that you abstain from the vote, Lord Talin. Are we agreed?"

The Housemen murmured their agreement.

"As you wish, my Prince," Talin said.

The lords of Houses Fellbond, Khalbond, and Xanbond sat immediately. Salasar remained standing, of course. The Guardian of Gai, representing House Grebond, puffed out his chest and stood proud.

The others hesitated. Mina watched them, marking each face as Prince Ravel did, either as a supporter of King Khaled or a potential enemy.

After a few minutes' conversation with their sorrans and the other members of their House in attendance, the lords of the other two Soland Houses, Darabond and Nasbond, took their seats. The head of House Baibond—a Duslander—remained standing.

The three priestesses were given a vote, to Mina's surprise. Leila kept her seat, which wasn't to her surprise. The High Priestess of Gai stood and, with some difficulty, she helped Lady Sarabond, the High Priestess of Lune, to stand as well.

Only three Gaislander Houses remained.

To Mina's relief, Raj's mother stood. The lord of House Orabond, however, did not.

And so it was down to House Myrbond. Alistar's family. Neu Bosan by birth and blood. Sandarian by choice. And soon to marry their son into the Bright Solara, if King Khaled's will should prevail.

Alistar squirmed. His father twitched, as though being physically torn between king and prince. Mina had never met him, but he was a renowned merchant and politician. An ambitious man, becoming head of a Sandarian House despite his foreign lineage and securing an ambassadorship for himself. And now, potentially, securing a royal wife for his son and heir. There could be no doubt he'd thrived under King Khaled's rule.

But that only meant he had a lot to lose.

If he stood now, only for the King to die and the throne to fall to Prince Ravel anyway, he might as well usher his entire family aboard a boat to Neu Bosa. Everything he'd built in Sandair would be lost. But if he sided with Prince Ravel, the Prince was certain to reward him generously, and for years to come.

Alistar's father, Lord of House Myrbond, rose slowly from his chair. And in doing so, damned his House.

"A tie, my Prince," Talin said.

"Perhaps a recount is in order, Lord Talin."

"Not needed, my Prince," Salasar said. An odd smile played on his lips. "The Code of Honor states that the reigning tournament champion may cast a deciding vote in times of strife. Isn't that so, Lord Talin?"

The embers in her gut stirred, and a rush of warmth left her mouth dry.

"Should the tournament champion be a *man*, Lord Salasar," Prince Ravel spluttered.

"The Code of Honor makes no reference to sex in this case, my Prince. Or should we summon the Academy scholars and pour over every line?"

"Cast your vote, Tamina," Talin said with calm reassurance, as though this decision meant nothing.

She looked straight at the Prince as she walked around to House Arlbond's seat at the table. His expression twisted with whatever poison burned in his veins. She placed her hands on the back of the chair and moved her gaze to Salasar. The Sword of Solus. A man she'd considered to be a living legend like her father, until she'd met him and learned that honor came cheap. He'd once warned her against denying the Prince in the tournament, but now... his one eye widened, bright with answer.

Gods, she could kiss him.

Oh, Prince Ravel thought himself so clever, dragging her here to witness his crowning moment. Hadn't he learned yet? So long as she drew breath, she'd deny his crown. She didn't need to become queen to stop him. Nor did she need to shed blood.

She casually tipped her chair onto its side. The clatter as it hit the tiled floor was the sweetest music she'd ever heard.

"I vote in King Khaled's favor."

A deep sigh rumbled through the room.

"If this matter is concluded, let us move on," Talin said. "We have a war to prepare for."

The Housemen shuffled back into their seats, grabbing wine or papers, their attention averted from the Prince.

Prince Ravel remained standing, his expression neutral. He inclined his head in polite defeat, though his sorran, Zavar, flinched. "As you will, Lord Talin. My father's success remains in your hands. May I make a request?"

"Of course, my Prince."

"Allow me to earn the respect of this Council and prove my worth. I request the opportunity to assist your campaigns. I mean not to steal your glory, Lord Talin, but to learn from you and contribute where necessary."

"That is acceptable, my Prince."

"With that in mind, I have a suggestion." Prince Ravel's amber eyes met hers. "It is only fitting that our tournament champion should fight beside our men to victory. And her sorran."

14

A PATH CHOSEN

Mina stiffened. Talin mirrored the movement. Salasar caught his expression. "Lady Arlbond is too young, my Prince, and far too inexperienced. She'd be a liability—"

"You dishonor our champion, Lord Salasar. If Lady Arlbond is man enough to enter our tournament and cast a vote in this Council, then she is well equipped for joining our men in battle. Is that not fair, Lady Sarabond?" His gaze shifted to the Priestess of Lune, who didn't take the bait or even raise an eyebrow.

Salasar offered Mina an apologetic smile. "I mean no offense, Lady Arlbond, but I think the Council can make an exception in this case. The first duty of a woman is to provide heirs for her husband. I believe Lady Arlbond is already betrothed."

Heat burned across her entire face. She hadn't even agreed to marry Prince Rais! How in Lune's name had he heard such nonsense?

This, at least, provoked a reaction from the Priestess of Lune, who snorted and shook her head.

"War isn't conducive to marriage, Lord Salasar," Prince Ravel said.

"A royal marriage would boost morale, my Prince."

"I'm not marrying anyone!" Mina yelled.

Farzad Fellbond thumped the table. "We're not here to discuss marriage plans." His leering gaze turned to her. "She beat me in the tournament. I'm a proud man, but if the King welcomes women in his tournament, then he must believe them competent enough to fight on a battlefield. Wouldn't you agree, Lord Talin? You chose to dress her up as a man, enter her into the Academy as a man, and parade her in the tournament as a man. Have faith in your daughter."

Talin's intense eyes found hers. "I have faith, do not mistake me. But the law is clear that only men can serve as soldiers."

"Oh, now you care what the law says about women and what they're allowed to be?" scoffed Lord Xanbond. "How convenient. However, the Code of Honor supersedes the law, and the Code is very clear about the responsibilities of our tournament champion."

Talin opened his mouth but no words came out.

It was Prince Ravel who spoke, grinning from ear to ear. "'Should the champion be unwilling or unable to answer the call of the king to battle, then he shall be champion no more and neither is he a warrior. All titles and honors shall be stripped of him, along with his sword.' Did I quote that correctly, Lord Talin? Or would you like to call for the Academy scholars?"

Talin's fury boiled hot through the blood bond. "The King did not call Mina to battle—"

"He called for war," snarled the Prince. "And in war, every warrior must answer the call of his king."

"The Code says nothing whatsoever about women being soldiers or serving in war. In this case, we can all agree that when the champion is a woman—"

"I don't agree," Farzad Fellbond said. "If the Code permits women to serve as champions, then the Code binds them to the rules and responsibilities that come with it. You can't have it both ways, Lord Talin."

In that moment, Mina felt something through her blood bond with Talin that she never thought she'd feel from him— helplessness. He looked to Salasar, then to Salasar's wife. Neither met his eye. Everyone in the room knew that the argument was over.

Prince Ravel smirked. "Take a seat, Lady Arlbond. Your sorran may stand."

Mina's chair still lay on its side. With the Housemen watching in silence, she righted the chair and slid into the seat, her knees weak. War, and she'd be at the front lines.

She'd denied Prince Ravel his crown once again, but he'd caught her in his trap in the end. Talin had wanted her to run back to Arlent because he knew this would happen. His anger no longer rattled through the bond, nor any sense of defeat. Only a solemn calm as if to say, *We'll survive this together.*

The Prince settled in his chair as though it was a throne. "Now, it's time we speak of strategy. One thing the Hartnords have made clear in recent weeks is how much they fear our Fire Walkers. We should exploit this fear. Our Fire Walkers should be on the forefront of the attack."

She sat up. "No."

Talin raised his hand for Mina to hold her tongue, but the Prince waved him off. "Allow Lady Arlbond to voice her objections."

She gripped the marble arms of her chair, nails scraping the stone. "King Khaled gave the Fire Walkers their freedom."

"And they used that freedom to murder a Hartnord king and damn us all to war."

"You cannot punish an entire group of people based on one person—"

"No one is being punished. Fire Walkers will be called to serve, same as any man."

She leaned over the table. "They're not your slaves!"

"Sit down. You're embarrassing yourself," Farzad Fellbond muttered.

"Forgive me, Lady Arlbond, but I'm confused." The Prince rubbed his chin. "I don't recall you representing the Fire Walkers as High Priestess of Rahn."

"Fire Walkers have always been called to assist during times of war," Salasar said.

She glared at him. "That was before they were freed!"

Now it was Leila's turn to raise her hand for silence. She waited until all eyes were upon her before she stood and said, "Our temple is a sanctuary, not a prison. And it is an honor, not a punishment, to serve our kingdom when war is upon us. As High Priestess of Rahn, I believe it is right and just for the Fire Walkers to march side by side with our soldiers."

"Well spoken," Prince Ravel said. "My lords and ladies, if this issue requires a vote, then we should vote."

"So be it," Talin said, as he rose from his chair. "For my part, I vote to let each Fire Walker make his own choice whether or not to serve. Let all who agree with me stand."

Of the Houses on the Council, only House Enaibond sided with him. Raj's mother stood, even as Alistar's father, Salasar, and all the rest remained in their seats.

The Fire Walkers would once again be rounded up and forced to march north. Forced to burn Hartnords and forced to die on Hartnord blades. There was nothing she could do about it.

The Priestesses of Gai and Lune, at least, supported the Fire Walkers, not that their votes counted for much. Lady Sarabond glowered at her husband across the table.

Once all votes were cast and recorded, Talin sank back into his chair. "If the Fire Walkers are to march with us to Hartnor, then I have a duty to perform as Right Arm of the King. I hereby relieve the High Priestess of Rahn of her position."

The Housemen groaned.

"This would place us in an awkward predicament, Lord Talin," Prince Ravel said. "Now is not the time to seek a replacement."

"On the contrary, my Prince, now is the ideal time. It was the High Priestess's own acolyte who murdered King Reinhart— during a ceremony that she herself was responsible for. Clearly, she has no control over her own people, even those closest to her. If we can't trust her to maintain order among the Fire Walkers here in our own Keep, then we dare not allow her to lead them into war." His eyes flickered to Mina, and she nodded in response.

Leila stood and swooped into a low bow. "My Prince, my

lords. I have served Rahn and the Bright Solara for many years. We have fought side by side as I led my Fire Walkers in battle. I'd hoped we'd never face another such conflict in my lifetime, and I am ashamed that it was one of my own who committed the atrocity which has led us back to war. I have prayed to Rahn for forgiveness, my lords, and now I humbly beg you for the same."

"I appreciate your testimony, but my command stands. We will choose a new High Priestess who can be trusted to act in the best interests of this Council."

Mina bit back a smirk. Now Leila would be no one but another Fire Walker.

Leila bowed again. "Of course, my Lord. There are many fine priestesses across Sandair. I could recommend any number."

Any priestess Leila recommended would treat the Fire Walkers with the same contempt. The same cowardice and subservience to those in power. It was dangerous enough in times of peace. In war, it would get hundreds killed, if not thousands. There was nothing Mina could do to stop this war, to stop the Fire Walkers from being dragged into it. But perhaps there were ways she could protect them, from the inside. The Prince wanted her thrown into harm's way regardless.

Mina stood. "I volunteer. I'll become your High Priestess."

The Housemen blinked at her.

"A priestess must be highly trained in our rituals with many years of service to the temple," Leila said, her nostrils flaring. "Neither of which fit you."

"I learn fast."

"The High Priestess is expected to command Fire Walkers in battle," Salasar said. "It's no easy path—"

"You expect your tournament champion to fight. Let me fight alongside my own kind."

Leila chuckled. "My lords, you cannot expect an untrained child to lead Fire Walkers. She'll burn half our own men before the battle starts."

A few Housemen added their own derision.

"She's just trying to get out of roughing it up on the front lines," Farzad Fellbond said with a snort.

Prince Ravel waved a hand. "Do not discount our champion. It is by her hand that the Fire Walkers gained their freedom to cause this war. By rights, she should be given the chance to fix her mess. Do you have the strength to lead Fire Walkers into battle, Lady Arlbond?" His eyebrow arched disbelievingly.

Unease rumbled through the bond.

"The path of a Fire Walker priestess requires celibacy," Talin said.

Her skin flushed at the implication. The choice. Become a priestess or marry a foolish prince. Both could help the Fire Walkers, but only one path offered her freedom. And she'd be allowed to keep her sword; the first time she met Leila was when she sword danced in a faraway Dusland town.

Mina gazed across the Council chamber to the corner where Tira watched on from inside a lantern's flames. Always watching. Her mother smiled and shrugged. *Your choice.*

Talin had asked her to consider the woman she wanted to be.

"This discussion is irrelevant, my lords," Leila said. "Throughout history, the temple has approved our own leaders before presenting them to the Council. No one else understands the unique demands of running the Temple of Rahn and training its Fire Walkers like our *experienced* acolytes. Nor can the matters of the temple be left to those whose motives do not align with our kingdom's laws." Leila's hardened stare moved to Mina, clearly marking her as one of those possessing such motives. "This is why you trust us to choose for ourselves and to choose wisely. If the Fire Walkers have no confidence in those who lead them, then they cannot be controlled effectively during times of war."

Leila's words stirred worried murmurs among the Housemen. None welcomed the threat of out-of-control Fire Walkers in the midst of battle.

Mina leaned back in her chair and crossed her arms. "Then let the Fire Walkers choose." She raised her brow in challenge at the former High Priestess. The Fire Walkers knew who'd won them their freedom—most of them did, anyhow.

But Leila merely smiled back, as though she knew something Mina didn't.

Farzad Fellbond thumped his wine glass on the table. "This meeting is running in circles. Give them their gods-damn vote and be done with it. Since our Sword of Solus holds jurisdiction over the Solus temple, let him handle it. I'm sure the Council can trust in Lord Salasar's... *familiarity* with Fire Walkers to agree on a suitable priestess." He exchanged a knowing glance with the other Solander Housemen. They still remembered when Salasar displayed his own blood fire at the Solend.

Salasar scowled. "Fine. I'll oversee a vote."

"Don't dally, Lord Salasar," Prince Ravel said. "We have little time to prepare. Our Fire Walkers began this war. They will end it."

Farzad Fellbond raised his glass in toast. "Hear, hear. Now can we wrap this meeting up? We have our queen to mourn."

"Yes, we've all had a trying morning." Talin rubbed his left hand across the bridge of his nose. "Let's adjourn and meet once we have rested and dealt with our grief, and when our new High Priestess has been chosen. A lurrite will need to be arranged for our Queen as soon as possible." He bowed his head toward Prince Ravel, who returned the respect. "The Temple of Rahn will also need time to adjust."

The Housemen gathered their papers and shuffled out of the room. Alistar ran after his father. Mina wanted to speak with Talin to discuss what being a High Priestess meant, but the Guardian of Gai demanded his attention.

Leila strode from the chamber with her chin held high—as though she'd already won.

This wasn't going to be easy, but Mina was the Fire Walkers' biggest advocate. As High Priestess, she'd give them a voice Leila refused. As a Houseman of House Arlbond, she could carry that voice with weight. And as Talin's daughter, the Council may listen.

All she needed to do was convince the Fire Walkers.

15

RAHN'S CALLING

In all of Mina's childhood, she'd never expected to find the Temple of Rahn welcoming. At first, she'd looked upon those red-stained doors as a prison crawling with Sandair's most horrifying monsters. Then, after discovering her own latent blood fire, she'd feared being locked inside, never being able to taste fresh air again. Talin had once tried to explain its purpose as a home to Rahn's children, but she'd not been able to see it until she'd been forced to sleep under its roof.

She entered the warm embrace of the temple with Fez tucked inside her sahn. But when she reached the main sanctum, any illusion of calm was shattered. Hundreds of men, women, and children were crowded into the cavernous sanctum. Angry, confused Fire Walkers who thought they'd escaped this place for good, only to be rounded up again twelve weeks later. They all rushed at her.

"What's going on? Why are we here?" one of them demanded.

She scanned the crowd for Leila—at least until the vote, she was still acting High Priestess, and this mob was hers to contain. But no help came.

The Fire Walkers erupted with questions.

Is the King dead?

Why are we here?

What happens if we leave?

Has the law been overturned?

Fez screeched at the commotion. He leaped from her sahn and ran for the tunnel.

A Solander woman jostled a small child in her arms. "They tried to snatch my baby! They threw me in here and tried to take her. My husband, he fought them off. They broke his nose and threw him in a cell. I don't even know where he is!"

If Leila wasn't here to calm her Fire Walkers' fears, then Mina needed to. She raised her palms. "I'll speak with the Sword of Solus and find your hus—"

"You can't lock him away again! You swore!" It was Kamran's mother. She held her boy close to her hip, his head still bandaged from where he'd been struck during the riot. "I won't leave my son!"

"I understand your concerns. I'll ask—"

"Are we going to war?" a Duslander yelled.

"Let me ex—"

"Where's Leila? Who are *you*?" another demanded. "You're nothing but a Houseman!"

"If you give me a chance, I'll—"

The doors burst open. Boots marched into the sanctum—Salasar and a handful of his guards. The Fire Walkers shrank back. Each guard had a hand to his sword hilt and watched the crowd with a wary face. Only the Sword of Solus looked unfazed.

"This is a waste of my time," he muttered. "Let's get it over with." He clapped his hands and his guards moved quickly to push the Fire Walkers away from the sanctum's center and to the stone steps surrounding it.

Leila emerged from the tunnel next with three of her female acolytes. The Fire Walkers shuffled aside as the High Priestess gracefully took her spot at the center of the sanctum. Leila raised her arms. "War is coming." Her voice cut through the Fire Walker's hushed conversations. "We have been asked once again to fight for the glory of Rahn and our great kingdom. You will all have a part to play in the battles to come. You will burn for Sandair. You will bleed for her. However, I will not be leading you."

The Fire Walkers broke out into fevered whispers: *Why this?*

Why now?

Gods, was Leila trying to terrify them?

Leila continued over their panicked voices, "Though I have served you all diligently these past twenty years, my diligence was not enough to prevent tragedy. The Council of the Great Houses has seen fit to replace me on the eve of war. Whoever shall wear these robes must act as I have—in accordance with Rahn's laws. The future of this temple rests in your hands." She bowed and moved to one side.

The fevered whispering renewed and anxiety sparked in the dusty air. Leila made no attempt to calm the crowds, as though she fed off their fears.

It took Salasar's booming voice to settle them. "What she said is true. You must all choose a new High Priestess to represent you. I'm not going to tell you who to choose—that's on your heads. But choose wisely. And quickly—"

"I will test them," Leila added. "To ensure only the brightest of Rahn's acolytes rise to represent his children. If you feel Rahn's calling, then step into his light." Flame flared from Leila's hand and spilled in a circle around the sanctum in one single *whoof*. Some of the Fire Walkers gasped and jumped back. Many just stared; their dark eyes hollow with despair.

They needed hope.

They needed to believe someone cared.

"I hope you'll be there for them, Mina Hawker, when the kingdom burns."

Mina hopped over Leila's flames into the center. "I'll serve as your High Priestess."

Jeers echoed in the sanctum.

Leila waved them off. "A Houseman has stepped before you to declare allegiance to Rahn. Allow her to speak."

The Fire Walkers muttered and exchanged wary glances. They repeated the word *Houseman*.

Most Fire Walkers standing here were city folk or street rats. No men in fancy clothes flashing gold stood among them. Certainly no Housemen.

This was her only chance to convince them she was on their side. "Yes, I'm a Houseman. But I wasn't always. I grew up on the streets. I watched helplessly when my uncle was cut down for being a Fire Walker. I, too, am a Fire Walker. I'm not ashamed of it." She rolled up her sleeves, showing off the silver tattoos, and let a flicker of flame burn in her palm. "And I'm your best chance of surviving a war none of us asked for."

A tall, gruff-looking Duslander stepped to the edge of Leila's simmering flames. "Since when do Housemen become priestesses?"

"Since now."

"Why bother? Housemen want us dead." He eyed up Salasar. "This war is just pretense."

Mina shook her flame out. "What's your name, my friend?"

"I'm not your friend," he spat. "And Housemen deserve none of our respect." The Duslander turned and jerked a thumb over his shoulder at thick scars splayed down his back. "Housemen did that to me in Khalbad's temple because I tried to stop them raping a girl. She ran so they killed her. What respect should we have for men like them?"

"You're from Khalbad?"

"Have you ever stepped foot in Khalbad's temple, Houseman? They have a column in their sanctum where they chain Fire Walkers who don't obey. Our High Priestess allowed it. Will you?"

Heat burned in her stomach and she glared at Leila. No emotion passed over the High Priestess's face. No denial. No remorse. Mina had never heard of Fire Walkers being tortured in the temples, but after witnessing the cruelty of Housemen herself, she could believe it. Especially under the rule of House Khalbond. "I want you there with me when we pull that column down."

The Duslander snorted in disbelief, but she meant every word.

A thin-looking Solander Fire Walker stepped beside him and waved casually. He reminded her of Raj with his twig-like arms. "I'm Bahri. I don't mean to intrude, but Dahn doesn't speak for all of us." He pointed at her and glanced to the many faces watching. "She's a Houseman, but she's not like them. It's because of her that we gained any freedom in the first place—"

"And for what?" The Duslander—Dahn—waved his arms toward the walls and ceiling of the temple. "To snatch that freedom away again! Look where we are!"

Some of the Fire Walkers murmured and nodded. Their angry glares made the heat rise in her blood. Mina glanced to Salasar, who picked dust from his sahn as though bored with it all, but Leila smirked. Fire Walkers held no love for Housemen. Mina understood that all too well.

"I was trapped inside the temple for being a Fire Walker, too," Mina said. "You call me a Houseman, but I'm no different from you. From all of you."

Dahn rolled his eyes. "Oh, spare me—"

"I was there," another man spoke up. A round Gaislander. "At the tournament. I was there when the Prince poisoned us. I watched my own friends burn." His voice broke. "I saw her argue against her own Housemen—against the Prince himself—for *us*."

At least some of these men believed she'd done the right thing.

"We all heard the King's declaration," Bahri shouted to the crowd. "None of that would have happened if it wasn't for her—for the Sand Dancer. Nothing would have changed. Those twelve weeks were a gift—"

"Nothing has changed!" Dahn snapped. "Don't you see? Our freedom was never going to last. The Housemen were never going to allow it. And you think *she* has the right to saunter in here and declare herself our High Priestess? To lead us into a war that Housemen declared?"

Mina stepped to the edge of Leila's flames. "I'm not asking you to like me, Dahn. I won't even ask you to respect me. But as a Houseman, I will do everything in my power to protect you. All of you. Under my House, Fire Walkers were given their freedom. I can't promise you that same freedom—*yet*. But my House will work toward it. Until then, what I *can* promise is that I'll use what power I have to navigate the Council, to protect you from *them*. Yes, I am a Houseman. It'll take a Houseman to understand them—and protect you from them."

The anger in Dahn's face slipped, if only for a heartbeat.

She shot a quick glance to Salasar to ensure she didn't overstep, and his eyes were narrowed. No doubt if any other House was standing here as witness, she'd have something to answer for, but she'd long suspected Salasar hated Houseman games as much as she did.

Leila clapped. "Strong words. But can you prove them in the eyes of Rahn?" She beckoned Mina closer. "Come and test yourself against his power."

Mina's heart sped up. Speaking in front of the Fire Walkers had been a test, so what was this?

Fire swirled around Leila's fists. "Only trained acolytes of Rahn possess the skills necessary to lead. If you wish to defend us, then summon a shield and show us how."

A shield. Gods, Mina had never learned how to summon a shield or otherwise defend herself against blood fire. It had taken weeks of Jonan's training just to maintain a steady flame, and they'd run out of time to progress further.

Samira and Saeed had observed her training—her failures. They'd have told Leila.

Mina had no choice but to try. She positioned her feet in the sand and thrust her fists out, ready to block. *I am the master of my own self and this fire is mine to control. I can do this.*

Fire flew toward Mina within the blink of an eye. She brought her fists close to her face and willed her own embers to spark. Heat surged through her veins, but not fast enough. Leila's flames burned Mina's sleeve and the fabric caught fire. She dove to the ground and used the sands to pat out the flames before they could do real harm.

Laugher filled the sanctum.

"I think we've all seen enough," Leila declared.

Mina stomped to the edge of Leila's flaming circle and blinked away hot tears. She'd failed in front of them all, just as Leila wanted. The roar of her own heartbeat thumped in her ears and she barely heard Leila call for other candidates to introduce and test themselves.

One, two, three female Fire Walkers she'd never seen inside the temple walked into the center. Each were able to summon a shield to guard against Leila's flames, though from the angle Mina stood, she could see that Leila held back her power, allowing the other candidates to display their blood fire with finesse. Their smug smirks made Mina's teeth grind. They were but puppets, all of them. Leila may have lost her position as High Priestess, but she'd seemingly found other ways of clawing back control.

Who acted the Houseman now?

Salasar patted her on the shoulder. "It's for the best, child. The path of a high priestess is no life. Trust me. I speak from experience."

"I think your wife would disagree."

He huffed and stepped into the center of the sanctum. The chatter of the Fire Walkers hushed once more. "We'll hold a vote on which acolyte to choose as your next high priestess. When I call each, you'll vote by raising your flame. You hear?"

The Fire Walkers mumbled their assent. Compared to the Council, this way of voting seemed more... visceral. Mina considered ducking out of the final vote, but she needed to see which of Leila's lackeys would be declared the new High Priestess. If only to know what new enemy she was up against.

Salasar called the first acolyte, and a smattering of flames sparked across the sanctum, including Dahn's. More flames rose for the second acolyte, a Solander woman with a dour face, but they fizzled out for the third. Many of the Fire Walkers sat back against the stone steps with their arms crossed, and their faces spoke a truth Mina knew in her gut: this vote didn't matter, so why vote at all?

"And for Lady Tamina Arlbond." Salasar waved a dismissive hand at her.

One by one, Fire Walkers raised their arms and summoned

Rahn's light. Fifty, a hundred, two hundred... They burned so brightly, Mina couldn't tell which fists the light emanated from. They were a forest of fire.

Across the sanctum, Dahn stared in disbelief. Bahri held his flaming arm aloft and grinned. Leila ducked into a bow, her flames snapping out, her hood hiding whatever anger seared through her.

Salasar gave her a wry smile. "It seems they've chosen their high priestess."

She! The High Priestess of Rahn!

Mina wanted to whoop and laugh, but Iman had trained her better than that. Instead, she bowed low. "I swear to serve each and every one of you as your high priestess. For now, we continue as normal. We give the Housemen and their Council no reason to punish us further. As long as you remain in these walls, you'll be safe. All of you. And if you have husbands, wives, or children who aren't Fire Walkers, then we'll accommodate them, too. I won't split up families. I know how Leila ran things, but I'm not her. We'll make room and get enough food and bedding for everyone."

Leila shot her head up at that.

Salasar approached and shook his head. "So be it. I'll inform the Council and start sending out orders to the other temples. Your duty is to this temple, first and foremost, but the Queen's lurrite takes precedence." He leaned close and whispered, "I'll give you until the lurrite to reconsider this farce. Think about it. You don't want to be responsible for their deaths."

She gave him a flat stare. "You're right. I don't."

"Lune's luck." He beckoned his guards and left the temple.

A few of the Fire Walkers rushed forward to speak with her, though some, she noted, kept a wary distance. It was those she'd need to win over next.

But she had one task to do first.

In the rush, Leila had slipped into the tunnel. Mina followed and found her in her glass chamber beside the wooden bookcase—

the only furniture in the room.

The former High Priestess kept her back turned. "Don't think this will be easy."

"I never said it would be."

"There's no one to help you. No one to train you. Saeed is dead, and Samira may as well be. If you have a heart, Mina Hawker, you'll exonerate her. She had nothing to do with Saeed's crimes."

Mina crossed her arms. "And you know that for a fact? You didn't know Saeed was about to murder King Reinhart. He was *your* acolyte. He acted on the lies and hatred from *your* mouth."

"I did my best to protect my people. You may not understand, but you soon will. You can't protect them from war. Nor can you protect them from death."

"I can at least burn their bones."

Leila pulled a silver bangle from the bookshelf and slid it around her wrist. "I acted under orders, and where do you think those orders came from? You may be High Priestess now, but you still bow to the crown."

"And Jahan's bones? What crime did he commit to be refused a lurrite?"

"Harboring a secret Rhaesbond and breaking a vow of celibacy."

"There is no reason to deny a man his afterlife. All bones need to be burned. As a Lunei, I'd expect you to understand that."

Leila's silver eyes met Mina's at last, and their depths seemed to stretch for eternity, as though they carried the entire weight of their shared tribe. A tribe Mina had never belonged to, and likely never would.

Only Leila knew their secrets. And she too was walking away.

Mina couldn't let her leave—not yet. There were too many questions. She grabbed Leila's wrist and her fingers brushed against the bangle.

A jolt of sky fire burned through her spine, and a dark whisper echoed in her mind—*You will lead them to their deaths.*

Mina staggered back. Not a silver bangle, but one made from

bone. "What is that?"

Leila rubbed her wrist. "Not all Shadows deserve an afterlife. War is coming to this land, Mina Hawker. There will be more death, more Shadows, and the two of us won't be enough. I'm returning to the Duslands to find our people. To find the Lunei."

The Lunei? Impossible. "The Lunei are gone."

"They're not gone. They're waiting for the end."

"What about the Queen's lurrite?"

"Perhaps you should look to the fire for guidance." She shoved past Mina and headed for the door. "It's your problem now."

16

LEECH

Blood pooled in the sands and began to congeal. The bodies needed to be burned, and soon. I cracked my knuckles and prayed.

"I don't understand why you're bothering," Talin said. "They killed men. They don't deserve to join Rahn in the afterlife."

I finished my prayer and shooed him out of the way. "Do you want to be chased halfway across the desert by wraiths?"

Talin fetched a water canteen from his saddlebags and held it ready for me. "I won't mourn them, that's all."

I bit back a smile and returned my attention to the bodies. Talin was right. These were raiders, slavers, and worse. One had died at Talin's blade. Two at my own. They deserved their fate, but now their souls were my responsibility. It was my duty to return them to Rahn. And vengeful men in life often made vengeful spirits in death.

Fire tingled within my fingers. I whispered my mother's words, the mantra she'd taught me to guide my flame. "I am the master of my own self. This fire is mine to control."

A Shadow rippled across the bodies. I didn't flinch. This was normal for me now. I'd seen so many Shadows since I was a child, spoken to so many of their spirits. Talin couldn't see them. Thank the gods he couldn't. This was my burden alone, and I didn't need some foolish hot-headed Sanstrider disturbing the dead. Shadows tended to panic. Who wouldn't, when faced with their own mortality?

Sand stirred around my feet. These would form wraiths if given the chance, but by Lune's luck a Lunei had killed them. An Ash Maker would have left them to rot. It's because of them sand wraiths stalked the desert at all.

"Tira?" Talin's hand flinched by his sword hilt. The fact he hadn't drawn it yet was touching. He'd finally learned to let me take charge.

The sands whipped into a flurry. I'd discovered long ago that a soothing voice and a stable flame calmed even the most hateful of spirits. I couldn't afford to judge these souls for their sins. That wasn't my role. I was merely a guide, Lune's beacon in the darkness to lead them back to Rahn's light.

I cast my flame with my left hand and drew my blade with my other, readying a dance.

If words didn't calm them, a dance would.

"Lune guide you."

Mina woke to her mother watching over her. Tira floated within the lantern still burning on her bedside table and welcomed her back to the land of the living with a warm smile. Sometimes it was hard to separate dreams from reality, but that one had been her mother's memory. Gods, her father had looked so young. How old would they have been then? Mina's age now? The blood bond had pulled her through her mother's old lurrites and the steps she'd taken when dealing with the Shadows. And today, the day of the Queen's lurrite, she needed all the help she could get. As the new high priestess, the honor fell to her to burn the bones.

"Thank you, mother," Mina whispered.

Tira blew a kiss and vanished into the flame.

Mina sat up and groaned. Her head ached, and a familiar nausea cramped her stomach. The same discomfort as when she used too much blood fire. She glanced down at her red stained nightgown and cursed.

"That's going to be a problem." Iman came out of the cistern wearing a robe and a towel wrapped around her damp hair. She pointed to Mina's legs.

Mina peeled herself off the lounger and inspected it. She'd returned to the Keep to spend one last night with her aunt before moving back into the temple, but she wouldn't miss sleeping on this gods-damn thing. No blood had reached the fabric, thank the gods. "It's always a problem."

"You don't understand me. You'll need all your blood if you're to handle a lurrite."

Mina scowled. "What do you want me to do, put it back in? Why does Gai make us bleed if it weakens us? Men don't have some gods-damn weakness."

"Blood fire is stronger in women. The gods have to compensate somewhere. Why do you think the temples of Rahn are mostly filled with men?"

"Because men are foolish and get caught easier?"

Iman snorted. "Girls are taught from a young age to sit down, shut up, and resist their urges. They naturally suppress their emotions, and thus their blood fire, whereas boys run rampant and allow their emotions to manifest freely. Your bleed acts as a natural suppressor, and blood fire stops altogether during pregnancy. It's one reason why many women remain unaware of the power they possess, and why Fire Walker priestesses are meant to take a vow of celibacy."

"Blood fire doesn't work if a woman carries a child?"

"It would be too dangerous to the babe, so the body blocks the ability completely."

"But that means my mother…"

"She couldn't use her blood fire when she carried you. Although the ability comes back after the body recovers from birth, your mother lacked her gift when she was killed. She couldn't summon fire to protect herself."

Mina glanced to the lantern on her bedside table. Tira had returned, somehow aware of the conversation. With a sad smile, she nodded, confirming Iman's tale.

Guilt gnawed at Mina's stomach, as though it was her fault her mother couldn't fight back.

"Are you sure this is the path you want, girl? You're a little young for taking vows of celibacy."

Her cheeks burned. "That vow didn't stop Jonan from being born."

"You've lived among Housemen; you know vows mean little to them. They'll be watching you like a hawk and expect you to slip up."

Mina made a face. "No chance."

"Easy for you to say now. But in another year, when you're in the company of the right man…" Iman cocked one eyebrow in a way that made Mina blush again.

Vows meant nothing to dishonorable men, but Mina had more honor than that. And she doubted she'd ever find a reason to break *that* particular vow. A lifetime of celibacy sounded better than being forced into marriage.

"So how am I supposed to do this gods-damn lurrite?"

Iman sighed as though unimpressed with her change of topic. "It's not impossible to use blood fire when wounded, but the wound makes it more difficult to summon and maintain. You almost died the last time. You're not ready for this."

"Those were ten sets of bones. This is one. I can handle it."

"And how do you plan to do that, oh mighty priestess?"

Mina headed for the cistern and pulled a face over her shoulder. "I know the right man to help."

Jonan waited on a marble bench in the palace gardens. He sat awkwardly, as though being surrounded by so many flowers was beneath him, though he rose and swooped a deep bow at her approach.

"High Priestess."

"Don't you start."

He lifted his head and smirked. "I hear you are to thank for my freedom. Leila would have left me to rot."

Releasing Jonan had been Mina's first act as priestess. "Talin would have gotten you out."

"Talin has more important things to worry about. Like his

troublesome daughter. Last I heard, he wasn't preparing you for priesthood. You're not the pious type."

"I've spent enough time in the temple to learn that playing priest is more about looking angry than being pious, and I have plenty of experience at that."

He chuckled and sat on the bench. He didn't look any worse for his imprisonment.

She slouched beside him. So much had happened the past few days. This was her first chance to speak with Jonan and tell him the truth he deserved to know. "Your father's Shadow was among the bones we burned. Jahan."

His smile faded. "You saw him?"

"It was his Shadow who led us to the bones. And that wasn't the first time I saw him. He led me to the Rahn's Breath that Prince Ravel was growing."

Jonan leaned back and rubbed a hand over his bald head. "Jahan was a Green Hand. Before he was discovered and thrown in the Temple of Rahn. My mother, Ashira... she loved him because he was kind. He grew an herb garden underground using a single shaft of Rahnlight. We all loved that garden. Leila destroyed it."

She patted his shoulder. "I burned his bones. I saw his Shadow fade. He was happy to see you. He wished he could have named you his son."

"I'm grateful, High Priestess." He fumbled in his sahn and pulled out a small red felt hat—the same hat which had given Fez his name. "This was Jahan's. The High Priestess of Gai gave it to me after his death. One of the few possessions he left behind."

An echo of sadness and regret fluttered through the bond. Jonan carried that hat everywhere.

"If I ever cross paths with Leila again, I'll become the Rhaesbond curse they expect of me." His fists clenched in his lap.

"And give the Housemen reason to believe you're behind the rogue Fire Walkers and their alleged attacks?"

"They don't believe I'm involved. I bowed like a good dog and stood before Gareth and told them everything I know. Which is nothing. His Hartnord eyes confirmed I spoke the truth. Someone is using the Rhaesbond name to stoke fear. Can you think of any man who can't keep quiet about House Rhaesbond and how dangerous Fire Walkers are?"

"Prince Ravel," she seethed.

"I had the same thought. But his malice has always been directed toward the Fire Walkers. Not the Hartnords. Even if he is somehow faking the attacks by these rogue Fire Walkers and orchestrating riots in response, why would he want to drag the kingdom into a war?"

"I don't know," Mina admitted. Prince Ravel's greatest wish had seemed to be coming true, with riots against the Fire Walkers and lynchings in the street. Now, the entire kingdom was focused on the impending war with the Hartnords and relying on the Fire Walkers to help them win it. If nothing else, the threat of war had squelched the angry mobs like dumping a bucket of water on a matchstick. "We have no proof either way. And nowhere to start."

"We'll discover who it is and destroy them, Master Malik. I'm at your service."

"Wouldn't you rather be by Talin's side? As his sorran?"

"When a master releases his sorran, the bond is negated and broken forever. A sorran bond cannot be made twice."

A twinge of pain passed through the bond, through his words. "I… I didn't know that's how the bond worked. This is why I need you. You grew up in the temple. You know all the things I'm supposed to. How can I be High Priestess when I don't even know how blood bonds work?"

"I can do better than that. I trained to be a Fire Walker priest before my mother told me the truth of our bloodline."

"You should be the High Priest."

Jonan burst into laughter. "Can you imagine the outrage? It is a role meant for women. Besides, being High Priestess is more than rites and blood fire. You're expected to converse with the populace and win their hearts. Such a challenge is impossible for me. You're likely to stand a better chance... though maybe not." He grinned savagely.

She thumped his arm. "You need to help me with this gods-damn lurrite. It's the Queen—I can't afford to get this wrong." Gods, everyone will be there. "And I'm bleeding."

Jonan looked puzzled. "Are you hurt?" His eyes widened in comprehension. "Oh. This is, I, uh... Have you asked Iman?" he spluttered.

"She said it'll affect my blood fire. Someone needs to burn the Queen." She cringed as she said the words aloud. She didn't mean for it to sound so crass. "I *think* I can do the ceremony if someone can handle the fire part."

"I can't take your place. I doubt they'd allow a Rhaesbond anywhere near her."

"Then what do I do? The Queen's lurrite is this afternoon. It can't wait."

"Besides Leila, only approved acolytes can perform a royal lurrite. There is only one left in Solus... Samira. Release her from her cell, and if she's still in one piece, she can burn the body."

The way Jonan grimaced set her teeth on edge.

"Take me to her."

The crooked stone steps down to the dungeons held a cool stillness Mina never thought existed in Sandair. The underground tunnels in the Temple of Rahn were stifling as though Rahn wrapped them in his arms. Here, the tunnels were dank and the dampness caught in her lungs, causing her to cough. The dungeons were buried underneath the Keep's military court, tucked away where no one would find them or even dare to look, given the number of armed soldiers in residence.

Dim lamplight lit Mina's path. She fought the urge to summon her flame. Jonan hadn't, and he stared ahead lost in thought.

"You were held down here?" she asked.

"No. These cells are for city folk. Beggars. Pickpockets. Men with gold are kept in more glamorous cells."

"And they didn't hurt you?"

"You would have felt it if they did."

They reached the bottom of the steps and entered a cramped underground chamber. Talin had told her that Samira wasn't involved with the rogue Fire Walkers, so why hadn't anyone released her? Was she or Leila supposed to? Mina didn't know how the law worked, only that the rules for city folk didn't apply to Housemen. Criminals are criminals—if Samira had to suffer these cells, it was only fair Prince Ravel should have to as well.

A guard approached with a leer on his face. His expression changed as soon as his lantern's light revealed their sahns. He ignored Jonan and turned to her. "What can I do you for, my lord?"

In the dim light, he'd mistaken her for a man. She was happy not to correct him. "You have a Fire Walker woman held here. A Solander by the name of Samira. I want her released."

"On who's authority? We dun just hand over burners—"

"On mine, as High Priestess of Rahn."

The guard snorted. "*You*?"

Jonan tugged at his sahn, flashing its purple in the lamplight. "The Temple of Rahn is now under the control of House Arlbond. You speak to Lady Tamina Arlbond, the Sand Dancer, daughter of Lord Talin, and winner of the two-hundred and twenty-second Solaran Tournament. You may refer to her as High Priestess."

A thrill pulsed through her blood. She'd always assumed Jonan merely tolerated her as Talin's daughter, but she could feel his pride swell in the bond.

The guard's eyes went wide with comprehension and he fumbled a bow, almost dropping his lantern. "Yes, yes, of course. Right this way, High Priestess."

She clicked her tongue at the man and lifted her chin. She wasn't used to her new title yet—and to her, it wasn't as glamorous as being known as the Sand Dancer. The guard hurried ahead down a dark hall, and she followed.

"What do I call you now?" Jonan murmured. "'Malik' is not befitting of a priestess."

"You never asked what to call me before."

"You chose Malik back in the Duslands."

"Mina is fine."

"Mina it is." He smiled, a rare warm one from him.

Cells stretched on either side of the dungeon. Each had been cut from the stone, like the rooms in the temple, but these were blocked with heavy steel doors. Torches burned outside the occupied cells, but their flames seemed to cast more shadow than light.

A horrid smell replaced the dank moss, worse than the rotting streets of the lower city.

The guard gestured to a door. "This one, High Priestess."

The cell didn't look particularly secure for a Fire Walker. "You're not worried she'd break out?"

"We keep them subdued."

His leering expression sent a jolt in her stomach. She reached for the door, but Jonan grabbed her wrist and bent his head close. "You should wait outside. You don't want to see this."

"Which is exactly why I need to." She shrugged from Jonan's grip and entered the cell.

The stench hit her first—rot and piss and something much worse she couldn't place and held no desire to. Jonan stepped in behind her and snapped his fingers. Light burned away the darkness, and a figure on the floor skittered into the corner. Samira's Solander skin was smeared with dirt. She still wore nothing but strips of cloth across her chest and waist, though those too were smeared brown. Thick chains were wrapped around her wrists, ankles, and neck, and her Fire Walker tattoos shone red. Not with ink but… blood.

They'd carved her tattoos. Mina covered her mouth and swayed on her feet. They'd sliced Samira like fruit.

Samira raised her head slowly. "Are you here to kill me?" she croaked.

"Water," Mina said. "Get her water."

Jonan pulled a canteen from his belt and crouched down.

Samira jerked her head away. As she moved, black lines glistened on her arms, like swollen fat worms. Jonan recoiled, aghast.

"What are they?" Mina gasped.

"Leeches. They're not only used to drain a body of blood, this kind also has a numbing effect which can block blood fire. But... they haven't been used in years."

Bile rose to her mouth. Mina had felt the same leeches on her own neck from the Shadow's memory beneath the temple. She'd felt them suck the life from her.

She stormed out of the room, drawing her sword on the guard and raising it to his throat before he knew what was happening. "You tortured her."

The guard squealed and raised his arms in protest. "We were told to question her!"

She pushed Hawk closer until the sharp edge caressed his skin. "You tortured her!"

"It were orders!"

Jonan stepped behind her. "Mina. Stop."

She glared over her shoulder. "They sliced her up like a—like a—"

She lowered her sword.

This was her fault.

She'd told the guards to arrest Samira, to question her, but she'd never imagined they'd chain her so she could barely move, let her wallow in her own filth, carve the tattoos from her flesh, and drain her blood.

Tears burned in Mina's eyes. "Release her," she ordered the guard. "Take her to the Temple of Gai and place her in Rajesh Enaibond's care. *Now*."

The guard bobbed his head in a series of frantic motions and then shuffled away.

She sagged against the wall. "Tell me this isn't normal. Tell me the King doesn't sanction the torture of Fire Walkers. Tell me Leila didn't turn a blind eye to this."

Jonan placed a hand on her shoulder, the same comforting way Talin would. "I won't lie to you. But I will tell you a truth. You are High Priestess now. You have the power to stop this. And to make sure it never happens again."

17

THE LURRITE

The Bright Solara decided on a small private lurrite for the Queen, thank the gods. Lune had cursed Mina with a thick, heavy flow, as though the gods themselves were displeased with her. The sight of Samira's hunched and bleeding form would haunt her for the next season. She'd not been the one who wielded the knife, but she'd damned Samira regardless. How could Mina have been so naïve to believe a Fire Walker wouldn't be questioned with such brutality?

Mina kept her anger in check. It wouldn't help the grieving King or his family. And it certainly didn't help channel her blood fire.

She rushed a bath and changed into her black bondrite silks. She tried snapping her fingers to summon her flame, but as Iman predicted, no fire passed from her flesh. How in Lune's name was she supposed to perform this gods-damn lurrite?

This was her first test to prove herself as the newly appointed High Priestess of Rahn and it was already going wrong.

Iman had gone to the Temple of Gai to check on Samira at Mina's suggestion. No doubt Mina would be the last person Samira wanted to face, but someone needed to reassure her and explain everything that had happened.

A knock tapped at the door. Jonan's presence bloomed from the other side.

She finished adjusting her sahn and opened the door to him. He too dressed in his best Houseman wear and held a small vial in his hand.

"What's that?" she asked.

"Rahn's Breath."

"Are you out of your mind?"

"For generations, House Rhaesbond ingested small quantities every dawn until they could withstand its heat and use it to boost their powers. It will force your fire out."

"Until I burn to ash and the King needs another High Priestess."

"We'll stop before that happens. I'll be nearby."

Of all their ideas, this was by far the worst, though she had little choice and they'd run out of time. The Queen's lurrite couldn't wait. Bodies seldom smelled pleasant in Rahn's heat, and the longer Mina dallied, the more agitated the Queen's Shadow would become. In her mother's dreams, Shadows who'd suffered trauma were more likely to form wraiths and attack. She couldn't discount the possibility that her presence as a Lunei could disturb the Queen's Shadow even further. Lunei were known to have that effect on the dead.

Gods, she hoped not.

She snatched the vial and shoved it into her sahn next to Prince Rais's necklace—it would be poor form to wear it today.

Jonan led the way through the palace gardens to a private courtyard where the Bright Solara and a few choice Housemen would be present. A march would be held in the streets of Solus later for the people to mourn their queen. Mina had never gotten the chance to mourn her Uncle Dustan when he'd died. He'd never been granted a proper lurrite. The thought boiled in her blood. The Prince had cut down the man who had raised Mina as his daughter, unashamedly murdered him in the street, and now she would lead the ceremony to help him grieve the death of his mother.

I am the master of my own self.

She took a deep breath. This day wasn't about her.

A shallow fountain served as a centerpiece for the courtyard, its waters replaced with Dusland sand. In the middle of the sand lay the Queen on a pyre. A red shroud covered her body and face, and red tulips had been carefully placed around her. It wasn't the extravagant and gaudy decoration she would have expected. But from what she'd observed of the Queen, she'd never flaunted her wealth or power. It was a shame Mina never got a chance to know her.

Ceramic pots of all shapes and sizes filled the garden, some decorated in gemstones—rubies, emeralds, and sapphires—and multi-colored tulips filled the pots. It turned the yard into a dazzling rainbow of color to match the Housemen and their sahns, though the Housemen all wore brooches of one color only—mourning blue.

Rahn burned overhead, but Lune was with them in spirit.

This deep into Rahn's Dawn and with so many mourners crowding the courtyard, the air tasted as thick as rosewater syrup. The noble women fanned their faces, and the men's foreheads flushed with sweat. Alistar's father also stood in attendance, though Alistar wasn't with him.

Mina passed through the crowd and caught fragments of conversation.

Vida sent my wife flowers from this very garden when she was ill with my little one.

If it wasn't for Vida, the Temple of Gai would have struggled for funding last year.

I remember when Vida came to Enais and asked us to plant green grapes for the King as a surprise. She didn't like our white wines much, but the King did, and she suffered its taste for him.

That tale was shared by Raj's mother, who stood in the corner by a purple trellis. The head of House Enaibond was a short, fierce-looking woman. The complete opposite to shy Raj. He stood there too, looking slightly out of place. She wanted to ask him about Samira, but now wasn't the time.

"She was a good woman," Salasar said, coming up next to her.

He was dressed in the same smart clothes as during her bondrite. The High Priestess of Lune—his wife—sat on a nearby bench, dressed in her thick blue robes, the bulge at her stomach straining through the fabric. "She didn't take rule seriously. Don't get me wrong, she had her duties, but she didn't dance to politics like the rest of them. She understood struggle, not like these lot." Salasar drew in a breath. "Walk with me."

Salasar began to stroll through the garden and Mina stepped in line by his side. He wasn't usually this somber. "You liked her," she said.

"You'll be hard pressed to find a man who didn't, and mark my words, those Hartnords will pay." Hardness settled across his face. "She wasn't meant to be queen, you know. It was my House who originally provided a bride for the Bright Solara. One of my cousins. Not that we needed more power and riches, but my House is full of greedy bastards and pushed. Ah, I remember the marriage ceremony well. What a disaster." Salasar shook his head. "The bond didn't take. The marriage bond. Our bloodlines were too close. And so, Khaled was forced to marry another. We scrambled for another suitable bride, but House Xanbond got there first and offered Vida. She was young, then. Younger than you are now. She was a frightened little thing, frightened of leaving her home forever, frightened of the weight and responsibilities of queendom. But she shouldered it well. She blossomed into one of the strongest women I've ever met, and I've dealt with some tough wenches." He turned his sharp eye to her. "There's more strength in women who don't wield swords."

"Why are you telling me this?"

"Because Vida didn't think she could shoulder being a queen, but she was strong and she made a real difference. Thanks to her, the Temple of Gai can afford to provide care for the common man without demanding his gold. She elevated them and became their biggest champion, just as Princess Aniya elevated the Temple of Lune. We need another Vida, another Aniya, to champion the Temple of Rahn."

Mina didn't like the comparison to a dead princess and now a dead queen. "What do you think I'm doing?"

Salasar guided her into a shaded section of the garden. "Playing priestess will only get you so far. There is greater power and it's yours for the taking. Think about it, child."

He bowed and stepped aside, revealing a man dressed in blue silks. She bit back a curse. Salasar had led her straight to Prince Rais.

She bowed. "My Prince."

"Lady Arlbond." The Prince smiled, but there was no warmth there. "I hear you are High Priestess now. You don't look like a priestess."

Her cheeks flushed. She knew there were certain rules and rites involved in being a priestess, but she didn't know everything she was supposed to do. The priestesses of Lune and Gai wore appropriate robes, but Mina had no intention of dropping her leather armor, sahn, or sword. They'd take her as she was or get no high priestess at all. "I'm still new to this, my Prince. But I'm dedicated to serving Rahn."

"Are you." The statement came out flat. "I thought you were dedicated to serving me. You swore a promise to me before the tournament. Do you remember?"

"I remember, my Prince."

"But you are now serving as a priestess of Rahn. Do your words and loyalties mean so little?"

How could Prince Rais act like such a fool? He needed to be bigger than his brother. He needed to be seen as king. "The Fire Walkers need me, my Prince, especially now."

Prince Rais grabbed her upper arm and pinched tight. "I need you," he whispered. "Why are you choosing the Fire Walkers over me?"

If she'd chosen to marry him… it would have been for the Fire Walkers.

His grip tightened. "Didn't I say I'd support you? Didn't I give you my favor? You're not even wearing it."

"This is a lurrite, my Prince. It would be poor form—"

A door on the opposite end of the courtyard opened and the Prince stepped back, releasing her arm. Princess Aniya entered the yard, also in blue, and Mina's heart skipped a beat—her arm curled around Alistar's. He steered the Princess to a shaded part of the courtyard as she dabbed her eyes with a silk cloth. He looked somber, like the dignitary he pretended to be.

Gasps and mummers drew Mina's attention. The King walked slowly and leaned on a cane. His legs shook and his spare arm was wrapped around Talin, who guided him to a bench under the shade of a canopy. His Solander skin was pale, his ringlet beard flat, his expression lifeless. He stared at the pyre as though he was also a Shadow ready to pass onto the next life.

Prince Ravel stood at the King's other side, not stooping to help his father but radiating throughout the courtyard with his presence. He wore a mismatch of Solaran red with mourning blue and held his chin high. Compared to the deathly pale king and the slouching Prince Rais, Prince Ravel looked vibrant. Commanding. Manly.

Her stomach lurched. He looked like a king.

Jonan found her. "It's time. Do you remember what to do?"

"Say the words. Burn the queen. Vomit after."

"You can skip the final part."

She doubted it. Even with such a small group, the courtyard was packed full of Housemen, strangers she barely knew and strangers she did know, albeit from a distance, who were eager to watch her make a fool of herself. Disbelief shone in their faces as she strode between them, her hands tucked neatly behind her back to hide their tremble. A gentle tug in the bond brought her gaze to Talin's kind smile. She'd been able to ignore the faces watching her in the tournament. This was a different sort of battle. Her first duty as High Priestess.

Gods, what was she even doing? *Say the words. Burn the queen.* A Shadow rippled across the red shroud as she approached the pyre. The Queen's spirit was there. Did she understand what was going on? That she'd died, that these people were here to watch her return to Rahn? Mina hadn't given it much thought, but how terrifying must it be to view the world as a Shadow? To know your fate? If Fire Walkers weren't here to burn their bones, what would become of them?

The Queen hadn't deserved this fate. Talking to Shadows wasn't pleasant, but if Mina spoke to the Queen, maybe her Shadow would remember something important about how she died—what wine she drank, who brought it to her, if anyone was acting strangely...

This was her one chance before the Queen's Shadow was lost forever.

Mina reached her hand over the pyre. "My Queen, I know this must be hard for you, but I can see you," she whispered. "I can hear you. If you talk to me, I'll find who did this to you. I'll get justice."

The Shadow grasped her hand.

My baby, where's my baby? My child, where is he?

Wind burst around them and the courtyard fell into sudden darkness.

18

THE QUEEN'S LAMENT

"It's a boy!"

Tears ran down my face with blessed relief. A Green Hand took the babe as another wiped my sweat-soaked brow. A boy. A baby boy. Khaled's joy burst through the bond. "A son. Vida, we have a son."

"Are there no others?" Solaran children were supposed to come in threes. When the Green Hands had told us I carried just one child, I'd hoped they were mistaken. I'd hoped for more. But I felt empty. I'd failed in my duties as queen and wife.

A Green Hand examined me. "No others, my Queen."

Khaled took my hand and kissed it. "It doesn't matter."

"I failed you."

"This is a blessing, don't you see? Our son will grow to take the crown without bloodshed, without needing to kill his brothers to lay claim. We'll have peace for once." He kissed my hand again. "Rahn has blessed us."

The Green Hand brought the babe to my arms. He squirmed and cried but settled as I cradled him, and he looked at me for the first time. Khaled's amber, golden and pure. He was beautiful. "He has your eyes."

"He'll have your heart."

"What will you call him?"

We'd discussed names: Aniya for a girl, named for his sister, and perhaps Rais, a warrior's name, for a boy. But this little one didn't look like a Rais to me.

"I want him to grow wise. Too many kings rule by the sword, but I

*want more for him. More for Sandair. We'll name him for the wisest
king I know, the founder of our Academy."*
My son. A future king.
King Ravel.

Mina's eyes snapped open. The Queen's Shadow grasped her
sword hand and refused to let go.
My baby, where's my baby?
A fierce, swirling wind scattered sand from the fountain and
lashed at the crowd. Housemen cried out and covered their eyes.
Mina stood in the heart of a whirlwind. The sand began pulling
together in clumps, but there wasn't enough to form a body, to
become a complete wraith.
"My Queen—Vida—listen to me! You need to stop. You're
scaring them!"
She tried to pull herself free from the Shadow, but its cold grip
only tightened, crushing down to the bone. How could a spirit
possess such strength?
Throughout the courtyard, the flower pots rocked over and
crashed. Broken shards were swept up into the sandstorm and
covered the half-formed wraith in a patchwork armor of ceramic
and gemstones.
Two thick rubies formed the wraith's eyes.
Lune help me.
Salasar's voice called out, not to her, but ordering the
Housemen to flee. Talin was there, desperately trying to scramble
through the funnel of wind and sand—Jonan, too—but neither
could press through.
It was just her and the Queen.
With her sword hand trapped, Mina couldn't draw Hawk or
dance. Her mother had soothed the Shadow's spirits by absolving
them. It was the only plan she had. "Vida, you're hurt and angry,
I understand. Your baby was taken. It wasn't your fault."
The wraith howled and its voice whispered in the wind.
Where's my baby?

"He's waiting for you, Vida. He's waiting with Rahn. I can send you to him. Let me—"

A flying shard slapped across her face and sliced down her forehead.

Who took my baby?

"I'll find the man who did this to you, Vida, I swear it! But you need to let me go!"

The sandstorm wavered for a heartbeat, allowing a figure to push through. Too small to be either Talin or Jonan.

"Mama," a soft voice called. The Princess. Princess Aniya strode right up to the pyre. "Mama, you're scaring Dada. You're hurting him."

The wraith's ruby eyes turned to her daughter. How could Mina explain that the Queen wasn't in her right mind, that her Shadow was lost and confused and didn't mean to lash out?

"Mama. Listen to the Priestess. She's trying to help you." Princess Aniya didn't look afraid, though sand clung to her tear-stained cheeks.

"Your daughter speaks true, Vida. Let me help. Let me send you to your baby."

A sigh passed through the wind. *Take me to my baby.*

"I will. We will."

The ceramic shackle fell from Mina's hand, allowing her to stagger back. She shook the stiffness away. It was bruised, but no bones were broken, thank the gods. She tried to snap her fingers and summon flame, but her bleed and the cut to her forehead wouldn't yield. Nor was Jonan nearby to help.

The storm blew faster, impatient and agitated.

Only Rahn's Breath would help now, as foolish as that was.

She fumbled for the vial in her pocket. The wind snatched it from her grip and sent it crashing against the pyre. The glass smashed and joined the wraith's body. Gods damn it!

"What's wrong?" the Princess asked.

"I can't summon my blood fire." Mina cringed. Some priestess she made. "I need to get help."

A flicker of flame burst from the Princess's hand. "Tell me what to do."

Mina gawked. The Princess was a Fire Walker? Could that mean her twin, Prince Rais, also possessed blood fire? "Are you sure? You risk draining your blood." It would be her head if she got the gods-damn princess killed.

The Princess's amber eyes shone with a fierce determination. "Tell me what to do."

"Point your hand at the bod—at the Queen. She'll draw it from you. Let it flow."

The Princess did as instructed. Flame poured from her palm with an orange glow as bright as Jonan's. Mina took the Princess's wrist and guided her fire. She burned effortlessly, and with better control than Mina could claim. Had someone trained her? Did Prince Ravel know?

"Tell me when you start to feel weak. When it gets too much."

"Like when it hurts?"

"Yes." The last thing she wanted was the Princess collapsing from blood loss.

"Too late, I think."

Her eyes rolled back into her head and her fire cut short. The Princess fell. Mina cursed and grabbed her waist before she hit the floor.

Sand, gems, and ceramic shards collapsed into the charred fountain, revealing a fading Shadow. The wind stopped and dust fell over them like a sprinkling of dry rain. The Princess sank in Mina's arms, her body heavy. Her eyelids fluttered.

The King's Left Arm was first at their side. Gareth kneeled among the broken ceramic and took the Princess. "She used too much blood," he murmured.

Mina stilled. "You saw what happened?"

Gareth flashed a grim smile. "I trust you know how to keep a secret."

"Princess!" Salasar cried and ran toward them. "Rahn's blood, what happened?"

"The shock, it was too much for her," Gareth said. "She needs rest, that's all."

The two men carried the Princess out of the yard, flanked now by Alistar and Prince Rais, and followed by Salasar's wife, a Green Hand, and several of the royal guards.

Mina stood and surveyed the damage.

The Housemen had fled, leaving only the King, Prince Ravel, Talin, and Jonan. The courtyard lay ruined. Broken ceramic, gemstones, sand, and flowers were scattered everywhere. And at the center were the still-smoldering ashes of the Queen.

Her first lurrite as high priestess, and it had all gone wrong. It was her job to ease the Queen's passing and comfort those still mourning. Instead, she'd made a wraith of the Queen's Shadow, terrorized a grieving family, and left the Princess near death.

Jonan approached her. "It wasn't your fault."

"I failed."

"You burned the body."

"I *failed*."

She pushed past him and stomped into the hallway.

Footsteps followed. She ignored them and kept walking.

"High Priestess." The words came from Prince Ravel with such spite that they stopped her dead. She turned around and a hand lunged for her neck.

Prince Ravel shoved her against the wall.

She choked and fumbled at his hand, trying to pry it away. He lifted her to tiptoes, cutting off her air and voice.

"What chance does Sandair have when her High Priestess can't manage a simple lurrite? You let my mother suffer. My *mother*. I heard her cries!"

He'd heard his mother's Shadow? But that wasn't possible— only Lunei could speak to the dead. She tried to fight him off, but her head swam and her arms felt weak from breathlessness.

"Do you honestly believe you have the strength for war, Lady Arlbond?" His face was inches away and his breath stank of wine. "The strength to lead your Fire Walkers into battle and watch them die? You're a tiny girl meddling in the affairs of great men. You hold our kingdom back."

His grip lessened and she sucked in a breath. "I support my King," she said through clenched teeth.

"You support a dying past. You cannot deny me my future."

"I'll deny it with every breath."

The Prince's hand squeezed again, choking off her breath. "And for what, *Tamina*? My father's body is failing. My brother is no contender for the throne. I am the only man who can lead us into war—a war made necessary by your precious Fire Walkers. I warned them all again and again. And now, here we are. But it's not too late for Sandair. I will save her. Me!" His nails dug into her neck as he leaned closer. "One day soon, you'll kneel and pledge your blood in my name."

She glared into those amber eyes, filled with flecks of fire and blood and death. "I will *never* kneel before you. I'll nev—"

Prince Ravel pressed his lips to hers.

His teeth sank into her lower lip and pulled at the skin. Her inner embers flared. Flame burst from her hands and she shoved him away with all her strength.

He stumbled back and patted out his singed sleeve. "You dare burn me?"

Her flames vanished as quickly as they appeared. She rubbed a smear of blood from her lip and spat the taste of him out. "Touch me again and I'll burn every inch of you," she seethed.

She preferred him when she was Malik—when his games involved duels and insults, not whatever this had turned into. She couldn't stand the way his amber eyes watched her now, the way they seemed to roam over her body as though trying to think of new ways to humiliate her. He wore a smirk that only Housemen possessed—a smirk that said she didn't matter, that her existence didn't matter, that her dignity didn't matter, and she was little better than a rat in the street.

"Look at how casually you declare treason."

"Treason? I'm sure your father and the Council would want to know if their Prince was attacking the High Priestess. You think your mother would be pleased?"

"Don't speak of my mother. And it's your word against mine. Who would believe a woman?"

"I would." Alistar stood behind the Prince, arms crossed over his chest.

The Prince sneered. "And what would your father say about that? He's worked hard to place you in better company than Lady Arlbond and her pitiful House. You wouldn't side with some Fire Walker over your own family now, would you?" He placed a friendly hand on Alistar's shoulder and turned to her, smiling. "I'll have to warn my brother she tastes like ash. But I'll wager you already knew that."

19

THE ASH MAKER

New Fire Walkers arrived at the Temple of Rahn the next day.

Most had been rounded up in the city—stragglers found and sent by the Sword of Solus and his guards. Others arrived from the temples outside of Solus. All came bearing questions and demands. Mina tried to explain everything that had happened—the attack on King Reinhart, Prince Wulfhart's threats, the assassination of Queen Vida, the Council's decision to go to war with her father in charge, her own decision to step up and replace Leila as high priestess. And Samira's unjust imprisonment. They listened and understood the warning her words carried. The Fire Walkers were being punished and would be used as weapons. None of this came as a shock, but their reactions varied—confusion, betrayal, hurt, anger.

A young Solander man broke free from the crowd and swaggered toward her. "*This* is the High Priestess?" He spoke with an odd accent she'd not heard before.

She met his gaze and swallowed a scream. His eyes were startlingly amber. Prince Ravel's eyes. For a heartbeat she thought it *was* the Prince, here to infiltrate the temple and ruin her life. But no. Although he looked the same age and carried himself with the same arrogant poise, his Solander skin was paler, his dark hair shaggier, and his beard looked more a rough scruff. His amber eyes held mischief, not malice, and his baggy shalwar came from the lower city.

"What are you?" she blurted out.

He didn't get a chance to answer. A group of angry Fire Walkers led by Dahn marched past them at that moment.

"This is your fault!" Dahn yelled.

Everyone turned their heads. He wasn't shouting at Mina, to her surprise, but at Samira, who leaned against the wall beside the sanctum entrance. She wore a long beige robe, commoner style, and a thin layer of fuzz coated her head. She looked different in clothes. They hid her Fire Walker tattoos and the scars the guards had inflicted.

Dahn thrust a finger in Samira's face. "You and Saeed, you're the reason we're in here! The reason we're going to war."

Mina pushed past him and drew her sword. "That's enough. Samira had nothing to do with Saeed's crime—"

"You're defending her? They murdered the Hartnord King—"

"I was there, Dahn. I saw what happened. Samira's innocent—"

"And Saeed—"

"Is dead."

Samira drew a sharp breath, the pain clear on her face. "What Saeed did... it came from fear. We all know it well. I'll—I'll never forgive what he's done." She lowered her head.

Mina sheathed her sword. "Fighting each other isn't going to bring back the Hartnord king and stop this war. If we hope to survive, we have to trust each other. That starts with you, Dahn."

Dahn grumbled and returned to the sanctum's steps.

"Is this how the High Priestess commands her people?" said the man with the amber eyes. He gave her an assessing stare. "By threatening us with a sword?"

"It's how I'll protect them from fools." She placed a hand back on her sword hilt.

"Know how to use that, do you?"

"Care for a demonstration?"

The sanctum doors opened. Jonan entered. Mina wanted to

demand answers from the man with the amber eyes, but Jonan marched straight for her.

He frowned at the dispersing crowd. "Everything okay? You're needed. Council meeting."

"So soon?"

"We're at war. Expect many."

"How am I supposed to protect the temple if I have to go to Council meetings?"

"Council meetings are where you'll protect the temple."

Samira approached and bowed to her with seemingly genuine respect, though the effort made her legs wobble. "You are High Priestess now. I cannot claim to understand the Council's decision, but I accept it. Will you allow me to speak?"

"Of course, Samira."

"You're a gods-damn fool."

Well, some things didn't change.

"That is your High Priestess you speak of," Jonan said with a growl. "She saved you from the dungeons."

Samira gave Jonan a look of disgust. "And you, too, I see, though why they'd let a Rhaesbond out when it was your name that caused this—"

"My ancestors have not returned from the dead. And it was *you* who left Mina to bleed. Give me one reason why I shouldn't repay that courtesy?"

"I followed Leila's command. Though *you* should know better than to use cursed blood magic."

Mina stepped between them. "Will you both stop? If we're going to survive this war, we'll need to work together. All of us."

"If you're too lenient, you *will* incur the wrath of your fellow Housemen," Samira said. "There are rules and regulations that even you will need to follow, High Priestess. Regardless of the reasons why Fire Walkers are imprisoned—to protect society, to protect themselves—it doesn't matter. Housemen see Fire Walkers as lesser. As prisoners. They expect them to be treated as such. They certainly won't pay to feed the mouths of Fire Walker families, especially not when war will squeeze them dry. Where do you expect to find the gold?"

"My House will pay for any excess."

"That simple, is it?"

"That simple. Unless you're planning on running to the Keep to betray me?"

Samira shuddered. "I don't want to step foot outside here ever again. You—you know I had no idea what Saeed planned. We were both worried, and scared, but—"

"You left me for dead."

"It was Saeed's idea, you have to believe me! He—he and Leila. They met often behind my back and didn't tell me everything. I'll—I'll tell you anything else you want to know. Just let me stay in the temple, I'm begging. This is my home. You can't run it alone. You need me."

Mina rolled her eyes. She wasn't planning on throwing Samira out, not after the torture she'd endured. "I have a Council meeting. You two are in charge, if you can survive each other." She strode for the temple doors.

Samira hobbled after her. "You're going dressed like that?"

"Is there something wrong with my clothes?"

"You're High Priestess. You're supposed to wear robes and look the part. Don't tell me you're taking a sword? Gods forbid."

"Leila owned a sword—"

"Only so she could carry out the law as necessary. Is that the message you want to send?"

No, she didn't want Fire Walkers to see her as their potential executor. She wanted them to see her as their defender. "I'm a Houseman. And the Sand Dancer. I'm not going to scrimp and bow because the Council expect me to be some weak woman in robes."

"Oh gods, you're going to be the death of us all." Samira sagged against the stone steps. "Don't you understand yet? You *have* to follow procedure. If the Housemen catch any scent that the Fire Walkers are discontent, that they plan to rebel, you will be put down *swiftly*. That is what happened to Leila's predecessor." Her gaze shifted to Jonan. "Your mother was investigated because she broke her vow of celibacy and allowed her Fire Walkers the same freedom. It was unfortunate they discovered her Rhaesbond blood during their investigation. Then they moved in quickly for the kill."

Salasar was right. As High Priestess, she had power, but not the sort of power wielded by a queen. Casting aside too many rules and traditions too quickly would only rile the Housemen up against the temple and the people she'd sworn to protect. And wearing the sahn of House Arlbond would only exacerbate their fears. It was House Arlbond who'd pushed for Fire Walker freedom, who'd been harboring them freely in Arlent for twenty years.

Prince Ravel knew this.

One wrong step and he could blame her—and her House—for the crimes of any and every Fire Walker in Sandair, real or imagined. Always, he remained the true enemy. Not Hartnords, or mobs, or rogue Fire Walkers. Did no one else see that?

Rahn curse all princes to a pitiless death and their bones to the farthest depths of the desert.

"Sounds harsh," said a rough voice. The young man with the eerie amber eyes. He leaned on the wall beside the entrance brazier. "You people walk around half naked and can't even enjoy it? It's the only reason I joined. I heard your women like it hot."

Jonan drew his sword and thrust the flat edge against the man's chest. "Your kind are not welcome here."

The man chuckled. "Oh, you take that celibacy vow seriously?"

"Who is he? Do you know him?" Mina asked.

"His eyes give him away."

At that, the amber-eyed man stopped laughing and real concern flickered over his face.

"He's an Ash Maker," Jonan said.

An Ash Maker? That couldn't be possible. They were a Dusland tribe, brutal men who killed for sport. Even Housemen knew to fear them. "But he's Solander?"

"Not all Ash Makers are Duslander. Why are you here?"

"Are we talking spiritually or—"

Jonan pressed his blade into the man's chest and snarled.

"I'm one of you, aren't I?" the Ash Maker spluttered. "The guards were throwing anyone with fire magic in here—"

"Where are you from?"

"What business is it of yours?"

With a subtle twist of the wrist, Jonan's sword turned so the sharp edge pressed against the man's shirt and dug into the cloth.

"I was just passing through! You think I wanted to be trapped in here with the rest of you lot? Not like I have a choice, do I?"

"You're an Ash Maker? You?" she said.

He turned his grin to her. "I'm whatever you want me to be, Priestess."

She gave her best look of disgust. If he were an Ash Maker, he should have recognized her own silver eyes marking her as a Lunei—the tribe *his* people hunted down and murdered years ago. It was the Ash Makers who had forced the few remaining Lunei to scatter to the wind and hide. This one's teeth were crooked, as was his nose and some of his fingers—a scrapper. The mark of a street rat. Which meant he was likely trouble. "Do you have a name, Ash Maker?"

"That's a personal question."

"Answer it."

"So you can mark my grave?"

Grave? This stranger truly was an Ash Maker. Dustan's tales spoke of their odd perversion for leaving their dead to rot rather than burning them. It was an affront to Lune, he'd said, though she hadn't realized just how perverse it was until she'd embraced her Lunei blood and began to deal with the Shadows herself.

"We burn our dead in civilized society. As you're about to find out."

"Ouch. She bites. Careful, Priestess, I bite back." He winked.

Jonan sighed. "He's a fool. Do you want me to gut him? No one will miss him."

"Whoa now. My ma would."

Mina examined her nails. "You're right, he's a fool. I wasn't going to start my reign as High Priestess by scrubbing blood from the walls, but Rahn may appreciate the sacrifice."

"I wouldn't want to dirty your walls, Priestess. Drag me to your palace up the hill and gut me there. They seem like the sort to appreciate it."

Definitely a fool. But Ash Maker or not, he was a Fire Walker and that made him her responsibility. "Let him go. I'm sure Samira will keep an eye on him. And if he should try anything inappropriate, I'll personally paint these walls red. Understood?"

Jonan lowered his blade. The Ash Maker straightened his tunic. "Garr."

"Excuse me?"

"My name, Priestess." He held out his hand. "I'm Garr."

She looked at his hand and snorted. "You're no prince." She turned heel and headed for the temple doors, resisting the urge to glance back.

"You're not changing?" Samira called.

"I'm already late for this gods-damn meeting. But we'll do it your way. Later." She shoved the temple doors open.

Jonan followed her outside into the harsh Rahnlight. "Be careful with that one. Ash Makers are trouble."

"You don't need to tell me."

"Don't I?"

"They destroyed the Lunei. I'm aware of who they are and what they are capable of. How do *you* know so much about them?"

"They're my ancestors. House Rhaesbond. And the Bright Solara."

"Wait, House Rhaesbond and the Bright Solara are descended from the Ash Makers?"

"Long, long ago. All Sandarians are descended from one of the old tribes."

"So you're related to the Bright Solara?"

"Me? No. But House Rhaesbond came from the same tribe in

the early days of Sandair, and our women often married into the Bright Solara. Including many ancient queens."

Which meant Prince Ravel likely inherited Rhaesbond blood. No wonder he was so fascinated, and repulsed, by House Rhaesbond's history. His veins carried Ash Maker blood as well. Like Jonan's.

"That explains why you're so lovable. Why don't you have amber eyes?"

Jonan smirked. "My ancestors did. But it's not like there are many of us left to keep the bloodline pure. My great-grandmother was born with amber eyes. She's the last Rhaesbond who ever will be."

"And you're sure that fool isn't a Rhaesbond cousin, however distantly? He could be related to those rogue Fire Walkers."

"No. They're dead. All of them. But the Ash Makers could be involved in these alleged attacks. It might not be a coincidence that this Garr showed up in our temple. If so, things are about to get bloody."

20

THE WAR COUNCIL

By the time Mina arrived in the Council chamber, only one chair remained empty: between the High Priestess of Lune and Gai.

"You're late, High Priestess." Prince Ravel sat at the red corner of the table beside Talin. "Well, it's not because you changed attire."

Mina bowed. "Forgive me, my lords. I—"

"Spare us your excuses, woman," Farzad Fellbond said. His thick hand gripped a goblet. "Sit and take your place."

She fought the urge to grab her sword and remind Farzad Fellbond of his defeat in the last tournament. A sharp warning burned through the bond from Talin. She ducked her head and slid into her chair beside the High Priestess of Lune.

Salasar's wife took Mina's hand and squeezed it. "Don't mind him," she whispered. "It's the only way he can make himself feel important. I'm Karina, and that's Yasmin." She nodded to the Gaislander High Priestess, who nodded back. "We priestesses have to stick together."

Mina forced a smile and turned her attention to the meeting. Her first official Council meeting.

Talin resumed a discussion she'd apparently interrupted with her entrance—preparations for what each House would be doing to contribute to the war effort. Mina expected each House to take turns and discuss their positions like civilized adults. But this meeting was more like a rowdy bazaar.

Housemen jeered and argued with one another, shouting until the loudest voices—most often Farzad Fellbond or Salasar, she noted—dominated the rest. Insults were wielded as weapons. The smaller Housemen were brow-beaten into accepting whatever concessions were demanded of them.

She leaned her head close to Karina. "Is this normal?"

Karina rubbed her swollen belly. "Sadly."

"Do we get a say in what's going on?"

"When we're asked, which is rare. The King is good for including us, but your father... he looks tired."

Mina cast a glance to Talin, his head leaning against his left fist. Had he been sleeping these past few days? He was still the King's sorran—Lune knew why—and the King's weakness could have been affecting him. Prince Ravel conducted the meeting with vigor, content to let Talin watch from the sidelines. She nudged him through the bond, and his gaze met hers. He offered the briefest of smiles and sat up, returning to the meeting at hand.

Discussion moved on as Talin agreed with the Guardian of Gai that he should return to Gaisland to mobilize their men there, which annoyed the Prince, to Mina's satisfaction. She couldn't keep up with the military tactics they spoke of, but from what she grasped, they planned to march the bulk of Sandair's forces north, up the Cold Path, and to prepare for Hartnord ships landing on the Ruby Coast.

She was surprised by how quickly each House volunteered their resources. She'd lived under Houseman banners long enough to know they taxed their poor to feed their lavish lifestyles, but she'd never considered they'd offer their own gold so readily to help the war effort. Some were more generous than others. Many loved their Queen and wanted blood.

Others, such as House Fellbond, negotiated their contributions in a way that would profit their Houses later—loaning gold and lending steel to the Bright Solara. House Nasbond offered their horses as an investment. The Gaisland Houses offered a percentage of crops for free.

All were in agreement that they wanted this war over before the rains of Lune's Shadow arrived and made fighting miserable. Their cold efficiency at organizing war was impressive, but then, they'd fought these battles before.

Prince Ravel called them to order. "Our next item of business—the Fire Walkers."

Mina sat up.

"High Priestess of Rahn." Prince Ravel said the words with such scorn that it made her teeth grind. "This Council has three tasks for the temple. One, that you gather and organize your Fire Walkers in preparation for the march north. Two, that you lead the march personally and prepare them for battle. And three, that you publicly renounce the actions of your rogue acolyte and apologize."

"You expect me to apologize for something I didn't do?"

"I expect you to represent the Fire Walkers and apologize on their behalf. We must show the people that Fire Walkers are under our control. The law is still in effect. Any Fire Walker caught refusing submission should be put down. Are you prepared to uphold the law and execute deserters, High Priestess?"

Mina squeezed her hands in her lap. She had no intention of executing anyone, but she'd worry about that later. "If it becomes necessary, my Prince."

"More Fire Walkers are being brought to the temple each day. I believe your men are overseeing this effort in Solus, Lord Salasar?"

Salasar grunted in reply.

"We cannot afford to spare the city guard for rounding up Fire Walkers whilst they prepare for the march north," the Prince continued. "It's a waste of our resources at this critical time. You have three days, Lord Salasar, to flush them out. After that, any Fire Walker caught outside the temple must be assumed to be a rogue in league with House Rhaesbond, or whoever it is that's using their name."

Salasar hesitated, then jerked his head in agreement.

"Can we expect the High Priestess's support on this?" Farzad
Fellbond said with a leering grin. "After all, your House has a soft
spot for them."

She met Farzad's leer with her own scowl. "The law is the law.
If there are rogue Fire Walkers out there—and forgive me, my
Prince, but I've yet to see evidence—as High Priestess I'd sooner
handle it myself." At least if she led her own investigation, she
could determine the truth without violence and torture. Perhaps
Gareth could help.

The Prince raised an eyebrow. "You're offering to hunt down
these monsters personally?"

"If it please you, my Prince. The Temple of Rahn is my
responsibility."

The Prince smirked, and she couldn't help but feel she'd walked
into another one of his traps. "You heard our Priestess, Lord
Salasar. She is willing to bow to your command on this matter.
Make whatever arrangements you deem necessary. Whilst we're
on the subject of contributions, don't waste too much time
hunting, High Priestess. You're still needed to prepare your Fire
Walkers for battle. *All* Fire Walkers."

"Not all Fire Walkers are able to fight, my Prince—"

"But all can contribute to the war effort in some way. I expect
you to work with the temples of each House. Those inside Dusland
temples, for example, should be brought north. They serve no use
in the desert. I believe your House has an ample collection."

Her heart thumped. He wanted the people of Arlent on the
front lines, ready for the slaughter. He wasn't even disguising it.

Talin raised his hand. "There may be some suitable men
trained to fight, my Prince—"

"All are expected to contribute, Lord Talin. We cannot be seen
to show favoritism, can we?" The Prince's gaze moved between
Talin and Salasar. They'd both revealed their blood fire to the
King at the Solend. "Fire Walkers who refuse the needs of their
kingdom and the orders of their King are traitors. What use do
they offer us?"

Mina snorted. "Do you expect children and blind old men to fight your wars?"

Prince Ravel met her hard stare. "If they're Fire Walkers, yes. Children and blind old men can still tend the campfires and burn the dead. Even women have their uses."

She couldn't believe what he was saying. "You want women and children to march to the front lines? And to kill those who refuse?"

Prince Ravel leaned back in his chair. "Don't look so shocked, High Priestess. It was your Fire Walkers who attacked the Hartnord king—who started this war. And you are, by your own admission, responsible for them—"

"You can't send children to war!"

"Any young Sandarian would be proud to serve their kingdom. I expected you to handle this matter with more grace. Are we agreed, Lord Talin?"

There was no way Talin could allow this, especially not when Arlent—their people—would be dragged from their homes and marched to the border to die. Women and children, too. And she'd have no choice but to enforce it. She'd be expected to kill those who refused.

Gods. No. She couldn't.

Talin didn't even look at her as he spoke. "It will be done, my Prince."

No.

How could he say that? What had happened to her father?

"Make your arrangements soon, Lord Talin. We have only ten weeks until Lune's Shadow. We must be ready to march within five. That includes you too, High Priestess."

Five weeks. They'd be marching to their deaths in only five weeks.

It wasn't enough time!

Mina sat in a daze as the rest of the Council meeting progressed. She didn't even hear it come to an end or notice when the Housemen began to clear out.

A hand touched her shoulder. Talin. "Come. We'll talk."

"Why did you—"

"Not here."

He dragged her up and she dutifully followed him out of the Council chamber and through the halls. It was frantic here as men carried crates full of weapons, food, and gods-knew what else. Talin led her out into the main Keep, but instead of turning to the palace and the gardens, he headed for the Keep's gates and the city.

"Don't you need to return to the King?" she asked.

"He's sleeping." Talin tapped his chest. "He sleeps much these days. Gareth is watching over him."

"Is this why he hasn't released you as his sorran?"

"He's recovering, though slowly. You've read the Code of Honor. So long as I remain his Right Arm, I can lead the Council."

"Prince Ravel seems to be leading it."

"Oh yes, he's trying. But I'm keeping him in check."

"You're doing a *great* job."

Talin bristled, but said nothing. They stepped past the Keep wall, and he nodded a greeting to the guards. She'd never entered the city with him before, only Iman and Jonan. Talin rarely had the time, and what little time they had together was spent training.

As they strode down the hill, she expected Talin to head toward the Temple of Rahn, but he veered behind it, alongside the canal leading to the docks.

The blood bond warmed as they came across Iman standing in the shade and chewing on a kebob. "You took your time."

Above her, Jonan stuck his head out of a crevice in the stone—the same one she'd escaped from to confront Prince Ravel at the tournament. He jumped down and bent his knees on the landing.

"What's going on?" Mina asked.

"A House meeting," Iman said. "We're missing Fez, but we'll have to make do."

"Actually…" Jonan jerked his thumb at the crevice. Fez lingered by the stone hole and screeched. Then he scuttled back inside, deciding the height wasn't worth it. "He followed me."

Mina glanced down the culvert. It was quiet, but still out in the public. "You want to have a meeting *here*?"

"It's safe enough," Iman said. "Fewer ears than the Keep. Well?" Talin leaned against the wall. "We just came from a Council meeting. It should be of no surprise what's happening. Fire Walkers will be called to war. All of them. And our Prince will target Arlent."

"And you agreed to it!" Mina snapped.

"In a Council meeting in front of the other Houses? Of course I did. Or do you want to give them an excuse to sack our House now?"

Any anger in her veins instantly cooled. "What are you planning?"

"Iman, you'll return to Arlent under the guise of mobilizing our people. But you will do no such thing. There are vast caverns underneath Arlent, large enough to hide the entire populace, and they're kept stocked with a week's supplies in case of another raid. That won't be enough now. I want you to prepare to shelter everyone for an entire season, or longer if possible."

Iman tossed her kebob stick aside. "It'll be done."

"I've also contacted the Sanstriders. They'll be arriving at Arlent roughly the same time you are."

"Your tribe?" Mina asked.

"*Our* tribe. They've been our eyes and ears in the Sandsea for many years now, and most wish to settle down in Arlent. They'll fight to defend her should the worst happen."

"You trust them?"

"With my life. Their djharn is my half-brother. Your uncle. He's a good man and will keep his vows."

Her uncle? She'd forgotten she had a whole family on Talin's side. She was half Lunei, but also half Sandstrider. She'd never met them. Maybe soon she'd get the chance. "And the other cities? What about the Fire Walkers there? The Prince is going to force them all to war."

"We have a plan for that, Mina." Jonan pointed to the tunnel above them.

Talin placed a hand on her shoulder. "Seventeen years ago, Jonan and I were called to war. Arlent hadn't been established for long, so we didn't have many resources to contribute, but as Housemen, we were expected to fight. We did. We joined the King on the front lines. I fought side-by-side with Salasar. I watched good men die. I killed good men. I did it all for the King, for his sister, and for my oaths. War is ugly, but you know my past. Blood and battle don't bother me. What did bother me was how the Fire Walkers were treated.

"It was new for me, a tribesman, to see men with blood fire imprisoned. In the tribes, there are no restrictions on blood fire. Men and women who are born with the gift simply learn how to use it and manage it. There's no fear, no hate. When I arrived in Solus for the first time, I was confused by the law banning blood fire. Iman caught on quicker than I did and urged me to keep our own fire secret. Housemen tried to convince me that Fire Walkers voluntarily joined the temple—that they chose their own imprisonment. It wasn't until I met Jonan that he informed me of what life was really like. He opened my eyes to their suffering."

Jonan chuckled. "You were a fool."

Talin inclined his head. "That I was. When the war started, I saw Fire Walkers being forced to fight. They had no choice. Those who lacked the strength either burned through their blood and died or were cut down. Those who refused were killed, no questions asked, no chance to beg. It horrified me. With Iman's help, Jonan and I smuggled some of the Fire Walkers out of the camps and sent them to Arlent. It was then we turned her into a sanctuary."

"We used these tunnels." Jonan waved his hand above him. "We rescued Fire Walkers until Leila noticed and blocked them."

Talin squeezed her shoulder. "And we shall do so again with your support, High Priestess."

A thrill pulsed through her blood. "You're going to smuggle them out?"

"I'll run trips between here and Arlent," Iman said. "It worked well the first time."

"We'll get the children, the weak, and the elderly out safely," Jonan added. "It'll be easier without Leila breathing down our necks."

"Some will need to remain and fight," Talin said. "The strongest and those willing. You'll be expected to travel to the temples across Sandair and send Fire Walkers to war. Instead, you'll send them to Arlent. It won't be your fault if travelling Fire Walkers get lost on the way."

After days of fretting, she'd cling to any hope she could get. But would it be enough? "Why should any Fire Walker fight for the Bright Solara? Why not fight for our freedom instead? Arlent could be its own kingdom. Together, we have so much power; no army could march on us."

"That's treasonous talk, girl," Iman murmured.

"Fire Walkers have tried," Jonan said. "Throughout history, they have rebelled through peaceful means and violent means. Neither were successful. Violent rebellions ended in more death, more laws designed to keep us down. Without support, neither path will bear fruit."

"We need a king to fight for us," Talin added. "I'd hoped that would be Khaled. Now we must hope the correct prince rises to the throne." The way he looked at her sent a rush of heat through her stomach. "We're not here to tell the Fire Walkers what to do. They're not our pawns. Most want to be left alone to live as everyone else lives, as part of Sandair. And starting a civil war will only play into the Hartnords hands. We're still at war, after all."

One battle at a time, in other words, though if the wrong prince gained the throne, she knew where this would eventually end. "What about Prince Ravel?"

"Leave the Prince to me. So long as he believes he has power, or is gaining it, he won't notice us."

"You… You're making him believe you're weak so he can walk all over you."

Talin smirked. "I'm not a complete fool."

"Careful, Talin," Iman said. "Play that too hard and he'll challenge you."

"What do you mean?" Mina asked.

"The Prince could challenge Khaled for the throne," Talin explained. "A duel to the death. As the King's Right Arm, I would be allowed to fight on the King's behalf while he recovers. Prince Ravel is no fool either. He'd only make the challenge if he knew he could win." Talin's dark eyes sparkled. "It's almost tempting. But no, I'll keep him distracted. All I ask is you play your part and trust me. Don't let him goad you. We cannot allow him to suspect what we're doing."

Mina breathed deeply. "I'll try."

"Don't try too hard, girl," Iman said. "If you start acting all demure now, that'll raise his suspicion quicker than missing Fire Walkers."

Talin chuckled. "Iman is right. You can get angry. Just don't get carried away."

"Get angry. That, I can do."

"We have to work together. We have to trust each other. No more secrets. No more lies. We are House Arlbond and we'll survive this together."

Iman slapped Mina's back. "Together."

"Together," Jonan grunted.

Mina wrapped her arms around Talin's waist. "Together, then."

Talin kissed her forehead. "Lune guide us all."

Part Two

The High Priestess
of Rahn

21

LESSONS IN FLAME

The traditional robes of a Fire Walker high priestess were thick, heavy, and itched like sand. Its length restricted movement and would be useless in a fight. And they were a red as bright as Rahn himself.

But as Samira said, Mina needed to play the part. It wasn't just the hearts of Solus she needed to win, but the Fire Walkers themselves. Dressed in her black leathers and purple sahn, she looked like a Houseman. Now, she tucked her sahn neatly away, and for the first time since Arlent, she'd unbuckled Hawk and left her precious sword behind.

Gods, she'd never felt so naked.

Fire Walkers filled the sanctum—more than Mina could ever remember seeing. Solander and Duslander sat on the stone steps. Most were clothed as normal and chatting with one another. Men tossed dice, women stitched fabric, and the young played with wooden toys that certainly hadn't belonged to the temple before. It was a relaxed atmosphere compared to the harsh rule of Leila, but Mina didn't want them to become complacent. In only five short weeks, they'd be marching north, and they had enemies closer to home.

"There's our High Priestess," Samira declared with a beaming smile. The acolyte was back in her usual Fire Walker garb of breast-band and loincloth. Her head was clean shaven, and her arms bandage-free. She'd gone over her tattoos with fresh red coloring to hide the scars. "Though you'd look more welcoming if you didn't scowl."

Mina tugged at her robes. "I'm not scowling."

"All you do is scowl."

Jonan approached with a smirk. Mina shot him a glare, and his expression quickly changed to something more solemn, though his amusement tingled through the blood bond. She gave him a shove.

He chuckled and pointed to the center of the sanctum. "We're ready to begin."

Piles of wood were stacked and ready to be turned into campfires. Learning to start a fire, maintain it, and snuff it out was the first lesson Jonan had taught her—and the only one she'd managed successfully. It taught the necessities for controlling blood fire without letting it get out of hand: a perfect start for any Fire Walker who hadn't mastered their flame.

Training the Fire Walkers would appease the Council, although Mina had no intention of letting anyone use their skills on or near a battlefield. Instead, these were survival skills they could take with them in life—building campfires, cooking, remaining warm in dire situations, using blood fire to navigate through darkness, and protecting themselves from attack.

Waiting beside stacks of wood were five older men whom she'd carefully chosen to serve as her new acolytes—to guard her and assist her in performing rites about the city. They were the only men in the sanctum wearing the traditional loincloths of a Fire Walker.

She rolled up her sleeves, exposing her silver markings, and bowed before them. "I know the Housemen and their Council see us as weapons to be used in war, but that's not the side of you I want Sandair to see. I want them to see you for who you are." She raised her arm and twisted it to display her tattoos. "I'm a Fire Walker, but I'm also Mina. My markings say who I am: a Lunei."

She nodded to the tallest of her new acolytes, who eyed her with suspicion even now. "Who are you, my friend?"

"Dahn." He crossed his muscular arms. "I'm no one's friend."

"I'm Bahri," volunteered a thin-looking Solander, the same one who'd argued with Dahn before the vote, once again coming to her defense. "My flames are waves, see." He pointed to the markings on his chest, which were indeed the shape of waves. "Because I was a fisherman. Before all this."

"Bahri." She smiled. "I grew up beside a river, but I can't say I liked the fish."

"Ah, but did you ever try them smoked on a stick?" He nudged a Gaislander standing beside him. "You taught me that."

The Gaislander offered a sheepish smile. He was a round man and his tattoos stretched across his belly in thin, fiery strokes. He, too, had spoken out in her favor. "I ran a kebob stall and grilled them with my own flame, not that the city guards approved." He shook his head. "They liked my food, but not how I cooked. Everyone's a critic. I'm Qareem."

"Amin," said the next, a Solander who beamed and waved at the crowd. "My flames are the musical notes of the Dusland winds, after my blood-bonded, to prove we'll never be apart. And this—" He grabbed a Duslander by the shoulders and squeezed him— "is my blood-bonded husband, Marek."

The Duslander nudged him playfully. "My markings are for Amin's penchant for fine wine." His flames were designed in patterns of flowing water with dots of grapes. "Because I'd play my setar and he'd get drunk."

"How long have you both been in the temple?" she asked.

Marek snorted. "Too long."

Amin fluttered his eyelashes. "We married in the temple."

"Leila let you?"

"Oh no. We bonded in secret. She threatened to bury us in stone if we continued our relationship, but I told her we weren't doing any harm. It's not like we could make a child between us, and trust me, we tried! Many times!" Amin flashed a wicked grin. "She sent

Marek to the far end of the Duslands, to Baiasra. It was only after the King granted our freedom that we followed our bond and found each other again."

They gazed at each other like young lovers, and she thought of Raj. It warmed her heart to think a love like this might be in his future. Leila had tried to break them, but their bond held true. "So long as I am High Priestess, you'll stay together."

The pair of them nodded in appreciation.

Dahn rolled his eyes.

Mina turned to the Fire Walkers sitting on the stone steps. "Those of you gathered here are new to the temple and therefore new to our rules. Not all of you will know how to summon and control your blood fire. My acolytes and I will teach you."

"So we can fight in your war, Priestess?" Garr the Ash Maker called. He sat on the front step and was picking at his nail. "That's all you're training us for, isn't it? To burn and bleed for King and kingdom?"

Some of the Fire Walkers murmured.

She bit back a retort. "We'll teach you how to use your fire as a tool, not a weapon. Every Fire Walker must learn to control their flame for their own safety—"

"Because you fear we'll burn some poor Houseman?"

"So you don't die from blood loss."

Garr looked confused. Did Ash Makers not burn through their blood?

"Everyone inside the temple is expected to train as per the law," Samira called. "This has not changed. We'll begin with building campfires—"

"*Campfires?*" Garr said incredulously. "How is learning to make a campfire going to protect us when we're thrust into war?"

Mina ground her teeth. "Because it'll teach you control—"

"And then you'll teach us how to burn the enemy? That's the only reason we're here."

A flicker of warmth bloomed in her gut. If she were in that crowd sitting beside Garr, she'd probably be arguing the same sentiment.

"Are you a fool?" Samira snapped. "Do you understand anything of the law?"

Garr leaned forward with his hands on his knees. "Housemen write the laws and use their gold to enforce them on everybody but themselves. But gold is nothing compared to the fire we have in our veins. Any one of us could overcome any Houseman. And all of us together—"

"I fought in the last war," Jonan said. "Some of the Fire Walkers thought as you do. They thought there was strength in numbers. But Housemen have perfected the art of slaughtering Fire Walkers over generations. Those who resist face the sword."

Garr's amber eyes stared not a Jonan, but right at her. "Fire can melt steel."

Some of the Fire Walker men nodded, and anger flashed in their faces.

What was Garr's game?

To deliberately stir them into rebellion?

Mina swept her gaze across the many faces watching her. Most knew the reality of the law. They had suffered it all but twelve short weeks of their lives. "Once this war is over, I swear to you that the law will change. I won your freedom once, and I'll do so again. But you must have patience. My House will see to it that all cities of Sandair become like Arlent. You will not be prisoners or slaves. Just give us time."

Samira shot her a startled look.

Garr didn't look impressed. "Sounds like an empty promise, Priestess. You Housemen are full of them. And even if I did believe you, which I don't, how many of us will live through the war to see it happen?"

"You'll live a lot longer if you keep your mouth shut and train."

He nudged a Fire Walker next to him. "See? Housemen always want us kept quiet. Your training is wasted on me, Priestess. I'm already the most powerful Fire Walker in here."

"Are you now? Do you care to prove it?"

Jonan's unease passed through the bond. Garr's boasting could be true for all she knew. Ash Makers were feared for the strength of their blood fire, or so the tales said.

"I'm not your pet." A glint of mischief shone in his eyes. "But why don't you demonstrate for us? Surely our High Priestess can show us how it's done."

Trying to start a bonfire wouldn't win any hearts or minds. She was more likely to make a fool of herself in front of so many gods-damn people.

Jonan caught her eye. "Our High Priestess has better things to do with her time—"

"Oh, so the rest of us are required to train, but not the High Priestess?" Garr turned to another Fire Walker and mouthed *Housemen*.

"Fine." She snapped her fingers and summoned a single flame. If this would help to convince them she wasn't just another Houseman, then she'd dance to Garr's tune. She strode to the pile of wood and kneeled before it. Like in the tournament, she ignored the many eyes watching her and focused on the task at hand. "Blood fire is a gift from Rahn, not a punishment. It's as much a part of you as sand is a part of the Duslands. If you remember anything from training, remember this: you are the master of your own self and the fire is yours to control."

She lowered her palm to the wood and allowed her fire to flow with the gentle rhythm of her heartbeat. This was the key to control. The more erratic her emotions, the less control she had over her flame. Dancing was one way to calm, but the breathing exercises Talin and Jonan had taught her helped immensely. Finding that inner stillness took the edge off her temper, and with the Council breathing down her neck, she needed greater control now more than ever.

The raw power of her blood fire tingled in her veins. She'd feared it for so long, she'd never realized how pleasurable it felt— like a release.

She lifted her head and met Garr's stare. His amber eyes burned through her robes and skin, as though trying to find the embers hidden inside. Such scrutiny reminded her of Gareth, and the way he'd stared into her soul with his Sight. Her heart skipped a beat, and her flame flickered. Garr's lip quirked into an arrogant smirk that was all male.

It sent her pulse fluttering.

A whoosh of flame burst from her palm, earning a gasp from the crowd. Jonan nudged her through the bond. She bit her lip and tried to calm her breathing. An ache already throbbed in her head—the sign to pull back. She yanked her hand free and shook her fire out.

The campfire roared with a hearty flame. She'd been aiming for a slow, glowing burn, but at least there was no doubt of her power.

She stood and gestured to the campfire. "As you can see, blood fire can—"

A warning rang through the blood bond. She glanced to Jonan, who was subtly pointing at her legs.

Her robes had caught fire.

Flame raced up the fabric. Mina stumbled back with a curse, but Jonan was by her side in an instant. One press of his hand and the flames were gone, leaving her robes crumbling into ash and her legs exposed.

The Fire Walkers laughed.

"Is this the control you'll be teaching us, Priestess?" Garr called amid the laughter.

Samira ducked in front of her and tried to hide Mina's legs with what was left of her robes. "And this is why Fire Walkers shouldn't wear clothes."

Mina had worn the traditional loincloth and breast-band and hated it. She wasn't about to force it upon these newcomers. It was another rule change that Samira didn't approve of. "Continue training. I'm getting changed, and don't you argue about it." She stomped away before Samira could say anything, and laughter followed her out of the sanctum.

This was Garr's fault. He'd made her look a fool in front of her

Fire Walkers. How was she supposed to train them if he was going to undermine her? They needed to trust her if she were to have any hope of smuggling them out of the temple and across the desert to Arlent.

At least Garr had the courtesy to mark himself as a potential threat.

As he watched her, so Mina would watch him.

22

DUTIES

The temple was a sandstorm of activity. Fire Walkers paired off and learned the basics of summoning their flame under Jonan's instruction. Mina's acolytes watched, listened, and offered genuine praise. Her plan was for them to study Jonan's methods for a few days and then take over, allowing him the time needed to dig out more tunnels underneath the sanctum. Her only problems were Samira and Garr; she needed both of them out of the way.

She found the pair of them arguing with one another in the corner. Of course they were.

Garr saw her first and gave an exaggerated bow. "Priestess."

Samira whirled around, her brows knitted together. "Oh, thank Rahn. I'm *trying* to teach, but this fool keeps interrupting me."

His expression was the picture of innocence. "All I said was the food in here's terrible. I'd kill for a bit of meat."

Mina gawked at him. "You're complaining about the food?"

"It's all beans." He rubbed his stomach. "It messes with my insides something rotten."

"They fill you with air," Kamran said. The baker's boy sat with Fez on the nearest stone step. He no longer wore a bandage, though the cut on his forehead had left a scar. "That's what the old Fire Walkers say. You can't have fire without air. But sometimes it comes out elsewhere." Kamran giggled and wafted his behind. "I burned my pants once."

Garr grinned at the boy. "Is this how we're going to win the war, Priestess? By bending over and letting go?"

Samira lifted her nose high. "Beans help restore blood. Especially in women."

"I'm no healer, but meat restores what's lost easier *and* tastes better," Garr said.

"Well, I'm no economist, but beans cost not the whit of meat."

"And? You expect us to fight your wars on *beans*?"

"You expect Housemen to pay for anything else?"

Garr turned to Mina. "Is that so, Priestess?" It was just the opening he'd been waiting for, and he glanced around to make sure he held an audience. Sure enough, several Fire Walkers had stopped training and now waited for Mina's answer.

Mina bit back a sigh. Too many newcomers still saw her as a Houseman and not as the Sand Dancer who had liberated the Fire Walkers. "He has a point. Add better food to our budget," she told Samira. "I want every man, woman, and child in this temple to eat well."

Samira's mouth dropped open. "We cannot afford such a thing, High Priestess."

"My House will cover the cost if necessary." She shot Garr with her most dismissive glare. "If you'll excuse me, Ash Maker, I require a word with my acolyte. Shouldn't you be training?"

"By lighting campfires? I don't know, Priestess. Sounds too complex for me."

"It's not hard." Kamran jumped down from the step and Fez scurried away with a screech. "I'll show you." He grabbed Garr's sleeve and dragged him to a pile of wood.

Garr glanced over his shoulder and winked.

What was his game now? To poison the minds of Fire Walker children?

He could well be in league with Saeed and here to stir discontent. She waited until he was out of earshot and bent close to Samira.

"Keep an eye on him. I'll wager my sahn he's going to try something."

"Something like bankrupting the temple? Or riling up the Council against us with constant demands for better food and more gold?" Samira rolled her eyes. "You're not going to win over our people with bribes."

"Leila didn't win them over with threats. They feared her."

"Leila was only following the law, which is what *you* should be doing."

Mina cast her gaze across the sanctum. Kamran laughed as he summoned a shower of sparks that rained down on Garr's head. He might soon be ordered to unleash his fire against the enemy. "Did Leila keep any records of how she ran things? Food orders, kitchen staffing, laundry duties, any of that? There's too many new people here, and we can't start running out of bread or clean sheets."

"Leila kept it all in here." Samira tapped her forehead. "But I watched her work and ran her errands. I have an awareness of what needs doing."

This was the perfect way to keep Samira occupied. "Then I'll need you to keep things running smoothly. You're the only one who knows all the ins and out of the temple. And don't be miserly. We want our people to feel safe and well cared for. Can I count on you?"

Samira puffed out her chest. "It will be done, High Priestess."

Mina reached into her pocket and dug out the ruby necklace Prince Rais had given her. The gem alone would be worth a pot of seras. "This should fetch enough gold for now." She dropped it into Samira's hands. "Sell it and get whatever we need."

Kamran ran up to her. "Uh, Priestess? There's a Bosan outside the temple."

Mina excused herself and slid past the temple doors. The sudden change from soft brazier light to golden Rahnlight blinded her. She squinted at the broad silhouette.

"Stars, you really are the High Priestess." Alistar smiled

awkwardly. His dark hair had returned to a shaggy mess and he seemed closer to the boy Mina knew from her Academy days than some prince-in-training.

Mina tugged at her robes. "They're itchy and I hate them. But my people would rather listen to a priestess than a Houseman, so I have to look the part. What's this about? I didn't expect to see you again anytime soon."

"I thought we could get a drink." His usual lime beads were back in his braid, and he tugged on it absentmindedly—something he only did when nervous. "I'd ask Raj too, but he's busy running Green Hand errands. Up for it, Arl?"

Mina smirked at her old nickname. "On my gold, I assume?"

Alistar grinned. Together, they strode down the hill as Ali and Arl, and Mina left her worries at the temple doorstep.

Solus was busier than normal with soldiers rolling wagons full of crates and sacks up to Bloodstone Keep. Tents had been erected outside the walls, and carts were stashed in every patch of grass or alleyway they could fit into. Lines of men surrounded the Hall of Honor—city folk, young and old. Every Sandarian man had some idea how to duel, but the arena is where they'd train to use their swords together as an army.

All were called to war. Most had little choice.

Alistar watched them wearily, his thoughts likely reflecting her own.

The Council had sounded their war cry and made revenge for the murder of their Queen sound glamorous, but these men had nothing to win from battle. Many would die, and the rest would return home to the exact same ragged lives as before.

Still, Mina wished she could spend a few days among them at the arena learning military strategy and tactics. She knew nothing about arranging soldiers on the battlefield or how to direct them once the fighting began. Would she be expected to command her Fire Walkers during battle? Would Jonan be at her side to guide her?

She wrapped her arm around Alistar's and pulled him into the market to buy them both a lamb skewer. They wandered aimlessly while they ate and found themselves beside the city docks.

Lune sent a soothing breeze thick with the taste of brine as Rahn sank toward the horizon. Alistar stared out to sea as seagulls fought over a scrap of bread nearby. "Orders are coming in now. Lord Salasar will be mobilizing his men within the next few weeks. And then the march north begins."

Indeed. Iman would be leaving for Arlent soon.

"My father's returned to Myryn," Alistar continued. "And my brothers back to Neu Bosa."

"You're not joining them?" she asked.

"I've received my orders. I'll be leaving with Lord Salasar's company for the Ruby Coast within the next couple of days."

She choked on her lamb and tossed the skewer aside. The seagulls took flight in alarm. "But you're the ambassador's son!"

"Which means I've got to perform my duty and prove myself to be a true warrior. Prince Ravel made that very clear, and so my father can't wait to send me to the front lines."

"Maybe I can talk to my father," Mina suggested, but without hope.

"It's fine." He turned and shrugged. "What was all that Academy training for, if not this? It's not like I left early to join a tournament or anything." Alistar grinned, though there was something manic about it.

Gods, he was scared. Seeing the preparations for war and knowing her dearest friend would be in the thick of it made her heart ache.

She opened her mouth to suggest getting that drink when a flicker in a lamppost's lantern caught her eye. Tira was waving frantically at her. She pointed in the direction of the temple.

Oh gods, what now?

"I have to get back." She thrust a few coins into his hand. "Get a drink on me."

"You're leaving?"

"Fetch Raj and we'll drink tomorrow," she called over her

shoulder. She wove through the market crowds, then hoisted her robes and raced up the hill to the Temple of Rahn. Samira and Jonan stood outside the main doors arguing with Garr.

"What's going on?" she yelled.

"The baker's boy is missing," Jonan said.

Samira jabbed a finger at Garr. "Because of *that* fool! He scared the poor boy half to death by saying we're all going to die on the front lines—"

"At least I'm not hiding the truth from them!" Garr crossed his arms and scowled.

"And how is terrifying them going to help?"

"It's the *truth!*"

Mina held up her hand. "Where is Kamran?"

Samira rubbed her head. "He ran from the temple a short while ago. I needn't explain what will happen if we don't find him, High Priestess."

No, she didn't. Running from the temple was a crime worthy of death in the eyes of the law. If the city guards found Kamran first… he wouldn't make it to war.

23

THE RUNAWAY

Dusk would soon cover the city, which meant the guards would begin their evening patrols. Mina couldn't risk Kamran running into them. "Jonan and I will cover the lower city. Samira, fetch his mother and ask if there are any places he could have run to. And you—" She eyed Garr with disdain. "Get back inside. You've done enough."

The Ash Maker stood with his arms crossed. "I didn't mean to scare the boy. Let me help. The two of you can't search an entire city—"

"If the guards see you running around outside the temple, they'll cut you down."

Samira snorted. "Let him. If he gets cut down, so be it."

"Fine," Mina said. "We've wasted enough time."

Samira returned to the temple as Mina, Jonan, and Garr headed for the lower city. They split up, and Mina slid into one of the many dark alleyways with a hand to the dagger in her belt. She waited until she was alone and snapped her fingers, willing a flame to spread around her fist. In a heartbeat, flickering red and orange flames engulfed her hand, and in the center floated Tira.

"You need to help me," Mina whispered. "Can you see where Kamran is?"

Tira nodded and pointed down the alley.

"Take me to him."

Mina held out her hand like a torch and jogged through the cramped alleys. Tira pointed her this way and that. The lower city remained quiet as Rahn withdrew his light and allowed Lune to take his place.

As she searched the alleys, an ache began to spread over her forehead. She wouldn't be able to keep this up for much longer, and the lower city alleys lacked torches or lanterns. Where would a young Fire Walker hide?

A familiar screech sounded from around a corner. Gods, it couldn't be—

Fez darted across a courtyard, chasing a rat. And there was Kamran stumbling after him, trying to catch the fox.

"What are you doing?" Mina said, a little too loudly. Tira faded as Mina shook her flame away.

Fez barked and came to a halt, his ears flat. Kamran scooped the fox, who wiggled in his arms. "He followed you out of the temple. I tried to stop him, but he's too fast."

"You were—you didn't run away?"

Fez nipped Kamran's finger. He yelped and released his grip enough for Fez to scamper up to his shoulder and perch there. "No!" Kamran said with indignation. "I didn't want your pet to get lost or hurt."

"He's not a pet. He's—never mind." She rubbed the bridge of her nose. "You do remember what happens to Fire Walkers who leave the temple?"

"I'm not dumb. But he's only a runt. He could have got eaten by dogs—"

"He's a smart fox. He can take care of himself. Do not leave the temple for any reason, you hear me?"

Kamran thrust out his lip, ready to argue.

She raised her eyebrow in the perfect imitation of Iman. "That's an order."

He hung his head. "Yes, Priestess."

"Good. Let's get back."

She steered Kamran out of the courtyard and they shuffled through the alleyways at a brisk pace. They were almost out of the lower city unseen and the tip of temple's pyramid was just visible above the decrepit buildings when they turned a corner straight into a city guard.

Kamran wasn't dressed like a Fire Walker, but his head was shaved bare, a telltale sign even if his tattoos were covered.

The guardsman placed a hand on his sword hilt. "You boys lost?"

Normally, Mina was content to be mistaken for a male, but gods, what was the point of wearing these accursed robes if not to mark her as a Fire Walker priestess? She stepped in front of Kamran and met the guard's eye. "I am High Priestess Tamina of House Arlbond." She cringed at her own name. It didn't sound right to introduce herself so formally. "If you'll excuse me, we must return to the temple."

"Why are you outside?"

"Lighting the city's lanterns. Kamran here volunteered to assist me. He's young but eager to help." She slapped Kamran on the shoulder, and he winced.

The guard's eyes narrowed. "In the lower city?"

"We became lost." She fluttered her eyelashes in the same way she'd seen noble women pout in the Keep. "All these darn alleys look the same. Thank the gods we found you! Would you kindly escort us back?"

The guard released his sword. "This way, Priestess."

He led them back to the main street and toward the temple. Kamran stuck out his tongue behind the guard's back but stopped when she gave him a stern look.

City guardsmen awaited them outside the temple doors with their swords drawn, pointed at Garr. At the head of the guard stood a broad figure she certainly never expected nor wanted to see again. His beard flopped like a goat's.

Cyrus Fellbond.

The bully from her Academy days. He'd been one of Prince

Ravel's lackeys and had challenged her to a sorrite. A sorrite she'd barely won.

"Are we in trouble?" Kamran whispered.

If the Ash Maker was picking fights with the local guard and Cyrus Fellbond of all people, then it wouldn't end well for any of them. "Wait here. I'll handle this."

She approached the guards with her chin held high and put on her best commanding voice—again mimicking Iman when her aunt was displeased. "What's the meaning of this?"

Cyrus whirled around and his face lit up with delighted malice. "Malik of House Arlbond. I always knew you were a bitch."

"Such an original insult. Did you think of it yourself?" She rubbed the hilt of her mother's dagger in her belt and regretted leaving Hawk behind. "What are you doing here? I thought you'd run away."

Cyrus thumped his chest. "The Sword of Solus needed a sorran, and he only takes the best."

"You're his new sorran? *You?*"

"When I realized the Academy was no place for men of worth or honor, I returned home to Fellbani and trained with real warriors, men who'd killed their fair share of raiders and Hartnords. Sounds like I made the right decision. I can't believe they let a woman into the tournament. What a farce."

"I won the tournament."

"You cheated our Prince of his victory. First, the King let women into his Council, then into his tournament, and then he listened when they told him to let Fire Walkers run rampant. And now, we've got riots and war. You see what happens when women are allowed to open their mouths? The last war started because some foolish slut got herself killed."

Did men really believe that? "Why are you here?"

"My Lord Salasar requests your presence. I came to deliver his message personally, and then I found this worthless mutt loitering in the streets—"

"At the Priestess's command," Garr said.

"At *your* command, Arlbond?"

Heat tingled in her fingertips and she fought the urge to glare at Garr. She couldn't admit they were looking for a missing Fire Walker. "Yes, at my command. You are aware that our duty as Fire Walkers means we light the city's lanterns?" She waved a hand at the street. "As you can see, it's dusk."

Garr offered a subtle smirk. Gods, she was going to wipe that smirk off his face as soon as she dragged his sorry hide inside the temple. "Your Houseman friend tried to force his way inside the temple and make demands of us—"

"And who are you to refuse me?" Cyrus scoffed. "If a Houseman makes a demand, you obey it."

"We answer to no one but our Priestess."

"Is that what you're teaching these dogs, Arlbond? That they're yours to command and not the Bright Solara's? I'm sure this is a matter our Prince should be made aware of."

No, no, no!

She couldn't let the Fire Walkers be seen as rebellious. This was just like Cyrus to poke a scorpion's nest and scream foul when the scorpion stung back. "If you're harassing my Fire Walkers in their own home, Fellbond, then don't blame me if you play with fire and get burned. I'll be taking this matter up with Lord Salasar myself. I don't think your master will be pleased to hear his sorran is abusing the kingdom's greatest assets."

Cyrus sneered. "Lord Salasar summons you at dawn, *Priestess*." He sauntered past her and rammed into her shoulder. "Couldn't find a man to marry you so you joined the priesthood? I shouldn't be surprised. We're all betting on how many burners will die under your command." He waved his hand and his guards followed.

"Are all Housemen as charming as him?" Garr asked.

She thrust a finger an inch from his nose. "What game are you playing, Ash Maker?"

He raised his palms. "No game, Priestess. I'm trying to protect the Fire Walkers—"

"Protect them? By getting into fights with the city guard?"

"I found that mule and his guards trying to force their way into the temple. An inspection, he said. I barred them from entering. Isn't that your job, Priestess? To protect us? Or are you more concerned for your Housemen friends?"

"Fellbond isn't my friend," she snapped. "And you're not protecting anyone by openly defying the city guard! If they suspect for one moment that the Fire Walkers aren't under their thumb, they'll march on this temple and slaughter everyone inside. Are you listening to me? Your arrogance is going to cost *lives*."

"Arrogance? To demand we're treated like people and not rats?"

She rubbed a hand over her scalp. "Gods, how can you be this ignorant? You may have grown up among the tribes, Ash Maker, but this is a Houseman's world with Houseman laws. I've witnessed Fire Walkers—even children, even my own uncle—cut down in the streets right in front of me. So don't you dare open your mouth and say I don't understand what's at stake."

"Why do you hate Ash Makers?"

How could he ask such a ludicrous question? She jabbed her finger into his chest. "It was *your* people who killed mine! You hunted the Lunei down and slaughtered them! And you talk of trying to protect people?" She laughed bitterly. The gods cursed her the day they thrust this fool into her temple.

"I don't remember hunting down and killing anyone, Priestess."

She glared at him. "Get inside."

Garr bowed with a mocking smile, then retreated through the temple doors.

Mina didn't know who was going to be more trouble: the Ash Maker or the goat of Fellbani.

24

ORDERS

Bloodstone Keep was full to bursting the next morning with armed men, horses, and carts being loaded with supplies to make the journey north. Men dressed in bronze plate armor shouted commands that echoed across the open courtyards, and lines of younger men carrying crates or sacks hustled to and fro in some organized dance. It wasn't the same Keep Mina had left only days ago.

Salasar waited outside his office and glared with his one good eye. "You took your time, Arlbond. Get in here."

She followed Salasar into a quiet room away from the noise and sweat. It reminded Mina of her Academy days with the legendary Sword of Solus ready to scold her or point out her inadequacies.

The office walls were lined by dusty bookcases, and cobwebs hung from the ceiling. How often did Salasar sit in his own office? Only the turquoise drapes gave any indication that the lord of House Sarabond occupied this room.

Salasar leaned over his desk. A map of Sandair covered its entirety, and on top of that were markers, scrolls, and a half-empty wine cup. "I'll not mince words. The Prince wants you to lead the Fire Walkers on the front lines, but you're not trained, and I'll not risk a single man's life on your ignorance and ineptitude."

She stiffened. "I trained in the Academy—"

"For barely a season. What do you know of fighting as part of a unit? Of commanding men? Nothing, because you deemed those lessons unworthy of you. You could have learned them had you stayed, and maybe we wouldn't be in this gods-damn mess."

"So you'll disobey our Prince?"

Salasar narrowed his eye. "You're the High Priestess now. That's your choice, I don't care, but that puts you and your Fire Walkers under my command. I'm giving you as much time as I can spare to prepare them, so you and your Rhaesbond best get to work. You know the law. You heard what our Prince said. If any of them refuse, that's your responsibility. And if you refuse to perform your duty, well... that's on me."

She met his hardened stare. She had no doubt he had the guts for death, even to murder innocents, and the guts to defy Talin and punish her if he must.

He didn't blink. "Here's how this'll work, Arlbond. You'll serve under my direct command and order your Fire Walkers to do exactly what I tell you, when I tell you. I'm leading a third of our army to the Ruby Coast to arrange our defenses there. Then, I'll return here to Solus to lead the rest on the long march up the Cold Path and into Hartnord territory. You and your Fire Walkers will march with us. But there's something I need you to do first." He threw a scroll across the table. "We've caught wind of fires in Gaisland. The Guardian of Gai has specifically requested your aid in investigating this matter and mobilizing the temples there. Report to him in Grenai and deal with it."

From what she remembered of her maps, Grenai was located in the heart of Gaisland. Four weeks' worth of travel to get there and back, maybe longer. "You expect me to train my Fire Walkers *and* take a trip all the way to Gaisland?"

"And I expect you to be quick about it. Personally, I believe this merry chase is a waste of our time and resources, but the Prince says it's a priority. You volunteered to track down these rogue Fire Walkers, so here's your chance."

"I don't know anything about Gaisland." But Alistar did. She'd not formally released him as her sorran. If she demanded Alistar serve her once more, he'd be able to guide her on the quickest path there and back. "I need my sorran."

"Your sorran? You can't mean the Bosan?"

"He's still pledged in service to me."

"You're a priestess—"

"And a Houseman."

"Do you really want to walk this path, child? You've inherited your father's foolishness, but I'll make it clear for you: both the Bright Solara and House Myrbond will see your refusal to release him as an insult. Need I go on?"

"What of your own sorran? Are you so desperate that you chose Fellbond?"

"Don't be foolish. I didn't choose him. Our Prince is keeping a close eye on his father's allies."

"Where does your loyalty lie, Sword of Solus? Sounds like the Prince has you at heel."

Salasar rubbed the bridge of his nose. "Let me impart you with some advice. You're a stubborn little girl who thinks the world owes you something. It doesn't."

She bristled at his tone and opened her mouth to argue.

He held up his hand. "I'm not done. You won't get special treatment because of your dada. You don't get to follow in his footsteps and play hero. This is war, child. This is real. Whatever rivalry you had with the Prince in the Academy stays in the Academy. Do you hear me? I'll not let either of you use this war as your personal playground."

"You think it's just some rivalry? He's threatening Fire Walkers—"

"It's about them, is it? Not your father or your House?"

"You forget you're a Fire Walker, too."

"I don't forget. Nor do I forget my place. This war is bigger than you or I. Do you understand? This war will decide the future of our kingdom, and I want Sandair to be on the winning side."

He picked up a wooden marker and slammed it atop the Gaisland map—above Grenai. "There's more than rogue Fire Walkers to worry about on the road to Gaisland. You'll travel with a contingent of armed men at all times. For your protection."

For her protection or to spy on her? "I don't need protection. They'll slow me down—"

"This isn't up for debate. Take your Rhaesbond with you—"

"I can't take Jonan. Someone will need to train the Fire Walkers in my absence."

"Then take your best-trained Fire Walkers with you and be vigilant."

"My sorran?"

"I'll send him, but on your head be it. You've got five weeks until we march, Arlbond. I expect you back here and ready to lead your Fire Walkers by then." He waved her off. "You're dismissed."

Why Gaisland? And why now? It felt like an excuse to get her out of the way. Of course, that's what Prince Ravel would want.

Five weeks to travel to Gaisland and back.

Five weeks to ready her Fire Walkers for war.

It wasn't enough time. But… if there were rogue Fire Walkers in Gaisland, she'd find them. And if they held the answer to Queen Vida and King Reinhart's murders, then maybe she could dash water on this war before it had a chance to ignite.

Mina stopped by the palace and updated Talin and Iman on her new orders. As she left, Alistar found her by the Keep's gate.

He waved a scroll in his hand. "What's this all about? I'm packing for a fun trip to the coast when suddenly I get orders that my master is calling rank. My master, the *priestess*." He burst out laughing.

Her cheeks warmed. "If you're that eager to march with Salasar, I'm happy to release you."

Alistar shrugged and smiled. "I suppose I *could* be persuaded to come with you. Why Gaisland?"

"I need a guide who knows the geography. And the politics.

The Guardian of Gai has summoned me. You've met him before. What's he like?"

"My father would call him a complete and utter bastard, even for a Houseman. When do we leave?"

"Tomorrow at dawn. We'll need to take the quickest route to Grenai."

He pulled out a map from his sahn and straightened it out across the Keep's wall. "It would be quickest if we cut across the Soland plains. There's no road there, and no inns, which means we'll need to make camp almost the whole way. Speaking of which, we'll need gold."

Mina fumbled in her pocket. "I'm fresh out. It's your turn, Myrbond."

He looked at her with mock shock. "*Me?* A sorran providing for his master? That goes against the Code of Honor. My House would be appalled at such treatment."

She gave him a shove. "Your House would be appalled at the ale you drank on my coin."

"Right, I'll pack as my lady commands."

"Don't you start calling me that."

He skipped to one side and laughed, as though evading an imaginary punch.

Relief warmed her gut. She'd worried he'd be angry at her for calling rank when they weren't technically bonded, but not even war could force apart a master and their sorran.

But, apparently, it could force apart a Princess and her betrothed.

25

TRAVEL PLANS

"Gaisland?" Jonan rubbed his jaw. "That is quite the journey for our new High Priestess."

Mina leaned back on a stone step. Jonan shared the same thoughts—this trip was to get her out of the way, or possibly even killed by whatever threats lurked west.

"They mean to send you now?" Samira looked aghast. She stood in the sanctum sand with hands on hips. "How do they expect us to train and mobilize for war? Do they want us to fail?"

Mina raised her eyebrows at Samira's foolish question. "If someone's going to be out there searching for rogue Fire Walkers, I want it to be me. Leaving it to Housemen will only get a lot of innocent Fire Walkers killed. If you know anything about Saeed's plans or if he had allies, this is your last chance to spit it out."

Samira wrung her hands. "I don't know anything. Sometimes, Saeed and Leila would talk about Fire Walkers stirring up trouble in the city, or flaunting their power in Gaisland and even Hartnor. Leila was disgusted by them. And Saeed, too, or so I thought. He never said anything to make me think he was in league with those filth."

"Gaisland is a hard trip in Rahn's Dawn," Jonan mused. "It's damp heat. Not like the Dusland's dry heat. Thick and exhausting. It attracts all kinds of bugs—the blood-sucking kind. And the forests are dense. You could get lost for weeks trying to navigate them."

"I'll have a guide. My sorran—"

"Priestesses shouldn't have a sorran!" Samira shrieked.

"Oh, don't start. Whilst I'm gone, I'm trusting you two to run the temple. Jonan, you're in charge of training. And you—" She turned to Samira— "are in charge of everything else." Mina cast her gaze across the sanctum, looking for her acolytes. "And Salasar demands I bring someone along for protection. Who would you recommend?"

"I'm not sure our new acolytes are best suited for long journeys," Jonan said. "They're a little too..."

"Old?" Mina suggested.

"I was going to say *wizened*."

Mina gave a puzzled look.

"It means old."

"I need someone who won't slow me down. I can protect myself, no matter what Salasar says. Just give me someone who won't be missed. It's bad enough the Prince is forcing me to waste weeks travelling the full length of the kingdom and back. We can't let him steal away anyone who'd be more useful here."

"If only *we* could send our enemies traipsing across the kingdom on some pointless errand to keep them out of our hair," lamented Jonan.

Samira glanced at his cleanly shaven head.

"It's a figure of speech," he said.

But Mina's attention was elsewhere. Jonan might be onto something.

Garr sat in the far corner with Kamran and Fez. He ate a pistachio and flicked the shell into a small pile littering the sacred sand at his feet. *Disrespectful mule.*

Leaving the temple meant Mina was also leaving *him* to stir discontent and endanger her Fire Walkers. Only Lune knew what trouble he'd get up to without her.

But if he travelled with her, he'd be under her constant scrutiny.

"No," Jonan said, following her eye. "Anyone but that fool. He'll gut you the moment you step through Solus's gates and rob your corpse."

"He's the most powerful Fire Walker in this temple, or so he says."

"*No*." Jonan's irritation burned through the bond. "The tales of Ash Makers are true. I won't leave you alone with him."

"I'm perfectly capable of defending myself!"

Jonan scowled. "You need to stop being so reckless. You're the High Priestess now. You cannot afford to risk yourself."

"He's right," Samira said.

Jonan thrust his hands toward Mina as if to say, *See!*

"You are High Priestess of Rahn and it would look most inappropriate to be travelling and camping alone with men."

Jonan buried his face in his hands.

The insinuation that Mina would be anything but *proper* made her teeth grind. "Gods, I'm not riding all the way to Gaisland so I can frolic in the forests! Besides, that's what my vows are for."

"You never actually *said* the vows," Samira grumbled.

Jonan cast his scowl on Samira. "May I have a private word with the Priestess?"

Samira threw up her hands and walked away, muttering.

Mina rubbed the ache forming in her forehead. "This trip is a waste of time."

Jonan waited until the acolyte was out of earshot. "No. It works in our favor." His voice dropped to a whisper. "The Guardian of Gai will be mobilizing his Fire Walkers for war. You'll be able to escort them out of Gaisland personally. And divert their path to Arlent."

"You want me to steal Fire Walkers under the nose of Nazim Grebond?"

"Or convince him to aid our cause. He voted in support of the King—"

"And he voted against the Fire Walkers' freedom."

"He turned a blind eye to missing Fire Walkers in the last war.

And he argued against my father's imprisonment. We cannot save the Fire Walkers alone. We need allies."

"I'll see what I can do."

"You're serious about taking the Ash Maker?"

She stared across the sanctum to where Garr was still flicking shells. "I don't know if he's nothing more than a brazen fool or if he's actively working against us, but either way we need him out of this temple and out of Solus. Otherwise, he's going to keep stirring up trouble and bring an entire regiment of soldiers through our door."

"Then take him—and leave him in Gaisland. He's a liability." Jonan's hard stare sent a shudder down her spine.

"You mean kill him."

"Nothing so crass. Lose him in the forest. Let the wolves take care of him for you. Take Samira with you and lose her, too."

"You can't murder everyone that annoys you."

Jonan grinned. "No. That would take too long."

She tutted at Jonan and sauntered across the sanctum to where Garr and Kamran were relaxing. Tira floated in the flames of a nearby brazier. She was pointing at Garr and nodding. The last time she did that, she was encouraging Mina to travel with Talin to Arlent.

Surely her mother didn't trust an Ash Maker?

The Ash Maker flicked a pistachio at Fez, who screeched and dove after it. The Lunei's tales of monsters must surely have been exaggerated.

"What are you doing?"

Garr wore a lazy smile. "What does it look like? I'm watching over your pet."

"He's not a pet."

"Then what's the problem?" He offered a palmful of nuts to her. "Did you want some?"

She lifted her nose. "Kamran, will you give us a moment?"

"He's not in trouble, is he?"

"Not yet."

The baker's boy slid down the steps and joined a group of girls trying to light a bonfire. Mina watched him summon a flame with a snap of his fingers, then try to teach one of them how to do the same. He did have talent.

She turned her attention back to Garr. "Tomorrow, I'm leaving for Gaisland and I've been ordered to take a bodyguard. You'll be acting as that guard."

"Me?" He looked her up and down. "Are you ready to break your vow of celibacy so soon, Priestess? Well, I'm not surprised but I am flattered."

She placed a hand on her hip. "The Council claims that rogue Fire Walkers are starting fires in Gaisland. I volunteered to investigate."

"So you can track them down and murder them?"

"So I can prove that Fire Walkers aren't responsible."

He raised a brow. "What difference will that make? A Fire Walker killed the Hartnord king and brought on this war. No one can deny that. Who cares if few forest fires didn't really turn out to be our fault? They'll want us dead anyway."

"I want to know if the man who killed the Hartnord king acted alone. If we can prove it, there may be some hope we can prevent this war."

"Is that right?" Garr tapped his finger on his chin as if thinking. "Even if you could convince the Hartnords that one man alone assassinated their King, how do you convince your royals to forget the murder of their Queen?"

"I don't know yet. But King Khaled listens to my father. Our first step is to find the truth."

"And you think you'll find your answer in some forest?"

"Yes."

"Then why do you need me?"

"The Sword of Solus has ordered me to take an escort. You said you were the most powerful Fire Walker in this temple. Now's your chance to prove it."

He crossed a leg over his knee and leaned back. "So, you'll drag me to your forest and stab me in the back? Sounds like the ideal place to bury a body."

"If I wanted you dead, we wouldn't be having this conversation. I expect you ready to leave by dawn."

"*Dawn?*"

"No complaints."

"You really think you can stop this war, Priestess?"

"So long as I breathe, I'll do all I can to protect my people. All of them."

"Even if it meant defying your King?"

Defying royalty was her favorite pastime. "You wouldn't be thinking of treason, would you?"

"Not me. I don't want to die in some pointless war. Isn't that enough?"

"You tell me. Can I trust you, Ash Maker?"

Light danced in those amber eyes. "I guess we'll see."

26

TO THE SOURCE OF DUSK

The Hartnord threw himself to the pristine marble floor of the throne room. King Khaled drew his sword.

"Where is she?"

The golden-haired man stared up at him with silver eyes.

My wife's eyes.

"I don't know."

"Why did Reinhart do this?" Khaled placed the edge of his blade an inch from the Hartnord's nose. "You'll give me an answer, or by Rahn, I'll find it in your blood."

"She has fire magic," the Hartnord gasped. "I saw it in her, plain as day. I see it in you, too."

Gods.

Such words were blasphemy and treason combined. Khaled would lose his throne and then his head if the other Houses knew.

But the King questioned this prisoner alone, save only Salasar, Nazim, and myself as guards. All three of his wardens knew the truth. We needed to know in order to protect the King and act in his best interests. And the King knew our secrets in return. We all burned with fire. Even myself.

The King's sword hand twitched. "You see blood fire with your Sight? And yet you saw fit to take my sister to your people, knowing they could see it?"

"I wanted them to see it." The Hartnord's voice cracked and tears slid down his cheeks. "I wanted them to see her beauty, to see that those who burn aren't the monsters they fear. I thought... God forgive me, I

thought it would bring our people together." He hung his head. "I deserve death. I welcome it."

I knew I should leave this fool to his fate, but he was our only chance of finding Princess Aniya alive–if he could be trusted to keep the King's secret. And mine. "My King, if we are to find her, we need him and his Sight. He's the only one who can lead us to Reinhart. He's no use to us dead."

Salasar scowled, and even Nazim shook his head with dismay. But Khaled's amber glare softened for me. I alone dared nudge him. By some mercy of Lune, he listened.

"Will you serve me, Hartnord? Will you pledge your life and blood in my name and renounce your kingdom? That is the choice I offer you: service or death."

The same choice Khaled had once offered me.

Resolve burned in the Hartnord's silver eyes–the look of a man willing to cut through an entire kingdom and his own people, if it came to that. "I will do whatever it takes to find her, my King. I swear on my blood and my word."

The King lowered his sword. "Then go and find my sister."

The blood bond gently roused Mina awake. Only a single brazier burned in the women's dormitory, and Tira was there, watching and smiling as always.

Princess Aniya had been a Fire Walker. Not a surprise, given her brother's own blood fire. Was this why the Hartnords had killed her? It was uncomfortable watching history play out though Talin's memories, but the bond had chosen to show her these dreams for a reason.

Mina slid off her stone bed and pulled her clothes on in the dim light, trying to keep the noise down. Her bags were packed—all she needed were her head scarf and sword.

As High Priestess, she could have taken Leila's room for her own, and truth be told, she would have preferred the privacy. But sleeping among the others helped build trust; she didn't want them to see her as unapproachable like Leila. In the few days she'd spent as High Priestess, the temple had become filled with comfortable blankets, clothes, better food, musical instruments, and other minor comforts of home. Samira had argued against every one.

Mina was tempted to say goodbye to Fez, but he was likely to yip and whine and wake too many people up. Besides, she wasn't exactly sure where in the temple Kamran usually slept. She'd entrusted the baker's boy with Fez's care, and the fox had seemed perfectly content to follow him away to bed last night.

The blood bond pulled her outside into the pre-dawn Rahnlight. Talin stood waiting for her, holding Luna's reins. Iman held the reins to her own gelding, packed for her return to Arlent. And Jonan had brought a mangy-looking horse from the Keep's stables for Garr.

Her family.

Iman grabbed her in a crushing hug. "You better travel safe, girl. You hear me?" She held Mina at arm's length. "Swear you'll not risk anything foolish. Our House already has war heroes. It doesn't need any more."

Mina made a face. "I just want to keep my Fire Walkers safe. That's all."

"And you will." Talin placed a comforting hand on her shoulder. His eyes looked darker, heavier, as though he hadn't slept in days. "Listen to your aunt and don't go running off to play Malik the Merciless," he said with a wry smile.

"If there really are rogue Fire Walkers in Gaisland, I can't promise danger won't find me."

At that, Talin pulled her into a hug. "I wish I could travel with you," he murmured. "But you're a woman now, and I trust you to do what's right. We all have work ahead."

Iman tapped her chest. "We may be apart, but we'll always be together through the bond."

"The sands travel with us," Jonan added.

The bond warmed with the combined essence of House Arlbond, but a chill settled in Mina's bones. With Iman riding south and Mina heading west, they would be farther apart than ever. And this would be her first trip alone without Talin to guide her, or Fez nestled in her sahn.

If she found the rogue Fire Walkers, what would she do?

Kill them?

Join them?

Gods.

The sound of approaching hooves interrupted their last-minute House meeting. Two horses came trotting down the hill. Alistar and Raj.

Talin dug a coin pouch from his sahn. "For your journey. Don't dally in Gaisland. The Council is not known for their patience."

Iman shoved Talin aside and grabbed Mina for one last hug. "Though, if you get time, girl, bring back some of Grenai's finest. Nazim owes me a bottle."

After stating their goodbyes, the three of them left as Alistar and Raj drew near.

Raj dismounted his horse and jogged over to her with a giddy smile. "Ali says you're travelling to Grenai. So am I! We can go together. Um, if you don't mind."

"You're welcome to join us. Are you headed back home?"

"Not yet. I'm helping to coordinate the efforts of their Temple of Gai and ours."

"It's Lune's luck we're heading the same way," Alistar said. He sat on his horse, dressed for travel. "All set to go, Arl? I've got some food, but we'll do a little hunting on the way." He plucked a bow that was slung over his shoulder.

"Are you going to introduce me to your friends, Priestess?"

Mina jumped. She drew her sword and spun it at the voice.

Garr. He slid out of the shadows with his brows raised. "Is this how the High Priestess treats her greatest Fire Walker? I feel threatened."

She shoved Hawk back into its scabbard. "If you don't want to lose your head, try not sneaking up on people."

Garr ignored her and admired her horse. "A fine beast. Strong legs, but a nasty temper." He rubbed a hand along Luna's neck.

"She doesn't have a temper."

"I wasn't talking about the horse." He winked.

She shoved the reins of the mangy mare into his hands "This one is yours. I hope you know how to ride as I'm not waiting for you to learn."

Garr appraised his horse and frowned. "So you *are* trying to murder me. This thing will throw me off and break my neck before we leave the city."

Which was likely Jonan's intention.

She turned back to Alistar and Raj. "This is Garr. That's Alistar of House Myrbond, my sorran, and Rajesh of House Enaibond. He's a Green Hand."

"More Housemen? Wonderful."

"Your eyes," Raj gasped. "Are you related to the Bright Solara?"

"He's an Ash Maker," she hurried to say, before Garr could open his mouth and say something foolish.

"An Ash Maker?" Alistar shifted in his saddle. "The kind that drinks the blood of children?"

"Only when I've run out of ale," Garr quipped.

"Drink blood?" Raj asked.

"So the tales go," Alistar said. "Why are we bringing one with us?"

Garr thumped his chest. "Because I'm the best Fire Walker in the temple and someone needs to burn your enemies. Might as well be me."

Alistar cringed and shared an uneasy glance with Raj.

She understood their fears. Ash Makers stole blood to extend their own life and cast their dead into the sandsea to become wraiths, or so the tales said. She didn't want to know how true those tales were. "Salasar said I needed to bring a guard, so he's coming with us. Are we ready to leave?"

Garr swooped a bow, though his smile was all trouble. "As the High Priestess commands."

How soon would she regret bringing Garr on this trip?

ᘛ ᘛ ᘛ

The city of Solus sat atop a low mountain that rose from the Lapis Sea. Once out of the city, Mina and her companions followed the sea's northern coast until the Solands opened up to a vast green land. Mina breathed in crisp air through her headscarf as the wind whipped past. She'd never ventured this far north before.

Beside her, Alistar rode on a roan mare. Like her, he faced into the wind with a laugh in his throat. Raj was a skilled rider, to her surprise, and Garr even managed to control his beast and keep pace, though it tried to buck him off a few times and kept veering off course.

This was the adventure she'd always dreamed of: she was Malik the Merciless on a quest across the land to defeat evil with her two closest friends.

Alistar acted as their guide. Just as she knew the desert—what dangers lurked in the dunes, when to rest from Rahn's heat, and how to conserve water—Alistar knew the plains. The land here was rocky and the danger came not from unstable sand dunes, but from jagged outcrops of stone, pitfalls, and streams. Alistar had mapped the most direct route to Gaisland. No towns, no inns, no comforts save what the gods could offer them. At least they could follow the road west for another few hours yet before heading out across the open land. As long as Rahn hung in the sky, they would stop only to rest and water their horses.

"Can we slow down?" Garr called out from behind, once Rahn's heat shone from above. "This wonderful beast is giving me a bad back."

Mina slowed Luna to a trot and signaled the others to do the same. The road remained quiet except for the odd merchant wagon travelling the opposite direction toward Solus. Out on the plains, they would see horsemen galloping on patrol in service to the Sword of Solus. Raiders were creatures of the plains as well as the desert.

"So, what's a Bosan doing this far east?" Garr called out, breaking the silence. "Hunting for Sandarian gold?"

"I was born in Sandair, not that it's any of your business."

"What about you?" Garr called to Raj. "You're a Green Hand. You heal people?"

"Um, that's right."

"And the three of you met in the Academy when our High Priestess was a little boy?"

How did he know that? She hadn't mentioned it. "Concentrate on your horse."

Garr yanked his reins and the horse swerved. "Just trying to make conversation. The three of you are damper than a Bosan's armpit."

Alistar scowled over his shoulder.

If Garr was going to *make conversation* their entire journey to Gaisland, then she may just take up Jonan's suggestion and push him off the nearest ravine.

Up ahead, she spied a stable with golden banners adorned with horseshoes. She recognized the color from the Keep and the Council meetings.

"House Nasbond," she called. "Talin says they're the finest horse rearers in Sandair. Luna came from one of their stables."

But Alistar still pouted and Raj sat in uncomfortable silence. It seemed Garr had spoiled the idea of conversation entirely.

Garr caught her glaring and grinned. He cleared his throat and began to sing.

"My love was a Fire Walker with a heart made of flame. I wooed her by candlelight but she wouldn't speak her name. The smoky fire in her eyes turned me hard as a rock. And when I tried to kiss her, she reached down and burned my–"

"Will you stop!" she snapped.

"If you don't like my song, Priestess, go ahead and sing your own."

"Um, I know some songs," Raj offered.

"No more singing!"

"Let him sing. He'll scare away the mountain lions," Alistar said.

"And attract every raider between here and Gaisland?"

"Like those, Priestess?" Garr pointed ahead.

A thin line of smoke danced on the horizon. Trouble. She spurred Luna's flank and galloped ahead. Alistar cursed and gave chase.

The smoke led them to a Nasbond stable engulfed in flame. Panicked men ran from the building, calling out for water. Ashes floating in the air made her eyes sting, but it was the smell that truly hit her—burned meat.

She brought Luna to a halt, her grip tight around the leather reins.

Burning horses screeched and writhed on the ground as stable hands tried to end their suffering. Thank the gods it was horses and not men, but who would do such a thing?

Three men approached Mina on horseback. Each wore a bronze scale breastplate over leather. Not guardsmen, but not raiders either. Their armor was far too nice for either. Housemen, then. As they neared, she noted a turquoise sahn beneath each man's breastplate. House Sarabond.

"Where have you ridden from, my lord?" There was bitter anger in the rider's voice, but not, Mina guessed, at her or her companions.

"We left from Solus at Rahn's rise. What happened here?"

"Have you seen any fires along the way? Campfires or burning bushes? We hunt a runaway Fire Walker."

Her heart began to race. "A Fire Walker did this?"

Raj spoke up: "Do you need a Green Hand? I'm from the Temple of Gai."

The horseman inclined his head. "Any assistance would be welcome."

Raj dismounted, dug out a pack from his saddlebags, and ran for the stables. Alistar ran after him to help.

"Did the Sword of Solus order this pursuit?" she asked.

"Indeed, my lord. Lord Salasar insists no Fire Walkers escape to join the rebels."

If the rebels even exist. "Tell me everything you know."

"You needn't worry yourself, my lord. We can—"

"I am Tamina of House Arlbond, High Priestess of the Temple of Rahn. I travel with my sorran, Alistar of House Myrbond, and…" Gods, what name could she give for Garr? Bodyguard? Pain in the—

"Lord Garr of House Arlbond," he said with an exaggerated impression of what she'd once imagined a plumped-up Houseman to sound like.

She forced a smile. Rahn would fall from the sky before Garr joined her House.

The horsemen looked skeptical. Gods, Garr couldn't play a lord dressed as a street rat, and no one expected to see a priestess in leather and a sahn! She pulled Salasar's orders from her sahn and held them out. "From your lord."

The horseman examined the scroll and returned it with a frown. "Do you intend to join us on this hunt, High Priestess?"

Garr shot him a look. "Why do you hunt them?"

"The law, my lord."

"What happens to them if you find them?"

The horseman raised an eyebrow.

She considered kicking Garr off his horse. "Forgive my friend. He is ignorant and still learning about our Code of Honor. Tell me what you know."

"An old man, fifty years at least, ran from the temple in Nasiri. He took with him a boy no more than twelve, possibly his son. The old man bears markings, though he's believed to be clothed. Named Youssef. The boy is unmarked. We have no known name for him. They've been looting and burning stables as they go." The horseman snorted in disgust. "These are desperate runaways, High Priestess. I would advise caution and to leave this matter to us."

"We, too, are travelling west. We'll keep an eye open."

"Safe travels, High Priestess." He signaled his men and the three of them galloped away from the burning stable.

"You're letting them go?" Garr said. "They're hunting Fire Walkers. What happens when they catch them?"

"You've stayed in the temple long enough to understand the law."

"So they're going to murder them? An old man and a child?"

"That's the law."

"And you're just going to let it happen? You're going to let them be butchered?" His amber eyes flared.

"Of course I'm not." Mina watched the horsemen disappear over a hill. "We give them a head start. And then begin our own hunt."

27

THE HUNT

"Arl!" Alistar ran toward her. "Where are you going?"

"Hunting."

"Stars, are you serious? They burned a whole stable!"

"They're my responsibility."

Alistar strode for his horse.

"Stay here," she called. "Protect Raj."

"I'm your sorran. I should—"

"This is Fire Walker business," Garr said. "We'll handle it."

She didn't wait for Alistar to argue further. With a *hoyt*, Luna galloped west. Garr's horse did its best to keep up.

Where would a runaway Fire Walker hide? There were patches of woods across the plains, but little else to provide shelter or a hiding place. Had they stolen food and water from the stable before they burned it? Which direction would she run if she were on foot with only a few day's supplies?

She didn't know the land, but likely neither did they. So they couldn't be headed for anything in particular. They'd just want to keep headed west, preferably taking the hardest path possible for horses to follow...

The river.

If it were her, she'd want to get across the river.

She signaled Garr and guided Lune south. Trusting Garr to ride with her was a risk, but if these Fire Walkers were dangerous, she'd need the Ash Maker to prove his skill with flame. And for all his complaints, he did seem to care about the Fire Walkers.

The grassy plains turned to rocky gravel as they approached the edge of a ravine. Blue waters shimmered below. The Giant's Arm. The river ran larger here than the Giant's Tail as it meandered through Khalbad.

She dismounted and pretended to dig for something from her saddlebags. With her back to Garr, she summoned a single flame in her palm. Tira watched expectantly.

"There are two Fire Walkers on the run," Mina whispered. "Can you see them?"

Tira nodded and pointed west.

"Along the river?"

Tira shrugged. Yes and no. Close by it, at least.

Mina shook out her flame as Garr dismounted beside her.

"So what do we do when we find them?" he asked.

In truth, she didn't know. If she turned them over to Salasar's men with orders to deliver them safely to a temple, could she trust them to follow her command? Possibly.

Possibly not. The punishment for fleeing the temple was beheading. The only reason to leave them alive was if Salasar wanted them questioned—which might be worse than death.

She took Luna's reins and gently led her horse over a rocky ridge down to the river. Garr followed in silence.

Then she spotted the worst thing possible—smoke rising into the bright sky.

This pillar was smaller and whiter than the last. It was barely more than a thin, twisting line. Not a stable, then. The Housemen might not even notice it if they were far enough away. Mina followed the river toward the smoke until she came to a small fishing shack.

Smoke twirled from the remains of a campfire, not the building itself. Broken crates, lanterns, and clothes littered the yard—as if the shack had been ransacked.

"Looks like our boys have been here," Garr said.

"I can see that," snapped Mina. "But why would they bother lighting a campfire if—"

Not a campfire.

It looked like something from a butcher's counter, like a pig roasted to perfection, but as she edged closer, the shape revealed itself to be no animal. The wind carried the scent of a dead man.

She covered her mouth and crouched low, leaving Luna behind. Garr followed her lead, and they carefully picked their way across the yard.

A raggedy man was inspecting a net half-full of fish as a child shoved bread into his mouth. Mina straightened and approached with her palms up.

The old man noticed her first. Flames engulfed both fists and he moved into a brawler's stance. Red swirls were inked around his neck, but the rest he'd hidden with a dirty kameez. "Don't come any closer," he said with a raspy voice. The child ran behind his legs.

The way he stood, the way the child hid... it was just like Dustan Hawker protecting her from Prince Ravel and his men back in Khalbad.

She signaled for Garr to stay put and smiled in the calm way Talin used to reassure someone. "You must be Youssef. I'm a friend. Look." She rolled up a sleeve, exposing her own silver tattoos. "I'm one of you."

The man didn't flinch. Thin graying fuzz coated his head and chin, and his wrinkled face and sunken eyes told his tale. He'd come fresh from the Temple of Rahn and had likely spent most of his life there. "They're not red. Who are you?"

"My name is Mina. I'm the High Priestess of Rahn—"

"I'm not going back." The flames around his fists flared.

"There are horsemen searching for—"

"I'm not going back!" The man threw his fire at her. She skipped to one side, feeling the *whoosh* of heat as it flew past.

Garr raised his own fists.

"Stop! We're not here to fight!" Gods, she didn't even know *how* to fight with fire. It was far too late to draw Hawk without getting roasted to a crisp. This man wielded his fire like Jonan—like a trained warrior.

Which meant he'd likely fought in the last war.

"I'm not letting you take him!" he yelled. "Not to fight wars! He's just a boy!"

The boy cowered behind a barrel. No more than twelve, they'd said. Younger than Kamran. "He's yours?"

"My grandson. It was supposed to be our new beginning, you know? When the law changed. He started burning things when he was six. I took the blame for the fires and entered the temple to protect him. To *protect* him." His voice broke with raw sorrow that Mina couldn't mistake.

"There are horsemen searching for you. You'll never make it across the plains alone."

"We would if you gave us your horse."

Give Luna?

The old man grimaced. "No. You won't do that, will you."

"Take mine," Garr offered. "She's a grumpy beast, but if you can handle her, she's yours."

"*No*," she said a little too loudly. "They are trained soldiers who hunt you. Come with me and I'll guarantee your safety—"

"And then what? You'll lock us in your temple? March us to your wars? I've been there. It doesn't end well for us. I won't subject him to that."

The man's fists trembled and sweat ran down his brow. She knew his fear, and the bravery it took to stand against a monster, a Houseman. She hated being on the other side of that world, hated that there was little she could do to make it easier.

"I won't allow children in war." She held out her hand. "I swear on my blood."

"That's not what House Nasbond said—"

"I'm not House Nasbond. Come with me and you'll be safe."

The man's face contorted, as though torn between her promises and his own instincts. "I burned men." His gaze darted to the smoldering corpse. "Housemen will never let us live after this." Tears hissed down his cheeks. "I never meant to hurt anyone. I just wanted to keep my grandson safe."

Garr stepped to her side. "We won't judge you for protecting your boy. Everything you've done is to keep him safe. That's why we're here, too. We're the only ones who can help your boy now." The man lowered his fists.

Hooves thudded the ground behind her. Mina whirled around. Alistar. He must have seen the smoke and followed her. He held his bow with an arrow nocked and pointed at the old man.

"You tricked me!" A wall of fire erupted around him and the child, loud and bright. The flames spread across the ground and licked the shack walls.

She ran for Alistar. "Don't shoot!"

An arrow zipped past her and through the wall of fire. The flames disappeared in an instant. The arrow had impaled itself dead center in the man's chest. He stared down at the shaft sticking out of his own flesh, his eyes wide in shock, and staggered back.

"No!" Garr yelled.

Alistar lowered his bow—the arrow still nocked. Another two arrows whizzed past him and slammed into the man's abdomen and neck. He collapsed to the ground. Dead.

At last, Mina saw them. The three Sarabond Housemen on horseback. All three held bows, but only one still had his arrow nocked. The other two had found their mark.

"Granda!" the little boy shrieked and ran for the old man.

The third horseman readied his bow.

"Stop!" she screamed and raced toward him. His horse reared, and the shot flew wide.

Garr ran for the boy and skidded to a halt. As the child clung to his grandfather's body, his skin began glowing bright red from head to foot.

The boy burst with flame.

A whoosh of heat knocked Garr off his feet. The boy and his

grandfather lay in the middle of a raging ball of fire as though Rahn had fallen from the sky. Through the flames, she could just see the child's clothes burning to nothing. And the old man's body...

Dear gods.

"Don't shoot him!" she yelled at the horsemen. "The child is under my protection!" She approached the flames as close as she could, then crouched beside him, a few feet away. "Listen to me. You need to calm your fire. It's dangerous to burn so brightly. I know this is scary, but you could hurt yourself if you don't."

"They hurt Granda!" he cried, and his tears turned to steam.

"I know. And it's not right. But your Granda doesn't want you to be hurt. You need to calm down. You need—"

"No!"

Gods, what could she do? She knew nothing about children or how to calm them, but if he didn't stop, he'd burn through his blood—if the horsemen didn't unleash their arrows first.

She drew her mother's dagger. She didn't want to cut a child, but if it could save his life, she'd have no choice.

"Stand aside, Priestess," the horseman called.

"I'm handling it!" She turned to the boy and held out her hand, hiding the dagger behind her back. A quick cut to his palm would end this. "Let me help you. Breathe. You are the master of your own self."

The boy smacked her hand aside and screamed. The ball of flame erupted into a monstrous tower as Garr tackled her to the ground, knocking her clear of the expanding inferno. Even so, the flames scalded her bare arm, and for a heartbeat she panicked that her hair and clothes might have caught fire.

"God..." Garr whispered.

Slowly, they stood. Ash floated gently down around her and turned the grass white. Both the boy and his Granda were gone.

Burned to nothing but a black stain.

Garr stared at the ash collecting in his hands.

Mina snatched her dagger and stomped up to the men on horseback. "You murdered him!"

"We're under orders from the Sword of Solus to subdue any out-of-control Fire Walkers."

She wanted to laugh. "The Sword of Solus *is* a Fire Walker, you fools. Are you going to *subdue* him?"

The horsemen glanced at each other, visibly confused. Surely they knew Salasar was a Fire Walker? He'd demonstrated his own blood fire at the Solend when the King had been poisoned. Plenty of Salasar's own men would have seen the fire burn from his flesh. But no. Salasar would have hidden it somehow, bribed those who saw or manipulated their words. Others, like the Prince, would have gained some bargain for their silence. Because that's what Housemen did. One law for them, and another for everyone else.

May Rahn burn Salasar and his gods-damn House to dirt.

The horsemen still eyed her as though she were a threat. It didn't matter to them if she was High Priestess—a Fire Walker was still a Fire Walker. She lowered her dagger and thrust her chin high. "Your hunt is over."

The lead horseman looked her over one last time before shrugging and guiding their mounts back to the plains. Once they were out of earshot, she loosed a breath and turned to the glowing pile of ash. They'd passed to the next life. There were no bones left to burn. No lurrite to perform. Still, she approached them and bowed her head.

"Lune guide you back home to Rahn," Mina whispered.

Two Fire Walkers had died on her watch. How many more would she allow?

28

A NIGHT ON THE PLAINS

They rode in silence. As Rahn's golden glow deepened to orange, Alistar signaled for them to take shelter within a nearby gorge. The sharp cliff face cut down into the land, creating a natural outcrop to pitch their tents underneath. A thin stream curved between the gray rock walls, giving them ample water for their horses. There were only a few trees nearby, but Alistar declared this a good thing. Most travelers preferred to camp in the patches of woods, where there was plenty of firewood and the chance to hunt game. They'd be better off without any company, he said.

Mina stretched her legs as Alistar and Raj busied themselves unpacking the horses. Her thighs felt heavy and wooden from a hard day of riding. She pulled down her scarf. The northern breeze ruffled through the three inches of hair on her head, massaging the scalp. She was covered in dust from riding across gravel. So were the others.

Garr lingered by his horse. He hadn't moved or made any attempt to unpack his saddlebags. Instead, he stared east to where clouds dotted the evening sky in puffs resembling flame. He hadn't said a word either, which for him was unusual indeed.

"There's a tent in your saddlebags," she said. "If you want help—"

"Why did he burn?"

"The old man?"

"The child."

Alistar and Raj stilled and glanced over to her.

"I've never..." Garr paused as though struggling to find the words. "I've never seen anyone burn like that."

Were Ash Makers so skilled that they never lost control of their fire? "It happens to a Fire Walker who can't control their power. And I've seen it happen to those who were poisoned."

"Poisoned?"

"At the Solend. Surely you heard? Prince Ravel poisoned people at the tournament. Many Fire Walkers lost their lives. I've suffered its effects myself—it forces your fire to burn so quickly you can't control it. You just... explode."

"But you survived it?"

"Barely."

"Then—then the Hartnords could poison Fire Walkers and turn them against us."

"Hartnords wouldn't know how." Gods, she hoped so, but they knew enough about poison to kill the Queen.

Alistar strolled over. "It wasn't poison that killed the Hartnord king. A Fire Walker did that unprovoked."

She scowled at him. "He paid for his actions with his life."

"Um, can we discuss this later?" Raj waddled toward them with a sack in his hands. "We need to pitch the tents before it gets dark."

Together, they pitched a small tent each. They'd keep out the bugs and pests, though not the cold. As Rahn kissed the horizon, a chilly wind swept through the gorge, cooler than any night in Solus.

Alistar pulled a bow and quiver out of his saddleback. "You start the campfire. I'm going to do a little hunting."

"Why do you get all the fun?" Garr said, more his old self.

"Because I'm the only one sensible enough to bring tracking gear. And you're the Fire Walker. Fire is your thing."

Garr pulled a face.

Alistar made a rude gesture and headed for the trees. He didn't need to hunt. They had enough dried meat and other food to last for days.

"I'm going with him," Raj said. "I, um, I gave some of my herbs to the stable hands. I need to gather more before we reach Gaisland. You'll thank me later." He jogged after Alistar, leaving her alone with Garr.

Mina rubbed her forehead and sighed at the dirt that fell in flakes. "I'm going to wash. Get that fire lit."

"Why do I have to light it?"

"Because you're the greatest Fire Walker in all Sandair. And I'm your High Priestess."

He crossed his arms. "I'm not your pet."

"I'm not asking you to sit in my lap." Her cheeks warmed at the mental image and she cursed herself for saying something so foolish. "Just—do what I say."

She turned heel and strode for the stream before he could argue. It wasn't just dirt she needed to scrub from her face, but ash—remnants of two Fire Walkers she'd failed.

What kind of priestess did she make? So far, she hadn't helped any of them. The Fire Walkers of the temple didn't trust her, Garr outright despised her, none of the Housemen or guardsmen showed her title any respect, and two Fire Walkers had died as she watched. If it wasn't for her sahn, the horseman may well have shot her, too.

"What power do you think you have?"

None. Absolutely none.

She splashed water on her face and scrubbed until her cheeks stung. On her return, a campfire was smoldering—barely. "Did you put any effort into that at all?"

"I didn't want to use too much of my power and burn the whole campsite down." Garr rose to his feet and strode for the rocks.

"Where are you going?"

"I'm taking a piss, Priestess. Do you care to watch?"

She shot him a contemptuous look and kneeled beside the campfire. Lighting torches and campfires was the first thing Jonan had taught her. The ability to create light and warmth was a Fire Walker's greatest asset, and their main purpose back in Solus until the war rolled round. She didn't like to think of her blood fire being used to melt or harm. She much preferred Iman's usage—lighting candles, baking pies, and heating baths.

The thought of her aunt set a spasm of flame in her palm. This little flicker was stronger than fire created by mere oil or flint. Those fires didn't last without fuel and could be easily undone by strong winds or a spot of rain. Blood fire burned fiercer. Only sky fire—the weapon of the gods—could match it.

She lowered her palm to the carefully arranged wood and allowed her fire to flow until it took hold. Tira's face formed in the flames. Mina glanced over her shoulder, but no one had retuned yet. Good. She wanted a private word with her mother.

"You can see me in any fire, can't you? And you watch me all the time?"

Tira nodded and furrowed her brow—questioning. Mina had spent enough time having a one-sided conversation with her mother through the flames that she'd begun to translate Tira's rather expressive facial features. This one asked *yes, why?*

"I'm not complaining. I wonder... what else do you see? Can you see other people, and not just me?"

A nod. *Yes.*

"So you could, say, spy on other people?"

A nod and a raised brow. *I could.*

"Can you be my eyes? I have no way of knowing what's going on in the temple. If there's trouble, alert me somehow, like you did when Kamran got out. It's a lot to ask—"

Tira shook her head and smiled. *It's no trouble.*

"I... I wish I could speak to you." Gods, she did. "I miss you. And I never even knew you." Her mother. Murdered so brutally the House bond refused to show her those memories, even though she'd asked. Iman had once said some memories should never be shared.

And her father, forced to endure a life where he believed his daughter to be dead. She'd been cruelly stolen from the life she could have had, a life she was now trying to make up for, all because of her uncle's fears. Uncle Dustan. The man she'd called Father. "Is Dustan there? With you? Talin said he'd burned his body..."

Tira faded into the fire and was replaced with a familiar male face.

Dustan Hawker.

Her father—*uncle*—stared with an apologetic expression. He was exactly how Mina remembered him. Young, but weary, as though exhaustion filled his blood. Except now, a scar stretched across his neck.

She'd watched him bleed. And she'd dreamed his lies.

His lips moved in a silent plea. *Tamina.*

Mina leaped up and kicked dust into the campfire. The flames hissed, and the face of Dustan faded. She staggered back and tripped over a rock. Sparks flew from her hand as she fell and burst into life on a cloth tent.

Oh gods.

Flames crept up the tent with surprising speed. Mina smacked at the fire with her palms, but she had no idea how to *stop* a fire. Starting them was child's play! But her lessons hadn't progressed enough to know how to manipulate and halt their spread.

Water. That's what put flames out. Gods, she was being foolish! She ran to her saddlebags and drew out her canteen. By the time she returned, the flames had completely engulfed one tent and were now inching toward its neighbor. Why'd they have to pitch them so gods-damn close? She emptied her canteen on the flames now licking at the second tent—at least she could save that one—but the water barely had an effect.

Rahn curse the strength of blood fire!

Footsteps came running up from behind. Alistar reeled to a halt and stared agape. "Stars above! You burned the *tents*?"

"It was an accident, I swear—"

"Can't you do something?"

"I tried! They're burning too quickly—you bought the cheapest gods-damn tents from the market!"

"Don't blame this on me! You're the one with candles for fingers!"

The second tent collapsed into a heap. Alistar hissed a curse and skipped back. Both tents were little more than glowing ash.

Raj ran into the campsite with a bunch of flowers in his hands. He dropped them and dove for the tent. "My herbs!"

Alistar grabbed him before he could plunge into the burning remains. Mina kicked dirt over them, smothering the lingering glow in case they spread to the remaining two tents.

Garr scrambled into the campsite.

"And where were *you*?" Alistar yelled.

Garr blinked and barked a laugh.

Alistar scowled. "I don't see what's so amusing. We're down two tents!"

"Relax, Bosan, that's plenty enough." He grinned at Mina. "If you wanted to share, Priestess, you only needed to ask."

She crossed her arms. "I'm not sharing a tent with you."

"Well, I'm not sharing with him either!" Alistar said.

"I'll sleep outside," Raj offered.

"Don't worry yourself, Houseman," Garr said. "I'll sleep beside the fire and keep the rats away. You're short and he's tall, so the two of you fit together like dogs and fleas."

Alistar glared at him.

She forced a smile. "Did you, uh, manage to hunt anything?"

Alistar's glare turned to disbelief. "No! I saw fire and came running! And this is why we didn't camp in the gods-damn woods." He stomped over to the horses to calm them.

Raj whimpered and ran after him.

Garr nudged the remains of the tents with his boot. "So, did those campfire lessons help, Priestess?"

Mina didn't have an answer for that.

29

THE STEEL WALL

Mina couldn't sleep. It wasn't the howls of distant wolves that bothered her, or the buzz of insects trying to invade her tent. Such discomforts didn't compare to her early life sleeping in a dirty wooden shack in Khalbad. But every time she closed her eyes, two faces stared back. Two old men who'd died trying to protect their families from being captured and enslaved for the fire in their blood. Both had died right before her. One was a stranger who'd tried to escape from a temple in Nasiri with his grandson. The other was the father who'd died to save her.

Camping wasn't the same without Talin's calming presence nearby. She could feel her family's essence like her pulse. Iman slept to the south somewhere in the desert under her own tent. Jonan lay on hard stone in the dusty temple back east in Solus. And Talin... his essence hummed with vigor. Which meant her father wasn't sleeping either.

And she missed Fez. The fennec fox had slept by her side in the Academy, either at the foot of her bed or snuggled into her side. His soft warmth had been a constant comfort. His tiresome whines were company. Even with Alistar and Raj sleeping nearby, she felt alone.

Staring into the darkness didn't make dawn rise any quicker. With a groan, she rose to her feet and slipped out of the tent. Her muscles were sore from riding, but a dance under Lune would ease out the stiffness.

The campfire was still lit and she blinked as her eyes adjusted to the light. Its warmth kept the Soland chill at bay. A figure sat beside the fire, though at a sword's length. Lime green beads in his hair caught the light. Alistar.

"Where's Garr?"

His attention remained fixed elsewhere. "Don't know. Don't care."

If the Ash Maker had run in the night, it would be one less problem. She glanced over to the horses. Still four. He must be lurking in shadows, somewhere. She settled down next to Alistar. "You can't sleep either?"

He said nothing but stared at the night sky. Lune had woken, joined by her glittering children.

Heavy silence pushed between them, filled only by the crackle of flame. "I'll pay for the tents once we reach Darasus."

"It's fine."

"It was an accident—"

"They were cheap tents anyhow." He turned and wore a sheepish smile. "I doubt they'd be thick enough to stop Raj's snoring. He breathes like a camel."

"That's why you're awake?"

"You try sleeping with him."

"I'm not his kind of man."

"I tried to find his kind of man, but you turned out to be a woman."

She elbowed him.

He huffed a laugh and shuffled closer so that their knees touched. "Why aren't you sleeping?"

"Missing home, I guess."

He pointed to the western sky. "When I miss home, I look to the stars. See there? That's Neu Bosa. It's always in the same position so Bosan can find their way."

"Just as Sandarians can follow Rahn to Solus."

"Right. In Neu Bosa, it's customary to travel by starlight. To read them like a map. That's why so many of us are late risers. We like the night."

"Sounds like an excuse to sleep in."

"We can't all be hotheads that prefer to burn under the sun."

"The sun. That's what Hartnords call Rahn, isn't it?"

"That's right. There are some in Neu Bosa who believe the sun, Rahn, is a type of star. A big bright one. But you can't say that in Sandair or you'd be hanged for blasphemy."

It made sense. If stars were Lune's children, then Rahn must be their father—the biggest star of all. Dustan Hawker once told her that stars were the souls of the Lunei, and that's where her silver eyes came from. "You know a lot about this."

"All Bosan do. We can track and read the constellations—the patterns in the sky. That's how I know we're on the right path. Look, see that triangular pattern?" He traced his finger through the air. "That's the constellation of the fox. He heralds the end of Rahn's Dawn. Those born under different constellations are said to inherit their personalities and their fate."

"Like how being born in Gai's Dawn makes you a Green Hand?"

"Something like that."

"Sounds like nonsense."

He smirked. "Maybe it is."

A twig snapped in the night.

The smirk on his lips faded. Alistar scrambled to his feet. She drew her mother's dagger and faced the danger.

Garr leaned against a tree. "Looking rather cozy there, Priestess. Don't forget your vows."

Had he eavesdropped on their entire conversation? "Where were you?"

"Getting some air. If you're sharing your tent with your Bosan lover, would you mind keeping the noise down? Some of us need sleep."

Alistar clenched his fists and stepped toward Garr. "What did you say?"

"Ali, leave it." She grabbed Alistar's arm and pulled him back.

"What's going on?" Raj said. He stood barefoot in his robes and rubbed his eyes.

"Nothing," Alistar snapped. He returned to their tent and pushed Raj back inside.

Garr stretched out by the fire. "Your friends don't like me."

"Perhaps if you stopped antagonizing them, they would."

"Perhaps if they weren't such bores, I wouldn't need to."

He'd been acting this annoying... for *fun*? Gods.

What was Mina going to do with him?

It took almost a week to cross the plains.

Alistar and Raj kept their distance from Garr, though he reined in his tongue where they were concerned and chose to complain of his hard saddle or sore legs instead. Each night they camped, Alistar would hunt, Mina would tend the fire—for practice, more than anything—Raj would cook stews or skewers, and Garr would be Garr with his endless inane comments. And each dawn she'd wake with the hope that he'd abandoned them, but for all his complaining, the Ash Maker remained.

They followed the Giant's Arm west until they reached the road to Darasus.

Not even reading about the Houses and their cities could prepare her for the fabled steel wall of Darasus. The city was a circular fortress that curled into many layers, not too dissimilar from the isle that formed Solus or even her home back in Arlent. However, the lower wall was made from hundreds and thousands of swords melded together. Curved thick sabers, long thin scimitars, polearm blades, and javelin heads. Straight swords like the kind the Hartnords used. Smaller knives to fill the gaps. The jagged, twisted mess of metal nearest the earth looked a muddy rust color, though the reds and browns faded into grays and silvers toward the top. The glittering top edge of the wall kissed the sky, five times Mina's height at least.

Garr whistled.

Alistar eased his horse next to hers. "Impressive, isn't it?"

"Where did they get so many swords?" she asked.

"War."

That's right. She'd read the tales of Darasi warriors in one of Iman's books.

House Darabond was the youngest of the Solander Houses. They owned no mines and little land to harvest, and so chose to prove their value the Solander way—with battle. They were the first to charge to the front lines, the first to raise their swords and bleed for Sandair. They'd long been overshadowed by the other Solander Houses, mainly House Sarabond, but they'd made a name for themselves in the last war. Every sword in their wall belonged to a downed enemy.

A wall of trophies.

With another war on the way, how high would this wall reach? Tents had already been set up outside on the plain, along with wagons and horses. Soon they would march north to the Ruby Coast or the Cold Path.

Alistar nudged his horse forward and she copied. They weren't going to stay in Darasus long. They needed fresh supplies—food and two new tents—and she longed to sleep in a real bed, if just for one night, and to wash away the dirt and sweat. She supposed she needed to visit the Temple of Rahn and meet with the Fire Walkers there, though the thought of visiting another decaying prison to speak with tired and depressed faces didn't appeal.

They'd almost reached the town gates when a guard blocked their path. "Hold there, Duslander. Which House do you represent?"

"House Arlbond." She shifted in her saddle so the purple sahn was visible.

The guard sent for another. The two engaged in whispered conversation before turning back to her. "Wait whilst we summon our master."

She exchanged a glance with Alistar. The Darasi soldiers didn't open their gate or offer any further greeting or water. Instead, they watched her with unwelcome stares.

"Well, this is awkward," Garr commented behind her.

She hushed him.

A familiar face leaned over the wall. A Solander man in a blue sahn. Lord Darian Darabond, a member of the Council and a man who'd voted in Prince Ravel's favor.

"What do we have here?" he called. "A Fire Walker priestess who pretends to be a man, a Bosan who pretends to be a Sandarian, a Green Hand who pretends to be a lord. And whatever that street rat is pretending to be."

His tone made her bristle. "Is this how you welcome guests in your city, Lord Darian?"

"I welcome my guests with the respect they have earned. You, however, are outsiders. We do not grant access to Fire Walkers, Bosan, cowards, or thieves."

"You insult House Myrbond and House Enaibond—"

"A House of foreigners and a House of drunken weavers. And your own House is nothing but uneducated tribesmen. This is the Solands, *Lady* Arlbond. We care little for Gaislanders or Duslanders here."

"Houseman gold doesn't teach manners, then?" Garr whispered.

"They're Solanders," Alistar muttered. "What do you expect?"

"Um, we don't want to offend them," Raj said. "Lord Darian sits on the Council."

Mina bit the inside of her cheek and addressed the Lord atop his steel wall. "I'm the High Priestess of Rahn. Your Fire Walkers are my people. Would you deny me entry to the temple?"

"There are no Fire Walkers in Darasus."

She snorted. "Your Temple of Rahn is an actual temple?"

Lord Darian's expression hardened. "Our temple is a training ground in honor of Rahn. Fire Walkers are not permitted in our city."

"Then what do you do with them?"

"We kill them."

She hadn't read *that* in her books. "You—you kill them?"

"House Darabond has no need for blood fire." He waved a hand at the wall of swords. "We rule as Rahn intended us to, as true Sandarian warriors."

Garr snarled. "Your king lets you murder innocent men?"

"They're Fire Walkers. We have no obligation to house and feed them."

"They're people, not criminals!" she yelled.

"The law begs to differ on that, Lady Arlbond. But what would a woman understand of our Code of Honor?" He laughed and his men laughed with him.

Her grip tightened around Luna's reins. "What would you understand of honor, Lord Darian? I believe you fought in the tournament last Solend. Against Prince Ravel, wasn't it? What *real* man would throw their match?"

"Watch your words. You may be Talin's daughter, but our courtesy only travels so far."

"What courtesy? You've refused us entry and insulted us."

"The courtesy of leaving our land with your swords intact. The King may entertain Fire Walkers in his court, but we do not."

"And if the King or the Sword of Solus commanded you?"

"The King and his wardens are feeble old men. They tire of war games. It will be Fellbani steel, Nasiri horses, and Darasi blood that wins this war. And when the crown sits on our Prince's head, we'll march and win the battles to come against *his* enemies."

His words were a threat, and he made no attempt to disguise it.

Guards crowded around the city gates, gripping sword hilts or javelins. Their eyes washed over her with suspicion. It didn't matter that she was a Houseman, a priestess, or Talin's flesh and blood. To them, she was a Fire Walker.

A monster.

Samira had tried to warn her that Fire Walkers weren't just locked away for the protection of themselves and society—they *were* prisoners being punished for existing, blamed for Sandair's woes. They'd tortured her. The King had allowed it. Leila had ignored it.

Warmth tingled in Mina's fingertips and she wrung her reins. "How much fire would it take to melt your steel wall?"

"Consider your position," Lord Darian called. "We know how to track and kill Fire Walkers. We know how to make them bleed. We've become rather efficient at it." He raised his hand.

Something flashed in the Rahnlight. Arrowheads. More guardsmen leaned over the wall, their arrows nocked and pointed at her.

"We need to go," Alistar murmured. "Before this gets ugly."

She cast a scathing look at the men. "It's already ugly."

"Let's not make it worse, Arl."

"We still need supplies."

"We can ride elsewhere," Raj whispered, his voice panicked and urgent. "Saraani or Fellbani."

Either city would add extra days to their journey. And if the Houses of the Solands were allowed to kill their Fire Walkers with impunity, a place like Fellbani—home to Farzad Fellbond and his goat-offspring—was likely to seize the opportunity. How many more Houses murdered their own people for possessing Rahn's gift? How many Houses did the King allow to practice such depravity?

"Priestess," Garr said, his eyes bright. "As much as I'd like to burn these dogs to the ground, getting shot full of arrows won't help our cause. Not here. Not now."

He was right. Threatening to destroy their legendary city would only serve to damn her people. *I am the master of my own self.*

Mina turned Luna away from the steel wall but glared over her shoulder. "You defy Rahn by hurting his children. He watches over you and your dead. Let's hope your people fare well in this war, Lord Darian, because neither I nor my Fire Walkers will burn their rotting corpses."

30

THE EMERALD PATH

No matter how far they rode from Darasus, Mina couldn't forget the angry eyes that looked at her as less than human, or the hateful whispers that clung to her skin like an oil she couldn't wash off. The others said nothing, but they watched her. Alistar tugged on his braid and looked ready to bolt. Raj radiated guilt, as though he couldn't find the words to say, and Garr... Garr looked how she felt: a volcano ready to explode and burn the world down.

And so, on they rode west.

Three days passed. The sparse pockets of woodland grew thicker, and they abandoned both the road and the Giant's Arm to head directly west toward a different wall—not stone or steel, but wood. Thick trees as tall as the poles on Lune's Path.

They'd reached Gaisland.

Raj whooped a laugh. "We're here!"

Alistar sidled his horse into the shade. "It's all woodland from here on."

Garr followed suit. "So, is this the part where we hold hands and skip merrily among the flowers?"

Mina pulled a face. Rahnlight easily filtered between branches on the outskirts of the forest, but darkened farther in. How would they see? "It's all like this? For how far?"

"For days and days."

She couldn't stop herself from staring. "It's that big?"

"Don't worry. There are roads through the forest, you know. The Emerald Path should be easy to find if we keep travelling due west," Alistar explained.

"You've ridden this path before?"

"A few times. My family prefers sailing along the Ruby Coast to Saraani and riding from there. Will you be able to keep your fire under control?"

His question caught her off guard. "What?"

Alistar tugged on his braid. "Well, it's… the forests are thick. If any of the trees go up in flames, the fire will be able to move a lot quicker than we can."

His words churned in her stomach. "I've not lost control of my fire around you."

"You burned down our tents, Arl."

"That was an accident."

"Will you be having any other accidents?"

His expression looked innocent enough, though his eyes twitched to the trees. Gods, he wasn't even being subtle about it. During their travels across the Solands, she'd noticed the way he'd run off to hunt their supper the moment she summoned her flame. They'd barely shared a word since their encounter with House Sarabond. And after leaving Darasus, he couldn't even look her in the eye.

Raj chewed his lip and fidgeted in his seat. Garr smirked with his brows raised, and his face said everything: *See, this is what Housemen think of us.*

She snapped her fingers and a single flame sparked in her palm.

Alistar yelped and near fell off his horse. "Put that out!"

"Look at it! It's fire. It's gods-damn fire, and I'm not some monster. You *know* me, Ali."

He righted himself in his saddle and ran a calming hand across his horse's neck. "Do I, *Malik*? Stars, we trained together. We fought in the tournament together. I supported you against the Prince, of all people. I don't even care that you're a priestess now, whatever that even means, but the least you could do is not flaunt it."

"Flaunt it? Are you serious? You think I'm flaunting my fire?"

"Yes! Stars above, we got caught in a riot, House Sarabond almost shot you, those Darabond guards were itching for a fight, and you *burned down our tents!*"

"That's not fair, Ali," Raj said. "She didn't mean to burn them—"

"Exactly! What if next time it's a tree? And she sets fire to the entire Emerald Forest? What if next time—"

"It's you?" she said.

He sucked in a breath but said nothing. He didn't have to.

"You're scared of me."

Her flame fizzled out. There was a part of her that wanted to scream and burn. Blood fire was more common than the Houses cared to admit, and yet Housemen still thought they could lock them away and ignore the issue. It made her want to laugh. Even the gods-damn Princess was one of them. How would Alistar cope when he found out?

Another part of her, a deeper part, wanted to lie down and close her eyes. Gods, this was exhausting. All of it. And the war hadn't even started yet. She should have known things couldn't continue as before. In her eyes, Malik and Mina were no different. But the same old Malik wasn't who Alistar saw. Who Prince Rais saw. Who any of them saw.

A monster.

"Alistar of House Myrbond, I formally release you as my sorran. Go back to your princess." She cracked Luna's reins and passed the first trees, ignoring the open stares from Raj and Garr. She'd find the Emerald Path and make her own way.

It's not like the bond meant anything. Alistar had never truly been her sorran.

The hooves of a single horse thumped behind her. "Arl, stop. You can't get through this forest alone."

"Are you following me in case I burn it down?"

"No! Stars, I'm trying! Didn't I tell you about my helbond? When my sword master burned down my ship? You've seen my scars. He was careless with his fire, and it cost him *and* me. Have I asked you to stop using your fire? I'm just asking you to be careful."

She stopped her horse and scowled. "I *am* careful. And don't you dare mention the tents."

"Look, I…" He glanced back among the trees but neither Raj nor Garr had followed. "War is coming, and Fire Walkers don't always make the best judgment when under pressure."

"You're questioning my judgment now?"

"Well, you brought *him*. You know the tales of Ash Makers and how strong their fire magic is. And you brought one to Sandair's largest forest!"

"You don't trust him because he's a Fire Walker."

"I don't trust him because he acts like a pampered Solaran prince."

"Isn't that what you're about to become? A pampered Solaran prince?"

He grimaced. "You know about Princess Aniya?"

Why else would Mina have given him so much space? She edged Luna forward. "They asked me to release you as my sorran."

His horse trotted alongside hers. "But you didn't."

"You didn't ask me to. You didn't trust my *judgment* enough to talk to me."

"I—I was going to tell you. Stars, I've not been allowed to tell anyone. My father forced me to pander to the Bright Solara and win their favor. You know how miserable it is being trapped in that palace with them? They act like they've scraped me from their boot. Prince Ravel invents a new threat every day and I'm supposed to bow and thank him for it. I'm sure the Prince would be happier if I got myself killed in war. I'd sooner face a hundred Hartnords than marry his gods-damn sister." He sucked in a breath.

"You don't like the Princess?"

"Well, she's… she's kind, not like her brother. But marrying her? My family never cared about my future, until they could sell me to the royal family. I only agreed because you…" His cheeks turned red. "I said I'd do it if my father supported the Fire Walkers. That's why he voted in the King's favor."

"You did that for me?"

"I said I would." He fiddled with his horse's reins. "And what about *you?* The way Prince Rais speaks about you, it sounded like you were already betrothed, not that you told me. And then you become a priestess? I don't know what's going on with you, Arl."

"I never agreed to marry Prince Rais. The High Priestess takes a vow of celibacy, so he can push his delusions onto someone else."

Hooves thumped the ground behind them. Raj and Garr had caught up.

"You're going the wrong way," Raj called.

Garr glanced between her and Alistar. "Finished your lovers' quarrel?"

Alistar spluttered but Raj shushed him. "You can't go galloping off into the forest without understanding it first." He thrust out his lip in defiance, though it wobbled slightly. "At least listen to me before you start arguing again."

Mina nodded. "Go ahead, Raj."

Raj sagged in his saddle as though the effort of assuming command deflated him. "Okay. First, you can't use your fire. Not until we reach the Emerald Path. It's not about controlling your power; the light attracts flies." He rummaged in his sahn and pulled out a tiny bottle with a pale liquid. "This is lavender oil. It helps keep the bitey bugs away."

"The bitey bugs?" Garr asked.

"The ones that drink blood."

Alistar gave Garr a look. "We found your people, Ash Maker."

"If the bitey bugs get you, there'll be no blood left for me." Garr licked his lips. "And I'm feeling *so* thirsty."

Mina drummed her fingers against her saddle. "No fire, no bugs. What else?"

"Until we reach the Path, it's easy to get lost. We need to stick together."

"I know the way," Alistar said. "I've travelled this forest before."

Garr waved a hand. "Then lead on, but watch out for those bitey bugs." He gnashed his teeth.

Alistar took point. She was grateful he'd remained; they'd both said words they couldn't take back. Their friendship had changed, no matter how much they tried to ignore it and pretend it hadn't. Even if they both survived war, what then? Their friendship would end when he married, and then he'd be the Princess's problem.

The thick woods forced them to split into single file. Mina rode behind Alistar and left Raj and Garr to make up the rear. Soon they were wrapped in the embrace of Gai's forest. Moss, leaves, and tree roots covered the uneven ground, slowing Luna's pace. Eventually the trees thinned, and the sodden earth turned to stone underneath her horse's hooves.

Strange green lights danced ahead. A canopy of leaves blocked out natural Rahnlight, but the lights came from lanterns that marked a road of worn cobblestone.

"The Emerald Path," Alistar confirmed.

Each lantern dangled from a metal pole not unlike the ones on Lune's Path, but shorter and decorated in mosaic stones in a hundred shades of green. The lanterns' flames burned a bright emerald, reminding her of the undying brazier in the foyer of Talin's home in Arlent.

And Raj's warning rang true—the light drew in a miasma of flies.

"Is that lantern glowing green?" Garr asked.

"House Grebond," Alistar said. "It's their House flame which lights the path, and has done for hundreds of years."

"Whoever lights the lanterns rules the forest," Raj mused to himself.

"Aren't they worried anyone could force their way into their bond?" she said. House bonds were permanent; one couldn't just leave a House.

"The lanterns are secure," Alistar said. "And if opened, the light goes out. Only a member of House Grebond can relight it."

"And the Guardian of Gai patrols the path," Raj added.

The warden of Gaisland, and a man she needed to convince to help the Fire Walkers. Alistar pressed on ahead as their guide. Raj and Garr hung back. The two of them chatted as Raj searched for lavender and pointed out purple flowers along the way. Garr was the kind of fool who didn't stay quiet for long, and Raj was the sort to talk incessantly once the topic shifted to plants. At least the two of them found something to keep them occupied.

The air hugged her skin with no reprieve. Jonan was right—this was a damp sort of heat that clung to her back. She didn't want to imagine how miserable it would be during the rains of Lune's Shadow. Flies buzzed past and she swatted them away. Other insects chirped all around her as though Gai hummed a tune and the forest echoed it. She'd never seen so much green in her life, but this was a wild, untamed green compared to the Keep's cultivated gardens.

Fez would have loved hunting the bugs, but she'd lose him quicker than in a city bazaar.

They crossed a small cobblestone bridge over a river that wove through the forest. Reeds covered the riverbed, making it impossible to tell where the green ended and the murky brown water began, but the dancing green lights of the Emerald Path didn't lead them astray.

Then Gai's embrace opened into a clearing. Mina gasped aloud.

Shafts of Rahnlight highlighted a gigantic tree which filled the clearing, twice as tall as her mansion back in Arlent. Its leaves were as wide as her waist, and plump fruit hung from its branches in various shades of ripeness from lime green to dark purple. More littered the ground beneath.

Garr whistled. "That's one big god-damn tree."

"The Tree of Gai," Raj said as he came up behind her. "The largest tree in all Sandair."

"Neu Bosa has larger trees," Alistar said as he dropped from his horse.

Raj did the same. "One day you'll show me." He approached

the tree and grabbed a plump fruit. "Figs. It's considered good fortune to take one on your way past."

She dismounted and approached his side. The tree towered above her, even larger on foot. "What stops people from looting it?"

"The Guardian of Gai. Anyone caught defacing the tree faces a good flogging, or worse. But no one would dare. This is Gai's tree, and this is her forest."

She reached up to a branch but couldn't quite touch it, even on tiptoes. Raj grabbed the branch and angled it down for her. Her cheeks warmed, but she grabbed the nearest offering.

"Now you have to make a wish," Raj said. "It's part of the tradition."

"Malik the Merciless himself rode past this tree." Alistar snatched a fig and tossed it in his hand. "Malik took one fruit, no more, and offered a prayer to Gai. In return, Gai granted him a single wish."

A thrill fluttered in her stomach. Malik the Merciless came here on another of his adventures? She hadn't heard that tale, but she supposed her great Lunei ancestor had travelled all over Sandair. There'd be tales of him everywhere. She'd ask Alistar to share it later. "What do you wish for?"

Raj wiped juice from his chin. "To keep my family and friends safe in war."

One wish. What would she even wish for? She gazed up at the tree and its dizzying height dwarfed her. For most of her life, she grew up believing her mother was a Green Hand. She'd spent her early years in the Temple of Gai, once as a young babe, then later to earn scraps of bread. She'd sat through their sermons and had those teachings drilled into her.

Gai had been a force in her life as much as Rahn's fire and blood, and as much as Lune's guidance. Mina was a child of Gai's Seed, whether she liked it or not, though she still didn't believe that it made her anything less than who she wanted to be.

Garr picked up a fig and sniffed it as though he'd never seen one before. "Do Ash Makers get a wish?"

"Try it and see if Gai favors you," Raj said.

Garr bit into the fruit and hummed. "Then I wish for the coldest, finest ale to help me cope with this god-damn heat and its god-damn bugs." He swiped at a bug flying past.

Alistar snorted a laugh.

"There's good wine in Grenai," Raj said. "I've got a small bottle in my saddlebags with the lavender oil if you need it?"

Garr scratched his neck. "You're a messenger from god."

The two of them strode for Raj's horse, leaving her alone with Alistar.

"I don't know if the Sandarian gods care for Neu Bosan," he said, gazing up at Gai's tree. "But every time I've come here and made a wish, it's come true. I wished to join the Academy, and I did that. I wished to go on an adventure, and here we are." His emerald eyes shone brighter in Gai's domain.

"What do you wish for now?"

"Forgiveness." His cheeks reddened. "I was rude to you, and I shouldn't have been. I—I still want to be your sorran, Arl, if you'll have me."

"I'm the High Priestess of Rahn, Ali." She placed a hand on her hip. "This is who I am. If you're scared of my fire, if you can't accept it—"

"I can—I do."

She bit into her fig. Its fresh sweetness exploded in her mouth. Gods, it was the best fig she'd ever eaten. There were many things she *should* wish for—an end to war, to keep her family and Fire Walkers safe—but here, deep in the forest reflected inside her sorran's eyes, there was only one thing she hoped for.

"Priestess!" Garr yelled. "Do you smell that?"

Smoke. Something was burning.

She gripped her sword hilt and ran down the path. Bright red flames twirled into the sky from a wagon on fire, and its flames illuminated bodies lying nearby. Their faces were charred black beyond recognition.

A gust of wind whipped the flames toward the trees lining the road. Mina ran to stomp out the glowing red embers that skittered over the cobblestones; they burned too close to the dry leaves blanketing the forest floor. If they spread farther, the whole forest could blaze and even Gai's tree would be in danger. There was no sign of any attacker, but the trees were so dense that anyone could be hiding among them.

Only a Fire Walker could have caused this much damage.

Another gust of wind whirled about the wagon, scattering tiny pieces of burning wood high into the air. To Mina's amazement, these didn't fly off into the forest but swirled around her as if she were the center of a whirlwind. She shielded her eyes against the ash and smoke and grit that spun in tighter and tighter circles.

Clumps of soil and earth were pulled from the ground and clung to an unseen form only a few feet away. No, not unseen. Mina noticed the Shadow now, even as it surrounded itself in dirt and ash. Vines wrapped around its thick limbs and formed a robe of green leaves.

"What is that thing?" Garr said as he ran to her side.

"You've not seen a wraith before?"

His amber eyes went wide. "These are *normal?*"

Wraiths were weapons of the Ash Makers; all the tales said so. How did Garr not know what they were?

Alistar reeled behind her. "Stars above, is that a wraith? Here?"

"Oh Gai, is that another one?" Raj pointed to the wagon.

Another Shadow rose from the burning wagon and the fire moved with it, wrapping around it in a cloak of burning light.

Oh gods.

It was a wraith made of flame.

31

THE HUNT

The fire wraith spun in a flaming circle, scattering sparks that scorched the grass. Beside it, the hulking figure of the earth wraith slammed its fists on the ground, sending a shuddering pulse underneath Mina's feet. She drew her sword and raised it into the Solaran stance. Whilst the earth wraith would likely pummel her into tenderized meat, the fire wraith presented the greater danger. It could destroy this entire forest in a heartbeat.

Burning the bodies was the only way to calm the wraiths for good, but the wraiths blocked her path to the wagon where their bodies lay.

Lune help us.

Raj cowered behind her. "Oh Gai, what do we do?"

Garr raised his fists into a fighting stance. "Burn it."

"No!" Alistar drew his bow and nocked an arrow, though it shook in his hands. He'd witnessed sand wraiths at the Solend, but they didn't compare to a wraith made of flame. "If you attack with fire, you'll risk burning the forest!"

The earth wraith lumbered forward, each step a menacing thud.

Garr pointed. "It's a god-damn walking tree! Burn it!"

"Don't you dare!"

She took a step toward the wraiths. "You're scared. I know. But

I'm a Lunei, I can burn your bodies, I can send you back to Rahn. If you let—"

A whoosh of fire flew at them, forcing them to jump apart. The fire wraith shrieked an inhuman sound. Gods, it wasn't just made of flames; it could command them, too.

"So what do you propose we do about *that* thing?" Garr said.

"The river!" Raj exclaimed. "Lead it to the water!"

"It's too close to the Tree of Gai," Alistar said. "We can't risk it."

Mina felt that familiar tug in her blood—of Lune calling her to reach those bodies and burn them. "There's only one way to stop a wraith. I have to get to that wagon. Distract them!"

"*How?*" Alistar yelled.

"I don't know—shoot them!"

Alistar cursed and fired. His arrow whizzed past and struck the earth wraith in the chest. A second and third arrow sank into the wraith but didn't have an effect on the beast. It grabbed the shaft embedded in its chest and snapped it in half. Alistar fired another, and another.

Garr scooped a stone and threw it at the fire wraith. The stone fizzled into nothing as though made of paper, but it caught the wraith's attention. It turned on him and launched spears of flame. One caught his arm and he hissed in pain.

Mina ran for the wagon.

The earth wraith swerved from Alistar and swung its massive fist. She ducked under it and sliced Hawk clean through its arm. It fell as a clump of useless dirt. Wraiths were practically invincible, but she and Talin had subdued a whole cluster of them at the Solend by hacking them into manageable pieces. If she could reduce *this* thing down, it would be one less problem.

Her feet slipped into a steady rhythm as she danced around the wraith in circles. Its remaining arm was cumbersome and slow enough to evade, and it couldn't deflect her blade as she made quick cuts. Mud, leaves, and vines tumbled from its body with each slice.

She skipped back and admired her work. The wraith was little more than a muddy stump.

Garr was gawking at her.

She wiped sweat from her brow. "What, you've never seen a woman use a sword?"

"Not like that." He grinned.

"Oh Gai," Raj gasped, and pointed a shaking hand at the stump. Wind spun around the earth wraith. Mina crouched into a protective stance as roots were ripped from the forest floor and formed fresh limbs of thick wood.

She brought Hawk down on its new arm. The blade lodged halfway. She tried to yank it free, but it remained stuck. The wraith drew back its arm, ripping Hawk from her grip and sending her blade clattering down the path out of reach.

Its fist lunged. She ducked under but failed to spot its other fist heading straight for her. It slammed into her chest, knocking the breath from her lungs and flinging her through the air. She landed on her side with a painful thud.

Raj pulled her up. "Are you all right?"

Mina gasped and rubbed her ribs—bruised, but hopefully not broken. "I'll live."

Both wraiths approached her. They wanted her. They wanted her Lunei blood.

She'd never get to the wagon like this. "I can't send you back to Rahn if you don't let me!"

Alistar fired more arrows, but the earth wraith swatted them away. "I've got three left!"

Garr slipped away from the fire wraith and snatched her sword. He held it in an unfamiliar stance, but steel alone wasn't going to defeat these. She wouldn't have defeated Barahn Khalbond in the tournament with steel alone either. The only thing that defeated him was his own fire.

If she could summon a shield, maybe she could contain the fire wraith.

She snapped her fingers. A feeble puff of smoke rose from her palm, but no flame. She dug her heels into the dirt and thrust her fists out, willing her blood to spark. But no flame ignited. Her inner embers sputtered, as though she'd suffered a wound. Gods, was she bleeding? She yanked up her shirt to check. Tiny red dots spread across her stomach. Bug bites.

The bitey bugs had got her.

No wonder there were no gods-damn Fire Walkers in Gaisland!

"*Arl?*" Alistar was frantically waving his bow at the approaching earth wraith.

"Summon a shield!" she called to Garr.

"I can't!" Garr hopped between spears of flame as he held the fire wraith's attention. "I'm covered in bug bites! I can't burn!"

Gods-damn useless Ash Maker.

If their flame couldn't stop it, then she'd have to change tactics. She held out her empty sword hand as if still wielding Hawk and began to dance once more. "Ali, aim for its eyes!"

An arrow sank into the beast's earthen face, and then another. Was it possible to blind a wraith? She didn't know, but it didn't really matter. Alistar's arrows would at least distract it—keep it angry and raging and unaware.

She wove between its flailing arms and ducked into a roll as the earth wraith swung a heavy fist straight through the fire wraith, splitting it into two. Flames crept up the earth wraith's arm and it staggered backwards.

Now there were two smaller fire wraiths and a burning earth wraith.

"Got any better ideas, Priestess?" Garr muttered.

"Do it again!" she yelled.

"Stars, are you serious?" Alistar exclaimed. "You want to make *more?*"

"Make them smaller and I can get past them. Keep distracting them!"

Garr swung her sword at the earth wraith. Alistar tossed his bow aside, swapping it for rocks and whatever debris he could get his hands on. Together, he and Raj lobbed a barrage at the fire wraiths. Their attacks were futile but kept the wraiths occupied.

Mina charged between them.

There were two bodies littering the road, but the wraiths had come from the wagon itself. She raced toward the burning wreckage, but it was too hot, too dangerous. Perhaps her fire could reduce the whole thing and its occupants to ash—*if* she could summon it.

A horse lay in the grass, dead, and beside it was a Gaislander, or at least a man in the remains of Gaislander robes—his face was a charred mess. A blackened symbol had been burned upon the cobblestones of the road at his side: a three-forked flame.

The sigil of House Rhaesbond.

Gods, what did that mean?

A Shadow flickered across the man's body. Why hadn't this one formed a wraith and attacked? "I'm here to help you, but you need to help me. Who did this? Who attacked you?"

The Shadow rushed over her. Mina cried out as it wrapped around her like a cloak, drowning out the roar and heat of the fire and the shouts from her companions until nothing remained.

We stopped to rest, thank Gai. How my back was aching! I slid off my horse with a hushed groan. I didn't want them to know my back howled like it did or they'd think me old and not up to the task. I adjusted my sword in my belt and stretched. Gods, it hurt, and not even a few herbs would help this time. The Green Hands warned me riding wouldn't do my back any good, but as my old commander used to say, I'm useless at following orders.

And now we were heading to another gods-damn war. I hadn't recovered from the last one. Maybe I'd finally admit my back was all but useless once the conscription came. I ran a hand over my sword hilt. This had once seen blood, plenty of it, but now was little more than decoration and a deterrent to would-be thieves. I prayed I never had to use it again.

It would be worse for my companions. Much worse.

I climbed up the wagon. A polite knock on the door in the sequence we'd agreed—three short taps—and a man's head popped out. A thin layer of fuzz coated it, but it hadn't grown much in the weeks we'd travelled. He hid the red tattoos on his neck with a scarf.

"We'll take a quick break," I said. "The trees are thick here if you want to stretch your legs. No one will see."

He dipped his head in a submissive bow. It hurt my heart to see him react that way. "No, we thank you, but we'll remain hidden," he said. "Do—can we have water?"

"One moment."

I headed behind the wagon and rummaged through my supplies. We'd rationed well on our way from Nasiri. A noise behind me made me spin, and I peered into the trees. A bird. Just a bird. I chuckled to myself. Once we reached the safety of Grenai, I wouldn't be jumping at every sound. Easier to cross Gaisland and lose any pursuers in the forest than risk getting caught trying to board a ship in Saraani or Solus. I'd run this same trip many times, from Nasiri, Fellbani, and even dared Darasus, though now that war was upon us, their suspicion grew.

Something tapped my shoulder. I spun around again and swallowed a curse. A Duslander held out a purple bottle. He was shaved bare like the rest of them, but my eyes were drawn to the brand on his forehead—a three-forked flame.

Worse than Fire Walker markings. His brand told me a tale that he never could—because they'd cut his tongue out. That's why Neu Bosa was never an option for my companions. I'd heard the rumors of what befell Fire Walkers over there. A fate worse than the Temple of Rahn.

"Needed to stretch your legs? Can't say I blame you. We're safe enough here if anyone else wants out to walk a bit."

He pushed the bottle into my hands and nodded with insistence. They'd stolen his voice, but not his spirit.

"Many thanks, my friend." Odd. I didn't remember packing purple bottles. I carried it around to the back of the wagon and handed it through the window. "Here you are."

The Fire Walker took it with his head lowered. I hoped one day he'd learn his worth and not bow to any man, Houseman, or king for the life he'd suffered. This world owed him more.

He opened the purple bottle and took a long swallow.

Then his eyes went wide.

He dropped the bottle and a clear, oily liquid began to pour out onto the floor of the wagon. Whatever it was, it had an odd whiff to it, like smoke. Sweat poured down the Fire Walker's face and he gasped for air.

"What's wrong? Are you—"

The whole forest turned red. Flame seared through my skin and shredded through my flesh until—

Mina's eyes shot open and she sucked in air. She ran both hands down her face. Thank the gods, her skin was still intact. She'd felt it melt, felt the fire rip through her.

Rahn's Breath. That's what these men had drunk.

Their wraiths were hurt, terrified, and there'd be no stopping them. She needed to return them to Rahn's light *now*.

She snapped her fingers. Nothing. *Gods damn it.*

On the other side of the burning wagon, the earth wraith lunged for Garr, trying to seize him by the neck and failing—but knocking him harshly to the ground in the attempt. The twin fire wraiths tossed fireballs at Alistar and Raj, who did what they could to keep the flames from reaching the trees.

Amid the embers scattered about the wagon, a glint of purple caught her eye. The bottle she'd seen in the Shadow's memory.

She ran to the wagon and grabbed the scorching hot bottle from the ground. This had killed the Fire Walkers. Ignoring the pain, she swished the bottle around. Not quite empty. Gods, she was foolish for even considering it, but one drop would be enough to force her fire out.

Tira's face appeared before her—larger than she'd ever seen her, rising high above her in the wagon's flame. She looked down in fierce anger and shook her head in a resolute *no*.

"I don't have a choice."

The earth wraith had Garr pinned to the ground. If she didn't burn the bodies now, the Ash maker would be joining them.

Mina tipped three drops onto her tongue and swallowed.

Heat roared through her veins and burst across her body, dissolving yet another set of clothes she'd have to replace. Her scabbard fell to the ground, as did her mother's dagger. She dug her bare feet into the dirt and thrust the fire out. This time her flame came in a rolling wave.

Blood fire was strong, and a woman's fire burned stronger, if Iman spoke true. Mina could reduce this entire wagon to ashes and the bodies trapped inside.

She could do this.

She ignored the throb in her head, the rapid pulse in her veins, the flutter of nausea in her stomach, and concentrated all her power on the wagon. The roof caved in and released a torrent of white sparks into the air. But still the wraiths fought on. It wasn't enough.

Sweat poured down her forehead and hissed into steam. She could almost feel the blood pouring from her body in a river of fire, the life leaving her veins. Then she felt a cool hand on her cheek. The Shadow stood beside her now, arm lifted up, fingers cupping her face.

And then he vanished.

The battle was over.

The wraiths had disappeared, leaving only smoking black grass as evidence they existed at all. Raj fell to his knees in exhaustion. Ali sank down next to him and wrapped an arm around his friend's shoulders. A few feet away, Garr rolled onto his side and gasped for air. They'd live.

Mina took a deep breath and willed her flames to ease.

They wouldn't.

I am the master of my own self, and this fire is mine to control.

The river of fire continued to flow.

Rahn's Breath was burning through her blood.

Alistar staggered toward her, his mouth wide open.

Why was he staring at her? Because she scared him. Because she burned and he hated her for it. But there was no hate or fear in those emerald eyes—just shock.

Shock and something else.

"Ali?"

The trees blurred into a single dark green smudge. They grew darker and darker until Mina found herself falling into a bed of burned grass.

32

THE GUARDIAN OF GAI

The reports didn't look good. I thumbed through the scroll with my left hand and reached for the wine with my right. The glass spilled across the table.

I blinked. Even after seventeen years, I sometimes forgot my injury, most often when exhaustion settled in my bones.

"*Tired, Lord Talin?*" *Prince Ravel said.*

His comment seemed innocent enough, but it set off smirks from the handful of men in the room watching me: Farzad Fellbond, Khan Khalbond, and Zahir Xanbond. I couldn't afford to make a mistake when their talons were ready to strike.

Each held a grudge against me. And each had bent to Prince Ravel's will. Salasar, I thought I could trust, but his loyalty to the King only stretched so far if his wife and daughters were in danger. A feeling I knew all too well.

I sat up and straightened my sahn. "*Reading so many reports would make anyone weary, my Prince.*"

The Prince inclined his head. "*Especially considering their contents. Where do we stand on this matter? Our ambassador is not here to explain Neu Bosa's actions.*"

The Three-Pointed Star was refusing our summons, which was a first as far as I recalled. We needed their ships.

Farzad Fellbond snarled. "*Neu Bosa can't pick and choose when to honor our alliance. We must summon House Myrbond at once.*"

"*And if Myrbond isn't up to the task, then we'll send the High Priestess of Rahn to remind those Bosan bastards of their commitment,*"

Lord Khalbond said.

I bristled whenever anyone spoke of my daughter.

"What are your thoughts, Lord Talin?" the Prince asked. "You've been quiet on this matter. I must wonder if our High Priestess would be capable of sending a message to Neu Bosa given her, ah, affiliation with the ambassador's son."

There was a darkness in the Prince's eyes I'd never noticed before the Solend.

Even back in the Academy when Mina and the Prince fought, I'd not noticed it.

In the tournament when they clashed blades.

When he'd condemned her to the temple, and I'd been forced to reveal the truth of her mother.

And when he'd murdered Dustan.

I'd still not seen it. I'd still thought him capable of becoming the man Khaled needed him to be. I'd thought him misguided, yes, but what young male hadn't brushed shoulders with arrogance?

But then he'd held a sword at my daughter's throat. And I'd witnessed that darkness from her own eyes in my dreams, through her memories.

I'd splay his guts across the Council chamber now if it didn't mean endangering Arlent.

"Threatening our allies at the turn of war would not work in our favor, my Prince. If we wish them to honor their commitments to us, then so must we honor our commitments to them."

Prince Ravel inclined his head in acquiescence. "Then we must summon our ambassador to explain the Three-Pointed Star's position."

I rubbed a hand down my face and glanced to the window. Dusk already. The King hadn't slept, and his exhaustion weighed me down. That was the price of a sorran bond: to feel every gasp of a dying man.

Time. There wasn't enough of it.

My gaze pulled west, to where my daughter travelled. I'd wanted to spend time with her, to scrape back some of that time lost, but it was all a futile effort. It was falling away, but not for her. Every decision I made held just one purpose. To give her time.

Even if it came from my own.

The choice would come soon. My loyalty, my oaths, my blood debt to a king who gave me everything–honor, family, a home. Or my own

flesh and blood.
I knew in my heart which one I'd choose.
And Khaled knew it too, which was why he hadn't yet released me.
I sighed and set down the scroll. We'd become old men, and our
children would define Sandair, whatever future that held.

Mina jerked up and rubbed her eyes. *Talin.* That was his memory, and a recent one. Why hadn't he admitted to her that the King lay dying? And why had the bond chosen to show it to her now, when she was hundreds of miles away? His unease in the dream hollowed her stomach. If the King were truly facing the end of his days, then why start a war?

Webs of fresh vine crept across a gray stone wall and dangled from the ceiling. She sat in a dark alcove on a thin cot. Jars of many colors lined a shelf on the wall, and the door was little more than a moth-bitten cloth that failed to keep out the smell of damp moss or the sounds of glass phials clinking together, soft whispers, and restrained coughs of the sick.

Such sounds stirred memories of her childhood. She sat inside the Temple of Gai. But which one?

She stood and swayed on her feet. It came back to her like flashes of sky fire: the forest, the wraiths, the wagon she'd burned, Alistar's emerald eyes as he'd stared at her naked body when she burned...

"Oh gods." She sank back onto the bed.

He'd seen her naked.

Someone had dressed her in Green Hand robes. Her saddlebags had been left on a lounger beside Hawk and her mother's dagger, and she was glad she'd thought to pack a spare pair of boots. She grabbed a jug of water beside her cot and washed away her thirst, and then dressed. Each slight movement sent a spasm of pain in her head—she wouldn't be lighting any campfires for weeks. Jonan's scorn burned through the bond, tutting at her from afar.

The curtain rustled and Raj peered inside. "Thank Gai, you're awake. How are you feeling?"

She rubbed her head. "Alive. Where are we?"

"Grenai."

Gods. She must have slept through at least a day of travel. "*Grenai?*"

"A patrol from House Grebond followed the smoke and found us. They insisted on escorting us here. And, um, you'd passed out."

"Who—who dressed me?"

Raj stepped inside the room carrying a cup. "Me. I told them I'm your personal Green Hand, so they let me bring you here. I, um, I didn't think you'd mind. Drink this." He handed her the cup. "It'll help your head."

Thank the gods for Raj. It was better to be cared for by him than seen by either Alistar or Garr, gods forbid. She took the cup and grimaced at the murk swirling inside. "Many thanks."

"Make sure you eat plenty of lamb," he chided with a soft smile. "Lord Grebond asked me to fetch you when you feel up to it."

The Guardian of Gai. He was the reason she'd come all this way, to convince him to support the Fire Walkers, or to sneak them out from under him, somehow.

"Take me to him."

She downed the herbal drink with minimal gagging and grabbed her sword and dagger. Raj led her into the temple's sanctum. Other curtained alcoves lined the hall, and men and women in green robes passed between them. Green Hands.

The temple here felt as gloomy as the ones in Solus and Khalbad. Dim lamps provided the only light. More vines crept across the ceiling and curved into the main circular sanctum of the temple, which seemed to have been built around an herb garden in the center, filled with all kinds of plants, flowers, and mushrooms. Younger acolytes, apprentices, and orphans gathered beside it. Her legs shook with each step, a side effect of the blood she'd lost, but Raj's herbal concoction eased the throb in her head.

"Are Ali and Garr safe?" she asked.

"They're fine. Um, last I saw, they were arguing with each

other."

Of course they were arguing; it's all they'd done on this entire gods-damn journey.

She followed Raj out of the main temple doors. Before her lay the heart of the emerald forest. Each tree stood the size of a house, and among them were gray buildings decorated in vines or moss as though they were giant stones plucked from the earth. Yellow flowers dotted the vines like stars, and lanterns hung outside each house, casting an eerie golden light—the only indication that these were livable abodes at all.

Leaves covered the sky in a massive canopy of green and allowed only thin and scattered beams of Rahnlight to filter through. The lack of light echoed the gloom from the Temple of Gai. It was nothing like the open cities of the Solands and the Duslands. Even the market stalls in the center of Grenai needed to be lit.

"This is one of the oldest cities in Sandair, even older than Solus," Raj said.

She could tell. Everything about this place felt ancient, from the wide trees to the stone huts that had withstood the test of time. They all looked the same to her, though she could identify the other two temples easily enough from the small water fountains on either side of the entrance to the Temple of Lune and the fire braziers outside the Temple of Rahn.

Steps led down into the market and they headed for the biggest of the stone buildings at the far end. It dwarfed the others, and the green banners of House Grebond were draped over its vine-covered walls. She'd never seen so many trees or so much green in her life. It covered everything in an oppressive strangle, and yet, there was nothing malevolent about Gai's domain. Indeed, the vines and moss didn't choke the life from this place. Instead, they seemed to thrive in harmony with its people.

"You've met the Guardian of Gai, haven't you, Raj? What's he like?"

"He's nice."

"Nice? Ali said he's a bastard."

"Ali's family doesn't like him because he taxes the Gaisland Houses based on trade. Richer Houses are forced to pay more so poorer Houses don't, including House Myrbond. Sounds fair to me."

"Some Houses forget they're supposed to serve their people."

Raj smiled. "Not us."

There were few guards outside House Grebond's mansion. No wall or gate separated it from the rest of the city. Most towns were split between the rich homes of the Housemen and the common folk, but not here.

One of the guards relit a lantern on the wall with his own finger. He was a Fire Walker, but wasn't dressed or marked like one, nor was he banished to the Temple of Rahn. Surely he mustn't know who she was? But he did, and he welcomed her inside the mansion with a sly wink.

The walls here were painted in bright oranges and red, and countless paintings hung on the walls—portraits, landscapes of the forest, the Tree of Gai—as well as banners and tapestries. Golden-edged furniture filled the room, and every table held jeweled vases stuffed with flowers or odd-looking ceramic models. The effect was extravagant but too garish for her liking.

"I need to get back to the temple and help organize their potions for the soldiers," Raj said. "That *is* why I came all this way. And, um, I promised to return some books to the Grenai library." He gave a sheepish smile and waved at the guard on his way out.

The guard gestured for her to follow and she stepped through a corridor decorated in more gaudy vases. Nerves fluttered in her gut. This wasn't a social visit. The Guardian of Gai had demanded her attendance and her assistance in rallying the Fire Walkers. Not to mention the mission the Council had imposed on her; she could no longer deny there were rogue Fire Walkers stalking the Emerald Forest.

And Lord Nazim Grebond wasn't a man to be crossed.

The guard opened a marble door and she stepped into a bright study. A platter of food had been left out on a wooden desk edged in gold. Large windows allowed in light, though vines and flowers draped down the glass. Glass, because sandstorms didn't reach Gaisland.

The Guardian of Gai rose from his chair. He was a short, clean-shaven Gaislander wearing a green sahn and turban to match. "My lady, it's so good to finally meet you." His face was lit with a beaming smile. "I'm glad you chose to heed my summons. Are you hungry?" He waved a hand to his desk. "It's my pleasure."

His cheerful nature caught her off guard. "My—my lord, your summons sounded urgent."

Lord Nazim chuckled. "Oh yes, they always are. It's the only way one can get things done. Would you like wine or do you prefer tea? It's honeyed tea and pairs well with the lemon cakes."

All manner of tiny cakes spread across the platter, from cinnamon buns to lemon sponge and sticky date. Lamb skewers, cheese, figs, grapes, flatbread, and rice-stuffed grape leaves filled the remaining space. A pot of tea sat steaming to the side. Gods, she missed tea.

"The, uh, tea, if it please you."

Lord Nazim poured two cups. "It's a great pleasure to finally speak with you. Council meetings and tournaments don't afford time for idle chatter. But you are my good friend's daughter." He squeezed into his chair and let out a contented sigh. "My dear, it is simply delightful to have your company."

Mina sat and stared at the Guardian of Gai. "Your guardsman is a Fire Walker."

Lord Nazim took a sip from his cup and eyed her over the rim. "And I was hoping for pleasant conversation."

"We're at war, my lord."

"Indeed, we are." He placed his cup down. "Yes, some of my men are Fire Walkers. They don't hide it. Not after your efforts to grant their freedom. I told them they were foolish for being so brazen, but that's the arrogance of youth. In truth, they possess a bravery I do not."

Lord Nazim snapped his fingers and a single flame bloomed.

She almost choked on her tea. "Does the King know?"

"He does. And now so do you. I am entrusting you with my secret in exchange for your help."

"My help?"

He cut himself a thin slice of lemon cake. "Gaisland is my domain. I've already ordered the Fire Walkers from the temples of Oramar, Enais, and Myryn to gather here in Grenai and ready themselves for the long march for Solus. Every last one of them. I believe those are Prince Ravel's orders, correct? To mobilize *every* Fire Walker for war?"

"Those are his orders."

"And what are your orders?"

She blinked. "My lord?"

Crumbs caught in his beard and he dabbed them away with a cloth. "Do you intend to march women and children to the Ruby Coast? To the Cold Path? You are the High Priestess of Rahn. Your Fire Walkers will follow you."

This was a trap. He was trying to root out information for Prince Ravel. But then why admit his blood fire? "I assure you, my lord—"

"Call me Nazim. We're friends here."

"How many Fire Walkers do you have, Nazim? I'm told Gaislanders rarely possess blood fire. It would be detrimental to your forests."

"Yes, so we wish the world to believe. It's a misconception, isn't it, that only Duslanders and those from the tribes possess blood fire. I'd long thought this invention was derived to make Duslanders and tribesmen look untrustworthy. Perhaps even savage. Solanders don't possess blood fire because they are strong and enlightened. And Gaislanders don't possess blood fire because we are weak and impractical. And yet, how many Fire Walkers in your temple are Solander?"

"Most of them."

He raised his teacup in toast. "There you are. Truth is, Fire Walkers have always been a part of Gaisland. Their flame is needed to tame the forest and stop it from overrunning the towns, and some trees require heat to seed. But each year, fewer are admitted into our temples. Our scholars believe this is a blessing from Rahn—that he is taking back what was stolen from him and soon blood fire will die out entirely. Though some madmen assume the opposite—that Rahn is displeased with us."

"And you?"

"My belief? Blood fire is as strong and prevalent as ever before. Our people have just learned to hide their powers better. By relaxing the law, we enticed those who had hidden their blood fire to step out of the shadows. And now we have fresh talent ready for war."

He'd hit a nerve. During those brief few weeks of freedom, so many secret Fire Walkers had finally felt safe enough to share the truth with their families and communities, only to find themselves marched to the temple after the murder of King Reinhart.

And that was Mina's fault. She'd tried to help them, but all she'd done was expose and damn them to war.

"How many in Gaisland?" she whispered.

Nazim's dark eyes glittered. "Many. But not so many as you might fear. My people are no fools—they are used to the whims of Solander royalty. I've done my best to protect them over the years. In fact, had you come in better times, you'd have found our Temple of Rahn to be a thriving artists' community. It amuses me that prized Gaisland pottery and jewelry comes from the Fire Walkers here. Who better to craft ceramics or set silver than the hands of those who burn? And the gold from their art feeds back into the temples to give them whatever comforts they need. We hid this from your predecessor, though fortunately, Leila rarely left Solus to check."

"You—you defied Leila?" After witnessing how House Darabond handled their Fire Walkers, she couldn't believe anyone would treat them with kindness, least of all the Guardian of Gai.

He took a sip from his tea, hiding a smirk. "'Defy' is such a strong word. I daresay my Fire Walkers have had no ill bearing on Sandair. Though now..." He put his tea down. "They are my people. They are family to me. And I fear for them. The other Houses would never admit it, but we all share Fire Walker ancestors. My fathers killed their brethren with blood fire. I've seen the memories in my House bond, and I aim to repay that blood debt."

"The wagon travelling from Nasiri..." They were travelling to Grenai for a better life. "How many have you helped?"

"Not enough, my dear. Never enough. My men examined the wreckage after tending to you and your friends, but we couldn't see any evidence of sabotage—"

"They were poisoned with Rahn's Breath."

"Rahn's Breath? The same poison which the King ingested?"

"The very same."

He leaned back in his chair and stroked his chin. "It wasn't the first wagon to burst into flames. No doubt you've heard reports of Fire Walkers attacking travelers or burning trees? I never believed that Fire Walkers were behind these attacks. It was unimaginable to me. You say they were instead the targeted victims... yes, I can imagine that. Rahn's Breath, you say? A Rhaesbond poison, was it not? Where would one get such a thing?"

If someone were trying to frame House Rhaesbond, then Rahn's Breath would be an effective way. The plant was thought extinct, but Jonan had brought a few seeds to Arlent, where it now thrived and grew wild. She didn't want to admit that to the Guardian of Gai just yet. Not when Prince Ravel seemed a fair more likely source. After all, the Prince had grown a small crop of Rahn's Breath from the peppers he stole from her room, and who's to say he didn't hide away a few seeds when brewing his poison?

She opened her mouth to blame the Prince, then closed it again. There were incidents of Fire Walkers burning out of control even before the Prince had poisoned his own people on the Solend, such as Prince Rais's injury... Could it be that the art of cultivating Rahn's Breath wasn't a secret that had belonged to House Rhaesbond alone? Alistar had recognized its flower from his books. She needed to ask him.

"I don't know how or where it's being grown, but we must

spread the word. Make sure your Fire Walkers check their food and water for Rahn's Breath. It has no taste except heat, but it smells like charcoal and smoke."

"We appreciate the warning. So now I will ask again: what are your orders regarding my Fire Walkers?"

He wanted to help the Fire Walkers—and had done so. She couldn't protect all the Fire Walkers alone. Jonan had said they needed allies. "Can they march to the Duslands?"

"But of course. The Emerald Path stretches west to Enais. Hana—Lady Enaibond—is an ally. She would grant them safe passage around the mountains. From there, they could find their way to Lune's Path, avoiding Oramar. And once they reach the Duslands, where then?"

"Arlent."

"Of course." He waggled a finger. "I knew Talin was planning something, though I am saddened I had to drag you all the way here to get it out of you. Those Houses who support Khaled—the King—they are your allies. You know which ones can't be trusted."

House Khalbond and the Solander ones, bar House Sarabond, but even then... Talin's dream made her wary of the Sword of Solus. "Send the women, the children, the old, and the lame. Ask for volunteers, any healthy young men, to stay behind. Some must reach Solus or the Prince will get suspicious."

He inclined his head. "It will be done. And I thank you for your trust. I will send my best men to oversee their protection. Would you care for more tea?"

Mina held up her cup and the Guardian of Gai filled it. As she sipped, its warmth filled her chest with sweet honey and something far more satisfying. Progress.

33

WILDFIRE

Mina found Alistar slouching on a stone bench, staring up the road north. If Fire Walkers were being targeted by Rahn's Breath, then her sorran could know who was growing it—and where.

"The western road heads to Gai's End and Enais, where Raj comes from, but north..." Alistar sighed. "That's my home. Myryn."

She sat beside him. "We don't have time to visit."

"I know." He ran a hand through his hair. "Did you speak with the Guardian of Gai? News from Solus travelled faster than we did, and the Council is none too happy with my House."

"Did something happen?"

"In a manner of speaking." His shoulders sagged further. "It's the Three-Pointed Star. They're rebelling."

"The who?"

"It's the name for the Neu Bosan council. We don't have a king like Sandair. Instead, each of the three main isles is run by an elected leader, and those three decide the fate of all Bosan."

A country not run by a king? "And that works?"

"For the most part. My father gets news from their council, but he doesn't tell me everything. In the past, Neu Bosa has always dispatched its navy in defense of Sandair against Hartnord raids. Well, not this time. The Three-Pointed Star is refusing to support the war effort." He laughed nervously. "It's remarkable, really. The Three-Pointed Star has *never* refused Sandair. Stars, I didn't think they had the guts to say no."

His words stirred uncomfortable memories. Talin had mentioned something like this in her dream. The Council depended on Neu Bosan ships to help protect Solus and the Ruby Coast from invading Hartnords. From what she'd read of the last war, Hartnords were good in the water in a way they weren't, but Neu Bosan were even better and their ships often helped shift the tide of battle. "Why now? Why won't they help us in our time of need?"

"Because they're cowards," came a caustic voice from behind her. Garr. He leaned against a lamp pole, eyeing Alistar with an appraising stare.

Alistar straightened up from his slouch. "It has nothing to do with cowardice."

Garr pulled an apple from his pocket and rubbed it down his shirt. "So let's hear it from a Bosan."

"You've heard the same news as I."

Garr bit into the apple and spoke with his mouth full. "And I drew my conclusion: cowardice."

"Or Neu Bosa finally decided to stand up for itself and refuse to bow to every demand Sandair makes."

"Bosan can't handle the heat. Shall I prove it?" Garr tossed the apple aside and positioned his fingers as though about to summon flame.

"Don't you dare!" Alistar leaped off the bench and marched up to Garr with a hand on his sword hilt.

Mina stepped between them and put her hand on Alistar's chest, pushing him back gently. "Will either of you explain?"

Garr smirked. "Neu Bosa has declined to offer their assistance against Hartnor whilst Fire Walkers are involved."

Alistar threw Garr a look of contempt and stepped back, though he didn't release his sword. "Are you surprised? Fire Walkers have always been used to threaten and control Sandair's neighbors, and don't forget it was a Fire Walker who started this mess. Neu Bosa doesn't want to risk its ships or men fighting side by side with people who burn. So long as Sandair continues to use Fire Walkers, the Three-Pointed Star will withhold support."

His words stung. Even the Neu Bosan didn't trust Fire Walkers. "Do you think we want to be used as weapons in war?"

"Stars, Fire Walkers have *always* been weapons in war. Why do you think Neu Bosa always takes Sandair's side in conflict? Out of fear! Two hundred years ago, they burned my people's sacred forest so badly that we've bowed to every demand by a Sandarian king since. And in the last war, they destroyed so many Hartnord cities that they turned their fear of Fire Walkers into a gods-damn religion."

She'd not read such deeds in her history books. They'd always framed the alliance between Sandair and Neu Bosa as mutually beneficial. Iman's words echoed in her mind: *Who wrote those history books?*

"Sounds like Hartnor and Neu Bosa would make natural allies," Garr said whilst tapping his chin. "Your people are one step from siding with the enemy, I'd say."

"Oh, like an Ash Maker knows anything about Neu Bosa or Hartnor to make such accusations," Alistar snapped.

"You act so righteous, demanding that Fire Walkers stand down, but your people have used Fire Walkers as weapons in the past. Go on, tell her about the slaves they keep in Neu Bosa."

Alistar cringed.

She crossed her arms. "They keep *slaves*?"

"No!" He tugged his braid. "It's not like that—"

"Then what, Ali? What?"

"In Neu Bosa, sometimes Fire Walkers agree to become servants under a contract. Only, those contracts aren't always fair or easy to get out of—"

"They prey on people who've fled to Neu Bosa with nothing," Garr said with an undisguised growl in his voice. "They offer them 'contracts' to work for rich families—contracts no one but the most wretched and desperate would ever sign. But in Neu Bosa, Fire

Walkers have no choice but to sign away their freedom or starve to death in the streets. It's slavery. All completely legal under the Three-Pointed Star."

"Have you been to Neu Bosa? How would you know—"

"No, I've not travelled there, but I've talked to Fire Walkers who've escaped it. I've seen their scars and heard their stories," Garr spat. "And so, Houseman, I have little respect for you and your posturing. There's nowhere safe for Fire Walkers in this world—Neu Bosa would enslave us, Hartnor would kill us, and Sandair falls somewhere in the middle. Whose side are you on?"

Garr's amber eyes shone with a fierce determination that awoke her inner embers.

He truly cared for the Fire Walkers. The first person she'd ever met outside House Arlbond to speak with such open defiance.

"I support her," Alistar said, his voice little more than a whisper.

"Because she's your master—"

"Because I choose to."

Despite Alistar's fears and discomfort with her fire, he'd remained by her side and travelled with her through the forests of Gaisland to help the Fire Walkers. To help her.

He'd done all that even though there was no sorran bond to compel him.

Because he was her friend.

She scowled at Garr. "Alistar is my sorran. I don't appreciate your attempts at turning us against each other." That's what his game was: to turn her friends and her Fire Walkers against her for whatever petty or sinister reasons.

"I wouldn't dream of it—"

"Good. I'd hate to think you'd disrespect your High Priestess."

Garr swept a low bow.

Alistar smiled in thanks. The relief in his expression made her stomach flutter. She didn't know enough about Neu Bosan culture to decide whether Garr's words held any truth to them. An issue she'd rectify once she returned to Solus. But Alistar had chosen her. He chose to support the Fire Walkers. That was good enough.

If Neu Bosa didn't want to support Sandair because they used Fire Walkers as weapons, then perhaps the Council could be convinced to withhold Fire Walkers from the front lines in exchange for Neu Bosan ships? Sandair *needed* ships more than blood fire. After all, in the heart of every Sandarian burned a warrior. A man without a sword couldn't call himself a man. And battle ran through their blood.

Lord Nazim walked down the stone steps of his mansion and waved her over. "Ah, there you are. Would like to meet your Fire Walkers, Lady Arlbond? I was about to make arrangements for their travel if you'll join me on the way."

"I'd be happy to."

Alistar stepped to her side, and Garr followed like a sulking fox cub with his tail between his legs. Together they strode with Lord Nazim through the markets toward the Temple of Rahn.

As they walked, a flicker of fire caught her eye. Tira waved from one of the market lanterns, as though trying to catch Mina's attention. She pointed to the market, away from the temple, where wagons were gathered around a stockpile of crates and barrels. Tira wouldn't have drawn her attention to them without good reason.

"What's over there?" Mina asked Lord Nazim.

He glanced where she pointed. "Oh, those? That's our first batch of supplies for the Ruby Coast. Food, grain, healing salves, all donated generously by the good Houses of Gaisland and organized by the Temple of Gai. It's how we've always supported our kingdom in times of conflict. The Solanders send their horses and steel, the Duslanders send their muscle, and we send food and potions to keep everyone happy and healthy."

She strode over to one of the wagons and examined it. Many were packed and ready to go. "Is this all of them?"

"Most of it. We had to gather the harvest early to fill them. There won't be much left once Lune's Shadow arrives."

"You're not worried raiders will loot them?"

"Not at all. They'll be travelling with an armed guard, including whatever Fire Walkers we'll spare." Lord Nazim nodded to where a group of Fire Walkers had gathered by the wagons. She was about to approach them when she spotted something purple—a purple glass bottle. The same as she'd drunk from on the Emerald Path.

The bottle was tucked into an open crate—one of several lined up next to a half-filled wagon. No one waited nearby. Nothing else in the crate seemed remarkable: a mishmash of cooking utensils, small spice jars, and bottles of grapeseed oil.

She lifted the purple bottle, popped the stopper, and sniffed it. Charcoal.

Lord Nazim chuckled. "If you're thirsty, Lady Arlbond, I'm sure we can procure more tea."

"Rahn's Breath." She passed the bottle to Lord Nazim.

He took a sniff and recoiled. "We checked all the food and water at your suggestion—"

"Where did these come from?"

"I have no idea. These crates are part of the batch from House Myrbond."

Alistar snatched the bottle and examined the bottom. "Do you have the shipping records, Lord Nazim?"

"Sort that out later," she said. "We need to search every crate for bottles like this one, before someone—"

Flame burst from behind one of the wagons. Mina gripped her sword hilt and ran for the Fire Walkers.

"Mina, stop!" Alistar called. He caught up to her and grabbed her arm. "Think! There are healing salves in those crates. Flammable alcohol! We need to get—"

A rattling boom and a *whoof* of heat burst through the air.

One of the wagons exploded in a storm of fire and wood. Alistar shoved her to the ground and lay on top of her, shielding her from debris. Garr ran toward the explosion, but a wall of fire burst around them, knocking him back.

Lord Nazim had summoned a shield of flame. It flickered and pulsed, as though battling against the elements beyond it. He roared and kept his shield intact.

"Did anyone see where the explosion came from? Was it—was it a person?" Mina called.

"I don't—" Alistar began to answer, but was silenced by another roaring explosion.

And another.

And a dozen more.

Lord Nazim waited until the last echoes of the explosions subsided and then his shield fluttered out. The taste of ash and death hung in the air. Alistar dragged himself off of her and hoisted her up.

She almost cried at the sight.

The wagons and crates were a smoldering heap of black ash and bright flame. Plumes of smoke twirled in the air and fell as black rain. The Fire Walkers and any other Gaislanders who'd stood nearby were gone. Burned to the ashes that fell.

Townsfolk screamed and ran.

Garr staggered to his feet. "How—how did this happen?"

Alistar smeared sweat and soot across his brow, staining his three silver star tattoos black. His face sagged. He'd never looked so terrified.

Lord Nazim was staring at his hands in shock. Both palms had been burned beyond mere blisters—white bone shone amid the pulpy flesh.

Oh gods. "He needs a Green Hand." She took his arm and gently steered him from the chaos. He said nothing, too numb for words, as she guided him to the Temple of Gai.

Raj came running out and reeled at the sight of Lord Nazim. "Oh Gai, what happened?"

"My men," Lord Nazim mumbled. "I must order—"

"I'll go to them. Let Raj help you." She passed Lord Nazim into Raj's capable hands and jogged back to the market.

The fleet of wagons had been utterly destroyed, and the flames continued to burn, stubborn even against Fire Walker magic and Water Bearers. Garr worked with them and helped lift debris to search for anyone trapped underneath, but no bodies were found.

No lives were spared. She flitted between piles of smoldering and flaming wreckage but discovered no trace of Shadows, and no purple bottles.

Twenty minutes later, Alistar found her slouched against the temple wall. "Those bottles came through Myryn from Neu Bosa." His voice dropped to a whisper. "I recognized the merchant's mark."

"Why would Neu Bosa grow Rahn's Breath?" What use would anyone have for it... other than to poison, expose, or kill Fire Walkers?

"Rahn's Breath is illegal in Neu Bosa because it's so dangerous... except for official use by the Three-Pointed Star."

"What do they want with it?

He grimaced. "To test Fire Walkers."

She crossed her arms. "Like you tested me." Back during their Academy days, he'd once tossed a dried Rahn's Breath pepper in her face in order to provoke a reaction. She'd almost forgotten the incident.

"We don't have priests with blood fire to perform tests like you, nor do we have the Sight of the Hartnords. We just want a means of protecting ourselves, that's all. Many Sandarians make their home in Neu Bosa. It's a precaution."

She wanted to scream at him. "How much of it do your people grow, and how is it controlled?"

He tugged his braid. "I don't know. Honestly, I don't. Rahn's Breath is a closely guarded secret. Even the black market traders won't touch it. I don't understand how it even reached these shores."

"But your House would know?"

"I don't know. We check every ship that comes through Myryn, and those bottles were marked as coming through our port. But there's no chance my House would purposefully allow it through. It would be a betrayal of the Three-Pointed Star. My father would lose all his business contracts and destroy everything he's worked for his entire life."

Mina turned to the wall where Tira waited within a lantern. Her mother looked grim. She'd known something was wrong. Perhaps she even knew the identity of those responsible, but Mina would have to wait until she was alone before she could question her mother.

If nothing else, she could at least be certain it wasn't Prince Ravel. Mina doubted his reach extended this far into Gaisland, much less into Neu Bosa—and he definitely wouldn't sabotage his own war effort by destroying these wagons. Someone else wanted to turn Sandair against its own people and cripple the kingdom as it marched to war.

Alistar leaned against the wall next to her. "If a Bosan is responsible for this, then I need to know. My father needs to know. It could damage our alliance, especially if the Three-Pointed Star is threatening to betray our treaties."

She nodded. She wouldn't report this to the Council yet, not with the Prince in charge in Solus.

Not until she'd discovered the truth.

They waited outside the Temple of Gai until Raj came with news. His green robes were smeared with blood and his curly hair flat with sweat.

"How is he?" she asked.

"He'll live. But he may never be able to wield a sword again."

Her heart sank. The Guardian of Gai had protected them, saved their lives, but at the cost of his hands and likely his title. "I hate to say it, but we can't return to Solus yet."

"What's our next step?" Alistar asked.

The trail led north. Talin had warned her not to go chasing shadows, but these couldn't be ignored. "Myryn."

34

MYRYN

Two days of riding north and Mina left behind the Emerald Forest for the shimmering turquoise waters of the Neu Inlet coastline. The thick woods turned to palm trees, and a salty sea breeze replaced the damp heat, though the curious insects remained. Alistar fidgeted in his saddle the closer they travelled to his home, and his nervous excitement infected her. Raj had elected to stay behind and care for Lord Nazim, and she'd dragged Garr with them against Alistar's protests. The remaining Gaisland Fire Walkers were still leaving for Arlent, and she didn't trust Garr not to get in their way and sabotage their efforts.

Garr hadn't complained of their sudden diversion north. If he'd wanted to murder her on this trip, he'd had ample opportunity. He'd seen her incompetence with blood fire, witnessed her fighting style. What was he waiting for? What was *she* waiting for? The real Garr. The one hidden behind that foolish smirk. Her Lunei instincts told her there was more to the Ash Maker than simply riling her friends.

Bronze boats bobbed alongside them. More dotted the horizon with a multitude of colorful sails. And before them on the coast, a marina the size of Solus came into view. It was like no Sandarian city Mina had ever visited. Because it wasn't Sandarian.

It was Neu Bosan.

Half of the city seemed to be built right on top of the Neu Inlet's waters. Unlike the stoic gray stone of Grenai or the comforting sandstone of Solus and Khalbad, Myryn's buildings and homes were made from wood and sat on thick, moss-painted stilts, allowing the inlet's waters to slosh underneath. But these weren't simple wooden shacks. Some were tall like townhouses, with rooves that curved with upswept eaves or pointed to the skies like the bow of a ship. Seashells of blues, yellows, and greens decorated the walls in mosaics of waves and stars. And in place of decorative Sandarian linens and pottery were netting, bunting, and green flags bearing the three-pointed star of Neu Bosa.

"It's not much, but it's home," Alistar said.

Mina gasped aloud. "It looks—"

"Flammable," Garr said.

Alistar scowled. "*You're* not setting foot anywhere near those buildings. Whilst we're here, you can stay in the Temple of Rahn."

"Why do I have to be locked away inside the temple?"

"Because it's made of stone."

Garr pointed to a building covered in bunting. "That's made of stone."

"That's a tavern."

"So? You're not in charge. She is." Garr turned to her with mock innocence. "Give me a bag of gold and I'll keep myself out of trouble, Priestess. I swear on my father's grave." He placed his hand over his heart and fluttered his eyelashes. "I stink of lavender and I'm itching in places no man should itch. I *need* a drink."

She rolled her eyes and dug a pouch of coins from her sahn. "One drink. Any trouble from you, and the Sword of Solus himself will hunt you down and decorate the Keep with your rotting head." She tossed a single sera into his outstretched hands.

Garr grinned and guided his horse to the tavern.

Alistar's stare followed him all the way. "Are you sure that's wise?"

"Would you rather he follow us to your home?"

"I'd rather you dropped him into the ocean."

They left their horses at the city stables and made their way through the crowds. To her surprise, there were some Gaislanders and Duslanders among the sea of Neu Bosan, mostly wandering the docks as shiphands. Some of the Neu Bosan wore the flamboyant tunics of bright mismatched colors that were apparently common in their homeland, though most wore modest clothes no different from the street rats of Solus and chose to show off their Bosan colors in other ways—mostly tattoos on their cheeks, chests, or arms in the shape of serpents or stars. Some had even painted their lips and nails a lime green, including the men.

Alistar led her north and the buildings grew in size and extravagance. Bronze plating covered some of them, like the boats, and the glass lanterns hanging over the streets weren't Sandarian in design. They passed Lune's temple, which was made of stones and far more generously decorated in silver stars than was customary. The Temple of Gai was covered in pink flowering vines across the entirety its stone walls, so much so that it looked like a tree.

"Where's the Temple of Rahn?"

"The lighthouse." Alistar pointed beyond the docks to a stone tower separate from the city. There were no signs to indicate who lived inside, but the top burned bright with flame. "The Fire Walkers keep it lit so that boats can reach shore safely."

She'd never known a lighthouse to act as a temple. Neu Bosan culture surely was different.

They approached a tall brass gate decorated in the banners of House Myrbond: lime green with a three-pointed star. The guards stationed outside were dressed in Sandarian scale armor, but carried the two-forked scimitar of Alistar's House.

The guards bowed as Alistar walked past and he led her into his home.

House Myrbond. The exterior of the mansion was a mixture of Sandarian sandstone and light brown wood, with etched bronze panels like the Neu Bosan boats. The effect was rather cozy. A wide pond separated them from the rest of the courtyard, with a wooden bridge leading to the mansion.

"Wait here," Alistar said. "I don't want to drag you inside if my brothers are prowling."

"Would it be so bad if I met them?"

"Yes. I'll be a moment." He jogged across the bridge and slipped inside the mansion.

She tucked her hands behind her back and peered into the pond. Golden fish the size of her arm swam in the shallows. Did Neu Bosan eat *these*?

Guards walked by on their patrols and ignored her. It felt like an hour before Alistar returned with a scroll clutched in his hand.

"My father's in residence, but he's entertaining some foreign guests. He's invited us to come back for dinner. Just us. No Ash Maker."

She tugged at her dirty sahn. "Like this?" She couldn't turn down an invitation from the ambassador, but she didn't carry any clean clothes.

Alistar's cheeks reddened. "We can visit the market and get you something more suitable if, uh, you'd like. Speaking of..." He waved the scroll. "I couldn't get into my father's private records, but I dug out a list of merchant marks. Those bottles? They came from an apothecary in town."

"This apothecary is smuggling Rahn's Breath?"

"Maybe. I doubt my father knows." He dug out a coin from his sahn. "Want to hit the stalls? My treat." He flicked the coin at her.

She caught it and smirked. "Lead on, Myrbond."

Alistar led her back to the docks. They pushed their way through the crowds of sailors returning home with their catch and tradesmen counting their coin. Neu Bosan families argued as they threw their belongings onboard ships, preparing for departure.

"They're leaving for the isles," Alistar said, following her eye. "No one wants to stay in case war reaches us, though it rarely does. There's a lot of Sandair to conquer before the Hartnords reach Gaisland, and their ships don't travel this far out."

The atmosphere relaxed as they passed the larger boats and

came to a busier section of the docks. Even Alistar wore an easy smile and exchanged welcoming nods with those he recognized.

Canal boats bobbed peacefully in the waters, tethered to the docks. Hundreds of them. So many that Mina couldn't see the inlet beneath. Some Neu Bosan sat atop their boats, either drying out linens or angling a fishing rod. Children hopped between the boats, chasing one another, and their laughter drowned out the gulls. Scents of mint tea and cooked fish rose from a nearby boat, and colorful windchimes clinked in the breeze. It was so Bosan it almost didn't feel like she was still in Sandair.

Some of the boats were floating market stalls with canopies to keep out the flies. These almost seemed like a Sandarian market, except they bobbed to the gentle sway of water underneath her feet. Most offered a range of fruit, fish, grain, and cloth, and a few displayed foods she didn't recognize.

"Is there not enough dirt around here to build a real market on?"

Alistar huffed a laugh. "Beware: my people are the best merchants in all Sandair. They'll sell your own boots to you. The apothecary is somewhere in the middle."

She shielded her eyes against the golden Rahnlight and squinted at the boats. "How do we get to it?"

"You hop."

"Between the boats? Are you serious?"

Alistar leaped onto a merchant boat selling green silks. He grabbed a railing to steady himself as the boat rocked in the water, but neither he nor the Neu Bosan merchant seemed to care. "See? It's easy."

Hunting rogue Fire Walkers across Gaisland was nothing compared to climbing from boat to gods-damn boat. She'd hated Dustan Hawker's boat back in Khalbad. The motion made her sick, and after she'd fallen off and almost drowned in the river, she held no desire to ever set foot on one of the floating deathtraps again. These boats were at least nestled so close together that the likelihood of drowning seemed slim, but the gods were surely testing her.

There were many times in her life when she'd felt truly

uncomfortable: begging for food in the Temple of Gai, riding whilst covered in filth the first time Talin took her to Arlent, dealing with her bleed, suffering the rains of Lune's Shadow, bowing before a certain pompous prince, receiving her Fire Walker tattoos, and this. This was one of those times.

Alistar held out his hand. "I'll keep hold of you."

Mina muttered a curse and grabbed his wrist. He hoisted her forward. The world shifted underneath her, but not like the shifting dunes of the Duslands. "Oh gods." She stumbled into him, grabbing onto his sahn.

He wrapped an arm around her waist. "You're fine."

"Don't let me go or I swear I'll gut you."

"You won the tournament and you're scared of boats?" The silver stars of his brows crinkled with bemusement.

"I can't fight a boat."

She kept a firm grip of his wrist as he led her across another boat that sold barrels of brown rice. This too bobbed underneath her feet and she chewed her tongue to stop herself from unleashing a torrent of curses that would make Samira blush. Children hopped by and giggled as Mina stumbled like a drunken noblewoman.

As they jumped between boats, Alistar tried to explain what each merchant sold: potted plants, tea leaves, ginger root, coconuts, duck meat, pork buns, shrimp, and a pungent fish broth that was popular on the isles, so he said.

On the next boat Mina rested against a wooden railing. "Give me a moment," she gasped.

"I could go back and get some ginger? That's good for sickness."

She tried to shake her head but gagged instead.

"Look." He pointed to the center of the marina.

The floating stalls were all centered around three statues of serpents painted red, blue, and green, each as tall as a man. The same imagery repeated throughout Myryn and even the Neu Bosan quarter of Solus. "They're Bosan gods, aren't they?"

Alistar's face lit up. "That's right. They guard the different oceans of the world: the sea, the starsea in the sky, and the sagesea of our forests. And others like the sandsea of Sandair or the snowsea of Hartnor. We named our town after the first, Myr."

His chatter was meant to distract her, and any other time she'd want to learn more, but it didn't help. The motion of the boats and the intensity of the overlapping colors and smells made her stomach churn. She stared over the railing at the water sloshing underneath them.

A darkness rippled across the surface that wasn't the natural swell of waves. Her inner embers stirred.

Shadows. There were Shadows under the boats.

Bodies lay at the bottom of the marina. They might have been sailors who died in shipwrecks or drowned by accident, though in a city as large as this, these poor souls could have been murdered and dumped where no one would find them.

She couldn't help these Shadows, not without learning how to swim and burn underwater. But her presence could rouse them into forming wraiths, and if that happened, the entire marina was in danger. Wraiths could rip apart these boats in a heartbeat. Nor could she summon her fire and risk burning down the entirety of Myryn. She hung at the edge of a storm ready to break.

"We need to find that apothecary *now*."

"It's only a few boats farther in."

There wasn't any time to worry about her stomach, not when she could be leading wraiths to Neu Bosan homes and merchants. She followed Alistar's lead and leaped to the next boat, and the next. Her boots slipped on the wood and the whole boat rattled.

Alistar grabbed her shoulder to steady her. "We're here."

The apothecary's boat twinkled like a glittering gemstone among a sea of wood and bronze. Glass bottles of every shape, size, and color filled the shelves or dangled from the roof. A counter stocked with more bottles filled the center—including the familiar purple ones.

Hidden behind them sat a short Neu Bosan man. Two round glass orbs covered his eyes, an odd contraption she'd never seen anyone wear before. His attention remained fixed on a bottle he was polishing with a dirty rag, and he didn't once look up at their arrival. Instead, he muttered a few words in his Neu Bosan language and continued his work.

"He says he doesn't speak Sandarian," Alistar translated.

"Convenient." She drew Hawk and thrust the tip of her blade over the counter. "Do you speak Sandarian now?"

The man squealed and dropped his bottle with a crash. "Yes, yes, I speak it!"

"What are you doing?" Alistar said aghast.

"We don't have time to be polite. There are wraiths under the boats."

"Wraiths? Stars above."

She kept her sword steady. "You sell Rahn's Breath. Who did you sell it to?"

The man gripped the edge of his counter and the racks of bottles clinked together. "I don't know what you're speaking of—"

"Rahn's Breath has been appearing in bottles with your merchant mark." She stepped forward and lifted the curve of her blade close to the man's cheek. "Who bought it?"

Alistar cursed and thumped his fist onto the counter. "Look, my Sandarian friend doesn't play games. A merchant as well stocked as you must keep records, and you know the penalty for smuggling illegal contraband." Then he spoke more words in Neu Bosan and flashed his sahn.

The man's eyes opened wide, which through the glass orbs, looked comically large. "Yes, yes, I sold it! I beg you, lower your sword."

Alistar nodded to her.

She sheathed Hawk. "Who did you sell it to? How many bottles? Spare no detail."

"I—I sold them to a Water Bearer. Six of them. No more."

Six bottles? "From the Temple of Lune? Are you sure?"

"Yes, yes. There's nothing odd about that. They regularly buy potions, though I hadn't seen her before. A young girl. New to the temple."

"Why would a Water Bearer need Rahn's Breath?"

"I don't question my patrons—"

"You just sell deadly poisons to Sandarians for coin?"

"No, no, it's not like that!" The man yanked up the glass orbs and rubbed his eyes. "It came into my stock by accident. I never ordered it, it's not worth the risk. I wanted rid of it. The Water Bearer, she said she'd escaped from the isles for a better life and was being hounded by a Sandarian master who owned her contract. She needed something to protect herself from him, so I sold her my stock. That's the truth of it." He turned to Alistar. "I sold it to her. No one else."

"I believe you," Alistar said. "But that doesn't make it right. These bottles have fallen into the wrong hands and caused harm. Why didn't you destroy them?"

The man sank behind the counter. "I needed to recoup my losses."

"Your losses!" she shouted. "People have been losing their lives—"

It was the sea that interrupted her, as if churned by her fury, and the boat lurched sharply. Water splashed over the side, and the blood bond tugged—not her House bond, but her inner embers, and the guiding hand of Lune urging her to reach out for the Shadows.

If a Shadow grabbed her here, it would likely drag her underneath the floating market and to her death. Even if she avoided its grasp, there were plenty of Neu Bosan trinkets to gather to itself and create a wraith, let alone the wooden planks of the boats themselves. She had many more questions for the merchant, and she wanted the satisfaction of watching the city guard drag him away after she'd gotten the answers, but that would have to wait.

"Ali, we need to go."

He didn't need to be told twice. He skipped from one boat to another and she did her best to keep up.

The water bubbled underneath them, causing the boats to sway. Some of the Neu Bosan hissed in their language with curses she didn't understand, but she didn't mistake their tone.

"I'd never picture a Water Bearer as a killer," Alistar said as he pulled her onto a fisherman's boat.

No, neither would she. "You think the seller was speaking the truth?"

"Definitely. I threatened to have my father withdraw his merchant contracts. If you want answers from a Bosan, threaten his livelihood, not his life."

"I didn't realize you were so ruthless, Alistar Myrbond."

He smirked. "Business is war."

War. The mere word was enough to ruin his smile.

The boats settled as they neared the boardwalk, and relief swept through her. Alistar made the jump first, landing on shore with practiced finesse. She leaped right after him.

A dark hand shot out of the water and grabbed her ankle.

Black mist swept over her eyes. She gasped and reached out for Alistar, but he was gone; the boats, the docks, everything had disappeared under a veil of black, and the cold grip at her ankle crept up her leg and straight to her heart.

Cold water rushed into my throat and lungs. I thrashed and sank my nails into his wrist, but he wouldn't let go. I couldn't breathe, oh Myn and Myr, he was killing me! My lungs burned and I gurgled a scream, but there was no air, no air, oh Myn, there was no air. He said nothing, nothing. The shimmering lights faded to black. Why did he do this to me? I gave them the bottles; I did what they wanted! I couldn't breathe, I couldn't feel–

Something wrenched Mina out of the darkness. Alistar. He'd pulled her from the Shadow's grasp. She collapsed against a crate, and the wood burst into flame at her touch.

"Stars above!" Alistar threw a discarded rug over the crate, smothering the flames until only a gasp of smoke remained.

She backed away from the boats and shoved shaking hands into her pockets. A funnel of water spurted between the gap, but no wraith crawled out. The farther from the boats she walked, the calmer the boats settled. "It was an accident; I didn't mean to—"

"What happened? You just—collapsed."

How could she explain that a dead spirit had spoken to her? Gods, someone had drowned a girl; drowned her and stolen the bottles. Mina had felt her last gasping breaths. For as long as she lived, she'd never set foot near water again. "I—I think I saw something in the water. A body. A young girl. It could be the Water Bearer."

"Stars. Should we go back and—"

"No!" She kept walking, not looking him in the eye. "The Temple of Lune. We should go there."

"I'll speak with the priestess. See if any of their girls are missing."

She steadied her breathing. Her blood pumped frantically after her encounter with the Shadow, but there was nothing she could do for the girl. Gods, they were so close to finding the truth.

"Well, what do we have here? A couple of street rats up to no good."

Garr leaned against a tall crate and tossed a dagger from hand to hand. He'd changed into gray leather pants, shiny black boots, a dark blue Neu Bosan tunic, and a gaudy bright purple cloak slung over his shoulder. He'd even found somewhere to wash his face clean of muck and grime and to comb his hair back. Dressed this way, he looked like any well-off city man, and not a wretched street rat.

She snatched his dagger mid-throw. "You spent my gold on clothes?"

"A better investment than ale, wouldn't you say, Priestess? It's easier to hunt information when you're dressed to play the part and have the coin to flash."

"And what information have you been hunting with my coin?"

Light danced in his amber eyes. "Valuable information."

Alistar snorted. "Likely which Bosan boats to plunder."

She shoved the dagger into her own belt. The thought of letting him wander around with a weapon didn't comfort her. "Just tell me what you learned."

Garr inclined his head. "A Hartnord ship sailed into port this morning. Your Housemen are keeping it quiet. Rather odd, considering we're at war." He gave Alistar a hard stare. "Why are Hartnords in Myryn?"

35

AN INVITATION

Dusk came by the time Mina returned to the Myrbond mansion. She didn't have time to buy suitable clothing. Instead, she'd turned to the Temple of Rahn and borrowed a priestess's robe—too long, of course, but it had to do. Garr pouted at being left behind. She'd dragged his sorry carcass to the temple and dumped him there, though not before buying him a bottle of ale and some smoked kippers to keep him out of trouble.

If what Garr said were true, Hartnords were on Sandarian soil and Alistar's father knew.

The brisk walk through Myryn helped calm her nerves. They said the Gaisland evening skies were the most beautiful, and as Rahn cast his golden light across the inlet, she had to agree. Myryn was a paradise. She breathed in the scents of spice and life and reached out with her thoughts down the blood bond. It responded with a rush of warmth and Talin's essence. Even though they were far apart, her father travelled with her, always.

Alistar waited by the mansion gate, dressed in the fine clothing he'd worn for Prince Rais's helbond ceremony. He'd brushed his hair back, his braid tucked behind his ear, though he must have rushed his bath for a smudge of dirt still smeared his cheek. "Welcome to my humble abode, High Priestess." He bowed.

She licked her thumb and wiped his cheek. "You're a scruffy cub."

"Yes, Ma." He stifled a giggle. "Do you like fish?"

"I hate fish."

"Good. That's what's for supper." He offered his arm.

She looped her arm around his and entered his home. The inside of the mansion merged Sandarian styles, with Gaisland rugs and pottery, Solander oak furniture etched with gold, and wooden Dusland windows to keep out pests. But the Neu Bosan influence was obvious, too: the pots held tropical flowers she didn't recognize and the tapestries were filled with Neu Bosan serpents and silver stars. A marriage of all cultures. Her heart ached at the thought. This would one day be Princess Aniya's home.

She slid free from Alistar's arm. He was her sorran and hanging onto him wasn't proper for the High Priestess, nor for a man betrothed to the Bright Solara.

"I visited the Temple of Lune on my way back," Alistar said. "They weren't keen on a man questioning them, but loosened up when they saw my sahn. Their priestess is a family friend."

"Learn anything about the girl?"

"The apothecary didn't lie. The Water Bearers said they had a new girl—Jade, she was called—and she went missing some weeks ago. They went to the guards, but nothing came from it. Eyewitnesses saw her speaking to a Duslander man a couple of times before she disappeared. They never found her."

"He killed her." And dumped her body in the marina where no one would find it. "The guards didn't hunt the Duslander responsible?"

"There's too many Duslanders working as ship hands. Whoever he is, he left no trace." Alistar's voice dropped as they approached a man waiting outside a doorway. His father.

The ambassador to Neu Bosa was dressed in a flowing beige robe and the lime green sahn of his House. He bowed with reserved politeness. "Lady Arlbond, welcome. My son speaks favorably of you."

She returned the bow. "I appreciate the invitation, Lord Myrbond."

"You may call me by my Sandarian name, Hiram. If you don't mind, I ask you remove your sword in my home."

No one ever asked a Sandarian to remove their sword, but perhaps Neu Bosa held different customs. She placed a hand on Hawk's hilt and paused.

"I assure you, you're safe here," Hiram added with his brows raised.

"It's fine," Alistar murmured.

She swallowed her unease and unbuckled her belt.

Hiram took the scabbard and placed it carefully on a marble table. "And your knives, if you will."

She bit back a retort and dug out both her mother's dagger and the one she'd snatched off Garr. The ambassador had sharp eyes.

"Many thanks. We're serving tea in the green room whilst we wait for our other guests to finish their evening prayers."

She exchanged a glance with Alistar and followed Hiram into a circular room made of glass. Some of the panes were open to allow in the evening breeze. Flowering trellises covered the glass ceiling and broke up the evening Rahnlight. A high dining table took up most of the space, surrounded by raised wooden chairs—not Sandarian cushions. Five white ceramic teacups had already been placed around the table, accompanied by a steaming pot of tea.

Hiram gestured to the table. "Be seated. It has been many years since we last hosted the High Priestess."

She tucked her robes under her and slid into a chair. "Leila came here?"

"To inspect the temple and ensure her Fire Walkers couldn't escape. Though my son informs me that you aren't here for the same purpose. The tea, Ali."

Without uttering a word, Alistar poured tea for his father and filled her cup.

"Fire Walkers are being poisoned by Rahn's Breath, Lord Hiram."

"And you believe these peppers are coming from Myryn? That's quite an accusation—"

"It's a fact. Rahn's Breath is being smuggled under your nose and falling into the wrong hands. Isn't your House responsible for checking merchant goods?"

Hiram lifted his cup and blew over the rim. "Illegal goods filter through the markets during wartime; we can't track every shipment when our docks are in chaos. Each day, more of our people leave for the isles. This problem will resolve itself."

No, the problem would get worse. The Water Bearer's murderer possessed as many as four more bottles. Perhaps fewer if he were responsible for more of the alleged rogue Fire Walkers' attacks. Perhaps more if he had other sources of Rahn's Breath as well.

The door creaked open and two pale-faced men entered.

Mina leaped from her chair, knocking it back with a crash.

Prince Wulfhart stood before her.

"Lady Arlbond. I'd hoped we would cross paths again, though not in such dire circumstances."

Her hand twitched to her hip. *This* was why Hiram made her leave her gods-damn sword behind!

"Why are you here?" Of all the people she'd imagined bumping into in Myryn, the prince of Hartnor was not among them.

Prince Wulfhart raised his palms in submission. "To negotiate."

"What's there to negotiate? You murdered our queen."

"You murdered my father, but we had nothing to do with your queen's death. Would I risk travel to your kingdom if so? I come here unarmed in good faith. Look in my eyes and see I speak true."

His silver eyes were soft. Not menacing. He wore a simple blue tunic and carried no sword, nor a dagger at his waist or boots as far as she could tell. His companion stood a few inches taller and came unarmed, too, though there was something unnerving about him; his head and face were shaved bare, like a Fire Walker, and his eyes shone a bright sapphire.

Hiram placed his cup down. "Be seated so we may discuss this calmly."

"Does the Council know of your invited guests, Lord Hiram?"

"The Council is rushing to war without knowing the facts and demanding the Three-Pointed Star act on blind faith. My intention is to prevent unnecessary bloodshed. Something I believe we have in common, High Priestess. Sit, Ali."

Alistar sank into a chair and looked as bewildered as she felt. She righted her chair and sat, her gaze pinned on the Prince.

"The Council believes you are responsible for Queen Vida's death."

Prince Wulfhart and his companion sat across from her. "Whatever you think of me and my people, you cannot believe me cruel enough to murder a female carrying a child. I did not sanction such an order, and I could not believe my ears when I heard of it. I held my own investigation, my lady, in case someone thought to act in my name, but found evidence of no such crime. I prayed to my god, and his insight points south. To Sandair. We did not do this."

"We also looked into this matter," Hiram said. "The poison which murdered the Queen is called Lotus Bud." He slid a cup of tea across the table to her. "It's a Neu Bosan contraceptive taken by women throughout the isles. In Hartnor, it's illegal but still available to certain privileged families. Recently, it has become more common in Sandarian markets. They use it in the Temple of Lune, I believe."

Another nod to the Temple of Lune. She picked up her tea and gave it a quick sniff. Honey. Nothing smoky to suggest they'd brought her here to poison her, at least.

"My lord, I must correct you on one point," Prince Wulfhart said. "It is true our family used Lotus Bud in the past, but no longer. These days, it is not only against our law, but our faith also forbids its use. I say again: we did not poison your queen."

Mina leaned back in her chair. "Someone did."

"Someone who wants to drag our nations into war," Hiram said. "The Three-Pointed Star believes neither king would allow this war if the truth were known. And so, they do what they can to slow Sandair's rush to battle. As does House Myrbond."

"We too are hesitant," Prince Wulfhart said. "I was but a child seventeen years ago when Sandarian warriors last invaded our lands, but I read the accounts. We were all but defenseless against your fire magic. You could decimate us at any time, and our kingdom continues to exist only at the whim and mercy of whoever sits on the Sandarian throne. I have no desire to see my people burned and my kingdom destroyed." He studied her from across the table. "When we last spoke, my lady, you were adamant to paint your kin as innocent, yet it was one of your kin who killed my father. And now our host tells me you represent them as their leader. If Sandair invades my home, would you march on our cities and set them alight?"

"The Fire Walkers don't want to be used as weapons, Prince Wulfhart, I didn't lie about that. But the Council has given us no choice. I became high priestess to protect them, to prevent bloodshed wherever possible. But *you* threatened us with war."

"My father burned in front of my eyes. Can you forgive my clouded judgment? We came to Sandair because we were promised safety. The keepers of my faith warned my father of the dangers, but he did not heed them, nor did I. And when he burned before me...

"I admit I sought revenge, but revenge will only hurt my people. By this winter, I will be crowned the new king of Hartnor, and these decisions—and consequences—rest on my shoulders. I do not wish to begin my reign on a throne of ash, my lady." He stared Mina in the eye, not with judgment or fear, but with reserved concern. "Now your people won't listen to reason. They blame me for a sin I did not commit. Will you help me stop this war before it begins?"

Could there be a way to stop war?

No one in this room wanted Fire Walkers thrust into battle. But even if she could convince both kingdoms to back down, Fire Walkers would remain locked away, enslaved, and dragged into Sandair's next war whenever it may come. They needed more than that. They needed kings who saw them as people.

Perhaps if Prince Rais and Prince Wulfhart worked together, they stood a chance.

She leaned over the table. "Would Hartnor recognize Fire Walkers as free men? I can't support any king who would see them as less."

"So long as your kin burn freely, my people will fear them. We cannot abide to live in the shadow of a hostile neighbor who could destroy us at any time. But we may have a solution to that problem, my lady." He nodded to Hiram.

Hiram rang a tiny bell. A Neu Bosan servant entered, carrying a small wooden box. She placed it on the dining table, then lit glass lanterns around the room to ward off the dark. Tira appeared in a flickering lantern, her face taut with worry.

"If you will, Falkner?" Prince Wulfhart gestured to his companion.

The man with the sapphire eyes—Falkner—pulled a glass jar from the box, placing it on the table for the room to see. Something dark squirmed inside.

Leeches.

"Is this a trick?" Mina moved her stare from Prince Wulfhart to Hiram. "Do you know what these are and what they do?"

"Father?" Alistar pressed.

Hiram raised his hand. "I know what they are—"

"Your great plan is to force leeches on Fire Walkers? Is that it?"

"That would be impractical," said Hiram. "Leeches are native to our jungles; we understand them and their applications. My people have used them in the past to cure illness, and it is through our medical experimentation that we discovered their ability to suppress a Fire Walker's magic—"

"It was your people who invented them?"

"Discovered them, yes. And we gave them to the Bright Solara. We use them ourselves, as well. But they are not without limitation. Our greatest minds have studied their effects and narrowed it down to a particular toxin in the leech's saliva. We believe this toxin can be extracted."

"Meaning what?"

Prince Wulfhart pulled a tiny silver vial from his pocket. "Meaning, my lady, we can create a potion which blocks your fire magic, in much the same way Lotus Bud can be used to prevent conception. I call it Lune's Tears."

Such a potion could render blood fire inert. She sank back into her chair. "What do you plan to do with it?"

"My people want all Sandarians tested and those with fire magic to be locked away forever. There are some on your Council who want the same, do they not? But I believe there can be compromise. You do not wish to see your kin locked away or hurt. Lune's Tears can offer you freedom. With this, your kin will be prevented from using their magic, and my people will feel safe in that knowledge."

Fire Walkers wouldn't need to be locked away in the temple because they would no longer be a threat to themselves or others. Nor would they be forced to serve as slaves in war or peace. They'd be ordinary men. Free.

She glanced to her mother, who stared back, frowning. Using a potion to suppress blood fire didn't feel right. It didn't feel... natural. "Is it safe?"

"We've tried it on our own people. I can verify it is safe to ingest, but we cannot test its intended properties. We need your help, my lady. We need people with fire magic so we can refine the correct dose and its effectiveness."

She recoiled. "You want me to sacrifice Fire Walkers?"

"Not sacrifice. We mean them no harm. Hopefully, the potion can be refined quickly and safely. Then, the keepers of my faith will agree to end this war."

"They're your people, Prince. *You* tell them to end this war."

"Whilst your kin threaten to burn our homes, I can do no such thing. Our reports state your fire magickers are out of control and burning your own people—"

"They were poisoned—"

"Which is exactly why we need this potion," Hiram said. "If

someone *is* poisoning Fire Walkers, then Lune's Tears is the antidote."

Hiram had a point. There was no telling how much damage Rahn's Breath could inflict if someone meant Fire Walkers harm.

But was this Lune's Tears truly the solution? She couldn't think of a suitable counter argument and instead pulled at a stray thread on her robe.

"We all have much to consider," Hiram said. "The night is drawing, and you must be famished from your travels, Lady Arlbond." Hiram rang his tiny bell and the servant returned, balancing a large tray filled with bowls. She placed a steaming bowl with a repugnant smell in front of Mina. Silver scales floated in a thick brown sludge with vegetables. If she weren't sitting in the company of a foreign prince and ambassador, she'd kick Alistar where it hurt.

The servant placed wooden spoons and bread onto the dining table. Alistar snapped his bread in half, but paused when his father tutted in irritation.

Hiram bowed his head in prayer. "We give thanks to Gai and Mya for this bounty, and we pray that Rahn and Myr offer us guidance in these trying times."

Prince Wulfhart, with his hands clasped together, added more words. "We ask the Keepers of Light to guide us on the correct path."

The Prince and Hiram glanced to her. She didn't know any suitable prayers for the present company. "Lune guide us," she murmured.

Hiram tapped his bowl with his spoon. "Eat. We have plenty to spare."

Alistar shoved his bread into the bowl and scooped out a lump of fish with the eagerness of a starving man. Hiram ate with more dignity. Prince Wulfhart swallowed tiny polite mouthfuls, his silver eyes watching her.

She stared down at the sludge. The smell alone made her gag, but the Prince's potion and the leeches still sitting on the dining table stole her appetite.

"Are you eating, my lady?" the Prince asked.

A mouthful wouldn't kill her, with Lune's luck. She forced a smile and scooped the least offensive thing she could find, a carrot, and popped it in her mouth.

Only then did she spot Tira waving her arms and yelling a soundless warning.

The broth clinging to the carrot tasted saltier than sand and a cold jolt shuddered down her spine. The spoon almost slipped from her grip, and she placed it back down with polite restraint. "Forgive me, Lord Hiram, but my stomach is unsettled from my travels. And I must return to the Temple of Rahn and speak with the Fire Walkers."

She rose from her chair. Alistar hurried a mouthful to join her.

Prince Wulfhart stood. "I'm grateful we had this moment to speak, my lady. Time is against us. Return with me to Harvera, the heart of my kingdom, and you may oversee testing of Lune's Tears yourself. Help me bring peace to your people and mine." He held out his hand.

She gawked at him. "You want me to travel to Hartnor with you?"

"I have a ship docked at our host's private pier. Come and meet my people. Together we can prevent this war. I give you my word, and my trust."

Mina glanced to the lantern. Tira shook her head with a resounding *no*.

"That's—that's a generous offer, Prince Wulfhart, but my people need me here, and this is something we should bring to the Council—"

"No." Hiram's spoon clattered into his empty bowl. "I tried to reason with the Council and they dismissed me. I mean no offence, Lady Arlbond, but they have little respect for either of us. We must act alone, confirm this potion works, and bring our proposal to the King once he recovers."

If he recovers.

Prince Wulfhart's hand dropped to his side. "Whilst we make pleasantries, our people prepare for war. Many of your kin will die, and even more of mine. Or you could lead them to a future where they are no longer seen as monsters."

"The Three-Pointed Star supports this research," Hiram said. "They no longer wish to be threatened with Fire Walkers, either. Surely you must understand that this is in the best interest of you and your people, High Priestess?"

Preventing war. Ending the oppression of her people. The chance to live normal lives, to be normal people... It sounded too good to be true. So why did it make her insides squirm?

"Should you offer Fire Walkers this potion, would you demand everyone use it? Even those trained, such as priests? And what of those who refused?"

Prince Wulfhart inclined his head. "You once said it yourself: your kin would give up their power if they had the choice. The question is, would Sandair be willing to relinquish its power over its neighbors?"

Alistar made a non-committal sound.

She glanced to him. He'd not made a single comment all meeting. "Ali?"

He shifted in his seat, not quite meeting her eyes. "If you could give up your fire, wouldn't you?"

Prince Wulfhart studied her face, waiting for her answer, but what would a Hartnord or Neu Bosan know about blood fire? If she were still Malik, she would have gladly given up her fire in exchange for peace of mind.

But now, after joining the Temple of Rahn and training with Jonan? She'd begun to see her fire as a part of herself. In all honesty, she enjoyed the thrill of her power, of the heat in her blood. To never feel that again would leave her blood cool. Bereft.

Rahn gave them this gift. Could she force her people to give it up?

But could she condemn them to dying in a pointless war?

Prince Wulfhart had put her into an impossible position, with an impossible decision that she couldn't make. She needed Talin or Iman for this. Even Jonan. Gods, *anyone* more competent than her. What would Leila choose?

To take this potion and force it on the Fire Walkers, no doubt.

In the right hands, with the right control, Fire Walkers could save lives. *I am the master of my own self, never forget.*

Tira was shaking her head.

She knew something. The truth.

"Hartnor will act with or without your blessing, my lady," the Prince said. "The sooner you realize that this is the only chance of peace between our peoples, the more lives will be saved. My ship leaves tomorrow at dawn. I pray you make the right choice."

36

A QUESTION OF TRUST

As impressive as the Temple of Rahn in Myryn appeared from the outside, it left little space inside. Only a handful of Fire Walkers occupied the few rooms built into the lighthouse, and they needed to remain in the city to guide the many boats sailing through. The temple's main sanctum held a single burning brazier in the center, nothing else, and unlike the pyramid in Solus with its underground tunnels, here the staircase went up to the stars, not down.

Garr sat cross-legged beside the brazier and picked his nails. "Out for a romantic stroll? I was starting to worry you'd been kidnapped by Hartnords."

Alistar crossed his arms and scowled. Mina was in no mood for their petty arguments. She sank into the sand covering the sanctum floor—sand from the inlet beaches, not the Duslands. Hiram had offered her a room in the Myrbond mansion, but she'd not wasted another second in his presence. She didn't need a chaperone, but Alistar had insisted on escorting her and bought them both steamed pork buns on the walk back. Better than his father's salty fish broth.

"What happened?" Garr shuffled closer. "You look like you've seen the dead."

"We met Prince Wulfhart."

"The Prince? Here?" He shot a glance to Alistar. "You Bosan are jumping in bed with the Hartnords quicker than I imagined."

"We're not jumping in bed with anyone!" Alistar leaned against the temple wall and hit the back of his head with a *thunk*. "Stars above, I don't even know anymore. What in Myr's name is my father thinking? If the Council learns of this..." He rubbed his neck and grimaced.

"What did Wulfhart want?" Garr asked.

She rubbed a hand down the full length of her face. "He says he and his people had nothing to do with the Queen's murder."

"And you believe him?"

"I don't know." As soon as she was alone, she'd confirm Prince Wulfhart's testimony with her mother. "He has a potion. A method of suppressing blood fire. He wants to test it on Fire Walkers. He... he wants me to travel to Hartnor with him at dawn."

Garr studied her with a wary expression, as though meeting an enemy on a battlefield. "So you're going to force this potion on Fire Walkers. Is that it?"

"Course I'm not. But if what he says is true, his potion could stop this war. Would you give up your blood fire if you had the chance? If it meant you could live a normal life and not be seen as a weapon to be wielded by Housemen? To not have your friends look at you like—like you're a monster?" She glanced to Alistar and met his emerald eyes. "Fire Walkers should be given the choice whether to give up their fire or not. I'm obligated to try, aren't I?"

Garr made a disgusted sound. "Are you?"

"I'm the High Priestess. The safety of the Fire Walkers—their future happiness—is my responsibility."

"Even me, Priestess?"

"Even you."

He smiled, but the usual mirth that lit up his eyes had faded. "So, let me guess. Neu Bosa supports Wulfhart's potion? With that, they'd have even greater control of their slaves."

"Yes, it's about control," Alistar scoffed. "Or maybe it's so Fire Walkers have greater control over themselves? You don't know what it's like to worry that everyone around you could burst into flame at any—"

"That's what your people fear, isn't it? That the scary Fire Walkers will burn down your homes and children. Why do you hate them so much?"

Alistar bristled. "I don't hate them—"

"Fear, hate, it all leads to the same consequences—"

"*These* are the consequences." Alistar lifted his shirt and exposed his scars. "This is what happens when a Fire Walker loses control of their power. I was burned for my helbond by a Fire Walker I trusted—"

"Did becoming a man make you less of one?"

"See? You can belittle me all you like, and what can I do about it? You could burn me in a heartbeat. What defense do I have? Not even those Hartnords in their armor could protect their king. And you don't see why people fear you?"

"I used to fear blood fire," Mina croaked, her voice suddenly dry. "I hated it. But I've not used my fire to hurt anyone, Ali."

"Would you, though? Would you use your fire to attack someone?"

To attack someone? No. To defend herself? She'd sooner depend on her sword before the power in her veins. There was nothing honorable about burning a man in a one-on-one duel. And she couldn't be certain she'd be able to wield her fire with the same precision and control as her blade. "I've no intention of burning homes or children. I've never met a Fire Walker who does."

Alistar ran trembling fingers through his hair. "Even if you've no intention to, there's still a risk you could hurt your friends and family."

He still feared her, and that realization hurt like a punch to the gut. So long as she possessed blood fire, he'd never trust her. They'd never be Ali and Arl again. "You want me to go with Prince Wulfhart? You—you want me to take his potion?"

"Stars, Mina, they're your people. You decide what to do with them." He pushed from the wall. "I need to speak with my father. I'll be back at dawn." He slid out of the sanctum before she could say anything, but what could she say?

306 | TRUDIE SKIES

Her shoulders sagged and she ran her hands through the sand grains beneath her, letting them filter between her fingers. Gods, she missed Arlent and the sands of her home more than ever. Fire Walkers had enjoyed only a few weeks of freedom before being forced into a cage again. In those brief weeks, she'd felt *free*. For the first time, Jonan was teaching her how to master her abilities, not just ignore them.

Could she give that up? Was it selfish to hope for more?

"You don't want to join Wulfhart." Garr spoke so softly she barely heard him. "Believe me, Priestess, that is the last thing you want."

"And you would know that how?"

"Because your Bosan speaks true. The Hartnords are fanatics. They're devoted to their god, and that god hates us for the power we possess. Sandarians are rarely allowed in Hartnord cities, and only if they covert to their religion—denouncing blood fire, undergoing painful tests, and participating in barbaric rituals to *atone* for the sin of tainted blood." He scrunched his nose. "Those who fail are executed. Those who pass... They flee if they have any sense."

She'd not heard of Sandarians being treated that way, but there were few Hartnords in Sandair to ask. Just Gareth, and he'd abandoned his kingdom after Princess Aniya's death. Gods. Aniya had been killed for possessing blood fire. "You know a lot about Hartnords for an Ash Maker."

"What can I say? I keep my ear to the ground. When someone's got a knife at your back, it pays to know who's wielding it. Speaking of which, can I have my dagger?"

"The one you bought with *my* gold?"

"For my protection. You may have noticed there are Hartnords on the loose."

"That's what your blood fire is for."

"Oh, so now you admit our fire magic is a weapon?"

"It's not a weapon, and I'm not giving you one, either." She glanced to the wall where Alistar stood moments before. "You can't speak of this to anyone. It could endanger lives."

"Who'd believe a street rat like me?" He removed his purple cloak and spread it out beside the brazier. "Sleep easy, Priestess."

"You're sleeping here?"

"I'm no stranger to dirty floors. The Fire Walkers here may have offered up a room for you, but I'm no high and mighty priestess and so I've got to make due on my own."

"You could sleep with me."

Garr quirked a brow. "And break your vows?"

"I meant *sleep*, you oaf. You know what, never mind. I'm getting some air." She ignored his stifled giggling and strode up the curved steps leading to the top of the tower. No one stopped her as she went up and up, and she emerged out onto the roof to face a fire as bright as Rahn.

The bronze brazier in front of her was as big as a wagon and its flames rose to the height of five men. But to her surprise, the night air was cool and gentle; the fire's heat and smoke drifted off to the stars.

She pulled her collar close to ward off the chill. Tira waited for her in the fire, as large as life. Gods, it was good to see a friendly face. "Can you see Talin right now? And Iman and Jonan? Are they safe?"

Tira smiled and nodded.

Mina rolled her shoulders and loosed a breath. Thank Lune that Tira could watch over them. "You saw what happened at dinner. Prince Wulfhart said he didn't murder the Queen. Is he speaking the truth?"

Tira shrugged.

That wasn't the answer Mina expected. Speaking to her mother through the fire was a gift, but a damn annoying one at times because the gods couldn't allow them to communicate properly. "You don't know?"

Tira covered her eyes and pointed at Mina.

"You didn't see what happened to the Queen because you were watching me?"

Tira nodded.

At the time of the Queen's murder, Mina had been talking to Prince Rais. Of course her nosy mother would have been more interested in *that* conversation. Mina chewed her thumb. If Lotus Bud was available at markets across Sandair, it increased the number of suspects. She'd thought it odd that Prince Wulfhart would get his revenge in such a crass manner, but what if the assassin framed the Hartnords? What would they gain?

War.

A massacre of the Fire Walkers.

The death of an unborn Solaran prince.

And the likely death of King Khaled.

This had Prince Ravel's name scrawled all over it, but she had no way to prove it. He'd threatened his father in the tournament; who was to say he hadn't planned this war to force his father's early abdication? Was the Prince monstrous enough to murder his own mother? He certainly had a skill for poison.

The Prince had sent her all the way to Gaisland for a reason. What horror was he planning with her out of the way? "Someone is poisoning Fire Walkers. It's not a rogue Rhaesbond, is it?"

Tira shook her head.

"A Duslander murdered a Water Bearer. He's got Rahn's Breath. Is he working for Prince Ravel? The Hartnords?"

Tira shrugged. If not them, then who? Mina wasn't asking the right questions. "Is Saeed in the fire? Can I speak to him?"

Tira bobbed her head in a series of nods and shakes which Mina interpreted as yes, he was in the fire, but no, he couldn't speak for whatever reason. Perhaps because she could only commune with other Lunei or those she shared blood with, such as her mother and uncle. Mina rubbed her head. This was going nowhere. "Should I go with Prince Wulfhart at dawn?"

Tira shook her head with such force it blurred through the flames.

"I don't know what to do. This could prevent war. That's worth trying, isn't it?"

Tira wore a sympathetic smile and placed a hand over her

heart. Her eyes said, *trust yourself.* There was so much she needed to ask her mother, but a pang of guilt caught in her chest. "It feels like I only talk to you when I'm in trouble and need something. I should let you enjoy your afterlife."

Tira covered her mouth with an exaggerated yawn.

"You're saying the afterlife is *dull?*"

Tira laughed with soundless joy and nodded.

How could the afterlife be dull when all the great Sandarian heroes were there? The first kings like King Solus and King Shahsahan, and the first heroes like Malik the Merciless? Just what trouble was her mother getting up to in her death? "One last question. There's an Ash Maker called Garr. Can I trust him?"

Tira pursed her lips together and made kissing motions.

"*Mother,* this is serious!"

Tina winked and faded from the flames.

"Who are you talking to?"

Mina spun around. Garr stood by the stairs with his purple cloak wrapped around his shoulders.

"Myself. I, uh, I talk to myself when I need to think."

"Your nose twitches when you lie."

She rubbed her nose.

"Now I know you're lying." He grinned and glanced over her shoulder to the brazier. "Is that normal?"

Gods, he hadn't seen Tira? "Is—is what normal?"

"To feel drawn to the fire. Is it a Fire Walker thing? Or a Sandarian thing?"

It was an odd question, but Garr was an odd man. There was so much she didn't know about him, and much he didn't seem to know about his own people. She summoned a single flame in her palm and it danced in the wind. "Those who grew up in the shadow of Housemen were taught to fear fire... and fear those who cast it. So many of us suppressed our urges and ignored our calling to the fire. But it's always been there. It's part of me whether I like it or not." Not just a part of her; using her power felt good. It felt *right*.

Was taking pleasure in it so wrong?

Garr's amber eyes examined her flame, not with fear or disgust, but… awe. "You carry the sun inside of you. Why be afraid of that?"

The sun? "You mean Rahn?" She closed her fist shut on her flame and it burned back into her skin.

"Rahn. Right. Been spending too much time around Bosan." He sniffed his collar. "Starting to smell like one, too."

"Why do you hate Bosan?"

"I don't hate them. I'd sooner share ale with a Bosan than a Hartnord."

She placed a hand on her hip. "Then why are you such an insufferable mule? You've done nothing but antagonize my friends and rile up my Fire Walkers since the moment you first stepped foot in the temple."

"I don't like snotty nobles and haughty priests who think they can order around the rest of us." He tugged the cloak tight over his shoulders. "Your Bosan friend says Fire Walkers hold all the power, but his people aren't locked away in the temples and forced to eat horse feed. If Fire Walkers held real power, your precious Keep would be nothing but rubble."

"Is that your game, Ash Maker? Treason?"

He leaned forward with a glint in his eyes. "Isn't it yours?"

"Why would you assume that?"

"You bow to your King's whims and lock the Fire Walkers away whilst proclaiming to protect them, and then you travel halfway across your kingdom to bed with the Hartnords. At first, I thought you were another noble singing a pretty tune whilst lining your own pockets, but now… now I think you're more ambitious than that."

She stared at him. "Are you serious? My House is the smallest on the Council. What ambitions do you think we have?"

"A small House need grow, by fair or foul. Why else would a noble volunteer for the priesthood? What do you gain, *Lady Arlbond*? Power or gold?"

He couldn't honestly believe her House was protecting the Fire Walkers to gain status? "You're the biggest fool of the temple.

I became High Priestess to protect them. Everything I've done is for them! I fought against Prince Ravel in the tournament for them. I gave up the chance of wearing a crown for them! If I wanted gold or power, *that* would have been the path I chose, not to ride through a gods-damn forest with *you*."

He looked puzzled. "A crown?"

"You know nothing about me or my life. I've watched children get cut down for their blood fire. I witnessed my own uncle's death. I've seen Housemen use their status to hide their blood fire whilst condemning the rest of us who survive on the streets—"

"What would a lady understand about surviving on the streets? What would you know of cold and hunger?" He snorted. "Survive on the streets indeed!"

"You think I was born into this life? I was adopted into House Arlbond. Before then, I lived in a rotting shack and worked for whatever scraps I could. So don't you dare tell me I don't understand what it's like."

"You're a street rat?" he blurted out. "You're not a lady?"

"Do I look like a lady? It doesn't matter who or what I used to be. I'm the High Priestess of Rahn. And if you're planning on harming my Fire Walkers, it won't end well for you." The High Priestess. She wanted to laugh. If only her Uncle Dustan could see what she'd become.

"But you—you *dance* with a sword. That's not how a street rat fights."

"It's called sand dancing. It comes from my tribe. Surely an Ash Maker would know it?"

"Not me. Is this why they call you the Sword Dancer?"

"Sand Dancer. That's my title and don't you forget it." Everyone was so quick to call her a *lady* or *priestess*, yet they forgot the real title she'd earned for herself. All because she was *Mina* now instead of *Malik*.

"Then I was right."

"About *what*?"

"Your ambitions." He unraveled his cloak and tossed it at her.

"It's cold up here, Sword Dancer. Don't go wasting your blood."
He winked and headed down the stairs.

What had just happened? Had she finally gotten through to him?
She caught Tira watching her in the lighthouse's flame. Her
mother was giggling silently.

"He's a fool, you know."

Tira nodded and vanished once more with a grin.

Why did her mother trust an Ash Maker? And why, Lune help
her, did she trust the fool too? She wrapped Garr's cloak around
her shoulders and snuggled into the warm folds he'd bought with
her coin.

Come dawn, Prince Wulfhart would expect her. Another prince
who wanted to eliminate or control her people, as Garr had said.
Could Lune's Tears suppress blood fire? Was it right to try it?
Alistar thought so, but Alistar didn't understand the call and
pleasure of flame. But he was right about one thing: blood fire was
a responsibility.

Many would long for a potion that could take that responsibility off their shoulders.

How many? Enough to satisfy the Hartnords and prevent a war?

And what awaited those who insisted on keeping Rahn's Gift?
A life of freedom in Arlent, perhaps. Or would that just bring the
armies of three nations marching on her home?

She wouldn't find her answers in Myryn. The truth waited back
in Solus.

The Fire Walkers needed her. All of them.

Even an amber-eyed street rat.

Part Three

The Rogue and
the Wolf

37

AN APOLOGY

A pale-faced fool bumped into me. I almost drew my dagger. He stepped back with a hurried bob of apologies. "Forgive me, gentle lady. Do you know the way?"

The Hartnord spoke in broken Sandarian, his accent thick and with a slur like after a few glasses of wine, but I understood enough to point him down the corridor. He could well be drunk for the state of his tussled golden hair and the creased clothes he'd hastily thrown on. The sorry bastard skittered down the hall and glanced over his shoulder like a frightened rabbit.

Chuckling echoed behind me. The Princess leaned against her doorway, wearing nothing but a silk nightgown, her legs and feet bare. "I wasn't expecting you this early."

"It's mid-afternoon, my Princess."

"So it is. Come in then." Princess Aniya waved a bare arm, inviting me into her quarters. I was about to ask whether she'd prefer to get dressed first, but she poured two goblets of red and sat on the lounger, her slender legs crossed. I took my cup and swallowed a hasty gulp to stop myself from staring.

Gods, she was breathtaking. The most beautiful woman in all Sandair. She'd turned down every suitor that came begging at her feet, and I'd hoped she was my kind of woman. But no, it seemed our princess held a taste for pale men.

"You'll be the death of that man," I ventured.

She grinned that smug look only a Solaran could muster. "You're rather forward, Lady Arlbond."

"Iman, if it please you, my Princess."

Her amber eyes gleamed. "Then call me Anni and let us speak plainly. I do tire of politics. Have you met my nephew? He's a charming little boy. He's already won the Council over, even those that cursed his birth. At least Ravel will grow up without worrying about killing his brothers." She took a sip from her wine. "Listen to me ramble like an old spinster. Becoming an aunt has aged me. Are you likely to be joining me soon?"

"Talin's duties keep him from his marriage bed, though Tira doesn't want children yet. Not until she's entered the Academy." I raised my brow in question.

Princess Aniya sighed. "And so we return to politics, as if I could ever escape it. I'm afraid I don't bring joy. My dung-headed brother won't listen to reason. He won't allow either you or Talin's wife entrance."

That wasn't a surprise. I'd hoped Princess Aniya could convince the King, but if neither she nor Talin could, then that was that.

"I do have one idea." The Princess traced a finger around her goblet and her bloodstone ring caught the Rahnlight. "I could offer to marry Prince Garet in exchange for certain concessions."

I choked on my wine. "Marry a Hartnord?"

"Oh, come now, he's not that unattractive. Khaled will see the potential in a marriage between our kingdoms. No more conflicts at the border, and a chance to bring fresh trade. Even the Council would agree to that."

Too much bad blood had spilled between our kingdoms, and our visiting foreign prince had admitted his people feared our blood fire. A marriage between Sandair and Hartnor would surely end in tragedy.

Princess Aniya stared into the distance with that dreamy smile Talin and Tira often shared. Gods, she was in love. That would surely be the death of us all.

Mina woke with a jolt.

Princess Aniya had loved a Hartnord prince.

Which meant...

Garet. *Gareth.* Gods, the King's sorran was a prince. A Hartnord prince. That's why Prince Wulfhart recognized him. Why the two of them looked alike. Gareth hadn't just served as Hartnor's ambassador. He was one of them.

No wonder the Hartnords seemed to hate him. And no wonder Gareth had such intimate knowledge of them. Why hadn't Talin told her this detail? He must have realized its importance.

And why was the late Princess invading her dreams? It had something to do with this war and the Queen's death, Mina could feel it in her gut.

She slid off the stone bed and dressed in her travel leathers, boots, sahn, and sword. Garr's cloak hung over her arm as she stepped out into the main sanctum. It was empty. Where had that fool disappeared to now?

The temple doors opened a fraction and Alistar slipped inside carrying a wrapped bundle in his arms. "I brought food. Thought you'd be hungry." He unwrapped a round steaming bread bun and offered it. "Careful, it's hot."

She stared down at the bun. "Ali, I—"

"My father sent me to fetch you. It's almost dawn, and Prince Wulfhart is waiting on his ship. I told my father that I'm still your sorran, so… if you go, I go with you."

"Why would you go all the way to Hartnor with me? Are you worried I'd burn your father's new allies?"

Alistar's cheeks reddened. "Well, you can't speak Hartnord."

"I'm not going to Hartnor. The temple needs me back in Solus, and the Council needs to be made aware that someone's using Rahn's Breath before they accuse more Fire Walkers of crimes. I'll pass along Prince Wulfhart's testimony and convince the Council to delay the war, if only to hear what the Hartnords have to say."

"You think they'll listen?"

"I'll make them listen."

"Don't mention this to the Council," he blurted out. "I'm begging. You see how it looks, right? Like we're betraying the Bright Solara." He tugged his braid. "I'm worried my father is making a mistake by helping Prince Wulfhart. I know he has good intentions, but the Council won't care. They never liked our House or the King's decision to allow us on the Council, because they don't trust us." There was true fear in his emerald eyes. "If this news gets out, it's not just my House that could suffer. It's hard enough being a Bosan in Sandair. Everyone already looks down on us. If people start to think every Bosan is secretly in league with Hartnor... Stars, this could make things worse."

"What are you worried about? It's not like the Bright Solara would ignore the suffering of an entire group of people just to placate the powerful, the hateful, the ignorant, is it?"

He grimaced. "I didn't mean what I said last night. I'm a dung-headed fool. Forgive me?" He held up the bun.

She shoved the bun into her mouth and moaned at its sweetness. The Bosan fascination with fish-based dishes was repulsive, but their buns could put Iman's pies to shame. "You're forgiven, Myrbond." They both knew the cost of harboring a Hartnord Prince. If the Council found out, the entirety of House Myrbond could be destroyed, as House Rhaesbond was.

Alistar included.

But if she couldn't admit to meeting with Prince Wulfhart, then he'd be blamed for the Queen's death and there would be no chance of reconciliation. Her Fire Walkers would march to war. Smuggling the women and children to Arlent would have to be enough.

Politics was a whole new battlefield. How did her father stomach it?

Alistar smiled, and it warmed through her with relief. "I'll let my father know we're leaving and meet you at the stables."

Garr was already at the city stables, brushing his horse. "We're leaving, then? I was preparing Dancer for our long trip back."

"You named your horse *Dancer*?"

"The perfect name for a grumpy mare." Garr grinned.

She threw the purple cloak at him and checked in on her own horse. Luna was a calm girl who didn't mind sharing a stable with Garr's beast. "I saved a bit for you." Mina dug out leftover scraps and let Luna lick the crumbs. Fez would have stolen them from her sahn.

By the time Mina finished packing her saddlebags and checking Luna's hooves and mane, Alistar had returned dressed for travel with his own supplies.

"My father thinks we're foolish children out to destroy the Neu Bosan alliance with Sandair," Alistar announced with mock cheer. "Let's leave before he declares us enemies of the people."

Garr swung onto his saddle. "No complaints from me."

It wasn't how she wanted to leave Myryn, but so be it. She just hoped Hiram's involvement with the Hartnords wouldn't add a new front to the war they were trying to prevent.

They guided their horses along the empty boardwalk. Ships crowded the docks, but the dawn Rahnlight gave a lovely view of the inlet. Smoke twirled from some of the Neu Bosan boat-houses, though the city remained at rest. Prince Wulfhart's ship hid somewhere among them.

A Hartnord waited by the city gates. The Prince's companion, Falkner.

"Lost, Priestess?" he said with a rough, gravelly voice, as though he rarely spoke and found the habit distasteful. "My master's ship is the other way."

She brought Luna to a stop. "Tell you master that whilst I appreciate his invitation, I must return to Solus. I encourage Prince Wulfhart to contact the Council and advocate his innocence himself."

"We thought you cared for your fire kin. Does your heart desire war?"

"I care for my people, which is why I won't abandon them and head north. Tell your master that."

Falkner's sapphire eyes stared through her, as though probing her mind for the truth.

She placed her hand on Hawk's hilt and edged Luna forward an inch. Falkner stepped in front of her, blocking her exit. Though he carried no weapon, the way he held his body was that of a warrior, and she realized what he reminded her of—the Hartnord fist-fighters of Prince Rais's helbond ceremony. If Falkner was one of *those*, then he wouldn't need a weapon to stop her.

His lip quirked as though he'd read the realization in her mind. Gods, he was like Gareth. He had the Hartnord Sight. Falkner's stare moved to Alistar and then Garr. Alistar shifted in his seat, but Garr stared back without flinching. She half-expected some quip from the Ash Maker, but he remained uncharacteristically silent.

"My master wishes to make peace with your people, but peace will be impossible whilst *he* remains rooted in your city. He has sabotaged our efforts. He has attempted to lure my master to his death."

"Who?"

"You know him as Gareth. That wasn't his name when he served as our ambassador."

"I know who he is." Though she'd have *many* questions for Talin when she returned back to Solus.

"Do you?" Falkner studied her. "I wonder what lies and truths your King has told you? Gareth betrayed us, accused us of murdering his princess when we did no such thing. *He* manipulated your king into waging war against us, and now King Reinhart is cold as stone and we ready ourselves for war once more. Whilst Gareth breathes, peace will be impossible."

Prince Wulfhart *had* said his pleas to the Council went unheard. Could Gareth have intercepted them, and for what purpose? Revenge, or something more sinister? "I'll bring your concerns directly to the King." Or the next best thing, her father.

"Do not trust the traitor you call Gareth." Falkner stepped aside. "Safe travels, Priestess."

She nudged Luna and didn't dare look back. Alistar and Garr flanked her like two sorrans.

"You'd be a fool to trust *him*, Sword Dancer," Garr muttered under his breath.

Mina waited until she cleared the city gates and kicked Luna into a gallop.

~ ~ ~

Garr whistled and Mina slowed Luna's pace to allow him to catch up.

"We're being followed."

She hissed a curse and glanced over her shoulder to the trees. They'd travelled far enough from Myryn to join the northern point of the Emerald Forest. Plenty of thick woods for assailants to hide in. "Are you sure? Did you see them?"

"No, but I have a nose for these things."

Alistar dropped to their pace. "I don't see anything. You're being paranoid."

"Am I? They let us go too easily, and they didn't want to, trust me. Hartnords are skilled hunters. They're tracking us."

"Why would Hartnords be tracking us?"

Garr's crooked smile was grim.

"It doesn't matter," she said. "We keep riding, but watch your backs."

Rahn sank behind the trees, but no Hartnords burst from behind them. She'd kept a hand on Hawk's hilt the entire ride, and Alistar kept his bow strung, ready to fire if needed. Why would Prince Wulfhart send his men after her when they were on the same side?

They came to a stop within a clearing. No matter where they camped, they would be surrounded by trees. Together, they pitched three tents, though they jumped at every noise Gai made in the woods.

Garr gathered firewood.

"You're lighting a fire?" Alistar asked. "Won't that attract our hunters?"

"I'd like to see the man who guts me." Garr arranged wood into a pile and then clapped dirt and splinters from his hands. "My dagger, Sword Dancer? I'm off for a little hunting."

"With a dagger?" Alistar scoffed. "What kind of game are you after?"

"The kind that thinks it's the hunter and not the prey."

Alistar stole a glance at the tree line. "Oh."

"How do you expect to hunt them?" Mina asked.

"I don't. They'll come to you, and I'll be waiting. No one notices a rat unless it's on fire."

Alistar frowned. "We're bait?"

Garr winked. "Your words, not mine."

She pulled the dagger from her saddlebag. If Garr was planning on murdering them, he'd had ample opportunity to do so before now. "Don't die." She tossed the dagger at him.

Garr caught it in one hand. "Didn't know you cared. Build that campfire high, oh mighty Priestess. It'll draw them out." He stalked into the trees and she debated following him. Instead, she held her palm over the wood and waited for Alistar to leave. He didn't.

"Do you want to check the horses? I'm going to light the fire."

Alistar sat cross-legged on the ground. "I—I want to watch you."

She kept a respectable distance and let heat flow from her palm. The wood burst into flame, and Alistar's breath hitched. Maintaining control wasn't easy when he stared at her like some dam about to break. The last thing she wanted was to add to his fears. She chewed her lip. *I am the master of my own self.*

There was more to her power than killing. Why couldn't everyone else see that?

The campfire roared to life and glowed with warm orange amid their shelter of green. She shook her flames away and settled beside Alistar. The fear in his eyes had gone, and they were shadowed instead with grim determination.

"I'm trying." Alistar forced himself to watch the campfire as it flickered and danced. "It's… hard to overcome instinct. But I'm trying."

She offered her hand. "I won't hurt you, Ali."

He pressed his palm into hers, and his breath whooshed over her in a single exhale. "You're still warm."

"Sandarians are always warm."

His emerald eyes held a depth she'd never read as Malik, as though becoming Mina allowed her to see it. Or, it allowed him to shine.

Would Princess Aniya see it, too? He may not know it, but Mina was training Alistar to become more comfortable with his betrothed, not with her. The thought doused her inner embers. "Why would your father risk angering the Council when you're betrothed to the Princess?"

Alistar let go of her hand and tugged the braid dangling by his neck. "If the Three-Pointed Star won't send their ships to Sandair's aid, there won't be any betrothal."

"You could always marry a Hartnord."

He spluttered a laugh, and the beads in his braid clinked. He always tugged his braid when nervous, but the sound came alive when he was happiest. In truth, she liked his braid. Most men braided their beard, not random strands of hair, but that's what made Alistar different. Bosan, she supposed.

She lifted her fingers to his braid with a sudden urge to tug it.

His laughing slowed as her fingers brushed close to his neck.

"I, ah, I want a braid like that," she said. "With silver and purple beads."

"You need something to braid first." His fingers reached up her scalp and traced a line where her hair should be, sending a jolt of sky fire down her neck and into the pit of her stomach. "Don't drink Wulfhart's potion."

"It would stop my blood fire. That's what you want, isn't it?"

His palm rested on her nape, close to her fluttering pulse. "What I want doesn't matter. You can't let others dictate your life when you're the one who has to live it." There was a bitter edge to his tone and she wasn't sure who he was talking about. "The fears of dung-headed fools aren't your problem."

"Those dung-headed fools keep making it my problem with their laws and their war."

She bit her lower lip. Back in the Emerald Forest, she'd been

326 | TRUDIE SKIES

close to making her wish. The only wish that mattered in this moment.

For their friendship to survive no matter what the gods threw at them.

He smiled, though it wasn't any she'd seen him wear in the Academy with Raj, or with his own people in Myryn. It was a smile just for her. "I'm not scared of you, Mina. How could I be? Your eyes are made of stars."

When had he stopped calling her Arl? When had she become *Mina* to him?

Something flickered in the campfire. Tira was waving her arms and pointing to the trees. Mina scrambled to her feet.

Alistar let out a sigh. "What is it?"

"Trouble." She drew Hawk and snapped her attention to the woods.

No movement. No sound. Nothing but the stirring leaves in the wind and the crackle of burning wood, but she couldn't shake off the feeling that someone was watching her.

"Get to the horses," Alistar whispered. He grabbed his bow, but had left his quiver of arrows by his saddlebags.

A glint of silver shone beneath a branch.

"Wait—"

Something shot through the air with a single *fwip*.

Alistar yelped and crumbled to the ground.

"Ali!"

Blood ran down his leg and an arrow shaft protruded from his thigh. "Behind you," he gasped.

Mina spun round, lifting Hawk into the Solaran stance in one quick movement.

Five men emerged from the woods. They were dressed in black from head to toe and carried Sandarian scimitars. From this distance, she couldn't see their eyes to confirm if they were truly Sandarian.

At least one more man sat in a tree, with another arrow nocked and ready to fly.

Where was Garr?

"Run," Alistar moaned. "Get in the woods and hide."

There was no chance she'd outrun an arrow, and there was no chance she'd leave Alistar behind, either.

The men stalked forward. They expected her to fight.

Mina raised her left hand and let it glow. Instead, she'd give them what they feared most.

38

BLOOD IN THE WOODS

Flame burst from Mina's fist. "Who are you and what do you want?"

The raiders didn't answer. She glanced to the archer in the tree and did a double take. Garr was climbing up one branch at a time with his dagger between his teeth. Thank the gods he hadn't abandoned her. She needed to keep the raiders' attention and give Garr a chance to strike.

"You shot my sorran. I'd like to know your names for when I perform your lurrite."

She stepped forward and the archer's aim followed. Good. He hadn't noticed Garr take the dagger from his mouth.

"I'll ask one last time. Who are you and what do you want?"

The raiders spread out in a semi-circle. They were going to surround her. Five against one was no honorable battle, but this wasn't the Academy or the tournament.

This was life or death.

Garr swung up and plunged his dagger into the archer's neck. The man plummeted to the ground with a weak scream. One of his companions whirled around at the noise, but the remaining four charged right at her, their swords raised in an unknown stance.

She thrust her left arm out and scattered fire. Three leaped back, but the other swerved out of her way and swung his sword.

His blade met Hawk with a jarring clang.

Dark brown eyes opened wide in surprise. A Duslander. They narrowed into grim determination, and his blade cut through the air in a series of slices at her back and neck.

She eased her feet into a dance to parry each one.

A joyous song burst in her chest as she slipped into the rhythmic spins and curves of her dance. It had been days, weeks even, since she'd last been able to dance with abandon, and though her muscles ached from travel, her blood pumped fierce and fast.

The Duslander kept his distance as his blade searched for an opening, slicing at her wrist or legs. Timid. Uncertain. No, that wasn't it—his attacks weren't weak or slow. They were designed to render her unarmed rather than dead. But why?

"What do you want?" she yelled.

The Duslander swung his blade in answer.

She spun Hawk in wide circles to keep him at a distance, aware of his companions stalking slowly forward, their blades ready and eager to slip past Hawk should she give them the chance. She needed to keep them from Alistar; he lay sprawled and bleeding on the grass, defenseless.

Behind them, Garr came running with his bloodied dagger. The other four raiders turned their swords on Garr, likely deeming him the greater threat. Garr rolled under one raider's swing with impressive finesse and barged another out of his way.

A sharp sting caught her wrist, snapping her attention back to her assailant. The Duslander wasn't giving her chance to breathe.

"Focus!" Garr yelled, as he wove between blades.

The Duslander continued his barrage of swings, and she realized too late what he was doing: his attacks were pushing her away from Garr. Dividing them into easier targets.

Garr couldn't hold off four men alone; his dagger didn't have the reach of their scimitars.

She drew the Duslander into a feint and flashed a burst of fire at his face.

He raised his arm into a block and her attack disappeared in a puff of smoke, as though he'd absorbed it. His dark eyes crinkled into amusement.

Gods, he was a Fire Walker.

Garr broke free from the raiders and slipped to her side. "They're not Hartnords!"

"I know." She raised Hawk into the Solaran stance.

Garr copied with his dagger. "Leave one alive."

Her thoughts exactly.

The Duslander and his four companions circled them. Mina and Garr stood back-to-back. When the first raider lunged, Mina swept his blade away with a flowing parry. Garr crouched ready— while the raider's blade was locked with Mina's, he threw himself inside the man's reach and stabbed him through the shoulder.

It was a good strategy, and Mina stepped forward to engage the next assailant before their enemies caught on. Again, Mina parried the man's blade away while Garr rushed him with the dagger, this time stabbing the stomach.

Three and two now. Closer to a fair fight.

This time, Mina fell into a dance pattern that Talin had drilled with her a hundred times at the least. *Parry, parry, feint, slash.*

Hawk cut clean through the raider's neck, as easy as carving meat.

He fell with the familiar gurgled rasps of her nightmares.

Gods, she'd killed a man.

It was her sword that had spilled his life's blood and ripped the light from his eyes.

She had no time to dwell on it.

"Mina!" Alistar yelled. "The trees!"

Another raider had crept into the clearing and was crouched over the body of the dead archer. The bow! He had the dead man's bow! And his arrow aimed right at Garr.

"Garr!" she screamed, but he was locked in battle with a raider, unable to take his eyes off his enemy and see the danger. Mina launched herself into a run, ramming into Garr's side and knocking him down. He hissed as the arrow skimmed his arm and left a thin trail of blood. She stumbled over his legs and dropped Hawk.

A raider came up behind her, his blade poised to strike.

Garr flung his dagger. It struck the man in the face, tearing a chunk out of his cheek as it bounced away into the grass. Mina seized the moment to grab Hawk by the hilt and thrust its blade up into the raider's stomach.

She twisted her face to one side as a spurt of blood splashed her tunic.

Garr retrieved his dagger, panting for breath. "Did we get them all?" His amber eyes opened wide. "Guess not."

She followed his gaze and swallowed a curse.

The Duslander poured fire from his palms. Flames raced across the grass of the clearing and began to lick at the trunks of the closest trees. His threat was clear—he could destroy this entire forest.

She lowered Hawk. "Don't."

"The forest," Alistar groaned. "You can't let him—"

"Your companions are dead," she called. "It's over. What good will burning some trees do? Give it up and leave with your life."

The Duslander pointed at her sword, and then the ground. He wanted her to drop it and submit.

The bowman stepped up beside him, arrow nocked and drawn. His arrow pointed at Garr. He stood too close. There would be no chance to duck or dive out of the way this time.

The Duslander had her trapped and he knew it. Mina's eyes moved from Garr to Alistar and the arrow in his—

Gods. The arrow was gone from his thigh. He'd ripped it out himself. The bloody thing was nocked in his bow, and drawn back with shaking hands. His eyes were half-glossed over, but he released it with the last of his strength.

It shot true.

The Duslander summoned a shield of fire.

The arrow pierced through it. His shield snapped out and he fell against a tree, the arrow embedded in his upper arm. But before Mina could approach, the Duslander snapped the arrow in half and fled into the woods, followed by his companion. Gods damn it, she wanted to question at least one of them. Even if she took Luna, there was no chance she'd find them in such dense woods at night.

Alistar groaned and collapsed back onto the grass.

"Ali!" She ran to him and dropped to her knees.

His Bosan skin shone far paler than she'd ever seen it, and sweat beads dotted his face. He grimaced. "How bad does it look?"

Blood gushed down his leg. Far too much. She yanked off her sahn and pressed it to his wound. Alistar hissed and grabbed clumps of grass.

Garr stood over them. "Can you move it?"

"Does it look like I can move it?" Alistar gasped. "Why d'you care anyway?"

"Because I'm the one who'll end up carrying your carcass. What, you think our tiny priestess here could do it?"

She shot Garr a glare, but Alistar barked a laugh. Then his laughter choked into a hacking cough that sent shudders through his whole body. The blood had already soaked through her sahn and showed no signs of stopping.

"Get the bandages. All of them," she ordered Garr.

He ran to their horses. She drew her mother's dagger and cut away the red-stained cloth around his thigh. As she peeled it and her sahn away, the blood ran so thick that she could barely tell where the wound began.

Garr returned with bandages. She took them, but her fingers shook and were sticky with Alistar's blood. *Oh gods.*

"Here." Garr took her hand and guided it. "Let me."

Together, they pressed down on Alistar's leg.

Alistar hissed, but the flow didn't abate.

"He's losing too much," Garr murmured. "You need to cauterize it." There was no humor in his expression.

"What, no!" Alistar's voice was hoarse. "Stars above, you're not burning my leg!"

"If we don't stop the flow, he'll bleed to death."

"No!" Alistar yelled and tried to sit up on his elbows, but lacked the strength. "Wrap it up, take me to Myryn!"

"He won't make it back to Myryn."

Gods, she couldn't do that to him. She glanced to her mother's dagger. Jonan had warned her against sharing her blood, but he'd saved King Khaled's life with his blood, and hers as well. Alistar was her friend. She wasn't going to sit here and watch him bleed to death.

She snatched her dagger and cut clean across her palm.

"What are you doing?" Garr said.

She ignored him and pressed her palm to Ali's wound. Nothing happened. No surge of power passed through her veins to his.

Because he was Neu Bosan. Because he couldn't form that connection.

Garr grabbed her shoulder. "He's running out of time."

A sob shuddered through her. "I'm not burning him. I can't!" She grasped onto Garr's wrist. "You're an Ash Maker, you must know how to stop blood. You must know something!"

His amber eyes were kind. "Whatever you think I can do, I can't."

"Then you burn him."

Tears ran down Alistar's cheeks. "Mina, I'm begging, don't burn me. *Don't.*"

"I'm bleeding. I can't summon my fire." Garr rubbed his torn shirt and held up fingers smeared with his own blood. He'd been shot too. "I'll hold him steady. Just one quick burst of fire. That's all he needs."

"You're not burning me!" Alistar tried to shuffle away but Garr grabbed his wrists and pinned him down. "Get your hands off me!" Alistar writhed and hissed a flurry of words in his Neu Bosan language, but Garr held on until Alistar's strength waned and he slumped in Garr's arms.

"Now, Sword Dancer!"

"Mina! *Don't!*"

Alistar's eyes were filled with absolute terror. She was the monster of his fears, but if she didn't do this, if she didn't become that monster, he'd bleed to death and she'd lose her friend.

She took Alistar's thigh.

"Mina, Arl, *don't*—"

Flame burst from her palm.

Alistar shrieked. His leg spasmed, but Garr held it steady.

A heartbeat later and Alistar's screams cut off. He collapsed, unconscious.

She sat back and gaped at the steaming wound. The flesh looked red, raw, pulpy, and stank of cooked kabob, but the blood flow had stopped. Garr fetched a canteen from his horse and attempted to clean the wound, then dress it with a bandage.

Mina only watched, too numb for words.

Unconscious on the ground, Alistar seemed calm, almost serene as Garr worked, though his skin remained as pale as a Hartnord.

"I burned him." She stared at her hands stained with her friend's blood.

Garr wiped sweat from his brow, leaving a bloody smear. "You saved his life."

"He'll never trust me again."

"You *saved* him. But we're not out of this yet. Listen to me, we need to travel on—we need to get him to a healer."

"Myryn—"

"We can't go back there." Garr jerked his thumb at the bodies littered behind them." That's where *they* followed us from."

Gods, she'd forgotten about the bodies. Dark ripples were already crawling over their former selves. Shadows. She needed to question them, but not like this. Not with Alistar wounded and lifeless. Not with Garr watching.

The blood bond tugged; her Lunei instincts were already asking her to burn the bodies, but they'd hurt her sorran—what afterlife did these men deserve?

She scrambled to her feet. "I need to burn the bodies."

Garr looked at her, dumbfounded. "Forget the bodies. We don't have time—"

"That's exactly what an Ash Maker would say."

"The dead have a luxury the living don't. All the time in the world. Your Bosan needs a healer *now*."

He was right. They didn't have time to burn multiple bodies, and she couldn't stomach the thought of summoning her fire now, not when the stench of burned flesh and blood danced on her tongue—and with Alistar's screams fresh in her mind.

Garr stretched to his feet. "I'll take your Bosan. He's light enough to ride on Dancer with me. You can tether his horse to yours."

"Grenai. We ride south through the night." Raj would still be waiting in Grenai. There was no other Green Hand she'd trust with her sorran's life.

They gathered the horses quickly. As she approached the campfire to snuff it out, she noticed Garr pawing at one of the bodies.

"What are you doing?"

"Looking for coin."

"Seriously? You're looting the bodies? You're disgusting."

"What, you think they deserve to keep it? In case they need it in the afterlife?"

"We don't have time for this."

"What have we here?" Garr stood up with a bottle in his hand. Not purple but clear—with a silver liquid inside.

Lune's Tears.

Why did the raiders carry Lune's Tears? Were they working for Prince Wulfhart?

"Is this some sort of Sandarian liquor I've never heard of?" Garr popped open the top.

"Don't drink it, you fool!" She yanked the bottle from his hands. "It's—it's complicated. But it's not liquor."

Garr grunted his disappointment. "Fine. Help me get your friend onto my horse."

Mina shoved the bottle into her pocket and ignored the urgent pull of her blood. If Lune wanted these bodies burned so badly, she could fall from the sky and do it herself.

39

THE LONG PATH BACK

It took a night and half a day of hard riding before they reached Grenai. Alistar slept the entire way in Garr's arms, though the Ash Maker didn't once complain. With his help, Mina twice washed and changed Alistar's wound and tried to force some water past his lips, but Alistar tossed and turned in fitful dreams.

Of all the lessons she'd learned from the Green Hands during her childhood, she knew fever wasn't a good sign.

Raj waited inside the Temple of Gai, organizing shipments to Solus. He took in Alistar straight away. Mina sat outside Alistar's room on a stone bench, listening to his moans and the coughs of other sick Gaislanders occupying the temple. Her mouth was parched, her clothes dirty and bloody, and her body hollow, but she refused to move and instead stared at the shafts of Rahnlight that pierced between the vines covering the temple's glass windows.

Warmth bloomed through the blood bond. *Are you safe?* it seemed to ask.

Gods knew what emotions she'd been sending through the House bond to her family, but she tried to send her reassurances, even if half-hearted.

Garr had wandered off to find food or drink or something. On his return, his clothes were still bloody, like hers, but his arm had been wrapped with a fresh bandage. She'd been so concerned for her sorran, she'd forgotten Garr had been hurt too.

"How's your wound?"

He rolled his shoulder. "Just a scratch. You need to drink, Sword Dancer." He offered her a canteen from his belt.

She lifted it to her lips and caught a whiff of strong alcohol. "This isn't water."

"You haven't slept. The healers have a spare cot. That'll help you get started."

"I'm not leaving him."

"He's not going anywhere, and you're not helping him by wasting away here."

"Since when did you care?"

"Since you saved my life." His amber eyes held a sincerity that sent a rush of anger in her gut. Sure, she'd saved *his* life, but her sorran—her gods-damn friend—was sick with fever in the room beyond. She was his master; his life was her responsibility, and he'd cried and begged as she forced her own fire onto his flesh.

She was nothing but a monster.

The curtain to Alistar's room parted and Raj stepped out.

She pulled herself up onto shaking legs. "How is he?"

Raj rubbed a stray sweaty strand of hair from his eyeline. "His leg is, um, it's pretty bad. We're cutting away the infected skin, but... it's deep. We might need to amputate."

Amputate.

Amputate.

The word reverberated through her.

She slumped against the wall and the canteen slid from her hands.

If he lost his leg, he'd never walk again, never swing his sword, never jump on boats, never... never forgive her.

Garr scooped the canteen and offered it to her again. "You saved his life."

She smacked his hand aside. "You. You told me to burn him. You used him as bait. You wanted him dead!"

"If I wanted your Bosan friend dead, I would have let him bleed. *He* pulled the arrow out and made his injury worse. I'm no healer, but the blood's supposed to stay inside."

"You didn't burn."

"I was wounded—"

"A scratch, you called it. You brag of your legendary power, Ash Maker, but I've yet to see you summon a single flame. We were outnumbered by raiders, and you didn't even think to burn to protect us?"

"You didn't use your legendary power either, High Priestess."

"I burned my friend!" And his screams would haunt her dreams forever. "But you're as much a monster as I!"

"I bled for you. I killed for you. What more do you want?"

She shoved him aside and marched out of the temple. Raj called after her, but neither he nor the Ash Maker followed. She wandered and kept wandering, not paying attention to where she went, nor caring. Eventually, she found herself by the bench where had Alistar sat, staring north to Myryn. She sank onto the stone with her head cradled in her hands.

She'd burned her dearest friend.

Defenseless and screaming for her to stop.

She'd become the monster of her childhood tales.

She reached into her pocket and pulled out the tiny bottle of Lune's Tears. If she didn't have blood fire, none of this would have happened. Gods, they wouldn't even *be* here. If every Fire Walker drank this, they wouldn't be marching to war.

Rahn gave them the power to turn their own blood into deadly flame. Why?

For all of her proclamations that the Fire Walkers were innocent, there were enough of her kind that used blood fire to harm. Men like Saeed. Perhaps Prince Wulfhart and Hiram were right. So long as anyone in Sandair possessed blood fire, eventually someone would misuse it.

Or be misused because of it.

She turned the bottle over and it glittered with all the stars of the sky. Lune's Tears. With this, she wouldn't burn again. Alistar wouldn't fear her.

The tiny bottle shook in her grip.

A shadow fell upon her. She shoved the bottle into her pocket. Garr stood over her and offered his canteen without uttering a word. She snatched it and gulped a strong fruity red that sent fresh tears to her eyes.

Garr chewed his lip as though restraining himself from words that would make her yell. "Your healer friend wanted me to tell you that your Bosan is sleeping—"

"He has a name."

"—and that Grenai hosts the best healers in the world and they'll do all they can. But they'll have to keep him here for a few weeks. Maybe longer."

She couldn't afford to remain in Grenai for weeks. It had taken almost two weeks to reach Gaisland, and then another three days to ride to Myryn and back. The Fire Walkers still needed her, and they were running out of time.

Scarcely more than two weeks remained before she'd be expected to march to the front lines. There would be only days left, if even that, by the time she reached Solus. She was the only one who could appeal to the Council and stop war.

But she didn't want to leave Alistar. She couldn't bear it.

"You're not a monster," Garr murmured.

"Aren't I? I burned my friend. I killed two men."

"You saved your friend and protected him from bandits who would have cut his throat and robbed his corpse. That makes you a hero in most tales. I've met real monsters, Sword Dancer, and they're a lot uglier than you."

"Is that supposed to be comforting?"

"Supposed to be." He gave a slight smile, but the amber in his eyes dulled. "I've killed men." He tugged at his stained shirt. "That's their blood, and it doesn't fill me with joy."

She glanced down to her own shirt. Alistar's blood. Raider blood. All the same color, and she was no stranger to it, yet seeing it hadn't gotten any easier. It didn't make her feel like the hero of her childhood tales. Would Malik the Merciless have spared a thought for the lives he took? "I thought Ash Makers enjoyed killing."

"Like we enjoy drinking blood?"

"That's what the tales say."

Garr sat down beside her. "And how many of those tales are true?"

Perhaps the tales had been exaggerated. But the Lunei wouldn't have painted them as monsters without reason.

He rubbed a bloody smear from the back of his hand. "Monsters enjoy killing. Men don't."

What was Garr? More man than monster? *You're as much a monster as I.* "You're right. I'm no help to the Fire Walkers or Bosan by staying here. But you should stay. War won't come this far west." She dug out a coin pouch and tossed the entire thing into his lap. "What you do when I leave is none of my concern." He could return to Myryn and take the nearest boat to nowhere for all she cared, and at least then she'd have fulfilled her promise to Jonan to get rid of him forever.

He tossed the pouch back. "I'm your guardian, aren't I? That's why you dragged me to this bug-infested forest."

"I'm giving you a way out, you fool. Take it." She shoved the pouch back into his hands.

"We were attacked by six men. They could be tracking us still. You won't make it across the plains without me."

"Try me."

"Are you always this stubborn?"

"I could ask you the same. I thought you didn't want to fight in a pointless war?"

"I don't." He gently pushed the pouch into her lap. "Take your coins before I escort them to the nearest tavern."

"Fine, but we're riding at dawn." She shoved the coins into her sahn and passed him the canteen.

Garr took a long gulp and gasped. "At dawn, then."

ℳ ℳ ℳ

Mina stopped by the Temple of Gai before leaving. Raj informed her that Alistar was still sleeping, though she wasn't sure if this was a gentle lie and Alistar simply didn't want to see her. The Guardian of Gai also visited. His hands were wrapped in thick bandages, though he still intended to lead his men into war, even if he couldn't wield a sword himself. He offered to write to Hiram—or dictate a letter at least—and pass on news of his son. One less task for her to agonize over.

Her heart ached at the thought of returning without Alistar or Raj, but duty pulled her east.

Truth be told, she was glad Garr had chosen to journey with her. The nights were lonely without her friends, and camping in the forest was a jittery experience compared to the Duslands, where the only howls she needed to worry about were an oncoming dry storm. The trees and the bugs and the damp heat were Alistar and Raj's life, not hers.

Two nights later, she and Garr passed Gai's Tree and emerged out of the Emerald Forest into bright Rahnlight. The air brushed along Mina's scalp in a refreshing breeze, but she had no time to enjoy it.

They were back in the Solands. And in fourteen days, the kingdom's soldiers would march north with her Fire Walkers whether she made it in time or not.

She needed to ride fast.

They'd barely left the shade of Gaisland when Garr called out behind her, and as she slowed Luna's pace, the whistling wind was replaced with thunder.

Horses.

"We're being followed, Sword Dancer!"

Raiders. She drew her sword. "Get in front!"

Three men on horseback came bounding across the plains. She squinted in the Rahnlight: these wore the same headscarf and leather armor as the raiders in Gaisland. Whoever they were, they were gods-damn persistent.

She kicked Luna with a *hoyt* and led the raiders on a chase. They soon caught up—there was no outrunning them when she'd run her own horse ragged these past few weeks. And Garr's beast was hopeless as a racehorse besides.

Two raiders rode up on either side to pin her in, scimitars raised.

One she recognized immediately—the Duslander. He waved a hand in a command to *stop*.

Her lungs burned as she breathed into the wind. "What do you want?"

The Duslander pointed behind her.

She glanced to Garr. His horse flagged behind, and the third raider easily kept pace with him, with a steady bow aimed at his chest. Garr didn't stand a chance.

"Tell me what you want!" she yelled.

The Duslander sliced his sword down in signal.

The arrow flew through the air.

Garr yanked his horse back and the arrow whizzed inches in front of his face.

She barged Luna into the raider on her left. She ducked a slice of his sword, yanked hard on Luna's reins, and spun around to race back for Garr.

The next arrow pierced his horse's leg.

The horse screeched and bucked. Garr yelled and wrapped his arms around the horse's neck to keep from getting thrown. Another arrow hit the horse's abdomen, and another punctured its neck. The horse crashed into the dirt and tossed Garr clean from his saddle.

The archer stopped his horse in front of Garr and nocked an arrow.

"No!" Mina screamed. She was still five horse lengths away—too far—and the Duslander on his fast horse had caught up with her. He swung his scimitar at Luna's neck. Mina blocked it with

Hawk and hissed as the clang reverberated through her tired muscles.

The Duslander pushed down with his full strength, despite the injury to his arm from Alistar's arrow. These weren't just common raiders, that much was clear. Who were they?

From the corner of her eye, she watched Garr dive behind his still-thrashing horse to shield himself from a barrage of arrows. Then he threw his dagger at the bowman's horse and hit his mark.

The horse fell, throwing its owner. The Duslander jerked his head toward the commotion, distracted enough for Mina to pull her sword free.

Hawk shook in her grip and her heart battered at her chest. "Who sent you? A Hartnord or a Bosan?" Though there were many Houses who might have hired raiders to track her down and kill her, these raiders came from Myryn. They'd attacked with restraint, because they didn't want her killed. They wanted her alive.

And they carried Lune's Tears.

Not even Hiram would be callous enough to send assassins after his own son. Would he?

"Who's paying you? For what purpose?"

The Duslander watched her with wary eyes but didn't utter a single word.

"Emir!" the bowman yelled with a garbled voice.

The Duslander—Emir—whipped his head around to his companion as an arrow whooshed past his face.

Garr held the raider's bow in his hands. He fired another shot as the Duslander charged him—and missed.

The Duslander's horse moved fast and was upon Garr in an instant, sword raised to cut him down. She was too far behind to stop it.

But Garr held his nerve. His third and final arrow skimmed Emir's horse. The beast panicked and reared, throwing Emir back. He leaped from the saddle and landed with practiced finesse.

Mina didn't give him a chance to recover his breath.

Luna barreled into him and drove Emir down into the dust.

The other horseman charged, but she was ready. She allowed his blade to swing through empty air as she sliced Hawk clean across his chest. It wasn't close enough to draw blood, but it cut through his leather armor. She raised Hawk for another pass. The raider pulled back on his reins, took one look at his companions in the dirt, and galloped from the scene.

Mina scanned the ground and found the fallen bowman lying face down, unmoving. Dead.

She sheathed Hawk and dropped from her horse. Emir shuffled away from her in the dirt. Still alive.

Good.

Garr stomped his boot down by Emir's head. "You seemed so eager for our company. Why leave now?"

Emir reached for his belt.

She drew Hawk once more and brought the tip of her blade to his throat. "Don't move."

Emir's arms fell to his side and his chest rose and fell in stolen breaths.

She prodded his chin. "Who sent you and why?"

He grimaced, but said nothing.

"You might as well talk. Your friend abandoned you. That's low, even for your kind."

Garr yanked Emir's headscarf down, exposing his face.

A familiar symbol had been burned into the center of his forehead—a three-forked flame. She'd seen that symbol before.

This was the Duslander who'd handed her a purple bottle just before she died in a torrent of light and fire. The Duslander whose hands were around her neck, holding her down as she drowned in the turquoise waters of the Neu Inlet.

"You're—"

His hand shot out and grabbed her wrist. Flames engulfed both of their hands and singed her sleeve. She yelled and tried to yank her arm free, but his grip tightened.

A cruel smirk lit his face.

Her inner embers reacted on instinct, mingling their fire together so it didn't burn her. Is this how shields worked? By making the fire her own? Emir's flames pulsed as if with his heartbeat, and she could feel her blood drain from her veins. That's what Jonan had once described in their training—that maintaining a shield was to absorb another's fire and allow it to burn through your own blood. Painful pins and needles raced from her fingers to her shoulder. Emir's fire was overpowering hers.

Garr grabbed her arm and pulled her back, breaking them apart.

Emir leaped up and spun his fire in a dancer's circle. His flame snapped like a whip, forcing Mina and Garr to dive apart and leaving a black trail across the dirt between them.

"Now would be a good time to make your shield, Sword Dancer."

"Why can't *you* do it?"

"And burn him to a crisp? We need him alive."

She muttered a curse and shoved Hawk into its scabbard. Emir cast another line of fire. This time she knew what to do. She thrust her fists out and flame burst around her in a cocoon. Emir's power collided with hers, forcing her back a step. She grunted and held her shield firm.

Through the flames, she saw Garr raise his dagger and slowly creep toward Emir.

Raw heat swelled against her shield and exploded outward, forcing Garr to retreat behind her. Pain splintered her head and sent waves of agony through her arms. She chewed her lip until it bled. Every nerve was screeching in protest.

Emir was draining her blood at the cost of his own.

Who *was* this man? A trained Fire Walker, obviously. Experienced in battle with sword and flame. Whenever she tried to press forward, his torrent of flame pulsed harder against her defenses and pinned her in place. He had her trapped; if she dropped her shield now, he'd burn her and Garr to cinders. But if she didn't, she'd collapse from blood loss.

Steel cut through her shield and sent a violent shudder through her chest.

Her shield vanished in a puff of smoke, but so did Emir's; Garr's dagger was a molten lump at their enemy's feet.

Emir's dark eyes blinked at her, as though trying to convey some message or threat, and then he ran for his horse. She stumbled after him, but it was too late. He swooped into his saddle and galloped away.

"Gods damn it!" She dropped to her knees and gasped for breath. Her muscles cramped and she stretched to relieve them. Another few heartbeats of holding a shield would have ended her, but she'd done it—she'd finally managed to summon one.

She glanced over to Garr, who was crouched over his unmoving horse. "Are you hurt?"

His face was a mixture of annoyance and disgust. "Those bastards killed Dancer." He rubbed a palm over his horse's mane. "She deserved a better fate."

Mina scanned the horizon. The raiders—murderers—were long gone. And the body of their dead companion had crumpled to a pile of ash, thanks to Emir's flames, which meant they'd left no Shadow for her to question.

They were her rogue Fire Walkers, but why target her now? With his skill and power, Emir could have destroyed them both with a snap of his fingers, but he'd tried to weaken her instead, whittle her down and render her useless.

Why did they want her alive?

Part of her wanted to ride back to Myryn and demand answers from Hiram, but she'd wasted enough time. This could well be a distraction, a way of delaying her from returning to Solus. That's where she needed to be. They'd attacked her twice. Would they risk it again?

If it wasn't for them, Alistar wouldn't be laying up in Grenai. And her sore muscles wouldn't be aching as though she'd wrestled a mountain lion. She unleashed her temper on Garr. "You could have helped! Are you so lacking in control you can't even summon a shield? And you are completely worthless with a bow!"

Garr simply shrugged. "Are you any better?"

She leveled her harshest glare at him. She could count the number of times she'd fired an arrow on one hand.

"I saved us, didn't I?" he said. "In any case, we should leave before our attackers bring back friends. I'll fit into your saddle if you squeeze onto my lap."

She recoiled. "You want to share my horse?"

He smirked in that cocky way of his. "You expect me to walk? I know we're called Fire Walkers, but I didn't think the temple took that literally."

Now the gods were truly testing her. "Luna can't carry two people."

"Good thing one of us is small enough to count as half." He laughed at her glare, then started digging out supplies from his saddlebags.

They gathered what they could, including the raider's bow and leftover arrows should they face another attack upon the plains. She mounted Luna and shuffled as far forward as she dared without pinning the poor beast's ears with her knees.

Garr climbed behind and his groin pressed into her back. His arms reached around her sides and gripped Luna's saddle. Mina was wedged in by solid muscle and heat.

Gods.

"Ready when you are, Sword Dancer."

"I'm only agreeing to this because of the circumstance."

"Of course. The *circumstance.*"

The amusement in his voice made her teeth grind. "If you fall off, I'm leaving you behind."

"I wouldn't expect any less."

Mina snapped Luna's reins and silently cursed the gods—Sandarian, Hartnord, and Neu Bosan gods alike—for bringing fools into her life.

40

AN UNWELCOME RETURN

Many eyes blinked in the dark. Sandarian eyes. Their heads were shaved bare, but where their skin should have been inked with red markings, there were only scars. Lashings. And a single brand had been burned into each forehead in the shape of a three-forked flame. I knew that symbol. Every Lunei did.

The sigil of House Rhaesbond.

No shackles bound them, yet they hadn't summoned their flame to escape their wooden cage. Each was destined to spend their blood in servitude of a Bosan master. They were broken.

I ducked out of the wagon and turned to my Bosan companion. "What did they do to them?"

Her emerald eyes glossed over. "Whatever they wanted. They're slaves, Tira."

No. They were slaves no longer. My companion had explained how they were used: in homes to cook, clean, and warm baths; in factories and ships to power their odd steam contraptions; as weapons to destroy their enemies; and some were even bred, so she said. I believed every word. It was worse than what Housemen did to them. Much worse.

"We take them to Arlent." Talin would understand the necessity to protect them. Jonan certainly would. And Iman would help clothe and feed them. If not, then what was the point of building a House?

"If the Three-Pointed Star learns we're hiding their slaves—"

"They'll have to explain to King Khaled why they have slaves in the

first place. Do you think our alliance would survive if the Housemen

knew your people were stealing Sandarians with blood fire?"
My Bosan friend shuddered and rubbed the three silver stars above
her left eyebrow. "They're not my people. Not anymore."

"We're here, Sword Dancer."

Mina awoke to the rhythmic sway of Luna's trot beneath her. She sat up in her saddle and wiped drool from her mouth. "How long was I asleep?"

"Not sure. You purred like a fox." Garr leaned close and his warm breath tickled her neck. "I see where your pet learned it."

Heat burned under her skin. She'd never before suffered the indignity of falling asleep in her own gods-damn saddle, but her battle with Emir had left her drained. In the nine days since, they'd driven Luna with all possible haste across roadless fields until deep in the night, sleeping only minimally and one at a time, while the other kept watch for an ambush. Truly resting and restoring her body had been an impossibility.

Emir. He'd been branded with the same mark as the slaves in Tira's memory—Neu Bosan slaves, which meant Garr had been right all along about how her kingdom's supposed ally treated her people. And Emir served as one of those slaves. But why attack other Fire Walkers? For revenge? She needed to return to Jonan and ask him about the brand—and what connection Neu Bosa held to House Rhaesbond.

She twisted in her saddle and scowled up at Garr. "You should have woken me."

"Worried I'd dump you in the river and steal your horse?"

"Yes. How did you even know which direction to go?"

"Easy. I headed for that thing." He pointed ahead.

Bright fire burned far off on the horizon, but it wasn't Rahn—rather the stone depiction of him atop Bloodstone Keep. The real Rahn burned behind her, as though he watched over Alistar and Raj where she could not.

The muddied path was trampled by boots and hooves and

wagon wheels. They rode past a whole legion of Darasi soldiers heading west from Solus to the Ruby Coast, along with groups bearing the black banner of House Fellbond, the yellow of House Nasbond, and more. The march had begun without her. The whole of Sandair moved into position for war.

Lune's Shadow was less than twelve weeks away. Barely enough time to begin a war, much less end one.

Night had fallen by the time Mina and Garr crossed the bridge into Solus. They fought against lines of men and wagons pouring out of the city. Guardsmen checked every visitor entering. Those the guards couldn't verify were turned away.

They blocked her before she could pass. "Only men with a House seal are permitted entry."

"You're only letting Housemen inside?"

"Housemen or those with a *valid* seal."

"So, they close their gates on any street rats who need sanctuary," Garr whispered in her ear.

"This is the largest city in Sandair. Surely you have room?"

"Our orders come from the Sword of Solus," the guard grunted. "Turn back and return from where you came. There's no beds for the likes of you."

She yanked at her dirtied sahn. "I'm Lady Tamina of House Arlbond, you fool."

The guard snorted. "And I'm Prince Wulfhart."

"You look like a street rat," Garr whispered. "Take off your shirt and show them your colors, Sword Dancer."

She pinched his thigh and he hissed a laugh behind her. "I'm sure the Sword of Solus would be pleased to know his men prevented the High Priestess of Rahn from entering the city."

A hush rippled through the crowd. The men parted and a figure dressed in the golden scale armor of the royal guard approached. Prince Rais.

He patted the arm of the guardsman. "It's quite all right. I'll escort Lady Arlbond."

The Prince was the last person she'd expected to see. She wanted to race up the hill to Talin, but duty came first, she supposed. She dropped from her horse and her knees buckled. Prince Rais caught her arm before she could fall.

She forced an awkward smile and gestured for Garr to dismount. He followed, but the guards blocked his entrance.

"He's a Fire Walker. He's with me."

Prince Rais gave her an annoyed look but nodded, and the guards allowed Garr through. Once away from the tangled knot of travelers at the gate, Prince Rais guided her into the doorway of a closed trading post out of earshot from any wandering street rats. Garr included.

"My Prince, it's good to see—"

"Who is he?" The Prince shot a scathing look at Garr. "Why were you sharing a saddle?"

"He's a Fire Walker, my Prince. We were attacked by raiders, his horse was killed—"

"Why were you travelling alone with a man?" Prince Rais towered over her with fire in his amber eye. When had he grown so tall?

"Lord Salasar insisted I travel with a guard. I took my sorran and Raj—"

"You travelled with *three* men?"

She chewed her tongue. Why couldn't the raiders have murdered her in Gaisland?

Garr swaggered over with a smirk that meant trouble. "It was a tight squeeze fitting into the one tiny tent, but we managed."

"You shared a tent?" Prince Rais spluttered.

What was that fool thinking? Offending the Bright Solara would only result in losing his head. "Forgive my acolyte. He has trouble leashing his tongue, but I'll recommend the Sword of Solus cut it out."

Her words jarred a memory from her encounter with the Shadow in Gaisland.

Emir had been in that vision. And the smuggler had mentioned something about him not having a tongue... That was why Emir didn't speak to her. He couldn't.

She shoved Luna's reins into Garr's hands. "Take her to the stables and return to the temple."

He flourished a bow. "Your will is mine, High Priestess."

Prince Rais's hardened stare followed Garr every step. She almost expected the Ash Maker to burst into flames.

"You, uh, look different, my Prince." Indeed, he stood out in his golden armor.

"Lord Talin suggested I join the guard and help prepare Solus's defense. He also informed me of your return, which is why I saw fit to welcome you." The anger slipped from his face, though there was a restrained tightness in his voice. "I'll speak with Lord Salasar myself on what company he allows you to keep. Such men as *that* are beneath you."

She kept her polite smile neutral. She didn't need some prince, the Sword of Solus, or anyone else to dictate what company she kept. Garr was many things: Ash Maker, street rat, utter fool, terrible singer, but he was also—

"Have I offended you, Lady Arlbond?"

"My Prince?"

"We've not spoken since my mother's lurrite, and then you rode all the way to Gaisland without saying goodbye. Are you avoiding me?"

In truth, she hadn't thought about Prince Rais once since she left for Gaisland. "Not avoiding you, my Prince. But serving the temple has taken my time."

"You couldn't spare a moment to tell me? I thought we were friends."

"War is coming, my Prince. The time for frivolities is past." She moved to join the crowd.

He took her hand without asking, forcing her to a stop. "No. The time for frivolities is now, before the Hartnords kill us all. I've missed you." He squeezed her hand. "Do you still wear the ruby I gave you? It belonged to my mother."

His mother? Oh gods. She'd given the Queen's necklace to

Samira to sell. "I, uh, I left it in the temple for safe keeping. It would have been dangerous travelling with such a precious item."

"It would mean much to me if you wore it. I want the whole of Solus to see the High Priestess has my favor."

His favor, and what else? "I will. But I must return back to the temple, my Prince. The Fire Walkers need me."

"Will you come see me before you ride for your next adventure?"

This was more the Prince Rais she knew. "I swear it."

He lifted her hand to his lips and planted a soft kiss on her knuckles. "Then I await your tales eagerly."

She slid from his grasp and strode awkwardly for the temple.

Her heart thumped in her chest and she leaned against a wall to stop the dizzying flutter in her stomach.

The Prince had kissed her, albeit in the awkward way that noble boys courted noble girls—though if Iman were here, she'd waggle her finger and lecture Mina on what it meant.

Gods.

Garr stood waiting at the foot of the hill.

She jabbed a finger into his ribs. "That was Prince Rais, you fool."

Garr rubbed his chest. "Oh, he's a prince? I would never have guessed by the way he spoke of you like you're his property. Is he aware of your vows?"

Vows meant nothing to Housemen, and likely less to Solaran princes, but Prince Rais was different. She rubbed the imprint of his lips from her hand. "Angering him isn't going to help the Fire Walkers." She turned and headed up the hill.

Garr kept a leisurely pace by her side. "Nor is lying to him about his mother's heirloom, Sword Dancer."

"I don't appreciate you spying on me—"

"Not spying. Acting in your best interest as your hired guard. Though, you've yet to actually pay me—"

"I didn't hire you, you mule. And I've given you coin!" Against her better judgment. She didn't need an Ash Maker acting in her best interests, nor did she appreciate the casual way he joked with her. It didn't feel right when she should have been walking and laughing with Alistar and Raj instead.

"So you don't want help finding your Prince's necklace? I could track it, if you'd like. Assuming your acolyte sold it locally."

"You're a thief now?"

"I'm a man of many talents."

"Do any of your talents involve being quiet?"

He grinned, but his expression fell as they neared the temple. Cyrus waited outside the doors. Another fool she didn't wish to see.

Garr growled beside her.

She elbowed him. "Stay quiet and don't start trouble. Let me handle him."

"As you say, Sword Dancer," he whispered, and fell in line behind her.

Cyrus sneered at her approach. "You and your dog made it back in one piece, then. Heard your Bosan might lose a leg, though. Bosan always find ways to get out of their commitments, even if it means hacking their own limbs off."

His words brought fire to her chest. She gripped her sword hilt. "What do you want?"

"You've been summoned for a Council meeting at dawn, *Priestess*." He spat her title with distaste. "Sounds like you made a right mess in Gaisland. All of our supplies burned? We're dying to read your report." He sauntered past her.

"I could push him off the city walls," Garr murmured. "Make it look like an accident."

She didn't doubt it. The blood bond warmed as Jonan stepped out of the temple. He hadn't changed much in the weeks she'd been gone, and she fought the urge to run up and grab him in one of Iman's crushing hugs.

Jonan smiled, but his irritation whipped through the bond as he locked eyes on Garr.

Before she could say anything, Fez bounded out of the temple doors with a screech and ran circles around her legs.

Mina chuckled. "I wasn't gone that long."

Kamran stumbled out after him and scooped the squirming fox into his arms. "You're back! You were gone for weeks! Did you fight raiders?"

Garr ruffled the boy's hair. "Oh, we fought hundreds of raiders *and* scary monsters made from fire. Come on, I'll tell you all about it." He glanced over his shoulder and winked.

Jonan waited until Garr had guided Kamran inside before turning his flat stare to her. "He looks healthy. Alive, even."

Her cheeks warmed. "Alistar was injured. He and Raj are still in Grenai—"

"I know. I saw what happened in my dreams."

Good. Then she didn't need to relive Alistar's screams in her mind. She'd once hated how the House bond violated her privacy and displayed her memories like some curiosity, but now she appreciated its advantages. "How are things in the temple? Cyrus was here—"

"Yes. He's been making frequent visits on behalf of our Sword of Solus. We are grateful for his protection." His gaze moved to where a group of guards were standing nearby. "You look exhausted. You must rest from your long journey. I suggest you visit the Temple of Lune and bathe. Ask their Water Bearers to recommend oils that ease your muscles."

His words carried a hidden command through the bond. They were being watched.

She stretched with an exaggerated yawn. "You're right. My muscles are stiff and sore from riding." She sniffed her armpits. "And I stink."

Jonan patted her shoulder in an awkward imitation of Talin. "That you do. Bathe, and we'll speak soon."

Sooner rather than later. What trouble had befallen the temple whilst Mina had been away?

41

LUNE'S PRAYER

City folk filled the Temple of Lune. It held a different atmosphere at night as men and women visited not for bathing or religious reasons, but to relax and… *court*, as Iman once described it. Mina had only entered the temple a handful of times to bathe, and never in the evening. Even setting foot inside the temple at night would set tongues waggling.

Creeping heat prickled her skin, and not just from the saunas below. Giggling voices followed her into the main lobby. It was a pleasant, spacious room with white marble walls decorated in blue tile mosaics and lanterns that hung from the ceiling like stars. A generous number of loungers filled the space, and a fountain of Lune in all her glory drew attention to the center. Any reverence shown to the goddess was ruined by the half-naked city folk entering the mixed baths. A Solander girl leaned against the bath's archway and fluttered thick eyelashes.

Gods, Mina still wore her male garb. She could almost hear Garr's condescension, *What about your vows?*

One of the hooded Water Bearers approached, but this one carried a sword strapped to her waist. She pulled her hood down, revealing flowing black hair and two turquoise earrings in the shape of Lune's crescent. "Lady Tamina. I've been expecting you."

"Lady Kasara," Mina blurted out. She was the Solander girl

from Prince Rais's helbond ceremony—the one who'd asked her about joining the Academy. "You're a Water Bearer?"

"I guard the temple. It can become rowdy at night. If you'll follow me?"

Who was this woman? She spoke like a Houseman and walked with the casual grace of the noblewomen around the Keep, but none of them would volunteer to serve a temple. "I was told to ask for, uh, oil recommendations."

Lady Kasara glanced over her shoulder. "I know the oils you need."

Mina followed her down the steps to the private pools underneath the temple.

Bronze Neu Bosan pipes ran along the ceiling and occasionally hissed with a puff of steam, though this was masked by laughter and the splash of water above them. Mina wafted the humid air. This was a damp heat, like Gaisland's forest, but hidden in the heart of Solus. Lady Kasara stopped by an unusual tapestry of Lune hunting with a bow, which was not an image Mina had ever seen before. Hidden behind the tapestry was a marble door. Lady Kasara knocked on it three times and then pushed it open, beckoning Mina inside.

Mina entered what appeared to be a storage space filled with crates and ceramic pots. Jonan stood waiting in front of a deep purple tapestry that stirred from a breeze, though where the breeze came from this far underground, Mina had no idea.

How did *he* even get inside the temple?

Jonan gestured to the wall to Mina's right and only then did she realize they were not alone. Seated on separate loungers were two robed women—Yasmin, the High Priestess of Gai, and Lady Karina Sarabond, the High Priestess of Lune. The wife of Salasar rubbed her swollen belly. "High Priestess of Rahn. Come, sit with us and we'll drink tea."

Mina stared at them. "What's going on?"

"This." Jonan pulled the tapestry aside and a whoosh of warm air rushed over her.

A dark, gaping tunnel had been dug out of the wall.

He *had* been busy. "This connects to the Temple of Rahn? How did you manage to hide it from Samira?"

Jonan huffed a laugh. "I didn't have to. Fez kept her distracted. Someone kept leaving nuts in her bed, robes, and other strange places." He shrugged. "It seems she's allergic to fur."

Poor Samira. And poor Fez for being used against her.

"But we have a problem," Jonan continued. "Cyrus Fellbond and his men have been patrolling the canals, including the place where our favorite tunnel has a most fortunate crack. That route is no longer safe. And so, we must resort to an alternative plan. The Temples of Gai and Lune are sympathetic to our cause."

Her heart skipped a beat. She'd sat beside both priestesses in the Council meetings without saying a word to either of them, and one was Salasar's wife. Could they be trusted with this?

Lady Kasara gestured to a chair and Mina sat, while Jonan dragged a wooden crate into the center to act as a makeshift table. The High Priestess of Gai poured green tea, offering the first cup to Lady Sarabond.

Jonan declined the tea. "I've gathered you all because you understand the situation and have agreed to help. The call will come soon. Our Prince expects all Fire Walkers, including women, children, and those who are not physically able, to march to the front lines of war and contribute. We of House Arlbond reject this. As I speak, our stewardess is preparing our town, Arlent, to receive Fire Walkers from across Sandair. To hide them. We have long smuggled Fire Walkers out of the Temples of Rahn, and we were once assisted by you—the High Priestesses of Gai and Lune. We call upon your help once more."

Mina bit back her surprise. She had no idea that both priestesses had once helped Jonan and Talin smuggle Fire Walkers out.

"The game is more deadly this time, Jonan," the High Priestess of Gai said with a soothing voice. It was the first time Mina had ever heard her speak. "But for your father—for Jahan—we will do what we can." Yasmin smiled and her old eyes gleamed with a gentleness. "Jahan was my mentor. He taught me the skills needed to be a Green Hand. I watched him being dragged away to the Temple of Rahn all those years ago, when I was barely an acolyte. Those of us in the Temple of Gai see Fire Walkers as our brothers and sisters, not our enemy. We'll take the children. War creates orphans, so hiding them will not be a problem. But we'd prefer not to split them from mothers."

"The Temple of Lune supports women," Lady Sarabond said. "*All* women. If that smarmy princeling wants to risk Lune's anger by sending Fire Walker women to their deaths, then that's where we get involved."

Mina openly stared. She'd never heard anyone insult Prince Ravel with such blatant disrespect.

Jonan inclined his head. "Then at least we can provide a path to freedom for the women and children. House Arlent thanks you and is at your disposal. The Council has no idea how many Fire Walkers live in the temples. In this, their contempt of us works in our favor. As long as Leila kept the temple doors locked and the Fire Walkers docile, the Council was content to spend as little thought on us as possible."

"Thank Lune she's not with us." Lady Sarabond shuddered. "I never liked the woman. She'd be the first to run up the hill and rat on us whenever the temples did anything that wasn't by the books. Contrary to popular belief, the temples don't receive the funding they should. Not since the days of Princess Aniya. Seventeen years since her death have taken their toll on us, and I'm sick and tired of foolish Housemen dictating what we need as if we were children." She smiled at Mina. "No offense meant."

Mina bowed her head. "None taken."

"We must act before the call to march comes," Jonan said. "None of our plans leave this room. Assume you are being watched."

"What about Salasar?" Mina blurted out. "Are we keeping this from him?"

Lady Sarabond smirked. "You think we can trust my foolish

husband with something this delicate? What goes on in the temples stays in the temples. If he thought for one moment I was going behind the Council's back, he'd march me to Saraani and force me to give birth there." She flashed a wicked grin. "It's what he did last time."

Lady Kasara choked on her tea.

"Salasar would bow to pressure from the Prince and his House," Jonan added. "We cannot trust anyone outside of this room, bar Nazim Grebond."

"Nazim's injured," Mina said. "When I was in Gaisland."

"Jonan told us about your journey," Lady Sarabond said. "We are greatly relieved that you made it home safely and we offer prayers for the recovery of your sorran." She gestured to Lady Kasara. "We have stepped up our security measures, especially around the water supply to your temple and certain Houses known to be... sympathetic to Fire Walkers. Isn't that right, Kasara?"

"All water is tested by taste and smell, and all Water Bearers to the Temple of Rahn are escorted by armed guard, as you commanded, Mother," Lady Kasara said.

"Very good. You should double the guard now that the High Priestess of Rahn has returned."

Lady Kasara bowed out of the room. *She* was Salasar's daughter?

"Gods, I hope this war fizzles out soon. I don't think I can wait it out." Lady Sarabond rubbed her belly. "My little one is ready to burst. Another girl." She smiled. "I asked Lune to grant me daughters so I wouldn't lose them to war, and then Kasara goes and takes after her father. Well. I best get back to my patrons before I'm missed." She rose to her feet. Yasmin helped her up as she struggled. "If you ever need sanctuary, this temple will always be open to you. Lune's luck to you, High Priestess of Rahn, and to us all."

The High Priestess of Lune waddled out of the room. Yasmin guided her by the arm and whispered soothing advice for the baby.

Jonan lingered by the tunnel until they were gone, and then

fixed Mina with a look he must have learned from Iman. "You used too much blood."

"I'm still standing, aren't I?"

"Barely. I can feel your exhaustion. Get some meat on your way back to the temple. As rare as possible."

"We have more important things to worry about than my stomach. That raider who attacked me—Emir—he had a brand on his forehead. The sigil of House Rhaesbond. That means he was a slave, right? From Neu Bosa?"

"Sadly." Jonan lifted his tunic, exposing his chest, and pointed to the red Fire Walker markings inked into his skin.

A three-forked flame was mixed into swirls, subtle but unmistakable once it was pointed out. She hadn't noticed it before, but he'd covered them up after the Solend.

He rubbed a palm across the pattern. "The sigil of a House long dead. A reminder of who I am. And what I can never escape."

"Why would slaves have the same symbol?"

"Because their masters are arrogant. They aspire to capture and breed those with the strongest blood fire, and who has stronger blood than a Rhaesbond? I know this from experience. A Neu Bosan slave master once tried to take me. When I lived on Solus's streets as a child. First, he offered bribes of a better life. Then, he dangled knowledge of my Rhaesbond past. And when I still refused, he tried to take me by force. I barely escaped him. I learned later, when we established Arlent, that this was not rare. They prey on vulnerable Fire Walkers and take them to Neu Bosa. There are many in Arlent who we saved from that fate."

"My mother saved them." Tira's face appeared in a lantern on the wall and nodded. *This* was why Jonan disliked Neu Bosan. Did Alistar know what his people were doing? Did he even care? "Emir is our rogue Fire Walker. But why? We could help men like him!"

"We don't know his motives or where his loyalty lies. Which is why I'm speaking to you here, and not in the temple. There could be spies among our Fire Walkers. We must be careful what company we keep." He gave her a pointed look.

She crossed her arms. "Garr told me about the slaves."

"He's a liability."

"He fought by my side. He could have run or attacked me at any point, but he didn't—"

"And think, why is that? What is he trying to gain?"

"He wants to help the Fire Walkers, that's all—"

"Tira wasn't this naïve."

She glanced to the lantern, and Tira rolled her eyes. "I haven't told him anything he doesn't need to know."

"Make sure it remains that way." He rubbed his jaw. "What concerns me are the Hartnords. Do you have the vial?"

She handed over her bottle of Lune's Tears.

Jonan popped the stopper and sniffed it. "No scent." He allowed a single drop to spill on his tongue. His face scrunched and a violent shudder cracked through the bond. "Salty. House-men have tried various methods to suppress blood fire, from leeches to castration. All on the false belief that Fire Walkers are feral and can be tamed. This is no different." He shoved the bottle into his own pocket. "The Water Bearers already check our temple's water for Rahn's Breath. We'll begin checking for this as well."

"Prince Wulfhart thinks it could stop war."

"Stop war or turn it in his favor? I'm not surprised the Bosan are involved. They don't see Fire Walkers as people but as commodities. They want what any Houseman wants: control of our power because they lack their own. With this new Hartnord elixir, they may succeed."

Then Garr was right. Lune's Tears would be used to control them, not free them. Fire Walkers would never be seen as ordinary men and women, no matter how successfully they suppressed their power. Even if they never summoned another flame again, the fear might be gone but the hatred would remain. It was too engrained in their culture. And if she convinced her people to surrender their power to that hatred, she would only strengthen their enemies and weaken her people.

"I once warned you not to trust Myrbond," Jonan said. "If his House is involved with the Hartnords, be cautious."

"Alistar's my friend. He can be trusted."

"Can he? Your memories state otherwise."

The door opened and thankfully saved her from an awkward conversation. Lady Kasara entered. "Forgive me, High Priestess. You were seen entering our temple and should not disappear from view too long lest you raise suspicion."

Jonan tugged the tapestry open. "If you see anything or anyone suspicious, find me. Don't go looking for trouble." He raised an eyebrow in Mina's direction. "And Mina? You really should bathe. You *do* stink."

She stuck out her tongue.

He chuckled and entered the tunnel, merging with the darkness.

Lady Kasara bowed. "Lady Tamina—"

"You're Salasar's daughter."

Lady Kasara smiled. It was a subtle one, though full of warmth. She didn't look anything like the fabled Sword of Solus, though Mina didn't exactly look like her father either. "I didn't mean to hide that from you. Perhaps now we can talk freely."

Mina's cheeks burned. She'd snubbed Lady Kasara during the helbond ceremony. "You want to join the Academy, but I didn't lie—the King won't listen to me."

"I begged my father to petition the King long ago, but he refused. He trained me to use a sword—to fight as well as him. But he wouldn't even ask. He said the Academy wasn't the realm of women and it would never be allowed."

"Salasar trained you?"

Lady Kasara ran a hand along her sword hilt—a simple pommel with a single turquoise gemstone molded into the hilt. "To grant me the skills needed to protect myself from men. I think he rather enjoyed teaching me. My mother didn't allow it, but we ignored her and trained regardless. It was our secret. I... I've never had the chance to test my skills. To prove to him I'm talented enough for the Academy. But the temple needs guards—female guards—to protect our Water Bearers from patrons. That's why I'm here.

"We house women. Lost women, those from broken homes or marriages, or those who lost husbands to battle and cannot bear the soul wound. They *need* protection. Acting as the temple's guard may not be glamorous, the other Houses may not deem it worthwhile, but I care little for what they think of me." She lifted her chin. "Fire Walkers are Lune's children, too. If Housemen won't protect them, then... I will. My sword is yours, Lady Tamina, should you want it."

Mina grinned. Perhaps if she'd been born Malik, she would have married Lady Kasara after all. "Are you sure? It'll be dangerous."

"Do you promise? The last danger I faced was offending Lady Fellbond's choice of dress."

"Assassins could be hiding in Solus."

"Deadly ones?"

"The deadliest."

Lady Kasara's eyes sparked with a defiance that was all Salasar. "Where do we begin?"

If Emir and his men were targeting Fire Walkers, then he'd know they were being sent to Solus's temple. And with more Fire Walkers crowding the capital than ever before, it was only a matter of time before he struck again, this time close to home.

They needed allies. They needed Lune's luck, too. Who better than a Water Bearer?

"The temples. We protect the temples."

42

THE COUNCIL'S REPORT

The one place Mina could best protect the Temple of Rahn was the Council chamber. It wasn't her battlefield of choice, but the next day's meeting may well be her only chance to protect the Fire Walkers before the order came to march her people out of Solus.

But first, Mina found a quiet space underground and got to work constructing a report of her time in Gaisland. She'd never written a report like this during her Academy days and had no idea how to word it. She tried roping Jonan into helping her since he'd surely spent some time writing reports with Talin. But no, Jonan didn't care for bureaucracy and Talin could barely write with his left hand. Instead, both men were apparently gods-damn useless and had left such tasks for Iman.

Gods, she wished Iman were here.

Mina wrote through a whole stack of scrolls to get the wording right, and then re-wrote it again after Fez smudged her ink. She left her encounter with Prince Wulfhart out; Alistar had begged her not to mention his father's involvement and she intended to keep that promise. The Hartnords would need to find their own way of proving their innocence. She couldn't depend on them to prevent war.

Tira watched in the dwindling brazier light. Her mother waggled her finger.

Mina put down her quill and rubbed her eyes. "What? I'm trying to write, and I can't do that if you keep scowling at me."

Tira cocked her head with her tongue out in some silly imitation of a corpse, then snapped her fingers as though pretending to summon her flame.

"You're mad at me because I didn't burn those bodies in Gaisland."

Tira nodded.

"Lune forgive me if I prioritize my *bleeding friend* over some gods-damn raiders. You'd have done the same if it were Talin."

Tira pulled a face and vanished.

"Talking to yourself again, Sword Dancer?"

Garr leaned by the door with a cup in his hand. By the slight pink tinge on his cheeks, she doubted it contained water.

"It's *Sand* Dancer."

"That's what I said." He was dressed once more in his street rat rags, without the blood and dirt of the past few weeks. "You should be sleeping." He sauntered into the room and snatched one of her discarded scrolls. "What's this?"

"My report of our trip. Care to write it for me?"

He tossed it aside. "Can't help you there. Those squiggles mean nothing."

"The man of many talents can't read or write?"

"Do you know many street rats who can?"

She bit her tongue. It was only because of Iman that Mina could read and write as well as she did. "Let me know when it's dawn."

Garr left but returned only a heartbeat later.

"I said when it's dawn—"

"It's dawn, High Priestess." His eyebrow quirked.

So soon? She had only enough time to change clothes, grab a bread roll, and bolt up the hill to the Keep. The Council was already in session when she burst through the doors.

Prince Ravel shook his head. "So kind of you to join us, High Priestess."

Talin sat beside him, and his warmth spread through the blood bond. He offered a weak smile but looked gaunt, his cheek bones more prominent than ever. Gods. He looked as though he hadn't slept or eaten in weeks.

On the Prince's left sat Gareth the Hartnord. *Prince* Gareth. How many Housemen knew the truth? More of them filled the chamber than she expected, mostly from the Solander and Duslander Houses. The Gaisland chairs were empty.

"Your report, Priestess?" Salasar commanded.

She handed the scroll to his sorran. Cyrus snatched it with an undisguised sneer.

Salasar skimmed through her notes with a frown before passing it to the Prince. As the Prince read, Salasar gestured for her to sit with the other Priestesses. Lady Sarabond smiled as Mina took her place.

The Prince handed the scroll to Talin, and his amber eyes met hers. "Your report contains some... discrepancies, Priestess."

She took in a breath. "What discrepancies, my Prince?"

Salasar held up his hand. "Will you give the Council a verbal account of the events in Grenai, Priestess?"

What was the point in writing a gods-damn report if she had to repeat it all anyway? Nonetheless, she stood and related the tale of the burning wagon. And the cause. As the words 'Rahn's Breath' slipped from her lips, she turned to the Prince and awaited his reaction.

Prince Ravel looked nonplussed. "You believe the Fire Walkers were poisoned?"

"It's there in my report, my Prince. The supplies were checked, but someone was deliberately leaving out canteens of poisoned water, knowing the Fire Walkers would drink it. I believe there has been a misunderstanding—there are no rogue Fire Walkers, my lords. Only innocent Fire Walkers being deliberately poisoned, just as men were poisoned during the Solend."

He raised an eyebrow. "Are you implying *I* am responsible for these attacks?"

"It is an odd coincidence, my Prince."

Farzad Fellbond thumped his fist on the table. "Gai's teat, we're at war, woman. Do you honestly believe any man in this room would willingly risk our greatest assets?"

"Who else has experience growing Rahn's Breath and applying it?"

"Watch your words, Priestess. Your treasonous tongue is not welcome here."

The other Housemen murmured their agreement.

She met their scowls with her own. "Are you forgetting who poisoned innocent men during the tournament? Who poisoned your king?" She turned to Kahn Khalbond. "Who poisoned Barahn? Perhaps we should ask the King's Left Arm for *his* opinion."

Gareth had been the one to damn Prince Ravel with his Sight. If the Prince were involved with this, Gareth would uncover it.

"Allow me to put this matter to rest, my lords," Prince Ravel said. He stood, placing both palms atop his heart in some mockery of honesty. "I swear to each of you on the blood of the Bright Solara that I have not poisoned any Fire Walkers since my arrest. My own father held an investigation and destroyed any Rahn's Breath. I willingly aided him in his search and allowed guards to ransack my rooms and possessions. I did so as penance. And whilst I will not justify my actions, I will point out a truth: I once warned that our enemies could turn the Fire Walkers against us."

Gareth inclined his head. "He speaks the truth."

She ground her teeth. Gareth had lied before to protect her; could he be lying now to protect Prince Ravel? But why would he? Unless he was trying to sabotage their peace, as Prince Wulfhart's guard had claimed.

Farzad Fellbond raised his hand. "If I may, my Prince, these Rahn's Breath peppers—how could Hartnords grow them? Their cultivation is supposedly a closely guarded secret of House Rhaesbond, and Hartnord land is all but barren, so they'd have us believe."

The Prince took his seat. "You are correct, Lord Fellbond.

Rahn's Breath is rare and difficult to grow. I did not come by them easily. In fact—" he glanced to her. "They came from House Arlbond. They grow in abundance in the valley of Arlent. Is that not so, Lord Talin?"

How could the Prince possibly know that? She'd never told anyone about Rahn's Breath other than Alistar and Raj.

Talin raised his head, weariness in his dark eyes. "Never in abundance, my Prince, and not anymore."

"What, your House is growing them?" Farzad Fellbond spat. "This is what happens when we allow Rhaesbond blood to enter a House—"

"I already ordered their destruction, Farzad. If the Hartnords are using Rahn's Breath, it is not coming from our House."

She tried to catch Talin's eye, to see if his words were true, but he avoided her gaze and the bond remained quiet. The valley bloomed purple from the Rahn's Breath flowers her mother had planted. They were part of her history.

The Prince waved a dismissive hand. "Regardless. Thanks to our Priestess's investigation, we now know that our enemies have the knowledge and means to attack us through the Fire Walkers. This complicates matters."

This was her chance. She stood and placed both palms onto the Council table. "Rahn's Breath is indeed dangerous and can turn the Fire Walkers into a weapon against our own army. You all saw the devastation it caused at the Solend. Given the risks, we must remove Fire Walkers from the front lines of war."

A flicker of a smile graced Prince Ravel's lips. Almost as though he admired her effort. "Are you admitting that you cannot control your Fire Walkers, Priestess?"

"When poisoned, my Prince. Fire Walkers will be of no danger inside the temple."

"Not true, my Prince," Cyrus said. "They're an undisciplined lot that come and go when they please. And they're spending our gold on fresh lamb, wine, and clothing. Is this how the Priestess trains them? Is this how they're rewarded for causing this war?"

There it came. She'd been waiting for it since Cyrus first showed up.

"What is this farce?" Farzad Fellbond demanded. "Our coffers are being drained for extravagance inside the temple?"

She clenched her fists behind her back. "My House is covering the additional expense to feed the Fire Walkers a more adequate diet. Or would you have our 'greatest assets' faint on the front lines from a lack of nutrition?"

From across the table, Talin smiled at her, and his warmth bloomed in her stomach.

"And wine?" Farzad Fellbond snapped.

"There's no wine. Your son is seeing what he wishes to see."

"The Fire Walkers are being fed and trained on my orders," Salasar said. "And my sorran is explicitly forbidden from interfering with their training." He shot a glare at Cyrus.

"Lord Fellbond raises an important issue," the Prince said. "You allow your Fire Walkers to leave the temple, Priestess?"

"To light the city's lanterns as per the law, my Prince."

He stroked his chin. "If our enemies know how to poison the Fire Walkers, then this presents a few problems. We must keep them under close guard so they cannot be used against us. Guards should be placed inside and outside the temples, and any Fire Walker who leaves must be accompanied by an armed man at all times. Even you, Priestess."

She blinked. "I have a sorran."

"Your sorran is injured, and far way. Though from my understanding, a bond between a Sandarian and a Bosan rarely works." He leaned forward. "Did yours?"

Gods, he knew.

The game was up. Her eyes moved to Gareth—a dumb and revealing move, but she couldn't help it. The Hartnord stared back with his silver eyes.

Lying was not an option.

"No, my Prince."

Talin looked down at the table, but whatever he was feeling

didn't come to her through the bond. Was he angry? Disappointed? He only looked exhausted.

"I'm sure we can arrange for a suitable guard," Prince Ravel continued. "Furthermore, any Fire Walkers travelling to or from Solus should also be accompanied. For their safety."

This had nothing to do with their safety. Had he learned that Fire Walkers were being smuggled out of the temple already? "I don't require a chaperone, my Prince." She rubbed a hand over Hawk's hilt. "I'm capable of seeing to my own safety."

"It sends a message, Priestess. One I'm sure even you would appreciate. Especially as the Hartnords wish to negotiate with us and have requested your presence specifically, along with our resident Rhaesbond."

Her heart caught in her throat. "What—what do they want?"

Salasar pulled a scroll from his sahn. "A few days ago, the Hartnords made contact. They're requesting a meeting in a neutral location and apparently have evidence regarding Queen Vida's murder—they're saying they've caught the perpetrator."

"And you believe them?" Farzad Fellbond asked.

Salasar grimaced. "We'll have our own Hartnord to verify their evidence. It makes no strategic sense for them to request negotiations now. The delay only works in our favor as we seek to rebuild our supply lines and replace the rations and materials lost in Grenai. Neu Bosa has offered to lend us their embassy for the meeting."

"What, you're inviting them into Solus?" Farzad Fellbond barked. "You're blundering into a trap!"

"They'll be well guarded. And our High Priestess will position her Fire Walkers to deal with them should the worst happen."

So, her Fire Walkers were to serve as guards and soldiers at last. At least it was happening here in Solus and not far away on some Hartnord battlefield. And it was unlikely Prince Wulfhart planned violence. He was going to make his own case to bring this war to an end before it began. Not only that, if he'd discovered who killed the Queen, then they'd be able to bring her killer to justice and put thoughts of war behind them.

Thank the gods.

"I welcome any chance to avenge my mother's death," Prince Ravel said. "Though it's unfortunate that our Neu Bosan allies seem more interested in this meeting with the Hartnords than providing their promised ships. At least this delay will give our ambassador a chance to explain the Three-Pointed Star's position." The Prince's eyes met Mina's. "He has much to answer for."

"I've sent for Lord Hiram, my Prince," Salasar said. "We'll get our answers then."

"See that the embassy and Solus are prepared." His amber eyes burned through her skin as though trying to summon Gareth's Sight. "Is there a reason why the Hartnords have requested *you*, High Priestess? And Lord Jonan?"

"I couldn't fathom, my Prince. Perhaps Prince Wulfhart values a Fire Walker's perspective."

"Perhaps. Between now and Lune's Shadow, we'll all be tested under the eyes of Rahn. And we'll all need to make sacrifices. Prepare your Fire Walkers. To ensure their safety, their markings must be visible at all times."

She caught his meaning. He wanted them stripped and humiliated. She gave a brief jerk of her head. Breaking her promise to them left a sour taste in her mouth, but it was a small price for their freedom—and keeping them clothed made it easier for infiltrators like Emir to hide their brand.

The meeting drew to a conclusion and the Housemen shuffled out. Talin had said almost nothing the entire meeting. It was as if her father weren't there at all. A shadow. The Prince played the Council like his own personal battlefield and the Housemen were soldiers under his command. He'd trained for this his whole life and acted like the King he wished to be. No matter what she planned, Prince Ravel was always one step ahead.

For all her instruction by Iman, Mina had no idea how to navigate a Houseman's world and its Council. She couldn't play him at this game. She didn't even know the rules.

Talin lingered behind. "Tamina."

She waited until the last man had left and sat beside him, taking his hand in hers. It felt cold. Wrong. "You look terrible. *Talk to me.*" Gods, he wasn't dying because of the King? She couldn't bear it. Talin squeezed her hand. "Don't worry." He glanced to the door as it opened and Gareth strode back in.

"It's safe," Gareth said, and leaned on the edge of the Council table.

Mina studied her father's expression. "What's going on?"

"I dreamed your conversation with Prince Wulfhart in Myryn," Talin said. "Gareth and I have our concerns regarding their demands. Our priority remains the same—to smuggle the Fire Walkers to safety. Then, if the Hartnords are truly willing to work with us, our House will test Lune's Tears ourselves. I won't subject Fire Walkers to a potion which could do more harm than good. We use it on our terms, or not at all."

She glanced between her father and Gareth. Why was Talin speaking so carelessly about their plans in front of an outsider? A potential traitor?

The King's Hartnord sorran cocked his head. "You don't trust me. That's wise."

"Gareth is our ally," Talin said. "His Sight has proven valuable to us."

"You defended Prince Ravel! You said he was speaking the truth—"

"Because he was," Gareth said. "Or he knows how to manipulate the truth. That remains to be seen. As for Wulfhart, I am unsure what his intentions are, but if he has any information about the Queen, we must weigh it. I will need your protection, High Priestess. My talents don't include swordplay." He smiled with genuine warmth. The first time she'd ever seen him smile, and there was something disconcertingly familiar about it.

"And what of *your* intentions, Lord Gareth? You're one of them. A Hartnord prince. Is it revenge you want?"

His smile faded. "I'm no lord or prince. My life lost its worth long ago. I am here to see justice done."

Talin squeezed her hand. "Trust me on this."

She didn't trust any of these gods-damn Hartnords, allies or not, but she trusted Talin. "Tell me what to do."

Talin nodded his gratitude. "I'm not keen on sending you to this meeting, but it will act as the distraction we need to smuggle Fire Walkers from Solus, especially now that Prince Ravel is beginning to suspect something. Iman is on her way here. We must be ready to act as soon as Prince Wulfhart lands on our shores, which means Jonan cannot accompany you—he'll be needed in the temple. And we must tread carefully. Prince Ravel is going to have you watched. You can't step a foot out of line."

"I figured. How is the King?"

"Recovering. And what I tell you must not be repeated." He drew in a breath. "I have been giving Khaled my blood."

"What? Why?" No wonder Talin looked so tired. "Surely there must be someone else—"

"There's no one else. The Green Hands, even Jonan, tried, but the King's blood is rejecting them for some reason. He'll only accept mine. Perhaps because of the sorran bond. My blood is helping him to return to strength—"

"At the cost of your own! Look at yourself!"

"It's a sacrifice worth making, Mina."

"Not to me!"

"If the King dies, then Prince Ravel will gain the crown."

And Talin would die with him. "Prince Rais—"

"Isn't ready—*yet*," he added, as she opened her mouth to argue. "Prince Ravel is making his moves, and so I'm making mine. I'm telling you this so you will understand what games are being played, what is at stake, and what your role will be."

She leaned back in her chair.

"I'm listening."

"Prince Ravel builds relationships between Houses by bribing them with gold or power, or threatening those who don't comply. You see how the Solander Houses feed off his every word. They'll be the ones who profit from this war whilst their people are the ones who'll pay the price. The attack in Grenai and Nazim's injury are no coincidence."

"You think the Solander Houses are being spared on purpose?"

"I'm discounting nothing. Rais needs allies like Nazim. He's eager, but inexperienced. I'm giving him that experience. I've sent him to the city guard to work alongside them and build Solus's defenses. It's not a glamorous task, but he'll gain skills, become a leader, remain safe from any assassination attempts, and most importantly, he'll be seen working alongside the very men that Prince Ravel so callously endangered at the Solend. Whilst Prince Ravel cozies up to Housemen in Council meetings, Rais will be out there getting his hands dirty and winning the hearts and minds of the people."

It wasn't enough. "Is that all?"

"It's only the start. I have persuaded the King to name Rais as his heir."

She swallowed a gasp. "Truly?"

"Yes, but not immediately. To do so now, with war so close, would only drive the Solander Houses to publicly declare support for Prince Ravel's claim and cause more division. First, Prince Rais will formally challenge his father to the crown, as per the Code of Honor. Khaled will accept and duel his son, who will win and claim the crown for his own. This is why I must build Khaled's strength to at least be able to act out a duel."

"But won't Prince Ravel challenge Rais to a duel for the crown? It'd be his right."

"You're learning," Talin said with a hoarse chuckle. "But it's only the threat of war that gives Prince Ravel such a strong hold over the Council. Take away that threat, and none would dare to publicly oppose King Khaled's right to name his own heir, not even House Fellbond. Everything depends on negotiating peace with Prince Wulfhart before blood is spilled on the battlefield."

"We will speak with Hartnor on Prince Rais's behalf," Gareth said. "We must convince them that a lasting peace is possible with Rais on the throne."

"Prince Wulfhart doesn't trust you," she said.

"With good reason. But Wulfhart isn't yet king of Hartnor. If he isn't amenable, there is another Hartnord prince who may be."

Was there? She knew nothing about Hartnord royalty.

"Our hope is to convince the Hartnords that there is no threat to their kingdom so long as Sandair is under Prince Rais's leadership and the Fire Walkers are under *yours*," Talin said. "I'm depending on you to sway them. For better or worse, Prince Wulfhart wants you at the negotiating table. Tell him that Rais will refuse to use the Fire Walkers as weapons in war, which should also appease Neu Bosa as well. Under Prince Rais, we have a chance to unite all three nations into one alliance. With their support, Rais will be in the best possible position to rise. There is just one final piece."

It was a good, thought-out plan. A devious one that went behind Prince Ravel's back. They were finally turning his tricks against him. "Which is?"

"He'll need a queen to further solidify his position as a ready-made king. I know I gave you a choice, but we are running out of options."

"I'm the Priestess—"

"Which, ironically, makes you a powerful choice. It will demonstrate to Hartnor, and all of Sandair as well, the respected position of Fire Walkers in Rais's kingdom, as well as secure your ability to keep the Fire Walkers, and Arlent's people, safe for generations to come." Talin paused a moment as if to give Mina a chance to process the importance of his words. "Prince Rais cannot challenge his father until this war is averted. Then, we'll have to move quickly and you'll need to stand down as high priestess. It's either you or Salasar's eldest daughter."

"Lady Kasara?" she choked out.

"Yes. She was to wed Prince Ravel, if King Khaled had his way—and he would have eventually, although Salasar resisted the match. A marriage with Rais would be equally fruitful to the Bright Solara and more to Salasar's liking. One of you will need to make that sacrifice. Rais needs a queen."

Mina sank into her chair. It was too much to ask of her, and Talin knew it. She could barely follow the Council meetings or write a report, and he wanted her to be *queen*? Of all Sandair? It was ludicrous. She was a desert rat born in the sands, not some lady like Kasara—a woman who'd grown up with the intricacies of noble etiquette.

It was a sacrifice Mina couldn't make.

And yet Talin was sacrificing his own blood to put Prince Rais on the throne. To secure a better future for them all.

Though there was a dark part of her that wondered if Prince Rais was ready for this.

If he could carry the full weight of the crown.

Talin patted her shoulder. "Think on it. I have faith in you to do what's right." His belief in her warmed through the blood bond, but it left Mina feeling cold inside.

43

THE PLAN

Good news arrived with the scent of spice and wine. Mina ran out of the temple and into the arms of her aunt.

Iman laughed and squeezed her tight. "I wasn't gone that long, girl."

"I still missed you." Mina withdrew from the hug. "How's Arlent?"

"Ready." Her eyes shone with bright determination. "Show me what you and Jonan have been up to."

Mina led Iman inside the temple, past the watchful eye of the city guard, to where dozens of Fire Walkers were engaging in breathing and stretching exercises. This had been her idea—they always calmed her before a battle, and her Fire Walkers were likely to face all manner of dangers before the season ended. They needed to be prepared for anything. Samira lectured them while they stretched, though most weren't paying attention. Hundreds of years ago, the Temple of Rahn once served as an academy for Fire Walkers, to train them how to harness their gifts for the benefit of man. Samira certainly enjoyed her position as a lecturer and wasn't at all perturbed by her students' dismissive behavior. An unexpected guilt burned in Mina's stomach. Soon Samira would lose her Fire Walkers. Her home. Her purpose.

Garr pulled faces behind Samira's back to a giggling Kamran.

He winked as Mina strode past. She raised a critical eyebrow, though she had to bite back a smile. Whatever his game was, it brought distraction and laughter to the younger Fire Walkers, which was precious indeed.

"That one's got eyes for you, girl," Iman said, not missing a beat. "Does he know about your vow of celibacy?"

Mina's cheeks warmed. "Everyone knows I'm dedicated to Rahn."

Iman smirked. "I'm sure they do."

They found Jonan inside Leila's glass room. After warm greetings and lengthy discussions of their various preparations at the temples and in Arlent, the topic inevitably turned to politics.

"Do we truly have Hartnords on the way to negotiate?" Iman asked.

"The crown prince himself," Mina said. "He wants me and Jonan at the meeting."

"Why Jonan?"

Jonan shrugged. "Men who seek Rhaesbond blood rarely do so for good reason. Though I won't be indulging them. Not when I'm needed here. This negotiation will prove our best distraction."

"No doubt," Iman said. "In fact, I have a plan to empty the entire temple whilst Mina is busy entertaining our cold-blooded guests."

Mina stared at her. "You're taking them all? But—there are hundreds inside this temple. The Prince will suspect our House if they all disappear. He'll send half the army to—"

"Not if they're all dead. Poisoned. Incinerated to ashes." Iman tapped her nose.

"An attack on the temple in the middle of negotiations," pondered Jonan with a delighted grin. "It's exactly what our rogue Fire Walker would do."

"I thought you'd like that. And who could blame poor Mina when the Council forced her to take her best Fire Walkers to keep watch on the Hartnords and leave the temple undefended?"

"And naturally, the attackers would leave nothing behind but ash and dust," Jonan added.

"And don't forget a little evidence of Rahn's Breath." Iman pulled a purple pepper pod out of her sahn.

Could they truly pull off such a plan? "That would require a lot of fire to look convincing," Mina said.

Jonan cracked his knuckles. "Allow me."

"Whilst the entire city guard is running toward the Temple of Rahn, who will notice a flood of pilgrims pouring out of the Temple of Lune?" Iman said.

"Perhaps we should leave behind the Ash Maker and let him burn," Jonan mused. "His screams would add to the illusion."

Mina scowled. "We're not killing anyone."

Iman patted her shoulder. "We don't kill anyone unless they get in our way. Take the Ash Maker with you to the negotiations. I'll deal with Leila's acolyte."

What would the Council do if their "greatest assets" were wiped out on the eve of war? They were Sandarian; they could win this war with steel. But the cost in blood and lives would be catastrophic to the kingdom, likely for generations. The pressure on the Council to actually *listen* to Prince Wulfhart and reach a compromise would be tremendous. This could end the war.

Prince Ravel would be furious.

It was win-win.

Mina sat with Iman and Jonan and began to plan.

Iman burst into the temple and stomped across the sanctum. "What is this!" she bellowed and thrust a scroll in Samira's face. "Over a hundred seras! This cannot be accurate."

Samira batted the scroll away. "Our High Priestess said we could charge your House any excess—"

"Excess! Five seras is excess, not a hundred!" Iman waved Mina over. "You authorized this, girl?"

Mina snatched the scroll. It was a list of items charged to House Arlbond's personal treasury—clothing, food, bedding, cushions, lamb, toys for the children, and... "I didn't authorize wine."

"Not just any wine," Iman said. "A rare vintage. This alone cost half our budget!"

Samira's face turned bright red. "Well, I, ah, I've never drunk wine. I don't know what's rare, what's expensive, and—it was *his* idea!" She pointed a finger at Garr.

The Ash Maker lounged on a stone step with his arms crossed behind his head, Kamran by his knee, as usual. "I barely touched a drop. Your merry crew of temple dwellers finished nearly the entire shipment while you had me off galloping about the country. You need to teach your followers how to share, Sword Dancer."

Iman's anger rolled through the blood bond and she whirled on Samira. "Where are your books? Your records? I demand to see them at once."

Without saying a word, Samira turned heel and ran into the tunnel.

But this left only Mina to face the brunt of Iman's temper. "And you! You should know better, girl. Do you think our House can be throwing money around right now? When we expect so many..." Her voice dropped to a whisper. "So many *guests* at our door soon? We can't be funding all this luxury. Didn't I teach you the economics involved with running a House?"

"I wasn't expecting Samira to buy wine," Mina grumbled, though she didn't pay much attention to Iman's lessons when numbers were involved.

"The damage is done. Besides, it'll keep her occupied. You need to get that fool under control." Iman glared at Garr. "We need him out of the way, but it'll be no good if he sabotages this meeting with the Hartnords. He needs to at least act the part of a Fire Walker."

"What makes you think he'll listen to me?"

"Because the blood bond doesn't lie, girl."

Mina sighed. She didn't agree with Iman's assessment—that he'd listen to her, or had eyes for her, whatever that meant. She approached the Ash Maker.

He wore a playful smirk. "Am I in trouble, Sword Dancer? You look angry, but honestly, it's hard to tell."

"A word. Now." She jerked her thumb to the archway.

"He's not in trouble, is he?" Kamran asked.

"I'll bring him back alive."

Garr dragged himself up. He ruffled Kamran's hair and followed Mina into the hallway. "Is this about the wine?"

She marched down the corridor, searching the doors for an empty room.

"I tried to stop her. I said, listen, our High Priestess won't be happy if you drink all the wine, she'll want some too—"

"Do you ever stay quiet?"

"My ma says I could talk a corpse back to life."

"I bet." She shoved him inside one of the empty dormitories. The stone beds were covered with silk sheets and down-filled pillows. If Farzad Fellbond saw this, he'd die of shock. "Prince Wulfhart is coming to Solus to negotiate with the Council. I'll be part of the welcoming delegation, and I'll need guards to make sure nothing goes wrong. That means you."

"Prince Grayface couldn't convince you to sail all the way to Hartnor, so instead he's coming here to make time with his favorite Fire Walker?"

"He's coming to talk, that's all."

"That's all? And what if your Council gets so excited about his little antidote to fire magic that they decide they want it for themselves? Stabbing a Hartnord prince in the back is a small price to pay for the solution to all their problems. Then it'll be me and Kamran on our knees with poison in our blood."

"I told you—as high priestess, my duty is to protect the Fire Walkers, even against the Council if it comes to it."

"Giving the Hartnords a chance to brag about their new poison doesn't sound like a smart move, but I'll play. What are your orders?"

"It's time you started acting and looking like a Fire Walker."

"You mean like a simpering coward?"

"If you're willing to obey my commands, then obey this—take off your clothes."

He grinned. "So direct, Sword Dancer. Shall I fetch the wine?"

"This isn't a game. Fire Walkers are supposed to dress a certain way—"

His grin faded. "And why is that?"

"Because cloth is flammable, for one—"

"And forcing them to disfigure their own skin? It's humiliating."

"That's the point."

"I have my dignity."

She held her breath and counted ten heartbeats. "I'm a warrior, not a priestess or Houseman or lady—or whatever other title the Council gives me. I hate all of this cowering and posturing even more than you do. But I accept it, for now, because we can't carve a path out of Solus for the people in this temple with a blade. That's not how we win." Her own words surprised her. Patience and politics had never been her game. "If all you want is to save your own worthless skin, then go. Find your own way out of the city and never come back. But if you want to protect Kamran or anyone else in this temple besides yourself, then shut up and do as I command."

Garr opened his mouth to argue, then frowned. Defeated at last. "Fine. I'll do it your way, Sword Dancer. But I won't take the markings."

"The older Fire Walkers use red paint to touch up their tattoos. Use that."

"You want me to *paint* myself?"

"You said you were dedicated to the Fire Walkers." She placed a hand on her hip. "Prove it."

"I don't know what the chest markings are supposed to look like. Care to show me yours?" He leaned closer, and his amber eyes twinkled. "I'd need to get a good look to accurately copy the patterns."

"Nice try." She rummaged beside one of the beds and tossed a loincloth into his hands. "Put this on."

"*This* is supposed to cover all of me?" He waved the flimsy cloth.

"Do you need something smaller?"

He muttered and pulled off his shirt, tossing it to one side. She swallowed thick saliva. His bare torso was all chiseled muscle—the toned body of a warrior. Strong biceps. Broad shoulders. And dark hair covered his chest in a thick fluff. She'd seen plenty of men shirtless before, men like Talin and Salasar who'd been shaped by the sword, and even Alistar with his fascinating tattoos, but Garr... gods, he was the living depiction of Rahn in all his glory.

She averted her eyes and searched the dormitory for paint. Sure enough, she found a small jar. She approached Garr as he sat on one of the beds to remove his boots. "Here. Uh, you might want to shave your chest first."

He gawked up at her. "You want me to shave my chest?"

"So the markings are visible." She handed him the jar. "Use it sparingly. The designs don't need to be large or fancy, just noticeable."

"Your markings aren't visible."

"That's because I'm the High Priestess."

"So you're ashamed of them?"

"I was, once. But they're part of me, just as fire is a part of my blood. I won't hide either." She rolled up her sleeves and rubbed the silver patterns Samira had once inked into her skin. "I won't force Fire Walkers to accept the markings if they don't want them. But the Council will. They want us seen."

Garr kicked off his boots and stood. He opened the jar and gave it a sniff. "I'm supposed to rub this over my chest?" He scooped a small glob of paint onto his finger.

"Yes. If you—"

He smeared the paint across her nose.

She stared at him dumbfounded. He hadn't just...? She touched her nose and got red on her fingers.

"You're too serious, Sword Dancer. When was the last time you laughed?"

"What have I got to laugh about?"

"That settles it, then. I'll have to paint your entire face red."

She took a step back. "Don't you dare."

He grinned and leaped at her.

Mina squealed and dove behind one of the stone beds. "Get away from me!"

Garr scooped a handful of the red paint and chased her. She picked up a cushion and threw it at him, but he dodged with surprising finesse.

They zigzagged between the beds as she threw cushion after cushion. One smacked him square in the face. He looked stunned for a heartbeat, then threw it back.

She swerved and danced away from cushions and swipes of his paint-covered fingers. It was just like her days training with Talin and Iman in Arlent. Invigorating. Exhausting. She laughed as she caught a cushion and prepared to throw it back, but her arm struck the wall. She'd run out of space. He'd trapped her in the corner.

How had she dropped her guard enough for him to win this advantage? She backed against hard stone as he stalked toward her, a glop of paint in one hand and a predatory smile across his face.

"I'll burn you!" She brandished her cushion. "You touch me and I'll burn your hand clean off."

His playful smile vanished. "Do I scare you, Tamina?"

The way Garr said her name with his odd accent... Like the rolling storms of Lune's Shadow. She swallowed a breath. There was much she didn't know about him, and much she didn't understand—who he was, what games he played.

Her inner embers sparked and heat raced through her veins.

What was it about Garr that made her want to burn? Was it his amber eyes, so eerily like Prince Ravel's?

Garr was...

An Ash Maker. That's who he was.

The tales of the Ash Makers stalked her nightmares as a child. They'd hunted her tribe to near extinction. They were the reason she had no one save Leila to explain her connection with the Shadows. They were a perversion of everything the Lunei stood for. They didn't even burn their dead, but left them for the sands— to become Shadows forever.

Garr was one of them. So why didn't she hate him?

Footsteps approached the door. "I heard a scream," Jonan said. He had a hand on his sword, half-drawn from its scabbard.

Garr hurriedly stepped back.

She placed the cushion down. "Everything's fine. I was, uh, giving orders to my Fire Walker."

On cue, Garr fell into a deep bow. "Your command will be carried out, High Priestess."

Jonan looked wearily between her and Garr, but he nodded and stepped out of the room. She hurried after him.

"I'll play your games, Sword Dancer," Garr called as she reached the entrance. "But watch your back with these Hartnords. You can't trust them."

She turned around to address him and swallowed a gasp. Garr sat on one of the stone beds, his back to her. Multiple scars ran down his back and cut through his body hair in thick jagged lines.

How did he get those scars?

Mina opened her mouth to ask and paused. It was none of her business and it didn't change anything. He was still her Fire Walker.

Still an Ash Maker.

And they had work to do.

44

THE EMBASSY

The Neu Bosan embassy was Myryn itself plucked from Gaisland's shores and hidden amid Solus's docks. Its green tiled walls, wooden roof, and glass lanterns were unmistakably Neu Bosan. The Sword of Solus had already blocked off the major streets leading into the docks, and more guards would patrol the alleyways to chase off any loiterers. A handful would remain outside the embassy. Enough to escort the Hartnords, but not too many to scare them away.

Mina waited outside the embassy walls with her Fire Walker acolytes: Dahn, the grumpy Duslander who eyed everyone that walked by with suspicion; Bahri, the cheerful Solander fisherman; Qareem, the former Gaislander cook; and the two lovers, the Solander setar player Amin and his Duslander husband Marek.

All five stood with their tattoos proudly displayed. That's what she wanted Prince Wulfhart to see—normal men whose lives meant more than the fire in their blood.

Dahn squinted into the distance. "Who invited that fool?"

The sixth man of their group arrived late.

"What did you do?" she blurted out.

Garr puffed out his chest and flexed his muscles. "What you asked, Sword Dancer. My markings represent *strength*." He'd shaved his head, chin, and torso bare and painted what she supposed were meant to be swords on his chest, but his clumsy attempt at art looked more... phallic. It made her face burn hot.

Even if it were an attempt to embarrass her, she couldn't help but be drawn to the curve of his biceps and the sharp dip of his collar bone. Without the thick fluff of hair to mask them, his muscles were truly defined. Her gaze dipped down. The loincloth covered his hips, but his thighs were as sculpted as the rest of him. *He's just a foolish Ash Maker, remember?*

Shouts echoed across the docks. Salasar's men were on the march. The Hartnords had landed.

"If we're fighting Hartnords, they better cut *him* down first," Dahn muttered.

"We're not here to fight." Gods, she hoped not. "Stay behind and follow my lead. No one summons their fire without my command. And if they offer you food or drink, politely decline. Garr, you're with me."

"Why do I have to take point?"

"Because your markings represent *strength*."

Garr grumbled but came to her side. Together, they strode for the embassy doors. He walked awkwardly and adjusted the cord that kept his loincloth in place. "I feel like the biggest fool of this god-damn city," he whispered.

"That's because you are."

Gareth waited by the embassy gates. He'd come without guard and completely unarmed. How much faith did he have in her abilities?

She signaled for her Fire Walkers to stop and approached Gareth alone.

Gareth inclined his head. "They're moving this way." He tapped the side of his eye. "I see them."

A contingent of guards approached with both the royal red and gold banners of the Bright Solara and the silver and blue of Prince Wulfhart. This was why they needed Gareth: to check the Hartnords' words were true, assuming she could even trust Gareth to relay the truth. "How does your Sight work?"

"The Sight allows me to see in color."

In color? "Sandarians can see color."

"We see colors you cannot. Each person has a color belonging to their soul, but those colors change depending on their emotions or actions. We see those emotions."

"Like a House bond?"

"I hear it is similar, yes. Sandarians feel each other's emotions. We see it."

"Does every Hartnord sees the world that way?"

"Not all. The Sight is a skill which must be trained, though some bloodlines are more naturally gifted than others. My Sight is stronger than most. As is Wulf's. He'll know I'm here. We share... similar colors."

It didn't make any sense to her. "And these colors help you see the truth?"

"I see the emotion behind your actions. An intent to deceive is apparent in the mix of fear, caution, and hope you feel while speaking. A master of the Sight will know the intentions behind every word and action you are planning before you speak or act. Sandarians exercise little restraint on their emotions. Their colors are more vivid than Hartnords'."

"Sandarians have been suppressing our emotions for generations. It's the first thing a Fire Walker learns."

"But not you? You are a rainbow of emotion. A Hartnord with good Sight can read you like a book."

Her cheeks burned. "I can control my emotions. If you're so good at reading people, then why haven't you discovered who killed the Queen?"

"Whoever killed the Queen must have worn a guard."

"A what?"

"There are ways to guard against the Sight—by suppressing emotions. My Sight is useless on Wulf. He knows how to guard himself against it."

"But that's why you're here. To uncover the truth with your Sight." How could he do that if Prince Wulfhart were immune?

"The Council believes I am leading this negotiation, but this is down to you."

"To *me?*"

"Wulf doesn't trust me, but he'll trust someone untrained in the Sight and unable to guard against it. If anyone can convince them that Fire Walkers are no threat, it's you."

She was no politician or negotiator. Her entire life was proof of that. "You've chosen the wrong person for this."

"You're exactly the right person. You cannot lie."

"I've lied plenty." And gotten away with it for the most part.

"Sandarians see what they want to see. Wulf will read the truth of your conviction."

"I can't even speak properly in Council meetings—"

"I've watched you, Tamina Hawker. Since you first came into the Keep. I know your heart. I have since the moment my eyes first fell upon you. I've witnessed all of your plotting and secrets and machinations, and said nothing. But you... you're not afraid to speak. Words mean more to a Hartnord than blood. You will tell Wulf exactly what he needs to hear."

She wrung her hands. "And if I can't? If I can't convince Prince Wulf—"

"You will. Your Fire Walkers need you to."

This was too much. A duel or a dance she could do, but this? "And if I *can't?*"

"Then I will do what must be done. One way or another, we will stop this war before it begins."

She studied him as he no doubt studied her. A man who knew a thousand secrets. Possibly more. He'd known her greatest secrets from the moment she stepped foot in Bloodstone Keep, yet he'd kept them hidden for a blood debt owed to Talin.

There is another Hartnord prince, he'd said. Is that why Salasar wanted her Fire Walkers here? To murder Prince Wulfhart if it came to it? Would Gareth have the guts to assassinate his own nephew?

She had to convince the Hartnord prince to stand down. She

had no choice. Too many lives were depending on her, and not just Sandarian ones.

She steadied her breathing. *I am the master of my own self.*

"Don't," Gareth murmured. "Don't try to suppress your emotions. Show them everything you are. Your colors are brightest when you speak from your heart."

"What color am I now?"

"Muddy yellow." He smirked in an oddly familiar way. "It means anxiety."

The embassy gates opened with a loud clang. Neu Bosan guards exited the gates and formed a line against the wall. Their master followed and wore an uneasy smile.

Mina bowed. "Lord Hiram."

Hiram returned the courtesy. "We meet again, High Priestess, in similar circumstances."

"Have you heard any news of Ali—Alistar? Is he well?"

Hiram stiffened. "He is in much pain and cannot walk. The Green Hands tell me he'll require weeks of rest. I've brought him home to Myryn. I wished to stay by his side, but events have forced me here. Why didn't you remain in Grenai?" A darkness fell across Hiram's face. "You're his master. His life was your responsibility, yet you abandoned him?"

Her heart ached. "I left him in good hands, Lord Hiram." And truth was, she regretted leaving him behind. It pained her to think of Alistar suffering and alone in Myryn. As soon as this business with the Hartnords was concluded, she'd find a way to visit him.

"Now is not the time," Gareth said.

Hiram smoothed down his robes. "Of course." He gestured to the embassy gates. "We are ready, if you'll join us. We ask you leave your weapons and Fire Walkers behind."

Her hand curled around Hawk's hilt. She'd expected to remove her sword, but not leave her Fire Walkers. "They're my personal guard."

"You won't require them in the embassy. My own men will be on guard." He raised an eyebrow. "The point of this meeting is to speak on neutral ground, and we cannot do that if our guests feel threatened."

"My Fire Walkers are no threat. They're here to prove that."

"With all respect, High Priestess, it was a Fire Walker who killed the Hartnord king and attacked my son. They will remain outside these walls, or this meeting will not go ahead."

Gareth leaned close. "Allow this concession."

What if this were all some elaborate plot to trick her into walking into Prince Wulfhart's hands? What if Gareth and Hiram had been working against her all this time? The embassy walls didn't contain any braziers, and the glass lanterns weren't lit. She couldn't summon her flame in front of them and ask her mother to confirm if any of these fools could be trusted. "Fine. But they stay at the gate."

Hiram inclined his head in thanks.

Mina took another steadying breath—no matter Gareth's advice—and returned to her Fire Walkers to relay the news.

"You're going in there alone?" Garr said aghast. "With Hartnords?"

"I'll have Gareth—"

"Another Hartnord." He steered her out of earshot of the other Fire Walkers. "You can't trust them, Sword Dancer. They have this ability where they can see—"

"The Sight. I know of it."

"Do you? They can see your emotions and intent, which means they can manipulate you into doing whatever they want."

"Trust me. No man can make me do what I don't want to."

"You think you can out stubborn a Hartnord? They're practically made of stone."

"And I'm made of sand." She cringed at her own poor analogy. "Keep the Fire Walkers safe. If there's trouble, take them back to the temple and find Jonan."

"And leave you at their mercy?"

Hiram called her name. The Hartnords had already entered the embassy and were waiting on her. She unbuckled her scabbard and shoved Hawk into his hands. "Take it."

"Fire Walkers aren't supposed to be armed—"

"Fire Walkers aren't supposed to argue with their High Priestess either, and yet here we are. If you damage it, I'll have your head, do you hear me?" She turned to the embassy.

"Tamina," Garr called. "If danger comes, get the hell out of there."

Hell? Was that an Ash Maker word? She didn't have time to ask about it. She jogged to Gareth's side, and he looked at her with an odd expression.

"Who is that?" he asked.

The doubt in his voice made her pause. "One of my Fire Walkers. What do you see?"

"He's wearing a guard. Sandarians rarely know how. He either has incredible control of his emotions or someone taught him how to do that. A Hartnord."

Garr did name himself the most powerful Fire Walker in Solus. Controlling blood fire required emotional mastery. It was possible he had that level of control.

But Garr had belittled her position as High Priestess and only turned to her side after she'd revealed her somewhat treasonous stance. Could his warnings of Prince Wulfhart's manipulation be a deflection? Garr certainly had knowledge of the Hartnords, and the Neu Bosan as well. But even without her mother's flame to guide her, there was something about him that felt... safe.

Or Mina was turning into the biggest fool of the temple.

"If Hartnords know how to guard, then whoever killed the Queen—"

"Was a Hartnord, or in league with them," Gareth confirmed.

Thinking about it made Mina's head hurt. Gods, she hated politics. She didn't belong in Council meetings or negotiations with foreign kingdoms; this was Talin's world, not hers. But she'd chosen to join it, chosen to become the High Priestess.

It was time to start acting like one. "We'll question him later. We've got a war to stop."

45

A NEGOTIATION

Prince Wulfhart looked the same as when Mina had last seen him in Myryn. He was dressed in his blue tunic and carried no weapon or armor. He'd come alone except for Falkner by his side and stood in the center of the embassy's courtyard. "We meet again, my lady."

She cast a quick glance around the courtyard. It looked less of a defensive fort and more of a traditional Neu Bosan garden like at the Myrbond mansion, complete with a fish pond. Neu Bosan guards lined the edges, standing perfectly still in their green tunics like potted plants.

A stone wall separated Mina from Garr and the rest of her Fire Walkers, and from Salasar and his men. They were in Hiram's hands now.

She bowed. "I'm glad you decided to meet with us, Prince Wulfhart."

"You left us no choice, my lady. Although, as we have suffered this discussion before, perhaps we can forego the formalities." The Prince's eyes narrowed as they rested on Gareth. "You haven't brought your Rhaesbond friend? And yet you saw fit to bring my uncle. My kingdom's former ambassador. How droll."

Gareth bristled. "My past is irrelevant to this meeting—"

"On the contrary, the past has everything to do with this meeting. Seventeen years ago, a Sandarian princess was killed on our land and we were blamed for it. Fire scorched our cities and burned Hartnord bones to dust. And now, we are again blamed for the death of Sandarian royalty." The Prince's eyes turned to her. "Your Council wouldn't believe our innocence, but thanks to the Three-Pointed Star, we have found those responsible." He nodded to Hiram.

Hiram clapped his hands. The mansion doors opened and more guards poured into the courtyard. They dragged two Duslander men in their arms.

Emir and his companion.

Both men wore thick iron chains around their wrists and ankles. Their faces were flushed and dirty, and the three-forked flame had been branded into both their foreheads.

The guards kicked the backs of their shins and forced them to their knees.

"These men are responsible for your Queen's death, and for my father's," Prince Wulfhart said. "They are Rhaesbond."

That couldn't be possible. There were no Rhaesbond left, save Jonan.

Prince Wulfhart raised an eyebrow at her skepticism. "Do you see why we wished to speak with your Rhaesbond? But no matter. Hiram has verified it. Tell her what you know."

"We caught these men in the Emerald Forest," Hiram explained. "After I learned of my son's injury, I did not wait for Lord Nazim to act and sent my own men. We recovered evidence of Lotus Bud and Rahn's Breath—the same purple bottles you warned of, High Priestess. It was then that I made contact with the Three-Pointed Star and learned a sordid truth; these men are former slaves. They killed their masters and escaped, and chose to seek vengeance. They are Rhaesbond blood, bred over many generations."

Were these men truly in league with Saeed? Could it be this simple? Though she couldn't deny their crimes.

These men had attacked her, hurt Alistar.

They'd poisoned Fire Walkers, killed them, and hurt so many others.

They'd framed her people for treason and murder—stolen the freedom of Fire Walkers away again across Sandair—and plotted to murder a king and queen to bring two nations to war.

She should be pleased. Here was the proof of everything she'd tried to convince the Council of, everything they'd refused to believe. This could end the war. No Fire Walkers need march to their deaths. And Mina's family wouldn't need to risk their House to smuggle and safeguard refuges in Arlent.

But these men were slaves. Desperate men, forgotten by Sandair. Killing their masters was no crime in her eyes. And they hadn't tried to kill her. They wanted her alive. Why? To listen to a tale no one else would? Fire Walkers were her responsibility.

All Fire Walkers.

Even these. "Have you questioned them?"

"We cannot. They cut out their own tongues to prevent questioning."

No, that wasn't right. They hadn't been able to talk even before Hiram's men had caught them. Someone was lying. She glanced to Gareth.

Gareth caught her expression and shook his head. Had he seen something with his Sight?

"We have brought you this gift, my lady. You and your Council may dispose of them however you wish." Prince Wulfhart pulled a silver vial from his pocket. "Now we ask you to return the favor."

She locked her hands behind her back. "My House would be willing to test your potion and determine its safety—"

"We have already verified its safety." He waved a hand at Emir.

The Duslander was chained so tight he couldn't move, but no leech hung from his skin. His blood fire was strong enough to burn this courtyard down, especially if he possessed Rhaesbond blood, but he hadn't.

Falkner pulled a purple bottle from a pocket within his tunic.

Rahn's Breath.

"What are you doing?" Mina resisted the urge to slap the bottle from his hand. "Stop!"

Prince Wulfhart placed a gentle hand on her arm. "Your concern is touching, my lady, but this is merely a demonstration." One guard grabbed Emir's companion by the hair and yanked his head back. Another punched him in the stomach so that his mouth opened in a grunt. Falkner then forced Rahn's Breath down his throat. They hurried back, and within heartbeats the raider's skin began to glow red. Gods, he was going to explode and kill another Hartnord royal.

She tugged the Prince's arm. "This isn't safe. They'll burn—"

"Observe." Prince Wulfhart held out the vial of Lune's Tears.

Sweat poured down the raider's face as he struggled against the tide of pure heat pulsating through his veins. Falkner took the vial from his prince's hand and poured its silver contents into the writhing prisoner's mouth.

The raider coughed, spluttering a drop a silver down his chin, but his skin faded from red to his natural deep brown.

She stared at him. Lune's Tears had counteracted the effects of Rahn's Breath so easily?

"I see you are impressed, my lady. Lune's Tears works as intended, and leaves no ill lasting effects."

She shrugged from his touch and glared. "What right do you have to force Rahn's Breath on Fire Walkers as part of your tests?"

"What right?" Prince Wulfhart raised an eyebrow. "When your kin threaten mine, we have every right, my lady. These men killed my father and your queen—"

"And they're proof Lune's Tears are no longer needed. You've caught the men responsible—"

"But who is to say there aren't more of your kin vying for vengeance?"

"Sandair stands on a precipice," Gareth interrupted before she could argue further. "King Khaled is old, and ill, and ready to pass on his throne. Which son will seize the reins of our kingdom? One fears and hates Fire Walkers as you do. But in his fear, he would control and enslave the Fire Walkers, as his fathers have done for generations. They would be his tools and his weapons. Is this the path Hartnor wishes for Sandair to walk? The other son, Prince Rais, holds no desire to wield Fire Walkers as weapons. He would free them, yes… but freedom means they are no longer slaves of the king, in war or in peace. Support his claim, and both Hartnor and Neu Bosa will live at ease."

"Why should I trust your words, Uncle?"

"Because he speaks the truth," she said. "If you can't trust his words, then see mine. Fire Walkers don't want to fight. They want to live in peace! Prince Rais supports this."

Prince Wulfhart rubbed his chin. "We would be willing to meet with your Prince and reach a compromise. However, if you wish peace between our kingdoms, then you must listen to us. I see no other way for us to proceed."

The Hartnord idea of compromise differed from her own. "Then what are your demands?"

"They're quite simple, my lady. We ask that you volunteer a handful of your kin so we may prove that Lune's Tears works. When your Prince is satisfied with its effects, we ask that he apply it to every man, woman, and child in his kingdom. Only then will we support his claim."

He couldn't mean *every* Sandarian? "Not all are born with blood fire."

"Most are. I see it with my Sight. Your people carelessly walk the streets unaware that a taint lurks underneath their skin. Lune's Tears will cleanse that taint."

Taint. Curse. That's all they saw blood fire as.

"Women and children are no threat to you or your kingdom. Even if they possessed blood fire, what harm can they cause a kingdom hundreds of miles away?"

"When we first met, my lady, I spoke of my prophet's words. Our Keepers believe your kin are stealing the light and warmth from our land each time they cast their magic. Our prophet states there will come a time soon when darkness will reign unless your use of fire magic can cease. Even lighting a single candle by magic diminishes our sun's power."

Gareth snorted. "That's preposterous."

"Is it, Uncle? Our doctrine is clear on this."

"The doctrine is wrong. Open your eyes, Wulf. The Keepers are manipulating you like they used my brother."

Prince Wulfhart's silver eyes narrowed. "Don't you speak of my father. You have been gone for seventeen years. What would you understand of his beliefs or our prophecies? You abandoned us and chose Sandair over your own kingdom, your own blood. You're too close to these people to see them for what they are."

"I see them for what they are. They're no different from us."

"Us." Prince Wulfhart wore a sardonic smile. "Is that what you thought when you fucked your Sandarian princess? Or did the heat in her blood rise your own?"

For a heartbeat, silence gripped the courtyard.

Then Gareth leaped at the Prince.

Falkner rushed forward. In one quick movement, he grabbed Gareth's neck and twisted it with a sickening snap.

Gareth collapsed to the ground. His head lolled into an impossible angle.

Mina ran to his side and searched his silver eyes, but they stared at nothing.

He was already dead.

"You killed him!"

"He betrayed my father and our kingdom. His execution was long overdue. But now, my lady, we may proceed with our negotiation unimpeded."

Hiram stood on the sidelines, watching without emotion or reaction, his lips pursed into a grim line. He knew this would happen. He expected it.

Both she and Gareth had walked into a trap.

She closed Gareth's eyes and positioned his body carefully. As she fumbled to straighten his limbs and tunic, she reached for her mother's dagger. She stood slowly, slipping the blade into the folds of her sleeve. "Is this your idea of compromise, Prince? To murder the King's sorran who came here in peace to negotiate with you on his behalf?" She turned her glare on Hiram. "Is this how the Three-Pointed Star honors our alliance?"

"Fire Walkers are as much a danger to Neu Bosa as Hartnor," Hiram said.

"A danger to you? I've never seen a Fire Walker keep a Bosan as a slave!" She waved a hand at Emir, still shackled on his knees. "Do you care to explain that?"

"My House has never owned slaves. These men are property of the Three-Pointed Star."

"These men are Sandarian, and we are no man's property! Have you forgotten what kingdom you belong to? You're our gods-damn ambassador, and yet you hide the fact that Neu Bosa holds our people in slavery!"

Prince Wulfhart chuckled. "You're acting emotional, my lady. Hiram serves the best interests of his people, same as we. I understand this is difficult for you to accept, but the fire in your blood is not natural. It is a perversion. It *must* be contained." He pulled another silver vial from his pocket. "This is the antidote."

She took a step back. "This is supposed to be a negotiation. It's no compromise if you force it on others."

He cocked his head. "But it *is* a compromise. Without this, we would have no choice but to subdue your kin."

"What do you mean by *subdue*?"

Prince Wulfhart's fake smile was as practiced as Prince Ravel's, and in his silver eyes, Mina found her answer.

Gods. He was no different than Prince Ravel.

But he was right about one thing. Lune's Tears was the compromise. She could prevent this war—and beyond that, save her Fire Walkers from ever being used as weapons.

But at the cost of their blood fire, the magic that made them whole.

If she refused, she would have no choice but to march her Fire Walkers into Hartnor to fight, kill, and die as slaves. And probably ensure the victory and ascension of Prince Ravel to the throne in the process.

She knew what the Council would choose, what King Khaled would choose: to fight. To maintain their power. To keep the Fire Walkers under their thumb so they could dominate their neighbors to both north and west.

There had to be another way.

"This won't prevent war. Prince Ravel and the Council may fear the Fire Walkers, but they need us. They *will* march on Hartnor—"

"Our concerns go beyond this one war. Hartnor has survived a Sandarian invasion before, and we can survive losing this war as well. But we cannot survive forever if the Fire Walkers are allowed to burn away our sun. The *world* will not survive. The threat is not to one kingdom but to all humanity. Do you understand me? I'm waiting for your consent, my lady."

"My consent?"

He held up the vial. "You will be the first to give up your power and convince your Prince that this is the only solution. That is your role as High Priestess, is it not? To represent your kin?" He prowled toward her with the grace of a mountain lion. "But you like it, don't you? You like the power in your veins. You like the rush of heat in your blood. You like being able to summon flame and burn your enemies to ash."

The Prince read her like a book, and he was right. She gloried in her own blood fire, and she had enough power to scatter the ashes of his bones in the wind. There were at least ten guards between her and the embassy gates. They wouldn't be enough to stop Salasar's men if she sent the right signal to Talin through the House bond.

Talin's essence burned back with concern. It said, *Buy time.*

Falkner watched her through narrowed eyes. He'd snapped Gareth's neck in a heartbeat. Could he outrun her flames?

"I see what you're thinking, my lady," said the Prince. "Violence is not the answer."

Falkner stretched both arms into a fighting stance. His prince nodded to Hiram.

Hiram clapped his hands once more, and his guards drew their swords. They closed in, forming a tight circle around her and Prince Wulfhart. Now there was no chance of escape.

"I'm no threat to you, Prince."

"Don't you see, my lady? Every Fire Walker is a threat. All of them. Even the cultured ones. The well trained ones. The subdued ones. They're all dangerous." His silver eyes were as sharp and cold as a blade. "Even you."

Is that what her stare looked like? Pitiless and empty?

He popped the stopper from the vial. "Drink."

"You first."

He smiled like a wolf about to devour its prey. "I see what you're doing, my lady, but it won't work."

Her heart stilled. "What do you mean?"

"You're stalling for time. You believe somehow it will protect your people. You're waiting for the last possible moment to send a signal to the soldiers outside to storm this embassy. Am I right, my lady? Do I read you correctly? But here's what you don't understand. This meeting was always intended to be a waste of time. I knew from our dinner in Myryn that you would never consent to relinquishing your fire magic, even before you knew it yourself. No, my efforts are wasted on you."

"Then why are you here?"

He closed the vial, tucked it back into his pocket, and waved a hand at the prisoners.

Emir stood; his clanking chains echoed in the courtyard. Flame burst from his fists and melted through the iron. Metal dropped to the ground in a molten lump.

Neither Hiram nor Prince Wulfhart blinked.

Emir wasn't a prisoner.

She glared at Hiram. "You! You hired men to attack your own son?"

"That arrow was meant to take him out of the fight with minimal injury—it was *you* who burned my son," Hiram said with disgust. "Thanks to you, he'll be scarred for life, if not worse. But he placed himself in that position by choosing a Fire Walker over his own House. You both forced my hand."

She couldn't believe what he was saying. "The Rahn's Breath came from your House. *You* poisoned the Fire Walkers!"

"We wanted to show the Council what would happen if Fire Walkers were left uncontrolled. I believe we have made our point."

"When the Council learns the truth, your House and our alliance with Neu Bosa will fall. You're not preventing war—you've started a new one!"

Hiram rubbed his lips, hiding a shewed smile. "I don't know about that. I think Prince Ravel might be rather forgiving of my plan, don't you? Perhaps even... generous... to my House. Voting against his claim to the throne had been a foolish move on my part. I needed to earn back his favor somehow."

Gods, Neu Bosa was their closest ally and they'd conspired with an enemy. All because they feared Fire Walkers.

And Lord Hiram was at the heart of it.

She thrust her dagger at him.

Prince Wulfhart moved quicker. He grabbed her wrist and twisted it back, snatching the dagger from her grip. She grabbed his wrist with her other hand and flame burst from her palm.

The Prince plunged the dagger into her thigh.

Its sharp point tore through skin and muscle. She screamed and fell to one knee.

Prince Wulfhart withdrew the knife. Her shaking hands pressed against the wound as blood poured between her fingers. The embers in her gut crackled, sending a wave of nausea through her. But no flames came at her call. Her fire was lost to her.

The Prince turned the dagger in his hand as though admiring the crimson smeared there. "A Fire Walker cannot burn without her blood, no?" He cleaned the dagger with a cloth and shoved it into his belt. "My father taught me never to harm a lady, but then..." His lip curled into a smirk. "You are no lady."

"And you're no king," she seethed. Once the flow stopped,

she'd burn this embassy down, starting with Hiram and his gods-damn Hartnord allies.

A Shadow shimmered at her side. It lingered over Gareth's body.

Gods, she'd almost forgotten Hartnords could rise as Shadows.

"Curious," Prince Wulfhart remarked. "You can see it."

"You see the Shadows?"

"We call them ghosts. My Sight has always been able to perceive them, but they don't usually appear in daylight like this. What do they look like to you?"

"Dark, like... like shadow." How in Lune's name could a Hartnord see them? Was it due to his silver eyes, so eerily similar to hers?

"They appear white to us."

"Do they attack?"

"Attack?" He raised an eyebrow. "Ghosts don't attack. They merely haunt crypts."

His Hartnord words made no sense. "Hartnord Shadows may not attack, but Sandarian ones do."

"How fortunate for us that my dead uncle is a Hartnord."

She turned to Gareth's Shadow and willed him to listen. "He lived in Sandair for seventeen years. He's no Hartnord. Shadows form wraiths, take on a physical form and fight—"

"Irrelevant." Prince Wulfhart cupped her cheek. His touch felt smooth, none of the rough callouses of a man used to wielding a sword. "Our time is up. Thanks to Hiram's slave, we know there are tunnels hidden beneath your temple, and we know you plan to use them to smuggle your kin. Our boats came empty, ready to collect them and bring them to Harvera."

No.

They'd tricked her, drawn her to this gods-damn meeting and distracted her so they could steal the Fire Walkers from under her nose. And she was trapped here, along with half of Solus's guard and her most powerful Fire Walkers.

Jonan, Iman, Samira... Gods, they were all in danger.

She tried to stand, but Prince Wulfhart pushed down on her shoulder.

"I'd hoped you would join me, my lady, but your death won't be in vain. Our friend here will burn this courtyard and all inside it. Hiram and I will barely escape with our lives, and this attack—this insult—will not go unpunished. Sandair will acknowledge that it was your kin responsible for our failed negotiation. And your death will spur action. Truly, it's for the best."

She spat in his face.

The Prince wiped the saliva from his cheek and his smile twisted into something more sinister. "Burn her."

Flame flickered in Emir's hand. He took a menacing step forward.

A burst of wind blasted them both.

She shielded her eyes as Gareth's Shadow formed a whirlwind of grit and dirt in the heart of the courtyard.

Gareth had heard her words.

"Impossible!" the Prince yelled.

Falkner hissed Hartnord words and backed away. The guards began to scatter, but Hiram barked a command and most regained their composure. It was a fatal mistake not to run while they had the chance. Plants, rocks, tiles, pots—anything not secured to the ground or walls pelted them. The ones who dropped their swords saw the blades sucked away into the whirlwind to join the swirling mass. Their steel contorted and bent, forming jagged points in the shape of a man.

Gareth became a wraith of swords.

The guards yelled and ran as Gareth's blades began to cut a path through them. Falkner grabbed Prince Wulfhart and dragged him to safety. Mina crouched with her hands over her head, but Gareth's form didn't come near her. Instead, he tore through the guards and made a path straight for the Prince.

Emir seemed all but forgotten in the chaos, but he had not forgotten her. He stalked slowly toward her, a ball of flame in his hand.

She yanked her sahn free and hastily wrapped it around her thigh. A jolt of pain shot through her leg when she tried to stand and she sank back on one knee.

With a sudden shift in the driving wind, Gareth's wraith turned from the Prince to face Emir. But there was no fear in Emir's eyes, as though he'd seen wraiths before.

Gareth's bladed fingers slashed through a foolish guard who stood between him and Emir—slicing through his armor and flesh as though he were nothing.

Emir dove to the ground and scrambled to safety.

Gareth did not follow him. Instead, he reached out for Mina with his gleaming, jagged, mangled steel hand and grabbed her shoulder. A shock of sky fire surged through her blood.

And then all went dark.

46

THE BURNING TEMPLE

The wagon rattled onward. Anni leaned against my shoulder and slept on. Even in sleep, she looked so content. So beautiful. Her lips parted, her eyelashes fluttered, and she rested a hand over her stomach.

I saw the colors pulsing underneath. The life blooming inside.

She hadn't told me yet, and I hadn't dared ask. I didn't want to scare her with the extent of my Sight, with what I truly saw. We both knew this would cause problems. Her brother was wary of a Hartnord suitor, and I didn't blame him. My people still saw Sandarians as fire-breathing monsters and my own brothers had warned me that my venture south was foolhardy. I'd argued that it was ridiculous to assume that all Sandarians possessed devastating fire magic. I'd travelled to Sandair for the thrill of adventure and to see if our prophet spoke true.

I came to Sandair with an open mind, but I saw fire everywhere and thought I'd made a grave mistake.

And then I saw her.

God, she was so beautiful in heart and soul and mind. And she too burned with an inner fire beneath her skin. I couldn't help myself; I was drawn to her, despite the danger and warnings. She never summoned her fire once and I knew in my heart the prophet spoke lies.

I was in love.

Scared, too. Like a lost boy. I wanted to bring her home to my brothers, to show them proof that Sandarians weren't monstrous creatures. How would they react when they learned I planned to marry her? When they saw the seed I'd planted inside her?

We were growing something new together. Would the child have her fire magic? My Sight? Whose eyes would it take–my silver Hartsire or her golden Solaran?

Those eyes fluttered open. "Garet."

I couldn't stop myself from grinning like a fool. She still couldn't say my name right, not that I ever liked it. Gerhart. I'd long stopped being a Hartsire, and depending on how my brothers reacted, my name could well be chipped from the family monument. Perhaps it was time for a new one. Garet. Gareth, maybe.

The wagon carried on north across the border. She trusted me to keep her safe. By my word and honor, I would.

Reality snapped back into focus with a sharp pain in Mina's leg. Someone was pulling her up.

"We need to go, Sword Dancer."

The embassy was in chaos. The storm of Gareth's rage battered everything and everyone in the courtyard. The last surviving Neu Bosan guards were running for cover inside the embassy building. Prince Wulfhart and his lackey were nowhere in sight. Neither was Hiram.

Gareth's wrath allowed the final guards to flee. When they were gone, the violent winds came to a sudden stop, leaving swords and rocks hanging in midair. The Shadow within that deadly steel body was watching her. No, not her—Garr.

Words echoed in the wind. She couldn't understand what they meant.

"Do you hear that?" Garr asked.

"I hear… something. What is it?"

"I—I don't know what I hear."

The Shadow spoke Hartnord, the same few words over and over, but they meant nothing to her. With a thunderous clatter, the mangled hunks of steel crashed to the ground all at once, but the pure black Shadow remained before them. One dark hand reached for Garr.

Garr held out his palm and shuddered at the Shadow's touch.

"You can see it?" she whispered.

A mournful cry carried through the wind. As that sound filled her ears, colors appeared before her eyes, not shining out from the Shadow but clinging to it like steam clung to the damp earth in Lune's Shadow—dark blue and then gray. And she knew those colors for what they were: sorrow and regret and longing and loss and something else. Something stronger. The same emotion she'd felt from Talin when she'd joined House Arlbond.

Absolution.

Fire burst behind them. Mina turned to see Gareth's body crumbling to ash inside a brilliant red bonfire. And behind the flames stood Emir.

Garr drew Hawk and raised it. "Don't come any closer."

Gareth's Shadow no longer lingered with them. Gone forever. Would he join with Rahn? She had no time to ponder it.

Emir scooped one of the discarded scimitars.

Mina had neither flame nor blade, and Prince Wulfhart had run off with her mother's gods-damn dagger. But she'd strangle Emir with her bare hands if she had to.

But before either side could make their first move, the embassy gates crashed open. The Sword of Solus raced into the courtyard at the head of a dozen royal guards.

Once again, Emir turned heel and fled.

Mina launched herself up to pursue him, but her wounded leg buckled at the first step. Garr wrapped his spare arm around her waist to keep her from tumbling to the ground.

Salasar spotted her and came running. "Arlbond, report."

"The Hartnords are headed for—"

The temple.

Gods damn it, she couldn't tell Salasar that! He'd send half his guards running, right when Jonan was burning the whole thing to glass. If her House were caught trying to rescue the Fire Walkers on the eve of war, that'd be treason—and execution.

"I don't know, they said something about the Keep," she said. "Protect the King."

Was sending Salasar on a merry chase to the Keep the right thing to do? She didn't know, but she didn't have time to think of a better plan. She needed to get to the temple as fast as possible without dragging any of the royal guards along with her.

"Stay here. Green Hands are on the way." Salasar barked at one group of guards to secure the courtyard, then ordered another to follow as he ran for the embassy doors.

"Can you walk?" Garr asked.

She flexed her leg. Sharp pain caused her to dig her nails into his arm. "I'll walk it off."

"You're bleeding."

She snatched Hawk from his hand. "I said I'll walk it off!"

They pushed past the guards and she hobbled out of the embassy gate. She expected to find her acolytes waiting, but they were nowhere in sight. Only more of Salasar's guards.

"Did you send them back to the temple?"

Garr frowned. "No. They were here when I jumped the wall. Are you going to tell me what happened in there?"

"You jumped the wall?"

"Scrambled over it, really. We just faced a big metal demon made out of the swords of its enemies, and that's the part of the story you want to dwell on?"

She explained as best she could between gasps of pain as they staggered toward the temple. Each step sent an agonizing stab through her leg, but the bleeding had stopped at least. Through the House bond, she felt Jonan unleashing the full power of his Rhaesbond blood, but not in anger. He was still burning the temple, so the Hartnords hadn't interrupted their plans just yet. Iman's essence was on the move, likely in the tunnels, leading the Fire Walkers to the Temple of Lune. Talin remained farther north, still in the Keep.

As they made their way up the hill to the Temple of Rahn, thin tendrils of smoke seeped out the open doors of the pyramid and rose into the sky. There were no guards outside to raise the alarm. Had Salasar pulled them away to watch the Hartnords?

A scream came from inside the temple.

She hoped it was part of the game. Garr ran for the door in

genuine panic.

Gods damn it, he wasn't in on the plan! She stumbled after him. Flame filled the inner sanctum with a deafening roar. She almost slipped on the smooth floor. The whole room had been burned black and parts of the sand had turned to glass. Piles of bones were slowly disintegrating into glowing ash everywhere around her and up the stone steps—animal bones carefully placed to mimic a massacre.

She could sense Jonan inside the heart of the flames and it sent an odd thrill up her spine. She knew his blood fire dwarfed her own and the others in their House, but to see him work… he was an artist who painted in Rahn's colors.

Garr tried to push through the flaming wall, but Jonan's flames held him back. He glanced at her, his eyes wide and frantic. "Do something! You need to stop it!"

She held her palm against the fiery wall. The heat was incredible—no shield could stop it from scorching her skin. Hopefully, the bond would carry her intentions. She thrust her hand into the fire.

Alarm flared through the bond and the wall of fire fell before it could do real damage. Jonan slumped against one of the stone seats, his face and clothes covered in sweat and soot. Mina limped up to him and grasped his arm.

"Thank the gods you're safe!"

"You stopped my fire," he whispered. "What happened?"

"The Hartnords know what we're planning. They're—"

But Garr was now at her side. "Where are the Fire Walkers? Did the Hartnords to this?"

Jonan covered his face—the very picture of shock and grief. "Poisoned… Rahn's Breath… In the water. I did what I could to stop it—to absorb their fire. But it was too much."

Garr stared at the crumbling bones throughout the sanctum. "They're dead?" His voice cracked and he staggered on his feet. "They can't—they can't all be dead. They can't be…"

"Jonan—the Hartnords are coming!"

She reached out with the blood bond to make him feel the honesty and urgency of her warning.

"Back," she added, with a glance at Garr. "They're coming back. Through the *tunnels* this time."

Jonan's face and essence sparked with panicked understanding. "How?"

What could she say in front of Garr? She didn't have time to be subtle, even if she'd had any gods-damn talent at it. She spun on the Ash Maker. "Go find my acolytes!"

"What?"

"Find them. Find out if they're safe. They went missing right when this attack happened. It can't be coincidence."

"I can't leave, not when—"

"You have to. I can't go, not with my wounded leg, and someone has to find them." She needed him not to argue. She thought of the night Dustan Hawker died and drew tears to her eyes. "Find them. I'm trusting you with this."

The fire in his amber eyes softened. "I'll be quick." Garr gave her one last lingering look and ran for the temple doors.

Jonan was looking at her leg. "You're hurt."

"Never mind that. The Hartnords know about the tunnels, and they're coming to take Fire Walkers for their twisted tests. It was Hiram, he did this. He has Fire Walker slaves—Rhaesbond slaves, he said."

Jonan's eyes widened. "That's not possible."

She stretched her leg, trying to ease out the stiffness, but it just sent fresh waves of agony down her thigh. "We'll deal with him later. I need to warn Iman. Stay here and keep watch in case the Hartnords or Salasar come this way."

Jonan sank against the steps. His exhaustion wouldn't be for show should the guards turn up.

Mina hobbled down the corridor to the lower level and barged through the door to Leila's glass chamber. Iman beckoned the last of the Fire Walkers into the tunnel that usually lay hidden behind the room's only decoration—a wooden bookcase filled with jars of sand of every color of the Dusland desert.

"The Hartnords know about the tunnels—and our plans to use them," Mina declared. "They're coming to seize as many Fire Walkers as they can. I don't know which direction they're coming from. They could be in the tunnels right now."

Iman shot a panicked glance at the tunnel. "Kasara's at the front of the line, leading the way. Her mother's waiting at the Temple of Lune. But if the Hartnords know about the tunnels, they may have arranged another way inside."

"Emir was hiding in the temple, spying on us. It's anybody's guess how long he's been here and what he's discovered."

"Doesn't matter now," said Iman. "Everything's in motion. It's too late to change plans."

"If they know we're leaving the city, it won't take a spy to figure out we're headed to Arlent. But I don't think the Hartnords will dare chase us across the desert. If they want Fire Walkers, now's their one chance to get them."

Someone tugged her tunic and she turned around to Kamran holding Fez in his arms. "The big lady says we have to go soon. But Fez likes it here, and I've never been to the desert."

Mina tried to soften the panic from her expression and ran a calming hand over Fez's head. The fox cooed and leaned into her touch. He belonged in the desert. The real desert, and not some mockery of one. "Where I come from isn't all sand. There's a river with an oasis and lots of goats. Fez doesn't belong here. Someone needs to return him home. Can I trust you to look after him a little longer?"

"But my ma said we could return to our bakery after the war—"

"That big lady over there's called Iman. She's a baker, and she makes the best pies in all Sandair. We'll have hundreds of new mouths to feed soon. She'll need help baking if we're going to feed them all."

Kamran's eyes lit up. "I can do that! I know what food Fez likes—he likes little crusts of bread—"

"Don't give him too many of those," Mina warned.

Kamran's cheeks reddened. "No—no, I won't, I swear."

She gave him a gentle push. "Now go. Take him through the tunnel and find your mother."

"Yes, Priestess." He bowed his head. "Where's Garr? Isn't he coming, too?"

"Don't worry about him, he'll catch up."

Kamran looked skeptical but carried Fez into the tunnel.

What would she do with the Ash Maker? She couldn't offer him a place in Arlent. Jonan would never allow it, and Arlent was built by Lunei blood. She wouldn't desecrate her mother's home with his presence.

A warning seared through the bond. Someone had broken past Jonan and was coming. Mina placed a hand on Hawk's hilt as the door flew open.

"What are you doing!" Samira shrieked.

Mina cursed and released her weapon.

"Stop this madness. Stop it *now*." Samira grabbed Mina's arm and pinched sharp. "Rahn curse you both! Don't you know what this will do? They will be hunted down and killed for this! Every single one of them!"

"We're saving them!"

Mina yanked her arm free.

"*Saving* them?" Samira snorted a laugh. "There is nowhere safe for our kind except the temple!"

"They can't stay in the temple one way or the other," Mina said. "The Prince has ordered every last one of them to march to the front lines. Women, children, all of them."

Iman put on her calm voice, which was still twice as loud as Mina's normal voice. "My House is willing to take in these Fire Walkers—all of them—and give them shelter, food, and a future where they may live in peace."

"One House cannot do that alone."

"Try us."

"Samira, listen to me," Mina said. "They chose to leave. Don't take that choice—their freedom—from them. We won't let anything happen to them."

Samira slowly turned her gaze back to Mina and tears were in her eyes. "They're my family," she choked out. "They're all I have. Saeed, he... Gods, I loved him. I loved him more than a brother, and he loved me—" She covered her mouth with a repressed sob. "I don't know why he did what he did. The Hartnords were supposed to save us, to convince the King to return us back to where we belonged. Why would Saeed kill Reinhart? Why? Saeed loved this temple and its people more than anything. He had to think it was the right thing to do for our people."

"Prince Ravel thinks he's doing the right thing for his people to, by sending ours to die on the front lines. I'm sick of these men claiming to protect one people by imprisoning and slaughtering others. Saeed was wrong. What he did was evil." Mina took Samira's hand and met her eye. "You've got to let him go."

Samira's look of despair made Mina's heart ache. "I only want to keep my family safe."

Iman placed a hand on Samira's shoulder. "In Rahn's name, I pledge my blood to ensure their safety. Always."

"Go with them," Mina said. "Help us keep them safe."

Samira looked startled. "Leave the temple?"

"There's a temple in Arlent."

"You—you would invite me to your home?"

"We'll have hundreds of new Fire Walkers to care for. We'll need all the help we can get."

Samira bowed her head in submission. "Then I will go where my people need me."

Mina almost laughed in relief. She never thought she'd see the day she'd win Samira to her side, but this *was* a win. At least now Mina didn't need to worry about Samira betraying them.

No one had to die. And no one would be left behind.

Screams came from behind her.

From the tunnels.

Kasara stumbled out. "Hartnords!"

47

DEATH IN THE TUNNELS

Mina drew Hawk and raced into the tunnel. The first thing she saw was the half-naked bodies. Dead Fire Walkers. And standing over them, five Hartnord soldiers.

No, no, no!

Kasara slid to her side and drew her own sword, a plain blade that had likely never seen blood.

A Hartnord barked commands in their language and all five prowled forward.

"Back to the chamber," hissed Mina. "There's no room to fight here."

The moment Mina turned her back, the Hartnords charged.

Mina and Kasara broke apart as they stepped through the doorway into the glass chamber, and the Hartnords raced between them, blades first. Pain in her leg flared, causing her to buckle and lose balance. She brought Hawk up in a hasty block, just as a Hartnord sword thrust for her heart.

Two of the Hartnords marched on her, swords out like spears. Mina bit her lip and swung Hawk to keep them at bay. The Hartnords wore leather armor disguised to look Sandarian, though their pale faces and straight-pointed steel were anything but.

Ahead of her, Kasara parried an attack from another Hartnord, but her sword arm shook between blocks and couldn't find an opening to counter.

Heat burst from behind them. Mina ducked as a ball of flame shot at the nearest Hartnord, causing him to screech and drop to the ground in a roll. Samira! She threw flame after flame.

Iman followed, knife in hand, and dove at another Hartnord. The man had no chance to react as Iman barged him into the wall with her knife in his gut.

Samira hit another in the chest, distracting him enough for Iman to run her blade across his throat.

The two remaining Hartnords fled back into the tunnel, no doubt to warn their friends.

The Hartnord who fell to Samira's flames still rolled on the ground. He fell still, suddenly aware he was now surrounded and outnumbered, and his Hartnord eyes—a dull blue—opened wide.

Mina pointed Hawk at the Hartnord. "You! I have a message for your gods-damn prince."

He shuffled back until he reached the glass wall, all whilst babbling incoherent nonsense in his language.

Samira swaggered to Mina's side, her fists still aflame. "He doesn't understand you, which makes him useless to us. Shall I kill him?"

"No. We don't kill unarmed men."

Iman kicked one of the Hartnord swords across the floor. It slid to a rest against his boot. "There. He's armed."

Flame cracked from Samira like a whip and swallowed the Hartnord whole. He let loose a single ear-wrenching scream. Mina cringed and shielded her eyes. The light dimmed, leaving a blackened smear and a pair of smoldering leather boots.

Mina scowled. "Was that necessary?"

Iman gave her a flat look. "Honor will do nothing but get you killed, girl. Did we get them all?"

"Two escaped."

Iman cursed. "We need to block these tunnels before more show up."

Mina tightened the sash around her leg. It had started bleeding again. "How many Fire Walkers did they take?"

"Take?" Kasara asked.

"That's why they're here. To capture Fire Walkers and steal them away on their boats."

"None that I saw," Kasara said. "Most of the Fire Walkers fled toward the Temple of Lune. A dozen or so stayed with me to block the Hartnords from following as best we could. But they weren't trained in combat, and—and they..." She fell silent.

Iman placed a comforting hand on Kasara's shoulder.

Kasara breathed slowly in and out before continuing. "When there were just five of us left, we fled this way, toward the Temple of Rahn, hoping the Hartnords would follow us instead of the main group. They took the bait. We were almost to your door when they caught up with us. The others... I was the only one who made it."

"You should stay here with Samira and Jonan. Iman and I will search the tunnels. We have to make sure our people made it through to the Temple of Lune."

"What if there are more Hartnords? I should go with you. I can still fight."

Iman didn't look convinced, so Mina answered. "Good. You're with me."

Mina limped to the tunnel, only to be pushed back by a gust of wind. "How..." she started to ask, but then she saw them.

Shadows stalked out from the tunnel, and they were none-too-pleased with their fate. A whirlwind spun around them, but the glass chamber was empty—nothing to form a body.

"Sand wraiths? Here?" Samira gasped.

"It's her blood." Iman nodded to Mina. "Lunei blood. It doesn't just attract them. It awakens them."

"Don't blame me!" Mina snapped. As though hearing her voice, the Shadows turned and looked right at her. Even without bodies, they could still do harm—and she didn't have the time or strength to placate angry spirits now. "We need to burn—"

Something smashed and Mina ducked, covering her head. It

came from beside the tunnel where Leila's old wooden bookcase stood. The jars of sand.

Each jar had been filled with a different color of sand representing the shifting moods of the Duslands. One by one, they fell and smashed to the ground, scattering glass shards and sand, and the wraiths began to take form.

"Burn the bodies!" she yelled.

Samira was there in an instant with her flame. "I'll handle them. Get into the tunnels and stop those Hartnords!"

Mina beckoned Iman and Kasara to follow and they charged through the miniature sandstorm as the wraths were still forming bodies. No more Hartnords yet, thank Lune, but they could be waiting in ambush. She needed to tread carefully.

"I'll take point." Iman snapped her fingers and summoned a bright flame.

These were the same tunnels Mina had almost lost herself in at the start of Rahn's Dawn during the Solaran Tournament. Fortunately, Iman's light shone brighter than her own and she led them with confidence from tunnel to tunnel.

Their footsteps echoed to the beat of Mina's own heart. Her leg ached, then throbbed, then burned as they kept walking. She didn't want to slow down the search, but she was close to collapsing when they came to a fork in the tunnel.

"This is where we first saw the Hartnords. They came from that tunnel." Kasara pointed to the right. "The temple is the other way. And... there are bodies." Her eyes went to Mina.

Iman huffed. "Best not let you near any more bodies today, girl. I'll burn them, then head on to the temple. Someone needs to find out where this other tunnel leads, and there's no one else for it but you two. But be careful. If you see any Hartnords, don't go rushing into a fight. Keep an eye on them, and that's it. Samira and I won't be around to save your worthless scalps if they come rushing at you with swords."

Mina rolled her eyes, hoping Iman could see it in the dimly lit space. Then she led Kasara down the right tunnel.

"It could be a trap," Kasara whispered, close at her heel.

It almost certainly was, but that didn't stop Mina from steering down it.

This tunnel was narrower than most, and she needed to angle her sword to keep it from scraping the walls. She summoned a faint glow in her fingers, which was enough to forge ahead. The pathetic, flickering light embarrassed her. She was supposed to be the High Priestess, the Sand Dancer, and it was all she could do to prevent herself from toppling over or walking straight into a wall.

"I, uh, I can normally make more light than this."

"I can see well enough," Kasara said with cheerful reassurance. Her scabbard was making an odd rattling sound.

Mina tuned her light around. Kasara's hands were shaking. "Are you okay?"

Kasara looked startled. "Oh. Forgive me, I..." She released her sword hilt and tucked a stray hair behind her ear. "I've never done that before. Fought in a real battle, I mean. It was a lot more chaotic than I expected. Not like the duels I watched in the tournament."

"For your first battle, you fought better than I." Mina resumed her slow, limping pace.

Kasara shuffled after her. "Ah, but you're injured. Perhaps you need a sorran, Lady Tamina."

"Are you volunteering?"

"Are you looking for one?"

The path suddenly lurched downward, and Mina skidded to keep her balance. A light shone ahead.

Rahnlight.

They emerged out onto a stone rampart overlooking the docks, not a canal as she'd been expecting. She was no stoneworker, but the slender entrance to the tunnel looked freshly chiseled—white, rough, and unweathered. How long had the Hartnords been planning this attack?

It was her fault if Emir and his men had been hiding in plain sight and spying on them. She'd insisted on allowing Fire Walkers to dress as they pleased.

"There!" Kasara pointed to a pier at the far side of the docks. Two huge ships were hoisting large white sails, preparing for launch. Hartnord ships. Mina scanned the docks. All of the usual fishermen and traders were gone, of course, per the King's orders for the Hartnords' visit. But where were Salasar's men? Shouldn't they be storming the docks by now, after the violence at the Neu Bosan embassy?

Gods damn it. She'd sent Salasar running off to the Keep, hadn't she?

Few guards patrolled the docks, and none Sandarian. Neu Bosan guards. Hiram's men.

She grabbed Kasara's arm and pulled her down behind a wall. Neu Bosan guards marched by, and with them... Hartnords. A whole group in silver armor were marching to the ships, escorting five men in chains.

Her acolytes.

Dahn, Bahri, Qareem, Amin, and Marek trudged along with iron chains binding their legs and arms. How had they been caught so easily, and why weren't they using their blood fire to resist? Unless they'd been poisoned with Lune's Tears.

Gods, they were being shipped to Hartnor.

If Hiram had cleared the docks of all guards but his own, then he could easily reach the harbor chain and lower it. "Find Salasar," whispered Mina. "He needs to get his men here *now*. We can't let the Hartnord ships get away."

"What about you?"

"I'll try and get a little closer. I can't run with this leg, but I'll stay out of sight."

Kasara nodded and carefully shuffled along the dock wall.

Mina copied, but in the opposite direction. She edged her way down the dock steps and headed for the Hartnord ships. Could she disable them somehow? She knew nothing about giant ocean galleons, except they were usually made of wood. A little fire could go a long way, assuming she could reach them before her acolytes were brought aboard.

She risked a glance over the wall to see if there was any way to approach without getting caught. How far did Hartnord Sight extend? It was one of many questions she wished she could have asked Gareth. No. Reaching the ships was a fool's dream. Running back to the tunnels to find Iman or anyone else was just as ridiculous—her acolytes would be gone with the Hartnord ships long before she could hope to return with help.

Her best bet was to buy Kasara as much time as possible to find Salasar and stop them from lowering the harbor chain. But how?

She grabbed a rock about the size of her fist and stood up. She hurled it at the closest silver giant and it pinged right off his armored head.

"Get your hands off them!"

The Hartnords turned, but none reached for their weapons. The one she'd hit with the rock pulled off his helmet and casually inspected it for dents. Then he looked up at her with a smile—what was he smiling about?

"We run into each other again, my lady. How fortunate."

Mina spun around.

Prince Wulfhart stood with Falkner amid another group of his silver giants. At least ten of them, maybe more. Falkner issued a command in Hartnord and the guards spread out, blocking all paths of escape.

She was trapped.

"Don't come any closer." She drew Hawk into the Solaran stance.

Prince Wulfhart's gaze trailed down to her bleeding leg. "All it takes is one wound to stop your fire magic, doesn't it? Then this will do the rest." He pulled a vial from his pocket. "And we'll see how you look in chains."

The image of Samira wrapped in chains in a dungeon cell as leeches sucked her life's blood made Mina's own blood run cold. She could try to burn—burn them all and run, but she'd never mastered her fire when wounded.

Not even Lune could get her out of this alive.

"What are you doing with my Fire Walkers?"

"Taking them to Harvera to test Lune's Tears, as I have already explained, my lady."

"You're a gods-damn fool if you think you're leaving these docks."

"Your attempts to waste my time are valiant, but pointless. I see your every thought as plainly as I see your face." He tapped at the corner of one silver eye. "You hope to delay us while the guards raise the harbor chain. They will not."

"What did you do to them? Are they dead?"

"Why would we kill Lord Hiram's own men?"

"Lord Salasar is responsible for the city guard, not Hiram Myrbond."

"Come now. You don't expect us to trust our lives and security to your Sword of Solus after what happened to my father on our last visit to your city, do you? Fortunately, the Neu Bosan ambassador came forward with the perfect compromise. Not only would he open his embassy to serve as a neutral meeting place, but he would also assume personal responsibility for the security of the docks, our delegation, and our ships."

No wonder Salasar's men were nowhere to be seen. She hadn't had time to warn him about Hiram's treachery at the embassy. She'd been too distracted worrying about the temple and protecting her House's own treason.

"Forget Salasar and his men. My House protects all Fire Walkers, everywhere. There's nowhere you can take them that we won't hunt you down."

"Ah yes, your House. Hiram informed me there is a living member of the Rhaesbond bloodline among you. I'd hoped you would bring him to our negotiation, but no matter. Hiram's slave is collecting him for me now."

Jonan.

No.

She sent her panicked warnings through the blood bond. They'd left Jonan alone in the temple sanctum, exhausted and with no blood left to fight.

Talin's dread burned back. He was on the move.

She needed to stop these Hartnords at any cost. "You touch my family, and I'll toss your bones into the ocean."

The Prince tutted. "Such an unladylike threat. You should thank us for removing this Rhaesbond from your midst. It is a cursed bloodline, the most dangerous and treacherous of your kind, the most hated by god, and the greatest threat to the light of the world."

"Jonan is none of those things! He had nothing to do with your father's death. What of Hiram's slaves? Emir? They orchestrated the attacks!"

"I know."

Her heart stilled. "You knew? Then you—you knew your own father would die?"

"My father didn't heed our prophet's warnings." His silver eyes gleamed with a danger she'd only witnessed in amber. "Falkner, escort our guest onto the ship."

Falkner charged—he was on her before she could even swing her sword. He grabbed her wrist and twisted it back with painful pressure. She yelped and dropped Hawk with a clang. He wrenched her arm up against her back and grabbed the other, squeezing her into a painful hold.

Heat built in her veins and the pulse of her inner embers flowed through her. Flame burst from her fist. Falkner released her and stumbled back.

He snarled and dove forward with blinding speed.

His fist slammed into her abdomen and knocked the breath from her lungs. She slumped against him and gasped for air. Pain rippled through her stomach and she could do nothing as Falkner pinned her arms, locking them into a tight hold once more.

"You'll enjoy Lune's Tears, my lady. Let it release your stress," Prince Wulfhart crooned.

The Prince strode forward and clawed at her mouth. She thrashed in Falkner's grip and tried to summon her flame, but panic squeezed her chest like thick chains, making it impossible to concentrate on her inner embers. The Prince saw her raw fear, saw all of it and fed off it like a leech.

I am the master of my own self. Calm, calm.

The Prince took a firm hold of her jaw and pressed a vial between her lips. He tilted her head back.

A thick salty syrup slivered between her clenched teeth and down her throat. She spluttered and tried to cough it up, but the Prince placed a hand over her mouth and pinched her nose until tiny black dots scattered across her vision.

Lune's Tears flooded through her blood with a cooling sensation like the day she'd fallen off Dustan's boat and swallowed water. It splashed over her inner embers, turning them to lifeless stone, and it left her skin feeling heavy and numb.

The fire inside died out. Extinguished. *Gone.*

She couldn't feel her House bond; she couldn't feel Talin or Jonan or Iman. Lune's Tears hadn't just suppressed her blood fire. It had doused everything that made her Sandarian.

They'd drowned her.

Someone hear me, feel me, anyone...

Prince Wulfhart placed a hand on Mina's cheek, but she didn't feel it. "You see, my lady, it's not harmful. You'll be a good girl for me now, won't you?" He turned to Falkner. "Chain her."

She didn't feel the chains clamp her limbs together.

Nor did she feel them drag her onto their ship.

She didn't feel the cool darkness of her wooden cell replace Rahn's bright warmth.

Mina didn't feel anything at all.

48

A NEGOTIATION

For the first time in Mina's life, the amber eyes of her nightmares were replaced with cold silver.

She sat in a dark room that swayed beneath her. The floors and walls were rough wood, but she could barely feel them. The cooling effect of Lune's Tears thickened her blood and made her nauseous. Not only sick, but empty inside. The Hartnords had cleaned and patched up her wounded leg, but none of them spoke a word of Sandarian or looked her in the eye. They'd wrapped her arms in chains and dragged her down into the belly of their ship. She'd tried to catch a glimpse of her Fire Walkers, to see if they were as defenseless as she was, but the Hartnords had plunged her into darkness.

And in darkness is where she remained.

The blood bond remained silent. No one answered her call. For a brief moment as Lune's Tears worked through her, she'd felt spikes of emotion—Talin's panic, Iman's fury, but they were muffled as though being held underwater. She couldn't sense where they were, and she'd tried to sleep, to bathe in their memories, but Lune's Tears blocked those as well, and all she had left were nightmares.

She stifled a sob. *I am the master of my own self.*

How long would the effects of Lune's Tears last? Did they mean to continuously drug her? It felt nothing like Rahn's Breath. She searched for her inner embers, but the gentle pulse and hum of her blood had quieted. Even if she could pull a thread of fire and burn her cage, there was nothing but sloshing water all around them.

No, her best chance of escape would be when they reached Hartnord shores. Then she'd truly be in enemy territory during the heat of war.

War. She'd not wanted it, but Prince Wulfhart left her no choice.

He'd attacked her people.

Taken them.

Taken Jonan.

And taken her blood fire.

Not only her fire, but the connection to her family, her bond, her mother, her *soul*. For all that and more, Prince Wulfhart deserved no mercy.

The door to her cell creaked open and light poured inside. She cringed and turned her eyes away. Boots tapped on the wood and someone placed a lantern down. Not a Sandarian or Neu Bosan one in design, but made of rustic iron. A man kneeled beside her and offered her a mug. She glanced up into dark eyes.

Emir.

She tried to shuffle away from him, but her chains held her tight against the wall. "Come near me and I'll bite your ears off."

Emir grimaced and lifted the mug.

"I'm not drinking any poison of yours. You killed the Queen!" She spat at him.

Emir grabbed her chains and yanked her still. The frustration was clear on his face. "Bon," he said in his garbled voice.

"What?"

Emir sighed through his nose. "Bon-uh."

"Why are you serving a Hartnord master? You're a Fire Walker, same as I! Do you know what they plan to do to us? You chose to betray your own kind. Do you hate us? Is that it? Do you hate what you are?"

Emir shook his head. "Bon."

"You murdered Fire Walkers! You tricked them, poisoned them—"

"*Bon.*" He gestured again to her chains.

"Why do you keep saying that? Bond?"

Emir's eyes lit up and he nodded.

The door burst open. Emir leaped to his feet and reached for his sword.

He gasped as the intruder thrust a knife into his throat. Blood spurted across her legs. Emir slumped to the ground beside her and choked with gurgling sounds. Dead.

"Sword Dancer!"

Garr stood over her, clutching the knife. He'd dressed in Hartnord clothes with a flat cap covering his head. He shoved the knife into his belt, smearing blood on his smock, and kneeled beside her. "Are you hurt?" He grabbed her wrists and fumbled with the shackles.

"What are you doing here? Did they take you with the others?"

"No. I saw the Hartnords take you, so I snuck aboard."

She grabbed his arm, forcing him to stare into her eyes. "Did you see the others? Are they here? And Jonan? Prince Wulfhart said they were taking him."

"Wulfhart is aboard the other ship. They took some Fire Walkers on that one, and the rest they left on this. I saw Dahn and the others, but not your friend."

She let go of his arm and her hands fell into her lap with a *clink*. "How many Hartnords on this ship?"

"Too many. But first, we need to get you out of these chains. I couldn't swipe a key. Can you burn through them?"

"They made me drink Lune's Tears. You'll need to burn them."

He stilled. "I can't."

"Now is not the time for your pride—"

"I can't control my fire. I'll sink this ship to the bottom of the ocean before I get through these chains."

"You wait until *now* to tell me you're useless?"

He offered a sheepish smile. "I figured you'd work it out."

A gust of wind blew off his cap. He shot to his feet and drew his knife.

But he couldn't see what she did. A Shadow pulled itself from Emir's bleeding corpse.

"You need to get rid of the body!"

Emir's Shadow swung its arm like a sword and his wind flung Garr against the wall. A dark hand grabbed her neck and the light from the lantern blew out.

"He doesn't have the eyes."

My captor forced my eyelids open wide and examined the color inside. I glared back into his bright green ones. That kernel of hate was all I had left. They'd bound me, forced leeches on my skin, and held me in the dirt with a sword at my neck.

"A defective Ash Maker still has the blood of one." He released my eye and stood back with his arms crossed. His skin was the smooth brown of a Gaislander, but his eyes and accent painted him as a Bosan. It wasn't uncommon to find crossbreeds in the isles, but he was the first I'd found who possessed blood fire strong enough to stop me.

"What's your story, boy? Did you run from the tribes, or were you thrown out?"

I kept my mouth closed.

My captor leered close. "Don't speak much, do you?"

"He killed two of our men," the other Bosan stated in perfect Sandarian.

"Did he? This one could make a fine assassin. You enjoy killing, don't you?"

Only when I needed to. Only when my life depended on it. I'd fought off my own people, raiders, and House guards alike to start a new life on the isles. I never thought I'd get caught by slavers. I never thought my blood would be taken from me again.

All I ever wanted was to be free.

My captor pulled a knife from his belt.

Gods no. He meant to kill me.

Instead, he sliced across his palm and offered his blood. "Drink, and we'll make a man out of you, Ash Maker."

ৠ ৠ ৠ

Mina opened her eyes and stared into Garr's amber. He didn't blink. Didn't breathe. She glanced around and the movement felt like wading through water. Everything had slowed down, even the motes of dust dancing in the air.

Emir's Shadow still gripped her neck and his words rumbled through her like the first rains of Lune's Shadow.

They force a sorran bond on their slaves. That is how we are controlled. We have no choice but to follow the commands of our Bosan master.

"You're an Ash Maker?" Her voice reverberated in the air.

Was. Your friend has freed me. His bitter amusement rumbled through her bones. *Why didn't you kill me? I gave you ample opportunity, Lunei.*

He'd recognized her eyes. Her tribal blood. "You wanted me to kill you?"

You Lunei are soft when it comes to death. My masters ordered you dead, but I resisted the command as much as I could. It would have defeated me in the end; no sorran can deny the commands of his master for long. I'd hoped you'd kill me first. Then we could finally speak, Tamina Hawker. As we are now.

He knew about the Shadows—he truly was an Ash Maker. "Then why did they call you a Rhaesbond?"

That lie was devised to lure your Rhaesbond into their trap. It didn't work, but I was ordered to capture him. He's not on this ship. You won't reach him.

They had Jonan. They'd caught him like they'd caught her. "You killed the Queen. You poisoned her with Lotus Bud."

No. A lie. My masters don't know who killed your Queen, but they turned it to their advantage. I felt her death. You did too. A Shadow ended her life.

A Shadow?

That wasn't possible. Shadows lay dormant until a Lunei was nearby—didn't they? There had been no wraith in the dining hall when the Queen had died, and yet… Mina had felt something. An odd stirring in the bond.

How could a Shadow have poisoned the Queen? There were no bones in the throne room. "You see the Shadows?"

We are different sides of the same coin, Lunei.

"The tales say Ash Makers can control them… That's true?" Gods, she didn't want to think about the implications. If Shadows could be controlled, then they were immortal assassins, warriors who could kill from beyond death.

Shadows can be compelled if you possess their bones. Whoever commanded the Queen's death would need a totem. Only Rhaesbond and Ash Makers know this. Why do you think we hunted your people? To hide our secrets from you.

"Then why are you telling me this?"

Because I hold no love for my people, and your Fire Walkers are in danger. My master is a member of the Three-Pointed Star. Hiram is but one of his many servants. He is the one who forged this secret alliance with the Hartnords.

"But how could a Bosan possibly command you? They can't form blood bonds—"

My master has Sandarian blood. He can form bonds, and has formed many. Solander. Gaislander. Duslander. Sanstrider. Ash Maker. Lunei. Hundreds of Fire Walkers in his palms. He's building a ready-made army for the Three-Pointed Star.

Gods. Only the King of Sandair was permitted to make two sorran bonds per the Code of Honor, but hundreds of bonds? It was obscene. And to do so by force! Forcing a bond on *any* man wasn't just a question of honor, but of dignity. It was slavery of body, mind, and soul.

If the Neu Bosan had been building their own secret army of Fire Walkers, then war would never end between their peoples— Bosan, Hartnord, and Sandarian alike. And they would truly turn her own people against her, as they'd done with Emir.

They don't care for Fire Walker lives. They'll use them and kill them when done. You must save those trapped here.

"How?"

Search my pockets for a way out. Don't burn my body. Let me fight them.

His Shadow vanished. All at once life sped up with a deafening roar of the waves.

Garr slumped against her. "What was that?" he gasped. "Your eyes—they turned *black*, Sword Dancer, as black as night. Like you weren't even here."

Black? She'd never heard of that before. "Never mind. Search his pockets!" She nodded to Emir's body.

"Oh, so now you want me ransacking corpses?" Garr turned Emir's body over and rummaged through his pockets. He pulled out a purple bottle.

Rahn's Breath.

She nudged Emir's body with her boot. "This is your idea of help? Gods, pass it here."

Garr handed her the bottle. "You sure about this?"

No, she wasn't sure at all, but if Lune's Tears was an antidote for Rahn's Breath, she had to trust Emir knew it also held the opposite effect. "If I start to lose control, cut me."

His brows raised in alarm. "Cut you?"

"To stop me from burning down this gods-damn ship. Don't balk on me now."

She fumbled the stopper and lifted the bottle with shaking hands, breathing in that familiar smoky scent. Garr cupped her hands to steady them, and the heat in his palms gave her the confidence she needed. She prayed to Lune and Rahn that her fire wouldn't rage out of control and took a deep gulp.

Heat rushed through her veins, sending tingles all over her skin. Raw power sang in her blood, and the warmth of her House bond came back with startling clarity; she could feel Jonan farther ahead on the other boat, confirming Emir's words. And she could feel Talin's terrifying rage from behind. A laugh escaped her lips.

She'd never felt so alive.

Flame sizzled around her wrists and her metal chains melted to shingles. Tira appeared in her flames and smiled with relief.

A cool breeze brushed over her shoulder. *They'll sense your fire. Act now.*

Garr stood with his knife poised. "Do I need to stab you, Sword Dancer?"

She stretched her leg. The power pumping through her veins eased its ache. "I'm good."

Emir's Shadow waited over his body. Her instincts tugged with panicked urgency, as though they knew he was an Ash Maker, a monster, and demanded she burn his taint away. She considered ending him there and then. But whilst Emir may have been an Ash Maker, he'd been abused the same as any Fire Walker, any true Rhaesbond. She couldn't blame the sins of an entire tribe on one man.

The Three-Pointed Star had forced a bond on him, turning him into nothing but a slave. He deserved a little revenge.

Garr grabbed the lantern. "What are your orders?"

Mina shook her flames away. "We save our Fire Walkers and get off this gods-damn boat."

49

THE BOAT TO NOWHERE

Garr peered out of the door, then signaled for her to follow. Together they slipped out into the dark underbelly of the ship. Wooden crates and barrels were tied to the walls with rope. It looked… flammable. Mina stumbled along, grabbing hold of a crate every couple of paces. The ship lurched and dipped worse than the floating market of Myryn.

Garr took her arm and steadied her. "You okay?" he whispered.

"I hate boats," she hissed back. The giddiness in her gut turned to nausea.

Narrow doors lined the far wall, each locked by a metal chain. This was where her Fire Walkers were trapped.

She grabbed the first chain and melted it enough to snap it in half. Garr kept watch as she stepped into the cell.

A half-naked Duslander was chained to the ground. Dahn. She kneeled beside him and began work on his chains. "You caused them trouble I see."

Dahn snapped his eyes to her. "Priestess. They poisoned us; we couldn't fight back—"

"Didn't I tell you not to accept food or drink?"

"Another Fire Walker offered us water. A Duslander. I thought he'd be safe."

She finished burning through Dahn's chains and helped him up. "Go outside and find weapons. Quietly."

From the other cells, she set free Bahri, Qareem, Amin, and Marek. By the time they were reunited, Dahn and Garr had recovered a collection of Hartnord knives and hammers and armed themselves. She took a short knife, but mourned Hawk. The Hartnords had taken her precious sword, which meant it might be on board somewhere.

There are more Fire Walkers at the other end of the ship, Emir's Shadow blew into her ear. *Save them.*

Footsteps hammered the wooden planks above them, along with muffled shouts.

She turned to her guard and pulled the bottle of Rahn's Breath from her sahn. "There are more of us back that way. Drink this— it'll restore your blood fire, and go find them. Dahn, Garr, and I will stay here and fight off the Hartnords."

Qareem took the bottle. "Will you be safe, Priestess?"

Dahn rolled his shoulders. "Question is, will these stone-faced bastards be safe?"

"What's our plan?" Amin asked. He had an arm wrapped around his husband.

"We're taking over this ship," she said. "Bahri, you were a fisherman. Can you steer it?"

"Well, ah, this is a lot bigger than my old boat." Bahri scratched the back of his head. "But between the seven of us, we'll manage."

She patted him on the shoulder. "Good. Get going."

"Lune's luck," Bahri said, and rushed ahead with the others.

She signaled for Dahn and Garr to take position underneath a wooden stairway that led to the upper level of the hold. They had to wait but moments before Hartnord feet trampled down the steps—and were met with a gust of wind. They shouted in alarm as their feet were whipped out from under them.

"Now!" she yelled.

Dahn and Garr sprang forward. The Hartnords had no time to regain their footing before Garr stabbed one in the neck and Dahn made quick work of the rest with his warhammer. He was a monster made of muscle that reminded her of the late Barahn Khalbond, and he took great joy in bludgeoning his unfortunate prey.

Five Hartnords down. But there were many more waiting.

Mina took point and stepped over the bodies to the upper level. Here, round glass windows allowed Rahnlight in. They couldn't have traveled far from Solus yet. A tug in her blood tried to pull her back to the Hartnord bodies, but she couldn't worry about Shadows now. She'd send them to the afterlife once it was safe.

Emir whispered directions, words that only she could hear. Garr and Dahn followed her without question. They passed wooden tables nailed to the floor. Dirty mugs and paper cards lay abandoned across the tables. Someone had left in a hurry.

They're waiting in ambush, Emir said. *I'll blow away their weapons.*

It felt perverse to rely on Emir's otherworldly power to fight the enemy—like something an Ash Maker would do. But she couldn't afford not to exploit this advantage. Prince Wulfhart and Hiram had used them both.

She'd make them regret it.

As they approached the steps to the deck of the ship, Emir's Shadow ruptured through the hold's roof and deck floor, scattering wood and splinters. Mina charged up the steps while the Hartnords above were scattered and bewildered.

As Emir had warned, a group of Hartnords had been lying in wait, but now their weapons had been ripped from their hands and were swirling in the air. Dahn, ever eager for blood, pushed past her and smashed the nearest Hartnord with his hammer.

Garr stared at her. "How are you doing this?"

"I'm not." She raised her dagger. Guilt surged within her— these men were now unarmed, and most were sprawled on the ground. But this was battle, not a duel.

A Hartnord swung a fist at her.

Mina plunged her dagger into his neck.

Garr followed her lead, and soon six more Hartnords were dead.

The surviving Hartnord sailors fled as a fully armored giant approached. He held a Sandarian scimitar in his gauntleted hand—Hawk.

"Cease your attack!" the giant bellowed.

"Give me back my gods-damn sword and I'll consider it."

The silver giant charged.

Mina skipped to one side and let him slice the air with Hawk. He swung at her with frustrated chops that didn't make use of her sword's reach; clearly he'd never trained with a Sandarian curved blade. She danced and weaved past each slice without making any counters of her own. His thick silver armor slowed him down.

Her inner embers surged with her heartbeat, then she hurled blasts of fire at his armor. She wasn't skilled enough at fighting with fire to melt it through, but soon the man was clawing at his scalding hot armor to wrench it off his body. He dropped Hawk to use both hands to save himself from cooking alive.

Mina took up her sword.

Shouts came from behind her. She turned to see her Fire Walker guard racing onto the deck with more of her people behind them. They threw flame at every Hartnord they saw, soldier and sailor alike.

The Hartnords didn't stand a chance.

Fire tore through their clothes, skin, and bone. They screamed inhuman sounds and writhed as they disintegrated into glowing ash.

Some dove from the ship into the turbulent water. Others flung themselves to their knees and begged for mercy.

Flame took them all.

Only the silver giant, half-stripped of his armor, remained. He'd tossed aside his helmet, revealing a gray-haired man flushed with sweat. "The Keepers see what demons you are!"

Her Fire Walkers surrounded him, each glowing with the power of every child's nightmare.

She raised her hand. "Stop."

They paused and turned to her. Even Emir's winds calmed. She was the High Priestess. Her word was their law.

"Kill him," Dahn urged. "Burn him like the monsters he thinks we are."

She stared into the Hartnord's defiant face, then her gaze moved among her Fire Walkers. All were hungry for revenge. Hadn't they earned it? She could taste the ashes of the Hartnord men in the air. It made her want to scream and vomit.

Her gaze settled on Garr. His eyes were wide, and she read one word there. *Enough.*

Talin wouldn't kill an unarmed prisoner.

"We need him alive. Prince Wulfhart still has Jonan and more on the other ship. We need information on where they're going and how to rescue our people."

"You're not taking me." The giant pulled a knife from his belt and lunged.

Fire burst from her palm and she swung it at the Hartnord by instinct.

Red and orange flame engulfed his outstretched arm, his chest, his face. His shrieks made her blood cold. Her fire snapped out, and she lowered her shaking hand.

His charred body fell to the smoldering wooden deck. His skin peeled away into flakes on the sea breeze, and his remaining armor fused into his blistered, pulpy flesh.

Mina recoiled. She'd done that in a single heartbeat.

Dahn slapped her on the back. "Good work!"

Her Fire Walker guards gathered around the body. Bahri absorbed the flames still licking the deck before they could spread and do real damage. Amin and Marek embraced each other as Qareem laughed with joy. She watched them, too numb for words.

How could they burn through flesh and carry on like it was nothing?

How could they take pleasure in it?

She stared at her tainted hands. They'd burned a man alive.

Her own life's blood had stolen another's.

A breeze blew against her neck. *You have a problem,* Emir said. *The Shadows below deck are growing restless.*

Gods, the bodies! "But they're Hartnord ghosts," she muttered. "They can't form wraiths, can they?"

I cannot say. In the presence of Lunei blood and an Ash Maker's Shadow, who knows what strength they may gather? You and I have a dangerous power over the dead.

She grabbed Hawk and ran for the hatch leading below.

Garr jogged beside her. "What's wrong?"

"The bodies, I have to burn—"

A deafening crash sounded below deck and the ship lurched to one side.

Bahri ran to the ship's railing. "There's a breach! We're going down! Get to the lifeboats!"

The Fire Walkers scrambled to obey his orders, but Mina ran down the stairs into the hold. The lurching ship made it hard to stay upright; mugs, bowls, and other debris skittered across the floor from side to side. She climbed over fallen chairs and scrambled for the lower deck.

Water lapped the stairs.

It's too late for me, Emir said. *Let me go.*

"I'm not letting you get stuck on the ocean floor for eternity!"

It's fitting, isn't it? It's what I deserve.

The water frothed as Shadows tried to reach her. The ship lurched again, and she fell forward.

Garr grabbed her arm and dragged her back. "Don't drown for the dead!"

"What are you doing here?" she shouted. "Get to the life—"

A funnel of water burst through the wood under Mina's feet. She screamed as the ship tilted sharply and threw her into the churning depths.

The ocean began to spin around her—a whirlpool that sucked her down, down and away from air and light. She held her breath and tried to grab at the walls or floor of the ship, but the waters were dark in the windowless lower hold and she couldn't see a thing. Her fingers met with nothing as she thrashed about. The more she struggled, the farther she sank.

Her lungs began to burn. No, no, no, she wasn't going to drown!

The whirlpool lessened and then dissolved as the Hartnord bodies sank, pulling their Shadows and Emir's with them. Rahnlight shimmered above through the waves—she too had been pulled free of the ship. She kicked upward, frantically, hopelessly. She didn't know how to coordinate her limbs. Hawk was still strapped to her belt and dragged her down into the dark.

She screamed and water rushed down her throat.

Something grabbed her tunic and hauled her up. She crashed out of the waves and gasped for air, spluttering the water that had filled her lungs.

Garr wrapped his arms under hers and hoisted her head above water. "Hold onto me and don't panic!"

She floundered in the water, kicking him with her flailing legs. "I can't swim, I can't—"

"Stop fighting me!"

She wrapped her arms around his torso and trembled against his chest. "Don't let me go. Gods, don't let me go."

"Never, Sword Dancer."

Behind her back, Garr clung to a floating piece of wood. They were surrounded by bobbing planks, tables, and crates. Twenty yards away, the prow of the ship was thrust up into the air and the stern was completely submerged. Lifeboats floated among the debris, and she offered a silent prayer to Lune that all of her Fire Walkers were aboard.

In the distance, Prince Wulfhart's ship rode the waves. It hadn't circled around to investigate or try to rescue any survivors. It sailed on for Hartnor, abandoning his men to their fate.

They'd never reach Jonan.

She leaned into Garr's damp chest and choked back tears. "They've got him. He's my brother by bond, my family, and they've got him."

Garr squeezed her tight. "We'll get him back. I swear to you, Tamina, we'll get him back."

She read the truth in his amber eyes and knew he meant it.

"Hoy hoy, do you need a hand?" called Bahri. He steered his lifeboat into their floating plank.

Bahri lifted her up first. She climbed into the raft and collapsed onto a seat. Garr followed and slumped beside her. The taste of saltwater filled her mouth like Lune's Tears. It made her tremble all over until Garr wrapped his arm around her shoulder and pulled her close. His warmth pressed through his own wet clothes and, somehow, it settled the rolling nausea inside.

"Where to, Captain?" Bahri asked.

Prince Wulfhart's ship disappeared over the horizon. There was nothing she could do for Jonan now, but she knew where the Prince was taking him.

The heart of Hartnor.

By all the gods, she swore she'd get him back.

For now, she turned the opposite direction. The city of Solus rose from the water in the far distance, a splotch of green and brown no bigger than her thumbnail. Talin's essence reeled her in like a fishing rod.

"Solus. Take us home."

50

LIES

Salasar's soldiers marched Mina and her Fire Walker guard to the Temple of Rahn, with Salasar and Cyrus leading the way. She wasn't sure if this was for their safety or arrest. Talin and Iman marched beside her, though neither dared speak in present company. They flooded the House bond with a cacophony of emotion—mostly relief for her escape and fear for Jonan's life.

Still, the House bond felt empty. The righteous light of Jonan's fire was missing—silenced by Lune's Tears.

The inside of the temple was a blackened mess of ash and glass. Samira waited for them, with Kamran at her side—Fez in his arms—and a handful of male Fire Walkers.

"They're gone," she said. "We are all that remain."

Mina understood her carefully chosen words. The Fire Walkers who had not been captured and carried away by Prince Wulfhart had escaped through the Temple of Lune and out the gates of Solus as planned. Salasar and the Council believed them dead.

How many? Mina wondered.

But this wasn't the time to ask.

Salasar studied the state of the sanctum with wide-eyed amazement. "Rahn's blood," he exclaimed.

Mina turned her gaze away and sagged against a stone step. Her exhaustion wasn't just for show. Her clothes were still damp and the lingering taste of Lune's Tears, Rahn's Breath, and the saltwater of the Lapis left her drained.

Marching footsteps sounded from the inner corridor and Lady Kasara appeared in the sanctum doorway.

Salasar's nostrils flared. "What are you doing here?"

Kasara glared up at her father. "The temple was on fire. The Water Bearers' duty is to help—"

"You are *not* a Water Bearer. You'll return to the Keep immediately—"

"My lord." Cyrus cleared his throat. "Lady Kasara is a witness to—"

"My daughter is no witness!" Salasar roared. He turned his glare on Talin. "Why is it that whenever something burns in Solus, your House is involved?"

Talin met Salasar's glare with a warrior's calm, but through the bond she felt his anger rise. "One of my House was attacked and taken. Don't forget."

"A gods-damn Rhaesbond. And the reason we're in this cursed mess—"

"Don't you insult Lord Jonan," Samira snarled. "He sacrificed his blood to stop these fires. If not for him, none of us would be alive."

Mina blinked. She'd never expected Samira of all people to leap to Jonan's defense.

Salasar scowled. "And just who are you, wench?"

Mina pushed herself to her feet and approached Salasar. "She's my acolyte and you'll show her and my people respect. Haven't we suffered enough?"

He huffed a laugh. "You expect me to believe this farce? A handful of survivors... out of hundreds?"

"They poisoned our water with Rahn's Breath as I warned you. You ignored my warning." She summoned all her hatred and disgust into her words. "This is your fault. All of it."

Cyrus sneered. "If my lord is to be blamed for anything, it's for putting command of our kingdom's greatest assets in *your* hands, Arlbond. It's thanks to you these men are dead."

Her Fire Walker guard edged closer to her in a protective circle and eyed Cyrus.

"If you speak horse dung about our Priestess, I'll show you what we did to those Hartnords," Dahn said with undisguised contempt.

"Is that a threat, dog?" Cyrus spat and put a hand on his sword hilt.

Salasar's men drew their swords. Flame flickered in Dahn's fist.

"Stand down!" Salasar raised his hand and his men sheathed their swords. "Fire Walkers, I command you to stand down."

The Fire Walkers didn't flinch.

She raised her own hand and her Fire Walkers retreated.

Salasar gave her a wry smile. "You've trained your Fire Walkers well, Arlbond. Or what's left of them. If I have to question every one of you, so be it."

"Save your questions for Lord Hiram. He's behind—"

Everything.

But Mina held her tongue.

In that moment, it occurred to her what Hiram Myrbond's guilt entailed—the sacking of his House and the execution of its members. Alistar included.

She couldn't let Hiram get away with it.

But she couldn't make herself say the words, either. She couldn't sentence her dearest friend to death.

"I've already questioned Hiram. He'll return to his House come dawn to speak with the Three-Pointed Star. We're still awaiting Neu Bosa's ships, and we need them now more than ever."

The Three-Pointed Star was the enemy.

But she couldn't say that, either.

Hiram Myrbond knew about the tunnels, about House Arlbond's plan to smuggle away the Fire Walkers through the Temple of Lune. If his House fell, he'd take hers with him. All of their secrets were entangled now. The executioner's axe would fall on them both alike.

"I wouldn't rely on them." She tried to mask the bitterness in her voice.

"Trust me, child, I don't. You'll meet with the Council and report."

Talin stepped to her side. "My daughter is injured and tired. She's going to the Temple of Gai, immediately. I'll handle the Council."

Salasar rubbed his jaw. "Go on then, man. As for the rest of you, my guards will keep you under watch until my investigation is complete. No one leaves this temple without my authority. Do you hear me?"

Mina nodded in acquiescence.

Salasar marched to the temple doors. "Kara. With me."

"Let me fetch my cloak. If you'd help me, High Priestess?" Kasara grabbed Mina's hand and dragged her into the archway before she could protest. She stopped when they were alone. "Make me your sorran."

Mina gaped at her. "What?"

Kasara pulled a small knife from her belt that looked more decorative than sharp. "I overheard Cyrus say that the Prince plans to force a sorran bond on you. They can't do that if you already have a sorran, and I—" She sucked in a breath. "My father cannot order me around if I am sorran to another."

Prince Ravel *had* threatened to make her sorran to him or one of his lackeys, and with her Fire Walkers gone, her protection as high priestess might be forfeit. She'd be bound to him in the same way Emir was bound to his slave master. The thought made her sick.

"Are you serious? We're heading for war, my lady. There's no avoiding it now."

"Which is why you need me for a sorran. I can fight."

She could. Mina had witnessed Kasara's skills for herself.

"And besides," added Kasara. "With me at your side, my father would be far more reluctant to send you or your followers to the front lines." Kasara offered the knife's handle. "Housemen believe we are silly women who know nothing of war, but they don't live the reality that women face. I've met enough widows in the temple to know it's our fight as well as theirs, and I won't stand by and watch war make more widows. Don't make me beg. I will."

"Are you prepared to face your father's wrath?"

Kasara laughed. A subtle, restrained laugh, as though her true wild nature hid behind the pomposity that came with a noble upbringing. "Are you? I've been defying him since the day I was born."

Mina couldn't believe she was doing this—Salasar would be livid when he found out, and she'd be risking Kasara's life.

Unlike Alistar, Kasara was Sandarian—the bond would work. Prince Ravel wouldn't be able to claim her as his sorran. And, having a female sorran made sense. She wouldn't need to hide herself or her bleed.

"Every true warrior has his own sorran," said Mina. She sliced the knife across her palm.

"Or *her* own." Kasara took Mina's hand and pressed her lips to the cut.

Mina couldn't feel anything happening, but Kasara's cheeks reddened and she began flexing her own hand as if it stung her. Then her left leg buckled—the same leg as Mina's wound. She felt Mina's injuries. The bond had worked.

"Oh, I should have warned you how badly my leg hurts right now."

"I can take it." Kasara winced. She drew her sword and kneeled into the sand, balancing the blade across her knees. "By the honor of House Sarabond and in the presence of Lune, I pledge my blood and blade to you and your House as your sorran."

Mina pulled her up. "And I swear to you, my lady, that I will never ask you to act in a way that would dishonor you or your House." Nor would she ever utter a command Kasara herself wouldn't make. Not after witnessing Emir's suffering.

"Call me Kara, Lady Tamina."

"Then call me Mina."

She smiled. "What's my first duty?"

Mina wiped her bleeding hand. "We lie to our betters."

The call came quicker than Mina had anticipated. She'd barely changed out of her damp clothes when Kasara came to collect her.

"Zavar Xanbond is outside the temple doors, demanding to speak with you."

Gods damn it, what did that fool want? She was supposed to be headed to the Temple of Gai. *Needed* to. Mina hobbled down the corridor with Kasara in tow.

Zavar stood in the sanctum with his arms crossed and his foot tapping. "Finally. Prince Ravel requests your presence in the Keep. I am to escort you for your own protection. And he wishes for me to personally offer my services as your new master."

Kasara was right—they'd been waiting to spring this on her. "You're already the Prince's sorran. You can't take a sorran when you serve as one. The Code of Hon—"

"States that a royal sorran may retain their own. Surely *you* must know that. Come now, Lady Arlbond—Priestess. We both know you won't survive this war without me." His sneer turned into a smarmy grin.

She ground her teeth. "I beat your master in the tournament. I don't need your help. Besides, I have a sorran—"

"Your Bosan doesn't count."

Mina raised her palm to show off the still-bleeding cut. To drive the point home, she balled her hand into a fist and dug her nails painfully into the cut.

Kasara yelped and shook her own hand.

"*You?*" Zavar spluttered.

Mina mouthed Kasara an apology.

"I will keep the High Priestess safe," Kasara said with more restraint that Mina would have shown.

Zavar forced a smile and inclined his head in some parody of politeness. "Lady Sarabond. War is no place for someone of your delicate—"

Kasara drew her sword and slashed it at Zavar, stopping an inch from his neck. "I am more than capable, Lord Zavar."

Zavar chuckled with nervous laughter, his eyes fixed on the sword. "Women don't serve as sorrans—"

"The Code of Honor says nothing about female sorrans one way or the other," Mina said. "Go and thank your prince for his concern for my welfare. It is most kind and noble of him. But as you can see, I already have a Sandarian sorran to guard me."

"Fine, it doesn't matter. The Prince still demands your presence. You'll come with me now, or would you prefer he march on the temple?"

Mina sighed. "Stay here, Kara. There's much to do, and I won't have both of us wasting our time with petty meetings."

Once again, she marched with Zavar on the summons of his master. She hid the limp in her leg as best she could as she climbed the steep hill to the Keep and tried to mentally prepare herself to face the onslaught of questions. But when Zavar opened the door to the Council chamber, only Prince Ravel stood inside, not a full Council meeting as she'd expected.

Zavar closed the door after her, leaving her alone with the Prince of Poison.

Prince Ravel sat on the edge of the table with the casual grace of a young Houseman—not a royal heir. His amber eyes looked thoughtful. "Sit."

She remained standing. "My Prince, there was a—"

"Lord Salasar has informed me of what has transpired. He states devastating losses. What confuses me is how?"

"Shouldn't we wait for the rest of the Council?"

"There's no need."

She tucked her hands behind her back. "Where's my father?" She couldn't feel Talin's essence nearby, though nothing out of the ordinary had passed through the bond.

"Lord Talin is waiting on my father in the palace. He spends

SAND DANCER | 449

rather a lot of time there, and not enough with the Council he is supposed to lead. As such, the decisions of the Council must fall on my shoulders. As heir, this is a burden I welcome."

Talin was giving not only too much time to the King but also too much blood. With each hour spent, he weakened himself and strengthened Prince Ravel's grip on the Council. Her anxiety passed through the bond and Talin's essence warmed in response— the scent of rain on sand.

"Priestess? I'm awaiting your explanation."

"Lord Salasar gave you a report—"

"I want to hear it from your own mouth."

Mina took a steadying breath. "The Fire Walkers were poisoned—"

"By Rahn's Breath." He raised an eyebrow.

"You of all people know its devastating effects. I warned you the Hartnords were poisoning my Fire Walkers to use them against our people. They used the negotiations as a diversion to invade the Temple of Rahn right under our noses. If you and the Council had listened, we could have stopped them and saved hundreds of lives!"

"There are tunnels leading outside, are there not? The Fire Walkers could have escaped."

How did he know about the tunnels? "Once, yes. Leila blocked them when she was high priestess."

"Historically, these tunnels connected the temples to one another."

She fought to keep her expression neutral. The Prince was a great student of history. He must have read about the tunnels in one of his books. How else would he know? "Historically, my Prince. The fact remains that the Hartnords chose to attack us, steal my Fire Walkers, take Jonan—"

"Yes, truly devastating." He stroked his chin. "How many of your Fire Walkers remain? Lord Sarabond reports a handful at best. A pity."

"Is that all you have to say?" She lowered her hands to her side and they curled into fists. "Hundreds of Fire Walkers died, and that's all you have to say?"

"Naturally, this loss will hinder our attack against the Hartnords—"

"They are not your weapons! They are people!"

Prince Ravel slid off the table. "They are the reason we are at war, Lady Arlbond, or have you forgotten already?"

"You continue to blame an entire group of people for the actions of one man—"

"Where Fire Walkers are concerned, the actions of one man can have reaching consequences. It was one man, one Rhaesbond, who almost destroyed my bloodline. It was one man, one delusional Fire Walker, who murdered a Hartnord king and destroyed any chance of peace between our nations. I believe in our laws, Priestess, because without them, all it would take is *one man* to destroy us."

She stepped an inch from his nose and eyed the crescent scar marring his cheek. "Are you so scared, my Prince?"

"For my people? Yes. It was they who scarred my brother for life—"

"And yet he is man enough to forgive them and move on."

"Man enough? He's no more a man than you, Lady Arlbond. He's nothing more than a little boy who pines for his Dusland whore and feels the need to win her affection by joining the town guard in order to prove he is *man* enough for her."

The Prince's words were like a slap across her face. She took a step back.

He grabbed her wrist and held her in place, the same way he'd held her the first time they met in Khalbad—the night he'd murdered her uncle.

"Let go of me."

He tugged her close enough for their breath to mingle. "You overreach yourself, Tamina. Do you honestly believe my brother has the fortitude to rule this kingdom? Or that its people would accept you as queen—a woman who, until recently, was a man?"

She tried to pull from his grip but it only tightened. "I won the tournament. And I'm the daughter of Lord Talin, a man whom everyone knows and adores."

"Ah, Lord Talin, a father who chose to dress up his daughter as a man, enter her into the Academy as a man, and parade her in the tournament as a *man*. Is it because you look in the mirror and see a man? Or by dressing as one, you hope to become one?"

"You seem fixated on sex, my Prince."

"I'm fixated on truth, Lady Arlbond. You and your House do nothing but lie. How many lies have spilled from those lips of yours? Should we count?"

"What of your own lies, my Prince? You poisoned your own people! Your own father!"

"I've always been honest about the dangers of the Fire Walkers and how far I'm willing to go to protect the people of Sandair from their kind. I admit to everything I've done. I serve the law and our Code of Honor. Do women even understand what that means?" He shook his head. "Duty comes first to any true warrior, *Malik*."

"Who would you poison next for your father's crown? Your brother? Sister?"

His nails dug into her skin. "My brother is a fool and a threat to no one. And my sister... I will destroy any Fire Walker who steps near her."

Gods, he didn't know his sister possessed blood fire. Mina would have to carry that secret to her death. Heat built in her hand and the Prince released her before she could burn him.

The Prince skipped back and chuckled as though this was all some new game. "The Council and Lord Sarabond have voted on our only course of action. We've invited the Hartnords into our city twice now, and twice they have betrayed us. Nor can we ignore the murder of my father's Left Arm. We must press forward and begin our attack on Hartnor immediately. What few Fire Walkers you have left will march for the Ruby Coast come dawn."

"*Dawn*? That's not enough time—"

"They will join with a battalion leaving the north gate. Each will be accompanied by a guard to ensure their protection and to prevent further attacks against them. I have ordered Zavar to assess each of your Fire Walkers and decide which to leave behind for Solus's defense."

He was going to identify every Fire Walker under her command and ensure none of them went missing. "There's hardly enough Fire Walkers left. We need them here, to protect Solus—"

"We need our most dangerous weapons on the front lines."

This wasn't about winning a war. It was about punishing them.

"Furthermore." The Prince grabbed a scroll from the table and passed it to her. "As I've said before, I believe it's only fitting that our High Priestess should lead the Fire Walkers into battle. Especially during these dark times. Lord Salasar will receive my orders separately and position you and your Fire Walkers accordingly. I do hate to waste a *talented* Fire Walker such as yourself, but think of the message it will send to our enemies—and the morale it will deliver to our soldiers. Our great High Priestess riding into battle—"

"But not you, my Prince? Are you not brave enough to lead your own men?"

"I will be on the battlefield, rest assured. Perhaps I'll even wave to you from some hilltop or another, where it is the place of commanders to sit in their comfortable pavilions to survey the field and arrange their troops. Such is the role of a prince." He cocked his head. "You seem displeased. We have the same enemies. Surely you wish to lead your Fire Walkers and save Lord Jonan? Are you no longer the fearless warrior you pretended to be as a man?"

She wanted nothing more than to save Jonan and make Prince Wulfhart suffer, but not at the expense of her Fire Walkers. Her first duty was to protect them—it's what Jonan would want. "Why the coast? Why aren't you sending us to the Cold Path?"

"Because Wulfhart will strike there first to test our defenses—"

"And Jonan? You've going to leave a Houseman in the hands of Hartnords?" How could they save Jonan if she was being pulled in the opposite direction?

"There's more than one life at stake in this war, Lady Arlbond."
Of course the Council didn't consider a Rhaesbond life worth
the rescue attempt. Any other Houseman, and they'd be burning
their way north already.

"Don't fret," the Prince said. "You and your Fire Walkers will
be put to task. Leave military strategy to those with an Academy
education."

She scrunched the scroll in her fist. "Is that all, my Prince?"

"Oh, I forgot. You received a letter from Rajesh Enaibond a few
days ago. I took the liberty of opening and destroying it for you."

"You read my letters?"

"Spies are everywhere. All correspondence must be checked."

It couldn't have included anything incriminating; otherwise,
she'd have been marched to the Council sooner. Raj was smarter
than that, though not smart enough to send his letter to the temple
instead of the Keep. At least now she knew she couldn't rely on a
courier to contact him or Alistar.

"What did the letter say?"

"*Nothing.*" The Prince rolled his eyes. "Pure drivel. He misses
you greatly and he's seen oh-so-many flowers and the temple's
food is terrible. I don't know how you tolerate those Gaislander
friends of yours." He waved his hand at her. "You're dismissed."

Mina stomped from the chamber and felt the Prince's eyes
follow her every step.

"Enjoy the coast, Lady Arlbond," Prince Ravel called. "It's
most lovely this time of year."

51

THE MARCH NORTH

Guards remained stationed outside the temple doors. Zavar stood inside the sanctum, watching her acolytes and eavesdropping on their every whisper. As soon as he saw her, he waved her over, his expression grim.

"As per our Prince's orders, I have counted and spoken to each of the Fire Walkers who survived the attack. I'm sad to say, our numbers are very little." He actually sounded remorseful, or he knew how to fake sincerity better than his cousin. "I've compiled a list of those who should remain and those who will be expected to march. Guards will arrive before dawn, and I'll personally assign one to each man for their protection."

He passed over a scroll and she quickly scanned the names of those to march with her to the coast—her five acolytes, Garr, and Kamran, but no mention of Samira or some of the other Fire Walkers who'd not managed to escape. "Kamran's a child—"

"He's old enough."

She scowled. "His mother has just burned to death and you want to march him to his own?"

"Those are your orders." Zavar strode for the temple doors, accompanied by two guards. Three more remained inside the temple on watch.

Gods curse all princes and Housemen.

"Sword Dancer." Garr leaned from the kitchen door and beckoned her to join him.

Kamran sat beside the kitchen hearth and was feeding Fez some leftover crumbs. Her guts twisted at the thought of sending him to war. He was just a boy—a boy who should have been leaving Solus with his mother. But now they were all trapped. The march to the Ruby Coast would take a week at least, and during that time, there'd be enough soldiers and commotion to lose track of one scrawny boy. Perhaps Iman could follow them secretly for a few days, then run off with Kamran in the night. It was the only plan she had.

"So, we're leaving for war," Garr said. "Your Council meetings are proving productive."

"We have no choice. The Hartnords took our people, burned half the temple—"

"Did they?" His brows raised.

She bit her lip.

Garr jerked a thumb over his shoulder at Kamran. "It's odd how his mother supposedly burned to death and he doesn't seem bothered by it. Does he look like a grieving boy to you?"

Fez nipped Kamran's finger and he giggled.

"He's in shock—"

"And Samira, she's positively glowing. Is she also in shock?"

"I won't tell people how to grieve."

Garr leaned close, his amber eyes so alike Prince Ravel's it made her want to scream. "All that time spent teaching your Fire Walkers how to make campfires. You should have been teaching them how to lie better."

"I don't know what you're talking about."

"It's easier to lie if you believe the lie to be true, Sword Dancer."

"Are you speaking from experience, Ash Maker?"

"From what I hear, you have more experience than I." He turned to watch Kamran play with Fez and his smile faded. "What's your intent?"

"My intent?"

"Will you march us to Hartnor and burn their cities? Burn their people? Your acolytes seemed happy to melt Hartnord flesh, but I've seen enough innocent people get caught up in battles to know war makes monsters of us all. I want no part in slaughter."

"You think I do?"

"They have your Houseman. Your brother by bond, you said. I'd burn a kingdom to the ground to save my family. I won't judge you for that."

She *thunked* her head against the wall. She wanted Jonan back, but she didn't want to sacrifice her Fire Walkers in exchange. What choice did any of them have?

She'd been gods-damn foolish to hope they could stop this war. Now her only hope was to end it quickly with minimal bloodshed.

You won't be able to save them all.

She met Garr's amber eyes. There was a fire hidden in those golden-brown swirls, but they didn't hold hate. He was an Ash Maker, not unlike Emir, and his past seemed to hide scars not so dissimilar. Were the Lunei's tales of Ash Makers true? Or were they as misunderstood as House Rhaesbond? She should hate Garr for his bloodline—and Emir, too, for that and so many reasons— but she didn't have the stomach for it.

Neither did Garr. He'd not once summoned his flame in all the time she'd watched him. "You're scared of your fire."

He jumped as though she'd startled him. "What—what makes you say that?"

"You've not used it once. You act the fool, but I see you, Ash Maker. I see your scars. What happened to you?"

The light in his eyes dimmed, and for a heartbeat she thought she'd never get her answer. "I have a sister back home. When I was fourteen, there was an... accident. I burned—I burned her face. Not as bad as your Prince Rais, but the scars are still there, four years later. I still have nightmares about it. I... I hear her screams. My scars are punishment."

"You were a child, and children rarely have control. That's why we train in the temple. You don't deserve to torture yourself for it. I've burned people, too."

"People you care about?"

She thought of Alistar. "Yes."

He ran a hand atop his bald head. "My sister didn't blame me, but I've yet to forgive myself. What monster deserves forgiveness?"

She put a hand on his arm. "Monsters enjoy inflicting pain, Ash Maker. We don't. I can teach you control, if you'll trust me. You are the master of your own self."

He put his hand over hers, rough with the callouses of a man who'd earned his strength. "I'll help you get your Houseman back. I'll join your march. Someone needs to keep *him* safe." He glanced to Kamran. "I swear to protect his life with mine, High Priestess."

Mina could ask for no more, but how many lives would she have to sacrifice to get Jonan back? Would anyone be left to return to her temple by the end? "I'm barely a priestess. I don't even know the prayers."

"You should learn some. We're going to need them."

The evening sky swirled with the murky pre-grays of Lune's Shadow and not the usual purple shades of Mina's House. Lune's rains would come before this war ended. She leaned over a railing at the docks and stared east. Endless water stared back. Being trapped inside it had terrified her, but staring at it now filled her with a sense of calm she'd surely need in the coming weeks. A warrior's calm.

And still the bond lacked Jonan's essence. She knew he still lived—she'd asked Tira to keep watch over him, but his absence hurt deep in her gut.

The bond warmed once more with the combined essence of rain on sand and sweet spice. She didn't take her eyes from the swell of the Lapis as Talin squeezed her shoulder and Iman wrapped an arm around her waist.

Mina squeezed them back. Her family.

"He's a tough nut, girl."

"That he is," Talin said, though concern ached through the bond. "We'll get him back."

"How can we get him back when I'm being sent west across the Solands to the Ruby Coast and not north into Hartnor?"

"Let me worry about that. You have enough to shoulder."

Mina wiped moisture from her eyes. "I'm scared. Not just for Jonan, but for the Fire Walkers."

"They'll be safe in their new home."

She turned to Iman. "When are you leaving?"

"At dawn. Through the south gate."

Mina's heart ached. She'd be marching the opposite direction with Salasar's men. When would she see Iman again? Or Arlent?

Talin pulled her into a hug and she clung onto his bony frame. Gods, how much weaker would he become in her absence? He withdrew and held her at arm's length. His dark eyes searched her, as though trying to memorize every dimple, mark, and scar on her face. "With Gareth gone, I cannot leave the King and march by your side, as much as I wish to."

"Gareth was a good man," Iman said. "He deserved a better end."

Gareth, a Hartnord Prince. The lover of Princess Aniya. And she'd been carrying his child. Did King Khaled know? Was that why she'd been killed? Those secrets hadn't died with his death; they'd become Mina's. Though she supposed they meant nothing now.

"We once invited him to join our House," Talin added. "He wouldn't have been able to make the bond, but he would have been one of us."

No one had never mentioned that before. "Why didn't he?"

"He was a stubborn old goat who couldn't move on from the regrets of his past." Iman gave Talin a pointed look. "Sound familiar?"

Talin grimaced. "Gareth felt it would be inappropriate for him to join a Sandarian House."

"Because he was Princess Aniya's lover or because he was a Hartnord prince?" Mina asked.

"Both, and other things besides. I'd almost convinced him this Solend, thanks to you turning the whole kingdom upside down, but then the Hartnords turned up." He rubbed a hand down his face. "Some men can't outrun their shadows."

Shadows. Gods, she still didn't know who killed the Queen, not that it mattered anymore. There was no chance of reconciliation with the Hartnords whilst Prince Wulfhart breathed, and Hiram as well. "Gareth was going to assassinate Wulfhart, wasn't he?" And pave the way for another.

"If things went wrong," Talin said. "Wulfhart has a younger brother—Prince Leonhart. There are rumors that this Leonhart is leading a coup against the keepers of their faith. Gareth wanted Leonhart and Rais to meet."

"What about Hiram? What do we do about him?"

"Political maneuvering is my battlefield. Let me deal with the Bosan. You must focus on the battles ahead. Listen to Salasar and follow his commands to the letter. He'll keep you safe. Especially when he learns you've taken his daughter for a sorran. Was that to spite him or me?" He gave her a wry smile.

"It wasn't to spite anyone. Kasara volunteered." It was just a coincidence that both of Prince Rais's potential queens were currently indisposed.

Iman barked a laugh. "She'll be good for you, girl."

Talin pulled her into another hug. "I'm sending help to the coast," he murmured. "They'll keep you safe where I can't."

She strained a look up. "Who?"

"You'll see." He kissed her forehead. "Lune guide you, always."

"Enough of this," Iman said. "I'm not spending my last night in Solus moping. You're both coming with me to the tea house, and by Rahn, you'll enjoy it."

Talin chuckled and wrapped an arm around Mina's shoulder. "You leave us no choice."

Mina squeezed him back. It had been too long since she'd

indulged in tea and cake with her aunt, and Lune knew Talin needed more meat on his bones. She'd spend the night with her father and aunt for possibly the last time.

Zavar and his men came to collect the Fire Walkers before dawn. Mina had done her best to prepare them. With Iman and Kasara's help, they'd procured adequate clothing and boots. Zavar, however, ordered them back inside to remove their clothes.

She stomped outside and met his foolish order with rage. "Prince Ravel expects the Fire Walkers to march naked and barefoot? They'll die of cold before they even make it to the coast! I refuse to authorize their travel unless they have wagons at least."

"They're Fire Walkers, not Fire Riders," Zavar said with a sneer. "Besides, if they cannot keep themselves warm, then what use are they in war?"

"None. So let them stay."

"Oh? Shall I inform our Prince that the High Priestess refuses to follow basic commands?"

Mina flexed her fingers into fists. "Even soldiers are allowed boots to protect their feet. My Fire Walkers will be useless in combat if they're crippled on a march."

Zavar's lips formed a tight line. Making the Fire Walkers suffer was the point of this foolish expedition, but there was also a war to be fought. Her Fire Walkers would be needed when Hartnord ships arrived on the Ruby Coast. "Boots, then. Nothing else."

"And Kamran rides in a wagon. He's barely a man. The walk will kill him."

Zavar jerked his head into the briefest bow. "Fine. Ready your men."

One by one her acolytes save Samira stepped through the temple doors into the cool dawn air. Dahn had volunteered to carry the Fire Walker's red banner, though she'd try and attach it to her horse as soon as she could. It felt wrong to ride Luna when her own men had to make the journey by foot.

Garr stepped out of the temple last and her jaw dropped. Gone were the awful red smears of paint from his chest, and in their place were real markings—tattoos in the shape of swirling flame with Rahn himself in red and gold.

The Fire Walkers were destined to attract attention, but Garr's markings were the colors of the Bright Solara and he would stand out like a king. He was a walking blasphemy.

Garr met her stare and winked.

She found Samira waiting in the pyramid's shade. "What did you do?" Mina said through clenched teeth.

Samira smirked. "I made art."

Fez snuck out of the temple doors and rubbed his head on Mina's leg. She scooped him up and gave him one last nuzzle. "Stay inside and be a good fox."

"I'll watch over him," Samira said.

"I thought you hated him."

"If he lives in the temple, then he's one of us, whether I like him or not." Samira bowed. "Rahn watch over you and our men, Priestess. Return to us whole."

Mina felt guilty for offering Samira the promise of a new life and then snatching it from her grasp. But Samira understood her place, and the temple would do well with her in charge.

Some duties were more important than blood and bonds.

A supply wagon rolled by and Kamran sat among the crates. He waved cheerfully as he passed, but her heart sank. Even he had been assigned a personal guard.

Another spied on her as well: a tall Solander with a face as expressionless as a rock. He stood across the street, not quite watching her, but she felt him follow her like a Shadow.

She mounted her horse and steered Luna toward Kasara, who sat waiting on her own horse—a beautiful golden mare in contrast to Mina's Lune-kissed white. They would be meeting Salasar and his battalion at the north gate. Kasara still hadn't told her father she was Mina's sorran, which meant he didn't know his daughter would be marching with them—yet.

There'd be trouble when he found out.

Mina gave the order, and her Fire Walkers began their march. They were not alone on the streets. Numerous other small bands of soldiers were on the march as well, all headed to the muster at the north gate. Soon there were hundreds of them crowding the streets together. A parade of soldiers. Women and children leaned from their windows as they passed, waving and calling. Some looked proud. Others looked grim.

Mina had been so focused on her own people and her own part in the war, she hadn't realized the enormity of this morning's departure. They were but nine soldiers among thousands, perhaps tens of thousands leaving home for possibly the last time. Most were Solanders, common folk of all ages from boys growing their first chin hairs to hardened soldiers whose braided beards had long since turned gray. Any Housemen were mounted, with bannermen marching before them: orange for House Khalbond, silver for Xanbond, and turquoise for Salasar's House.

If Mina were still Malik, she would have been marching as a warrior instead of a priestess. No, if Mina were still Malik, she'd be sitting comfortably at home as Talin's only male heir. Another privilege the Housemen could afford that common folk couldn't. How many sons wouldn't return from the Ruby Coast? How many fathers?

Prince Rais waited by the north gate. He gestured for her to dismount, and she did so, despite grumbling from the men around her. She was blocking the procession, but no one would deny a Solaran prince his whims.

He positioned Luna so the march could continue. "Were you about to sneak off and leave me for another adventure without saying goodbye?"

"No, my Prince, I—"

"I'm teasing you. I heard about the attack. I regret I wasn't there to help. Lord Talin wishes me to remain in Solus and prepare the defense, but I would sooner join the charge at the Cold Path and help rescue Lord Jonan." He glanced to the soldiers marching past. "I cannot wait here whilst our men take the fight north."

"It would be safer if you remained here, my Prince. Sandair needs you, and you can't serve her if you're dead."

"How can I serve her by hiding behind her skirts?" He smiled, but there was an edge to his words.

"We need you, my Prince. Sandair needs you. Alive and strong."

His smile widened. "And do you need me, Lady Arlbond?"

"Of course, my Prince."

"I can't tell if you're just saying what I want to hear or the truth. I wish you would speak plain." He took her hand. "That's why I wanted you for my sorran. Because you're honest. You didn't— you didn't hide the truth behind a mask."

"Malik was my mask."

"I think Tamina is your mask. Malik is who you really are."

What did he mean? Mina and Malik were the same. This was another game, so different from his brother's, but she needed to play it if Sandair were to crown a half-decent king. "I do need you. I need you to be more than Rais. More than some Solaran prince in a pretty palace. I need you to lead your people. I need you to become a king. And sometimes that means making hard choices and sacrifices. Sometimes it will mean sending your men to die so that you may continue to live. But you will make those hard choices because *you* will be king."

"You're wiser than Salasar."

She chuckled. "I don't think that's true."

Prince Rais lifted her hand to his lips. "The desires I have probably make me a bad king." He kissed her knuckles so gently, it sent a bolt of sky fire in her stomach. "If you were Malik, I would have made you my brother. I'm fortunate that you're Tamina so I can make you my wife."

The march of a thousand boots roared in her ears. "My—my Prince?"

He kissed her hand again and she fought the urge to fling herself onto the nearest javelin. "You are the Lune to my Rahn. I want what you want—a united Sandair. Together we can achieve it. You don't have to march. Come with me. Marry me now, today, and you won't need to leave. You'll remain in Solus and another can lead the Fire Walkers in your place."

She pulled her hand free from his grip. "It's my responsibility to lead them—"

"But that's what you were saying. A queen must make those hard decisions. And sometimes that means sending men to die in her place."

No, no, no! She wasn't a queen; she didn't want *anyone* to die in her place!

Talin couldn't still mean for her to make this choice? This sacrifice? Gods, he must know. Her father had likely sent him. Was this Talin's idea of help? To offer her a coward's way out? She searched the crowds and caught the flicker of their temple's banner, now far ahead of her. They were her men, and she wouldn't abandon them now.

Perhaps Prince Rais was right. She was more Malik than Mina. Malik wanted to fight.

Prince Rais cupped her cheek. "Isn't this what you want? To protect your Fire Walkers?" He puckered his lips and leaned forward.

She placed a finger on his lip. "I'll protect them. I'll fight for them, as I expect you to fight for us. And should we both still live at the end of this war, then—then you'll have a warrior queen who commanded her Fire Walkers in the defeat of our enemies. What better way to start your reign, my Prince?"

A lie. But a necessary one.

Gold glittered inside Prince Rais's amber eye. "Then go and win me a kingdom."

She bowed and mounted her horse with shaking hands. Prince Rais wasn't in love with either Malik or Mina. He only loved what she represented—power.

She trotted Luna to catch up with her Fire Walker guard. Dahn nodded as he hefted the red banner high. Bahri gave her horse a friendly pat as Qareem slipped Luna a pitted date.

Amin pounded his daf drum to the march, and Marek strummed his setar.

"The sands travel with us!" Dahn called, and the crowd echoed in reply.

The sands travel with you.

Garr glanced up with a smile. It wasn't one of fear, or malice, or mischief.

But hope.

These were her Fire Walkers and Mina would lead them with pride, even to their deaths.

SAND DANCER | BOOK THREE

Wraith Maker

COMING
FALL 2021

ABOUT THE AUTHOR

Author Trudie Skies lives in North East England but was born in Nottingham—Robin Hood country, she says. An IT administrator by day, she spends the majority of her free time imagining warmer climates and writing about them. *Sand Dancer* is her first novel.

If you love Jane Austen...
And also Blood Magic

One of Booklist's Top Ten
Best Debut Speculative Fiction
Novels of 2020

"Sure to win over fantasy readers."
-Publishers Weekly

Also from Uproar Books:

FORETOLD by Violet Lumani (2021)

As if OCD wasn't bad enough, a high school student begins seeing visions of the future, including her best friend's death, and must join a mysterious secret society to stop it.

WILD SUN: UNBOUND by Ehsan & Shakil Ahmad (2021)

In book two of the Wild Sun Series, a small band of escaped slaves looks for refuge and allies in their uprising against the interstellar empire that conquered their people.

THE WAY OUT by Armond Boudreaux (2020)

When a virus necessitates the use of artificial wombs for all pregnancies, two fearless women discover the horrifying truth behind this world-changing technology.

WORLDS OF LIGHT AND DARKNESS (2021)

The best science-fiction short stories from the pages of DreamForge and Space & Time magazines, including works by Jane Lindskold, Scott Edelman, and more.

For more information, visit UproarBooks.com